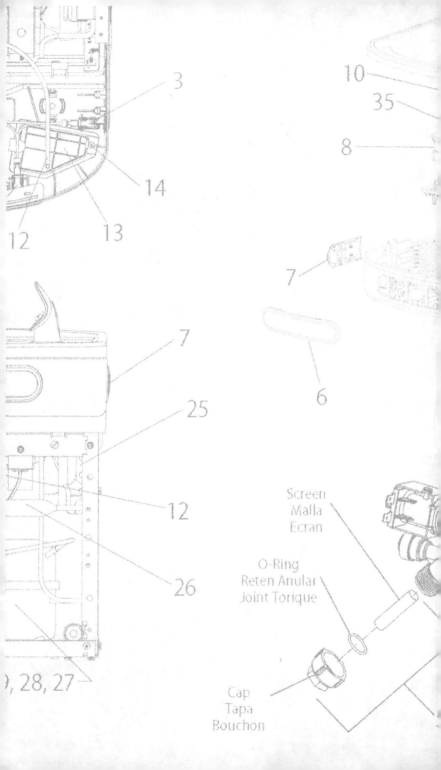

3

14

12

13

10

35

8

7

6

7

25

12

26

0, 28, 27

Screen
Malla
Ecran

O-Ring
Reten Anular
Joint Torique

Cap
Tapa
Bouchon

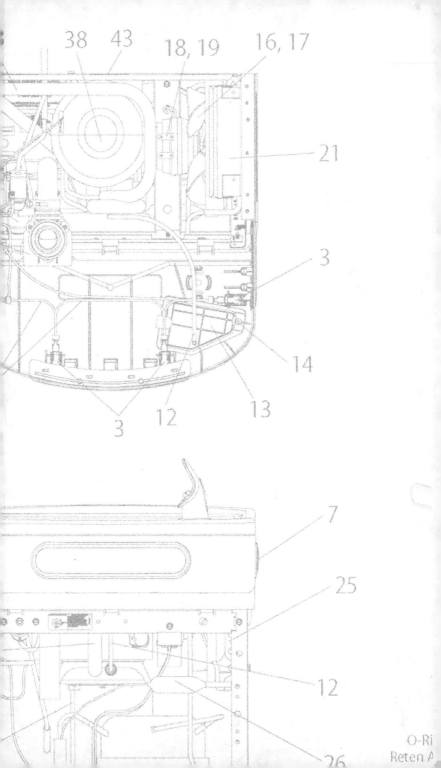

The FOUNTAIN

David Scott Hay

Whisk(e)y Tit
VT & NYC

Published in the United States by Whisk(e)y Tit: www.whiskeytit.com. If you wish to use or reproduce all or part of this book for any means, please let the author and publisher know. You're pretty much required to, legally.

The Fountain ©2021 By David Scott Hay. All Rights Reserved.
ISBN 978-1-952600-04-3
Library Of Congress Control Number: 2020946539
First Whiskey Tit Paperback Edition

Cover Art By Sebastien Derenoncourt
Cover And Book Design By Sebastien Derenoncourt

NO
To: WE ARE
IMMORTAL
UNTIL OUR
WORK IS DONE

BROOKLYN BOOK FESTIVAL '21

foreword to The Fountain

First things first: the novel you're about to read is hugely enjoyable. It deals with weighty subjects like art and originality and taste and what makes life worth living, and there's a (perhaps surprising) amount of lust and gore and violence—but the book is also truly engaging and funny. Genuine hilarity in literature is very much to be prized. We'd do better as a culture if our "serious" writers could learn to be funnier.

David Scott Hay is very funny indeed. Who but a man with an irrepressible desire for mordant laughter, the sort of freakish gallows humor possessed by the likes of Kurt Vonnegut and Philip Dick, could imagine a fountain in an art museum that magically grants, momentarily, monumental talent? And that this magical wish-granting fountain would herald the death of art itself, and that the cost of its magic would be humiliation, agony, and death—and that it would all in the end be quite droll? It's a book that makes me chuckle when (spoiler alert, but it won't really spoil anything) a little boy gets run over. That's a neat trick.

The book's central thesis—that "we're all going to die... surrounded by indescribable pieces of beauty"—is nonetheless quite a troubling one: a revelation, an apocalypse, and this is a story of apocalyptic, epic proportion. There is more than a little bit of Old Testament seriousness to backstop the novel's abundant absurdity. Hay creates many flesh-crawling (of the good variety) moments, moments that shocked me when I read them and that linger in the mind still. "He brushes B's hair with a clawed hand, the tender loving touch of Grendel's mother." I love such moments for their terrible nature, and for the callouts they frequently make to our great, ancient stories. Much of literature's success lies in the wise employment of allusion, and there are many such good, smart allusions here.

David Scott Hay possesses a cinematic sense of timing and pacing. It's one of his great strengths as a writer, to be able to propel the narrative powerfully forward, with immense authority. That authority is an unusual gift, and the quality that we prize above all others, in our narratives. And it must be assumed by the writer, because such a thing truly cannot be earned: it's priceless. Almost anything can happen in a book, in almost any way, without limits, so long as the writer takes responsibility. Hay does that very well, moving effortlessly in and out of the points of view of various of his characters, and also further out, into an omniscient but still opinionated, wry narrative voice.

The novel's narrative strategy is in fact very much like a free-roaming camera, putting the freedom and authority of the writer to excellent use. I admire and envy the twists and turns in a line like "Big Tim looks to Duckworth for guidance, because, come on, a fucking clown." It's truly funny, and it's truly fine writing, and it demands attention and discernment from the reader, and derives so directly out of the integrity of the writer, that the sentence would make me like any novel that contains it, even if I were not already so disposed.

The book has the feel of something that's been created out of inspiration and then honed and refined with a gem-cutter's eye. The connections among the broad cast of characters all are drawn marvelously tight. The working out of the numerous intricately strung plotlines is clever in the extreme; and I mean clever not in the sense of precious, but in the sense of thrilling, as the workings of an expensive watch, or any ingeniously crafted device, are thrilling. I deeply appreciated the thrills of recognition I experienced as I met in one chapter characters whom I knew from another chapter, and worked out who they were and how they belonged to that moment in the narrative. Hay is a master of plot, and there were many moments when I wanted to cheer, to see how craftily he had arranged things.

The great question the novel poses is what it means to be a hack, and what it might mean to be authentic. The Fountain uses a deliberately glib prose style to inquire into this subject, which is a smart gambit: it asks the reader to decide whether it is possible to write critically and incisively about hackery when you yourself use the tools of the hack: the quick sardonic wit, the slick prose, the swiftly-moving camera, the amped-up plot (since artists, sad to say, are never anything like as interesting and as frightening as these people are).

Usually issues of art are addressed in dull and lugubrious tones, in order to point up the seriousness of the questions that are being asked and the answers that are being essayed. Hay has taken the opposite and much more original tack of creating something that looks like hackwork (to an untrained or uninterested eye) to probe the problem of hackwork, of fraud and inauthenticity. The book is a spirited engagement with the central conundrums of our discipline, and a booming and extended *ars poetica*. My hat's off to David Scott Hay for the howling success he's managed to create while working at a very difficult task.

— Pinckney Benedict, 2020

Pinckney Benedict grew up on his family's dairy farm in Greenbrier County, West Virginia. He attended Princeton University and the

Iowa Writers' Workshop. He has published a novel (*Dogs of God*) and three collections of short fiction, the most recent of which is *Miracle Boy and Other Stories*. His work has been published in, among other magazines and anthologies, Esquire, Zoetrope: All-Story, the O. Henry Award series, the Pushcart Prize series, the Best New Stories from the South series, Apocalypse Now: Poems and Prose from the End of Days, The Ecco Anthology of Contemporary American Short Fiction, and The Oxford Book of the American Short Story, edited by Joyce Carol Oates. Benedict is the recipient of, among other awards and honors, a Literature Fellowship from the National Endowment for the Arts, a fiction grant from the Illinois Arts Council, two Plattner Awards for fiction from Appalachian Heritage magazine, a Literary Fellowship from the West Virginia Commission on the Arts, and the Chicago Tribune's Nelson Algren Award. Benedict has taught on the writing faculties of Oberlin College, Princeton University, Davidson College, and Hollins University, and he now serves as a professor in the MFA program at Southern Illinois University Carbondale and on the core faculty of the low-residency MFA program at Queens University in Charlotte, NC.

Allison

Matthew

Min Min

K-Girl

Steven

Dad + Mom

art (n.)

Early 13c., "skill as a result of learning or practice," from Old French art (10c.), from Latin artem (nominative ars) "Work of art, practical skill; a business, craft."

Akin to Latin arma "weapons."

— Etymology Online

"Fuck art."

— Harriet "Jawbone" Walker

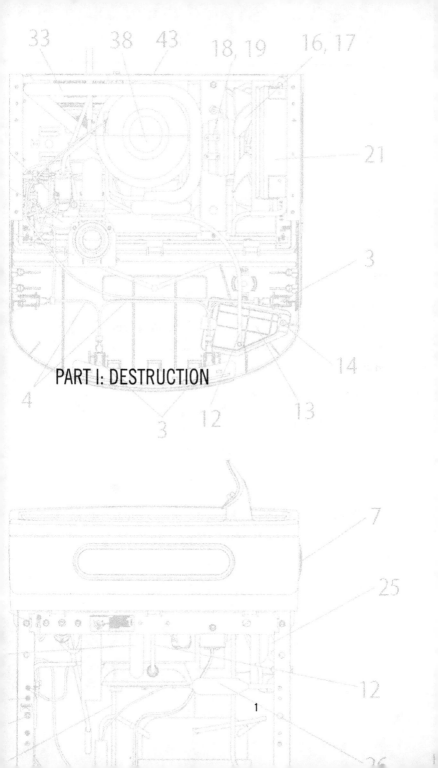

PART I: DESTRUCTION

The Exhibit

Everything will change in six minutes.

The bomb is built by a ten-year-old boy in a museum of contemporary art. It is not constructed from store-bought shrapnel encased in a counter-top kitchen appliance, but from modeling clay and various kiddie playtime accouterments. No bomb-sniffing dog will detect it. An art critic's nose, however, is twitching and his mouth salivating. He is on High Alert. Adults talk as the boy builds his bomb.

"Rebirth," the critic says.

"Maybe," the photographer says.

"Innovative," the critic says.

"Inventive, maybe?" the photographer says.

"*Reinventive,*" the critic corrects, adjusting his bow tie.

The bomb is a metaphorical bomb, but a bomb nonetheless. One that will detonate here in Chicago on a Thursday afternoon.[1]

The two men murmur words to each other, each leaning in to examine the boy's freshly minted work of art. Their whispers float around the otherwise still room, floating off the white walls (Gardenia #AF-10) of the BE AN ARTIST™ exhibit at the Museum of Contemporary Art in Chicago, Illinois. The exhibit is tucked away on the second floor an appropriate distance from the flow of main

---

1. Serendipitously, Brian Eno's classic ambient recording Thursday Afternoon plays on a 61 minute loop.

exhibits. Away from the fêted, the studied, the prosaic. The museum is a celebration of a new way of thinking, of experimentation, of dreams, and years spent finding a voice that will challenge the status quo.

However, for a ten-dollar donation, a patron can step into this side room and become an artist. Buckets and trays of colors and plastic doodads at your disposal. And you get your picture taken to be hanged on the wall. Or on the MCA's website[2].

"Is this not a rebirth? Of form, of structure?" the critic, Jasper P. Duckworth, asks of no one. He is the Associate Media Critic from the local *Chicago Shoulders*. He is on a 'feel good' assignment. Having drawn the shortest straw. "Am I crazy?"[3]

"Maybe," the photographer says, undecided. His Texas accent is almost undetectable. He is the exhibit's photographer *du jour*. And is now realizing his purist's ethics and vintage equipment are wasted on this gig.

"He's a prodigy," Duckworth the admirer says, as he snaps his pencil in half and tosses it in surrender. One of the halves hits the photographer. The other lands on the table. "I can't describe it,"

---

2. The exhibit copy is a little unclear. Budget crunch collateral damage.

3. At first, Duckworth cannot draw a bead on this piece. Why would he even try this child's thing? At first it is a dragon or a snake wrapped around a bridge. Or is this bridge the dragon? Then he sees it, the partial head of a warrior. The warrior could be from any age. It is a young anguished face with eyes somewhere between pathos and ethos, between the river and the boat. The moment between conscious and unconscious. The moment between ignorance and bliss. The instant before numbness and space set in. He's studied photos of his father's great war. His father's father's war. The cracked and ashen photos, he recognizes this moment, but not what it means in, say, a contemporary or artistic context. Thus begins Duckworth's lamentation.

Duckworth the critic says. "I don't have the words." But he does have a slight accent. British, perhaps.

The other half of the broken pencil rolls to the edge of the table. It is a standard rectangular plastic table with metal legs that might require a swift kick to shut. The boy at the end of the table picks up the pencil.

"Get a camera," Duckworth says to the photographer holding a camera. He does not take his eyes off the boy's sculpture. "We must photograph it."

∞

As the boy who has paid his ten dollars contemplates the jagged pencil, Waylon the skeptic photographer moves to the side of the boy's art project, switching lenses on his weapon of choice. Suddenly, he feels that he is no longer an observer. Or safe. The sculpture's eyes follow him. The abyss stares back. Waylon can feel it track him even as he stands behind the sculpture. Then a crisis of faith. The camera weighs heavy in his hands.[4]

Am I truly a hunter?

---

4. *Waylon contemplates the sculpture: a great wounded saber tooth cat still considering its cornered prey, while heightened big cat senses tingle with imminent danger from beyond. Perhaps, waiting for the asteroid, waiting for the end of faith.*

   Would I raise my primitive spear in aggression or would I accept a fate of digesting in the belly of the beast? What will I do in the final moment at the end of it all? Who will capture that moment, record our legacy? Our testament. Love or kill. All we are is all we are.

   Waylon's thoughts are usually minimalist, but he allows himself these sudden deep ponderings.

∞

The boy's name is Tim. Timothy, according to his paper nametag scrawled with the bright deliberate handwriting of a ten-year-old. He wears a white and purple football jersey and a plastic Viking helmet complete with yellow yarn braids that drape over his slight shoulders.

"OUTFUCKINGSTANDING," he says, and spears the broken pencil into his clay structure and current center of attention.

∞

"ACK!" What have you done, Timmy? Duckworth thinks. You've ruined this masterpiece and turned it into the media's culpability in war, genocide, and homelessness. Duckworth staggers, just a step or two. He sees it now, clearly. The media's culpability in war. It stops him cold, and his mouth goes to his hand. He swallows the sour burning in his gullet. He feels shame— indicted, but then a bellwether of a notion:

I've got an exclusive.

∞

In the corner, quiet and out of her depth, is Timmy's teacher. A buttoned-up, youngish looking woman, wearing a what-the-bloody-hell-is-that Dutch dress. Her name is Erma or Emily or Emma or something like that (introductions have not been made). She too is fixated on the boy's creation. She seems a bit uncomfortable here and mute as well, but in her head, behind clear eyes, the eyes of a giant beast stare back at her.[5]

∞

And next to her, slightly offstage, is a guest art critic with the *LA Times*, taking a break from staring at his umpteenth video montage exhibit with no discernable message. He looks away and discreetly pinches off one of his contact lenses and flicks it away. But pay him no mind for now, as he seems bored and above it all.[6]

∞

To recap this madcap macédoine: Duckworth (and if Duckworth were editing this list, it would read: Duckworth and his supporting cast consisting of... because Duckworth is clearly *the* leading man)[7], a photographer, an out of town critic and the little house on the prairie woman whose name starts with an E. And Timmy, the main attraction.

They've been staring at the end of the long table. On the table are a number of arts and crafts materials: clay, pen & ink, paper, Tinkertoy˙, string, balsa wood, charcoal, chalk, water colors, and LEGO˙. Every type of "craft" is equally represented.

---

5. *It is Skull Island, vibrating with Fay Wray's reluctant ecstasy. The great silverback's primal pull, to an age of hunting, eating, sleeping, fucking. She feels the nails dragging against her back shredding her clothing, exposing her flesh. The sun hot, the wind chill. Being taken. Driven to that place in her head where body and instinct purge shame and scream in pure stimulus and response. To that place where pagan gods are born.*

6. *Seriously. Pay him no mind.*

7. *Quite the opposite. See Chapter B.*

∞

Timothy O'Donnell hops in place and smacks his lips, pleased at the addition of a No. 2 pencil. Pleased and satisfied with his work and awash, if you will, in the calm of knowing that there is a balance to the hybrid of Tinkertoy˚ and Play-Doh˚ before him, his own version of the Rainbow Bridge to Asgard. The adults are pleased as well. That much is evident with their whispers, although the one man throwing the pencil puzzles him— but only for the brief second before he realizes that only a broken No. 2 pencil ("a found object" is how they will describe it later in the newspaper and magazine articles) would be the last and perfect piece for his Valhalla project.

Surely, he'll get an A. Outfuckingstanding, indeed.

And although he doesn't realize it now, in the short time Timmy will live, he will never again be this satisfied.

∞

Duckworth pulls loose his trademark Scottish plaid bow tie. All the better to breathe. Perhaps there is a fingerprint on the pencil, something that would tie Jasper P. Duckworth forever, physically, to the pencil, to this Work of Art. Despite this flash of impure thoughts, his knees waver and weaken with humility. He will not be swayed by anyone, not his colleagues or those college *art fags*[8] that

---

8. "art fag" being a term Duckworth co-opted from The Dead Milkmen. During his short, but formative punk phase. He now covers his fading Black Flag tattoo, which was, for a short time, a guaranteed free pass for microaggressions against incoming freshmen.

doze through his adjunct lectures and evening classes, with their funky haircuts and air of disaffected coolness.

Timmy's art is important.

And a ticket out of short straw assignments.

> *Think bigger.*

But dare he say the M-word?

What other word could he possibly use?

> *I have discovered a generational talent.*
>
> *I've been preparing for this my whole career.*
>
> *I can guide him.*

The LA critic shrugs off Timmy's work with a tear-producing yawn. The LA critic is lousy at poker.

Duckworth goes all in. "This is a Masterpiece."

Sacred & Profane

Oh God, what if Timothy— how to name him? "Tim" or "Timothy"? Would he use a middle name or middle initial? No middle initial. (They are pretentious and he knows it, but with

Google they are necessary so as to differentiate oneself from others with your name. There are over six billion people in the world after all.)

"Timmy," perhaps. But then he would always be known as "Timmy." Would it be fair for the adult Tim to have to compete with the shadow of his childhood? No... we'll go with his given name. Full, first, and last.

He tests it under his breath. "Timothy O'Donnell." *Artiste.*

Yes, it's falling into place. Books, lectures as a keynote speaker, a career studying this piece. Perhaps tenure at a university in another big city. But first Jasper P. Duckworth would lead a great historic convention in, say, Sweden. He would passionately dissect and bisect and deconstruct only to reconstruct this landmark piece of art in the history of art landmarks before their very eyes. He would abandon his dream of being a playwright (his longest held dream) for this, a higher calling. He would burn the letter in his jacket pocket next to his heart from the Julie Harris Playwriting Competition. It contains three copies of three reader comments on his submitted play ("Play").

1. "The violence was gratuitous and why was the man speaking in Pidgin English?" 30/100 *(He was faking the accent. Did you read the thing?)*

2. "The main character has no arc nor is likeable." 60/100 *(His goal is to resist the horrors of the world around him. He's an American hero. Did you read it?)*

3. "Decent read. Ambition far outweighs the talent. Nothing special." 71/100. *(I'm 49 and nothing special.)*

Yes, they would say later, perhaps years later:

I was there.

I was there at the Duckworth convention.

The boy Timothy O'Donnell was there as well.

They seemed close.

Like a father and son.

You could see the bond between them.

Duckworth, they would think, yes, an odd name for a man who was a master in the bedroom, their eyes glazing over with drifting memories of unbelievable orgasms, memories tainted with the sharp tug of heartache when he left to travel to other parts of the world with Timmy and *Untitled #9.*

Not *Untitled.* UN*TILTED*, Timothy might insist. LIKE PINBALL.

That is what Timmy would wish for and he was, after all, the Artiste. There would be black-tie parties. Duckworth and Timmy would be the toast. All those questions and flashbulbs popping, requests to be on the cover of magazines, but Duckworth imagines himself soon growing weary of that. They would part ways. A bittersweet chat along the Thames, capped by a hearty double-back clap hug, and Duckworth would force himself not to look back, even when he hears Timmy's footsteps hesitate. Oh, Duckworth would be sought out by other artists for his opinion, his blessing. But he would become a recluse. They'd have trouble finding him, papers would be written, hypotheses of where he might be now.

Gossip.

Rumors.

In a cabin in Montana painting.

Writing a *new* play.

A sighting in Tibet. Japan. The South of France. Stockholm.

He settled down with Swedish twins. Inga and Gretchen.

He dropped the middle initial from his name.

Duckworth wonders if he can get Timmy a ribbon now. Or a certificate, one with a gold stamp made of real foil. One that would be worth badgering his mom to get framed. Maybe even one of those special frames with, what was it, non-reflective glass. Timmy must sense it, Duckworth thinks, this *victory*.

Timmy farts and says: "YOU GOT ANY FUCKING CHOW IN THIS JOINT? MAYBE A GRILLED CHEESE?"

Waylon the photographer taps Duckworth's shoulder. "The kid wants to know if you can get a grilled cheese here at the restaurant out back."

"Timmy," Duckworth says. "Grilled cheese soon. But first, what do you call your masterpiece— er, art project?"

"RAGNARÖK," Timmy says. He chugs a good third of a cup of water from the fountain upstairs, dumps the rest on his face, hoists his project above his head like the Stanley Cup and screams: "RAGNARÖK AND ROLL!" And tears out of the room and into the museum proper, yellow braids streaming like the chem trails of a low flying jet.[9]

Duckworth, who is not prone to impulse or action, cannot make sense of what Timmy is screaming about, but realizes he has left the room and taken his Art into a large area filled with gawking tourists and thus Duckworth gives chase as he calls out to his subservient photographer: "Waylon!"[10]

∞

Waylon breaks out of his introspection with close, but not quite, side-clutching laughter. But now echoing from the hall where Duckworth and Timmy have disappeared, Waylon hears Timmy exclaim: "MAN OVERBOARD!" Waylon realizes they are on the second level, overlooking the museum foyer. Waylon realizes he

---

9. *Or like fake braids attached to a fake Viking helmet. Worn by a boy running.*

10. *Photographers fall into two types if you pay attention. You get the t-shirt/flannel, jeans, cargo shorts, mini-Maglite, Gerber all-in-one tool, tech types. A subset of these would be the photographers with the vests and an alarming number of pockets. These seem to be involved more in taking pictures of wars or sporting events. Both events requiring the use of ambulances and medics. They are usually grounded and workman-like. Minimalist.*

The second is the fashion-centric all-in-black types, usually with fashionably out of fashion hair. Much like those hairdressers who seemed to flaunt the very rules and trends of style they are recommending and selling. And always with spectacular eyeglasses you secretly wish you would be able to pull off, but know your friends and family would never let you live down. They are allowed to exhibit eccentric, if not questionable, behavior.

Waylon belongs to the former set.

has not landed THE SHOT of Timmy's piece, and professionally, though not morally, he, too, is obligated to give chase.

∞

Timmy darts in and out of tourists and staff, all of whom are overcome with bystander apathy. All except the children who point and the tweens who text and the teens who tweet.

"Stop, Timmy! Stop!" Duckworth screams. "For the love of Art! Please stop!"

Timmy runs, the wind in his face, and he kicks off his shoes mid-stride and sock skates. He is now an American college ice hockey player. They have finally slain the Great Bear and he is now looking for his dad in the stands, while hoisting his handmade Olympic Stanley Cup. (We will refrain from correcting Timmy's trophy knowledge, as it is not our place.)

∞

Waylon runs past Duckworth easily as people seem to clear the way for Waylon whereas Duckworth seems to be encountering his share of elbows and shoulder checks. Waylon clicks on the auto shutter and zooms in which, as every photographer, regardless of type, knows, means you have to be extra steady.

Timmy stops, pausing momentarily to spin in place, showing off his trophy. Timmy, as you can see, is more interested in trophies than medals. "U.S.A.! U.S.A.! U.S.A.!"

14

Waylon slides to a knee.

Fires off eight shots.

Out of focus.

Overexposed.

He adjusts. Fires two more shots as Timmy spins and breaks into a sprint.

Duckworth passes Waylon. "Timmy, please stop."

Timmy hauls ass. "DO YOU BELIEVE IN MIRACLES?"

Waylon pops up. Technically, it's his knee that pops. He cannot run, only hobble now. And Duckworth blocks a clear field of fire to Timmy, even with Timmy holding his masterpiece aloft.

Finally a clear shot.

Then: **BLACK OUT.**

"No photography in the museum, sir." A Latino kid with a high and tight military haircut wearing baggy pants and an ill-fitting polo shirt has put his hand in front of Waylon's camera. With the other, he points a walkie-talkie sideways gangsta style at him. His name tag reads: HECTOR.

Waylon smiles. "Sure, no problem." And holds the camera above his head and goes auto fire. He sidesteps Hector, and then gambles, taking the stairs down below by way of a heroic bannister slide. He tumbles and slides on his knees as if a genuflecting Elvis (pompadour and all), and points the camera straight up focusing on the railing. He cannot miss the shot.

Timmy stops against the railing of the museum foyer. Then he is standing on it. The game changes and Timmy screams: "OOGA CHAKA. OOGA CHAKA. VIRGIN SACRIFICE!"

"No, Timmy," Duckworth says. "Take me instead!"

But Timmy, a Ritalin-free kid, flips channels faster than a machine gun and pulls out a cigar torch and ignites the pencil. The fuse is lit.

Duckworth just reaches him, leans his body over the railing to catch the masterpiece as Timmy O'Donnell of Lake Forest, IL becomes the bastard son of Thomas Ferebee and Robert Oppenheimer. His art project is the Little Boy. He lets it fly.

"BOMBS AWAY, BITCHES!"

Through his lens, Waylon watches it tumble down, this death from above.

WHIRL CLICK

WHIRL CLICK

WHIRL CLICK

WHIRL CLICK

WHIRL CLICK

WHIRL CLICK

WHIRL CLICK

Until the point of impact on Waylon Nagasaki's face.

It is a tiny isolated nuclear blow.

The fallout of which will reach from here to Mars.[11]

B

"Don't be the coward of your own life," his dad had said.

But, B is a middle-aged man and couldn't give a shit about the missing sculpture. What can you do about another City Hall fuck-up? Except it represents time and money. He loaned the sculpture to the City as part of a neighborhood-centric display. They rotated it around the City, but by the time a serious buyer made inquiries, it had gone into city storage. And now it is missing. The City has no paperwork to even prove they had it; consequently they are not even looking. No sculpture. No sale. No reparations. He is broke. He stares at his cell phone, an old flip version, which sits silently on his bar table. An object of stillness.

Any minute he will receive a text message: *GO/NO GO.* If *GO* then a new commission will be official and he will be solvent for the next six months. Working. Creating. Living the life. If only for six months.

---

11. *Yes. Mars.*

If *NO GO*, he is fucked, and this will be his Last Meal.

∞

A pink-haired waitress in a tight white t-shirt zips past.

"Say, waiter! Water, please?" Bellio slurs. He raises a finger pointing to his empty hand-blown Chihuly knock-off water glass, but she's already gone. B adjusts his greasy overalls and repositions his greasy ball cap, the one with the big red "B." He resettles on the bar stool at a bar table at the back of the ArtBar. It wobbles despite the matchbooks, folded menus, and moldy napkins shoved under the legs. They all wobble. B had a deal with the old owner of the ArtBar to make and install a new shock-absorber system to keep them all level and look cool, a new retro steampunk look to the ArtBar. It would have been a nice paycheck, nice exposure, and a permanent marketing installation for B. But the owner became the old owner and the new owner was more interested in a new menu. Even when B offered him the same for 50% off.

A curtain of darkened glass lines the edge of the round table. He knows the artisan who made them. Everything here at the ArtBar is handcrafted. Or was. His eyes blur with a numbing buzz. B belches and slams down another empty. A few drops shoot out of his glass like glitter on a pounded snare drum. They dot the greasy fingerprinted copy of the *Chicago Shoulders*, one of the free newspapers stacked by the bar door. This edition contains the Duckworth column about new geniuses Duckworth discovered at the MCA.

Timmy — 10.

Tabby — 72.

It's a puff piece, and "genius" is used ironically. He thinks. Still. A ten-year-old is getting more press than I have in five years, B thinks. But of course. B is not the oldest, or the youngest, nor does he have the most bizarre backstory.

> *It used to be you could roll up your sleeves and do the work. Not anymore.*

B wads up the newspaper column and starts to drop it under the table. He stops. Smoothes it flat(ish) and sets it across from him. He checks his phone. The battery meter ticks down to the last bar. Three city blocks away his charger sits silently. Another object of stillness.

∞

The bar is quiet tonight.

An image catches his eye on the TVs above the bar. The new owner has inexplicably installed TVs. As if someone would say, hey, let's go down to the ArtBar and watch TV. (But Chicago is a sports town, and these things matter during a playoff run.)

The image is of a round, creased, and cratered moon of a face, beaming with positive energy and a splatter of paint. The camera pans along his face to his silver hair to the impossibly long trademark ponytail, to the dowel in his hand, to the tip of the ponytail being used as a paintbrush. Pans again to the canvas where it reads: CAN I BE A PART OF ROSS ROBARDS' 30th ANNIVERSARY PARTY? The camera tilts down. B looks away, sways a bit. The unseen words already echoing in his head with the sing-song melodic hook of the world's worst three note jingle: YES, YOU CAN!

B tries one more bite of his pulled pork sandwich. It's a new item on the new menu. He puts it down and lets the half chewed bite fall to his plate. He nibbles on the bun, trying to get something down to soak up his booze-filled gut.

"Do I know you?" It's the pink-haired waitress. She's outflanked him. The pink-haired waitress is new. He's never seen her here before, and she seems a little shy or plain evasive. Her customer service banter is non-existent and B thinks she knows him from somewhere. You can tell because she doesn't ask "Do I know you?" with a smile or a flirty practiced wink that experienced waitresses know means an additional five percent tip, but with an irritated I-can't-remember-who-sang-that-song tone. Her silk-screened tight white t-shirt sports an unfamiliar logo: BITHA. And she is braless, wearing her pert carefree nipples like jewelry. "Are you sure I don't know you?" she says, again.

Her question elicits a weak smile from B. He doesn't ignore her, but he wants solitude, but he doesn't want to be ignored, but he wants to be near people, be near life, be near alcohol. He wants that phone to vibrate, and he wants a glass of water. He wants to go back in time to that internship interview in 1983 with Ross Robards. He wants to do things differently. He wants to pinpoint that moment in his life where it all went sideways. Where he should have taken that left turn at Albuquerque.

If he could only redo that moment.

If he only had a time machine.

If.

"Don't I know you?"

B shrugs. "I come in here all the time," he says. He adjusts his greasy baseball cap with the red "B" on it. B wants to lay his weary head against her chest and fall into a carefree sleep. Of all the things he wants, he would settle for that.

"I'm new," she says.

"I'm Bob Bellio."

"You're trouble, I heard."

He smiles. She splits into two for a moment, a comic book blur of speed. He adjusts his greasy Buddy Holly glasses. "Where'd you hear that from?"

"Jawbone. She says you're trouble. Capital T. And a hack. Capital H."

"Jawbone says that about everyone."

"No, Jawbone mentioned you by name."

"I'd like more water, Pinky Lee," he says.

She frowns. The frown that says someone else is in charge of water, and that refilling your water does not help me with the current song in my head problem. Before she can walk away, B snags the back pocket of her impossibly tight jeans with their stitched logo: SPANK!

"And my sandwich is off," B says, letting go of her jeans and noticing he's left a greasy fingerprint.

"Pulled pork?"

"Yeah, but taste it."

"What's wrong?"

"Just taste it."

"I can't," she says, making an icky face, staring at the half eaten bit that's landed half on his plate and half on his newspaper. "I'm a vegan."

"Bullshit," he says. "Taste it." He pulls a small bite for her. "I don't have cooties," he says, but she eyes the dirt and grime under his fingernails, occupationally and permanently stained black. "Taste it."

She pauses. But she has three older brothers and takes a bite. She's eaten worse. "It's good."

B shakes his head. "No no no no. Taste it."

"It's good."

"No no."

"Yes yes."

"No. No. The sauce. The hell kind of sauce is that?"

"BBQ."

"*That* is not BBQ sauce. It's—"

"East coast BBQ sauce."

"What?"

"It's vinegar based."

"Oh."

"Yeah."

B collects himself. "It's an abomination," he says. "Can I get real sauce? KC, or Texas?"

"I'll check, but I don't think we have it."

"You don't," B assures her.

"Then why are you asking?"

"I'm trying to spread awareness."

"Start a revolution?"

"Yes," B slurs. There are five of her. Ten pert carefree breasts. Enough to stretch from head to toe if B were to line them up and nap. Then three of her. B speaks to the one in the middle. He wishes the one in the middle would shut up and climb into his lap and he would hold her and lay his head against her neck and make that non-ringing, non-vibrating phone not matter. Make his old chipped glasses not matter. Make not crossing that stream not matter. Make time travel to 1983 not matter.

"Bring in your own next time," she says.

"Maybe I will," B says. "I'll make my own damn BBQ sauce. How's that?"[12]

"You do that, Farmer B." She winks and walks off.

"I will make my own dang BBQ," he says to the mutilated and dejected pulled pork sandwich. "From scratch. And I'm not a farmer. Heh."

He grabs his hand-blown Chihuly knock-off water glass. Still empty. "Uh, water," he says, looking up. But she's gone, taking sanctuary with her. B checks his phone as he turns off the backlight to conserve energy, angling it in the light of the dusty Wurlitzer. Still one battery bar.

The Ross Robards commercial plays again. This time it's different. This time it tells B that it's never too late to become an artist. That millions of people have become artists with Ross Robards' books. His tapes. His DVDs. Now there's a new podcast. B doubts that Ross Robards, his red eyes most likely whitened with digital technology, knows what the fuck a podcast is. Millions sold. Three different kits. Three different price points. B does a number of quick calculations in his head. Fuck. Me. is the bottom line each time.

B pulls out his wallet. A few gas station singles. A carbon piece of paper.

---

12. Years later, B will look back at this moment and chuckle. At the time it didn't seem worthy of a footnote.

Name: Robert Bellio
Bank: Bank One
Account number: 092734-9283
Balance: −1,509

It's temporary, he tells himself. Only temporary.

How different would it have been: success?

B sits there. Object of stillness.

And then he asks out loud: How can City Hall lose a twenty-foot sculpture?

The Ring of Fire

It is a heart attack. Duckworth knows it. This tapping in his chest.

This is the end.

At least I'm in an art museum, he thinks. His wife would bring flowers every month, a permanent installation piece.

If he'd ever been married.

Oh, Inga, oh, Gretchen.

Erma or Emily or Emma gasps, tightening her thighs.

"I didn't get the shot," Waylon says. He pushes his shattered $3,000 dollar lens aside as he pulls the still smoking jagged end of the No. 2 pencil out of his cheek. "I didn't get it. I didn't get the shot."

The *LA Times* critic takes a small step back from the crowd and produces another tear-producing yawn.[13]

Duckworth takes a deep breath. The pain fades to a mild heartburn, and the roll of Tums in his pocket should alleviate that.

Waylon taps Duckworth's shoulder.

Duckworth takes Waylon's hand. Grips it. "Oh God, Waylon, you scruffy but loyal cameraman."

"I didn't get the shot."

"It's going to be okay, Waylon."

"I didn't get the—" Waylon stops mid-sentence and takes Duckworth's head in his large callused hands. Why are they callused so, Duckworth wonders— and turns Duckworth to the staircase.

∞

Descending the staircase, Tabby Masterson, another patron of the BE AN ARTIST™ exhibit, balances on the palm of her hand a creation of wire and tissue and paper so delicate that using the words ephemeral and ethereal would be too harsh. Tabby, a tomboyish woman in her early seventies, was widowed five years ago and has recently joined a women's group that plays cards and takes advantage

---

13. Though instant reply may reveal the tear was produced prior to the yawn, the call stands.

of Chicago's many sights. The Museum of Contemporary Art is on that list (#6). Her jaw hangs slightly open, not because it is easier to breathe, but in disbelief and dismay at Timothy O'Donnell's possible destruction of one of the most beautiful things she's ever seen. She feels shame for the pride she feels for her own recently completed work from the BE AN ARTIST™ exhibit. A mobile of paper-thin thread-like creatures in flight returning home for the mating season: *Migration.*

∞

The din of the major metropolitan museum and the Timmy chaos and the instant cursing of slow up-loads to video sites and the gawking of tourists and the scrambling of security guards not equipped for this type of commotion hits an eerie silence where everyone is synched with the same inward breath.

Their collective exhale nudges *Migration* into action. The birds drift in flight over and under one another, soaring and diving over her hand, until they synch up into a perfect V pattern. Though mesmerized, people clear a path for Tabby. The din surges back like a wave, rolling with gasps and monotheistic proclamations, then recedes back to an ocean of silence. Waylon looks at the mobile sculpture. His palms sweat. He can think of no angle at which he could capture the beauty of the object. He curses his own shortcomings and array of photographic tricks and lighting he's built his career on.

I am a hack.

But the professional in him takes over. He switches to a short lens, replacing the ruined lens, and his finger depresses the button. *CLICK. EER, EEERR, EEERRR, EEEEERRRR.* He is out of film, the last frame exposed for Timmy's makeshift Atomic Asgardian Olympic Stanley Cup. The advantages of going digital become all too clear.

∞

Tabby is pleased they want to take her picture, as that was part of the senior tour package for the BE AN ARTIST™ exhibit here at the MCA. She is flattered by the attention, especially from Duckworth. It's a name she thinks odd, and must have been cause for concern for him in his youth on the playgrounds of wherever. Yes, he really is the Associate Media Critic from the *Chicago Shoulders*. She actually reads his column, but only on Super Bowl Sundays, right before the obituaries.

Another fellow is here from LA. She wonders how big an art scene there is in LA, since all she knows about LA is that they make tons and tons of movies there. She wonders how anything gets done in that town, if everyone works in the industry as she suspects they do. She has heard that everyone is an actor or writing a screenplay. She is going to write one someday about growing up in the oil fields of Kansas.

At the moment, she only wants to know if Timmy did the unthinkable, as she could only hear him screaming as he ran. Right now she balances *Migration* on her hand, only because the long arcing wires will not allow her to set it down without destroying it.

She'd built the thing with one hand while the master post dug into the palm of her other hand. A small drop of blood pools there. A dimpled stigmata. Over the railing, she sees Timmy's piece in ruins and her heart breaks.

∞

Duckworth feels exposed, as naked as a newborn. He cannot look away or offer any deflective wry commentary about Tabby Masterson. Tabby Masterson, who has in the span of forty-five minutes created a Work of Art. A masterpiece.

Another masterpiece.

With each half step Tabby takes down the staircase, a hush radiates out until the entire foyer is quiet as a winter's night. A clique of art students stop their sarcastic commentary. One, two, then six drop to their knees, leaning her way. Towards Tabby. They call her by name.

"Goddess."

Axiom

Duckworth leads a quick meeting in an upstairs office between Les the curator who is a trim, affable fellow and apparently, by his tan and thinning blonde hair, an avid golfer and the *LA Times* critic, who finally introduces himself. His name is Eyal (a name Duckworth finds challenging to pronounce). Waylon putters around in the back of the office in despair. It is a huddle during a thirty-second time out.

"Two masterpieces in one day?" Les says.

"A ten-year-old," Duckworth says. His cell phone vibrates. He ignores it. "And a seventy-year-old."

"Must be something in the water," Eyal the LA critic says, yawning again.

"Two—"

"Yes, two."

"Two in one day?"

"Two."

"We're certainly pleased the exhibit is inspiring such success, er, inspiration across a nice demographic," Les says. "The exhibit designer will be happy to know. I'll pass along your kudos. I think, however, the term *masterpiece*—"

"It's subjective," Eyal says, blowing his nose.

"Thank God we preserved both," Duckworth says. "One on film, the other with loose plastic wrap. If we can procure any. It's downstairs."

Les asks: "And what about the first one?"

"The first was destroyed by the artist, Timmy (and with it the dreams of the Duckworth Convention in Sweden). But we have a picture of it," Duckworth says, gesturing to Waylon, who paces and shakes his head in shock. A small streak of blood from the pencil puncture makes it look like he has been shot in the face with a small caliber firearm.

"It was the inferior piece," says the LA critic.

Waylon looks up defensively, as if the LA critic is judging his skills.

"I think not," Duckworth says.

"That's your opinion."

"My opinion?" says Duckworth.

"Yes, *your* opinion," the LA critic says. "Art is subjective."

"*My* opinion? I'm the Media Critic of the *Shoulders*." (He omits "Associate.")

"I'm the *Chief* Art Critic of the *LA Times*."

"You're in Chicago now," Duckworth says. His cell phone vibrates again. Again he ignores it.

The curator smiles politely.

Duckworth hates that.

Les nods.

"I say there are—"

"Were—"

"Two genius pieces in your BE AN ARTIST™ exhibit. Please, come down and look at them—"

"It."

Duckworth imagines jabbing his spare pencil through Eyal's eyeball. The pencil that has drafted many witty and clever media reviews of the best and worst TV commercials of the last several years. "Waylon, how long before you can get that film developed to show them Timmy's piece?"

Waylon raises his camera with a weary sigh. "I didn't get the—"

"Couple of hours?" Duckworth offers. Then to Les: "He uses real film." Duckworth pulls out his cell phone and sees the text from his younger boss at the *Chicago Shoulders*.

CUT BACKZ. NEED A KILLER STORY OR UR OUT

"Shall we, shall we..." Duckworth pauses, gathering himself, as he imagines sticking another pencil in Eyal's eyeball. "Shall we go find Tabby, er, Tabitha?" Duckworth wonders which name she'll prefer. He also wonders if she has a current passport. *Migration* would do well in Sweden.

∞

"My God," Duckworth repeats on viewing Tabby Masterson's piece.

"My gosh, you boys lay it on a bit thick," Tabby says. "Don't you think?" *Migration* draws blood from her palm, one drop at a time.

She's afraid to set the piece down and damage it. An art student with fake angel wings who has followed them back to the exhibit catches a drop with a blue shop towel. "I certainly feel I've gotten my money's worth," Tabby says.

Les, a wide smile under a perfectly trimmed cigar mustache, takes it from her. He snaps his fingers and two white gloved, white lab-coated museum assistants whisk the piece away. "We'll properly box it up to ship home to you," Les says. "In four to six weeks."

You can see this idea frightens Tabby, but the presence of an authority figure with a tan and mustache keeps her silent.

Les seems pleased with the audience and the art students, whereas Duckworth seems to eye them with suspicion, despite the fact this would be a large percentage of his fan base at the Duckworth Convention.

∞

"Run along," Duckworth says, feeling vaguely like a character out of a Dickens novel or short story or whatever it was Dickens wrote.

The other patrons and the clique of art students and their phone cameras and videos (in clear violation of museum policies) in the BE AN ARTIST™ exhibit are escorted out by Hector, though the posted sign for the exhibit clearly states that it is to remain open for another hour. A fact pointed out by Timmy with a shiny new watch from the gift store. "TIME CHECK!"

∞

They've now cleared the room save for Tabby and Timmy (the similarity in the names now starting to dawn on Waylon, who could foresee problems with the photo's caption, if he can muster the strength of will for a simple medium two shot), the curator Les, and Duckworth. And that teacher, Erma or Emma or Emily. Duckworth can't remember and she wears no nametag, having taken it off and tossing it after spilling Kool-Aid (Double Double Cherry) on it earlier.

The *LA Times* critic Eyal has begged off, citing his angina. No one notices Timmy's own sock-skating exit in Eyal's wake.

Duckworth doesn't seem thrilled about Erma or Emma or Emily's stoic presence, but as she points out, she has to stay if Timmy is going to miss the bus back to school. They do have a legal responsibility to watch after the children, after all. She laughs as she explains this to him, thinking that an adult wearing a bow tie, albeit an untied one, would take this as a matter of course. But perhaps the bow tie moved Duckworth into that eccentric range of people for whom such things had to be explained. She herself would appreciate an explanation, as she doesn't understand what is going on, being distracted by the realization that her panties are damp.

"Tell me again," Erma or Emma or Emily says, watching her hand reach out on its own and touch Les' shoulder.

"We, that is, myself," Les the curator says, "and these two gentleman would like to give Tabby and Timmy—"

"He's my student," Erma or Emma or Emily says.

34

"Ah, yes, very good," Les says, with a wink. He leans forward, puts his hand on her back. "So, we're going to give Tabby and Timmy a couple of hours alone."

Erma or Emma or Emily nods, her panties now wet.

Duckworth nods.

Les nods.

Waylon wonders aloud if he's picked the right f-stop.

Erma or Emma or Emily leans closer to Les.

Les' voice drops to a whisper. "We want them to work on another piece of art much as they did earlier. These two gentlemen as you know are from the paper and believe these two may have T-A-L-E-N-T." He spells it out like that as his hand on her back slips an inch or two lower than appropriate, right at the curve of her ass.

"I'm sorry," Erma or Emma or Emily says, flushing with shame and asking for clarification as her panties are now horrifically soaked.

"Talent," the curator whispers.

A jolt runs through her body. "Oh. I see," Erma or Emma or Emily says, stepping away from Les to get her bearings. "Timmy's always been a dabbler. I'm his homeroom teacher," she says with a tinge of pride for the first time.

"GOOD CHRIST," Timmy says, with a mouthful of grilled cheese as he sock-skates back into the exhibit. "WHAT SMELLS LIKE POON?"

The curator and Duckworth exchange glances.

Waylon fishes around in his camera bag for another 35mm lens.

Duckworth turns and faces Tabby and Timmy. "We'll give you an hour and then come back and check on you."

Tabby and Timmy look at each other. Tabby's stomach growls and she blushes. "I'd like more water," she says. "Please."

Duckworth looks to delegate.

Waylon picks up a large Styrofoam cup. Hands it to Timmy's teacher. "Please..." Waylon indicates his camera as if it means something of rank.

"There's a fountain on the third floor," Tabby says.

"Yes, the third floor," Les says to Duckworth.

Tapping his chin and smiling at Tabby, Duckworth says: "Ethel, if you would please."

"THAT WATER IS SHIT WARM," Timmy says. "SHIT WARM, I TELL YA."

Caesura Forte-Piano

Emma wanders the halls of the MCA, the Styrofoam cup in her hand now an afterthought. She wanders through a wing of the museum, her eyes drifting into what she and her girlfriends call the Museum Stare. Too much to think about and ponder. A half-century of art reduced to a blur in the peripheral vision, but in her mind's eye: Timmy's project; a primal vision of Chaos. And Tabby's project; an ethereal (or is that too harsh?) one of Order. She thinks of her stepfather, Morton. He would appreciate both, but gravitate towards the intricacies of Tabby's.

Ooga chaka ooga chaka

A yellow placard sign off to the side blocks her way to the water fountain. It says: WET FLOOR. She decides she is thirty-years-old and Tabby is thirsty and no sign is going to stop her. She feels ramped with this decision, this ne'er-do-well attitude, an echoing déjà vu of when she refused more piano lessons when she was Timmy's age. (Posture did her in.) It powers her forward to the water fountain in the corner, where she takes a few gulps and wipes a drop of water from her chin. Timmy was right. Shit warm.

The movement of a butterfly inside the museum catches her attention. It flits about an African statue for a moment and then disappears into the shadows. The stature is of two men in an embrace, or women, their sex undeterminable as they join at the crotch. She touches the piece. Her chest flushes.

∞

The summer of her thirteenth year when her friends were upgrading their bras, she slouched her shoulders, not hiding new breasts, but concealing a lack of. Only her hips grew. She felt awkwardly out of proportion, falling outside the bell curve. So she took to wearing jackets. Army, Navy. Thrift store shopping. It was unique without standing out. She kept her head down, navigating the crowds of her school with invisible ease. The river of students, the moving dots of color all trained by the bell. She felt comfortable in the crowd, in this slipstream of invisibility, at prom and homecoming dances, always slipping the stream. Always being the fourth or sixth choice of the boys who wanted to dance, but who only had three choices in mind.

∞

And now she is in her seventh year of teaching, at home again in the slipstream. The confined halls, the moving streams of students with eyes only for each other. She embraces technology in her classes: webcasts, podcasts, films, and movies. Situating herself at the back of the class, a voice in the darkness. Unseen. The darkness, her chrysalis. Her first year teaching she was excited to take center stage. Until the stabbings. A pencil. A pair of scissors. A protractor. Now she struggles to get through the day, the weeks, the months until the next extended school break.

∞

She almost went into entomology. Studying insects, specifically butterflies. She had a delicate collection as a child. Her killing jar and pins arranged meticulously on her dresser. Her stepdad, Morton, made her a frame of wood to hold and hang her specimens. He was younger than the other dads. Handsome. Raising her as his own.

"Don't worry, darlin'," Morton said, when he caught her posing in the mirror looking for change that summer. Wiping his hands on his greasy overalls. The oils never coming out of his clothes, no matter how hard she scrubbed. Or from under his fingernails. "My little caterpillar will get her wings. Be more beautiful than a Monarch."

That summer she wanted him to take her to prom. She wanted to ride shotgun in the monster truck he tinkered with on evenings and weekends, even when she found the dirty magazines in a metal tool box in the barn.

She snuck glances at them, leafing through the oil fingerprinted pages. They seem so quaint now. Classy almost. Years later, she confiscated a similar magazine from a young student. Same girl posing. Same hair. Same measurements. Only the shade of eye shadow was different. And the shape of the breasts. Was it a genetic thing? Or a trendy thing in publishing tastes?

Morton caught her again that summer staring at the mirror wearing one of his tight undershirts. A wife beater. He saw one of his magazines spread on her bed. He said nothing, but kissed her forehead and cooked her favorite meal: plank-grilled salmon on the outdoor Weber. Later that week she noticed the ashes and pieces of burned magazine in the bottom of the grill. Had he burned his whole collection?

That summer change never came. She never got her wings. And at the State Fair of Minnesota, as a B.J. Thomas song played over the PA system, Morton ended up fifty feet from his upside down monster truck, his helmet and skull cracked on a concrete barrier.

∞

The school where she currently teaches has nixed the Vo-Tech programs and most of the shop classes. Instead of preparing young people for the jobs that keep the country running (keep the cars and trucks on the road, the bridges safe, the gears and cogs of the American machine lubed), she now preps young students for the jobs that will profit corporations by placing factories overseas, appeasing their shareholders as the last generation of Americans who knew what MADE IN USA meant watch their children become digital slaves.

In the back of her desk drawer in her classroom is a greasy eighteen-inch adjustable crescent wrench. *Craftsman*. MADE IN USA. Lifetime guarantee. Her stepdad's helmet had no such guarantee.

∞

And now here in the MCA, she unbuttons the first front two buttons of her frilly outfit. The HVAC kicks on and the cool air ripples her breasts with goose pimples. Her nipples press against her cheap utilitarian brassiere.

The African statue now seems to be earth to Tabby's heaven and Timmy's hell. Her hand flits down to her crotch. A butterfly to her diving bell. She catches herself and looks briefly over her shoulder to make sure no one is watching, especially one of those annoying part-time student security guards with the matching shirts and walkie-talkies.

But someone is. There in the shadows. A black woman. In ill-fitting overalls with a tool bag. Dreadlocks. The woman stares at her.

Emma smiles. Wets her lips. She says: "My name is Emma." Bites her lower lip.

The woman in overalls smirks and museum light glints off her silver teeth. She takes a swig from a metal water bottle. Emma even sees the logo: FUCK ART.

Ooga chaka ooga chaka

Smiling back at the woman with dreadlocks, Emma's butterfly fingers flit here and there. Searching in vain for nectar through the thick cotton dress. Her other hand follows the contours of the sculpture, then she unbuttons another button. The slight swell of her cleavage now exposed. The plain white edge of her bra now shockingly visible for anyone to see.

She half expects a slap of guilt. Damnation. Discipline.

Bad, bad girl.

She closes her eyes. Imagines—

A *squawk* of a walkie-talkie brings Emma back to earth. She adjusts her dress. She makes eye contact with the woman in overalls, and looks away in anticipation of crushing shame. It does not come. Emma smiles, relieved, and blows her a kiss.

Emma ducks into the bathroom, giddy with her naughtiness, her *brazenness*. She chooses the second stall on the right, a chrysalis pale green fiberglass box. Her thighs are damp and not with sweat. She unhooks her bra from the back, wrestles with the front/back combination of the dress buttons and back clasp of the bra and shoves her hand roughly under the wire, grasping her breast, twisting her hard nipple. Her head spins, she grasps the stall wall and sits down, planting her feet at latch level on either side of the door. Emma imagines she is a third participant in the sculpture while that cute photographer Waylon takes pictures. She hopes the FUCK ART woman outside will follow her in. She is dripping, the fingers of her left hand circling her slick clit, her nail catching in her untrimmed bush, and then dipping into her wetness and again circling her clit, circles smaller and bigger Sol LeWitt style. She does not hope when she imagines, but wills them to come in and join her. The stall can no longer contain her. This is not a harmless fantasy, but commitment. Emma swears to her god that if the restroom door opens, she will give them a show. Any man. Any woman. Any beast. Will be embraced in an orgy of flesh and become a living breathing sculpture. She will let them do anything. Anything. Anywhere. She will obey. Give herself over. Submit. Now she finds the right angle, the right pressure, but she hesitates, fighting her body to maintain a holding teasing pattern, waiting while the world outside the restroom finds the spirit to join her, but it is the middle of the week during the day and nothing happens. She decides she will no longer wait for anyone or anything. Ever again. Seven seconds later, a surge ripples through her body in wave after glorious wave of colored energy.

Oh Morton.

∞

Emma will tell this scenario to her cousin Archie at a family reunion. And again in an alley, in the back seat of his squad car. Handcuffed. Where he will no doubt give her the punishment she deserves.

Ooga chaka ooga chaka

Having lost all sense of time and despite the weakness in her knees, Emma power-walks up to the museum foyer, holding the cup of water out like a giant egg on a spoon at a state fair race. Though Timmy seems to have an acute sense of smell, she vaguely wonders if the others can smell the sex on her fingers. And then she wonders if butterflies have a sense of smell.

∞

Duckworth looks at his watch. Clucks his tongue.

Emma positions herself closer to Waylon.

"You smell nice," he says.

"Thank you."

Duckworth clucks his tongue again.

The curator, Les, strolls up, his presence announced by the tapping of his faux alligator shoes on the floor.

Duckworth looks at his watch.

An hour has elapsed. The allotted time for the Artists in Residence. That's how Les spoke of them, and though it started with a more sarcastic tone, it is now sincere.

"Shall we?" Duckworth says.

They take a collective deep breath and head to the BE AN ARTIST™ exhibit's entrance. But Tabby and Timmy are gone, and the door to the exhibit locked. Our friend Hector, the zealous Latino security guard, having closed the exhibit at the posted time.

To hide his frustration, Duckworth turns to the MCA window facing Seneca Park. Three Monarch butterflies thud mutedly again and again against the window. Suddenly, one, then two hungry cardinals crash into the window and fall to the ground, their beaks crushed and necks broken.

Duckworth stares at the avian corpses.

Oh mum, oh dad.

Stepping in front of him, Emma puts her hand on the glass, eyes upward, tracking the floating butterflies.

Junk Yard Dogs

This fucking chair is going to kill me.

"Keep looking," Jawbone says, digging through the collected junk in the bed of a rusting pick-up truck parked at a scrap yard. She pauses to take a swig of Chicago's finest tap water from her FUCK ART bottle. There are curious watchers; Mexicans mostly, with beat-up trucks, their beds built up simply and haphazardly on the sides with old sheets of plywood and wire and filled with a "*miscellany*"— good word, thinks Jawbone, a miscellany of scrap metal. Anything from old appliances to unused pipe to too-lazy-to-repair furniture are piled high with this morning's treasures found along Dumpsters and alleys. "It's gotta be about yea big," she says, putting a loose band around her dreads. "Half moon. Crescent moon. I want it found, not fabbed."

"I don't see nothing looking like that," Hector says, wearing his MCA shirt, though untucked and now terminally stained with the juice of discarded fruit, oil, dirt, and grime.

"Keep digging."

"No, I don't see nothing like that chair in this picture." Hector holds up a page ripped from a magazine sporting a cool modern Higby-designed chair produced by Laxmie's.

"That picture is just a suggestion," Jawbone says. Her ass itches. She scratches it once, and then wipes her hands on her overalls.[14] She hates the new pair. Two weeks and counting. She should wash them more to break them in. The other pair, my lord, that other pair was like slipping into an old love: comfortable, familiar, knew where to touch you and always took your call. The initial decision of jeans vs.

---

14. *This is our leading lady.*

overalls for the plumber vocation was an easy one, considering all the plumber's crack jokes. And, well, it was true, you spend your day bending over and snaking drains your pants are going to slip, belt or no belt. And suspenders? Well, you can forget them, they'll put your arms to sleep inside a country minute. And let me ask you this, friend, are you sure you want your plumber at $64.99 an hour to spend one minute out of every ten hitching her britches?

I think not.

So overalls it was. Been that way for her at Walker & Sons Plumbing for the last fifteen years. (There are no sons, only her.) But that's her day job. Jawbone is attending to more important matters right now.

This fucking chair.

Hector pauses, staring again at the jagged magazine page. "I thought you said she wanted a chair just like this."

"She *thinks* she wants one just like that," Jawbone says.

"Didn't she give you a deposit?"

"Watch it," Jawbone grunts. She heaves a piece of scrap pipe into the back of her new-to-her F-150 pickup. It bangs against her truck bed tool boxes, but not as loudly as you might expect, due to her new professionally sprayed-on Rhino-bed liner. She's been thinking about having a sculpture sprayed with it. But it's a fleeting cart-before-horse thought. Everything now is about that fucking chair.

She shifts through the other morning loads.

Hector shadows Jawbone, commenting on Jawbone's rejects, mostly agreeing. Sometimes not.

Jawbone's arrangement with the scrap place and the scrappers gives her right of first refusal on their loads. Then she pays more cash to the scrappers than they would have received if they'd sold by the pound. The owner of the scrap place sits on the board of the MCA and other hoity-toity places with hoity-toity people, but genuinely likes Jawbone and loves to hear the *Home Depot Polaroid Art Project* toilet story. The owner loves hanging out with most artists and getting to know them personally. He finds the real ones to be appreciative of things meriting appreciation and disdainful of things that need searing and, additionally, such artists are generally entertaining folks and will switch it up occasionally searing genuine things and praising shit. "Just to keep'em on their toes," Jawbone would say with a wink.

"By the way," Jawbone says. "I wanna check out that new exhibit."

"Be An Artist? Eh, it's kiddie bullshit," Hector says. "They got uppity critics coming in tomorrow. Doing a softie on Arts Education."

"*Uppity critics?*"

"You know, *villainous.*"

"Maybe I'll swing by soon for a look-see," she says, her metal mouth gleaming.

"I'll be working that wing after lunch." [15] Hector's head tick-tocks between the magazine picture and the scattered junk.

---

15. Hector likes the quiet Zen of the museum, but recently has come to loathe Brian Eno.

"Well, helloooo, baby," Jawbone says, picking up two scarred skillet lids. "I think these'll work."

"You think?" Hector doesn't.

"I can see it," Jawbone says.

"Can you?" Hector can't.

"Starting to take shape." She taps her head.

"Hey," Hector says. "I'm so confused. Which chair you making? Because nothing you're grabbing looks like the chair in this picture. Won't your client be pissed?"

The Good, the Bad and the Ugly sounds off in the front pocket of Jawbone's overalls.

Hector is prescient.

Jawbone flips open her cell phone. Before she can answer, a female voice screams at her. Screaming not in volume, but in tone. Akin to a Lincoln Park white woman, which she is, asking to speak to a manager.

"*Where is my chair?*"

"It's in, uh, process," Jawbone says.

"In *process?*"

"I'm noodling on a few variations I'd like to show you."

"*Noodling?*"

"Maybe something a little more original."

"Original? Oh God."

"Luv 'n' Haight" starts to play in her other pocket.

Hector says, "Hey man. Your plumber's phone is ringing. Is that Sly? I got *There's A Riot Goin' On* on vinyl. Just this week."

Jawbone pulls out the other phone, a six shooter in each hand.

"*Original?* Have you even started building it, Ms. Jawbone?"

"One sec," Jawbone says. "You're breaking up."

"Don't you dare—"

Click (on hold).

"Walker Plumbing," Jawbone says into the other cell phone.

"Thank God I caught you, Harriet. It's our upstairs toilet."

"I can't, Jackie. I'm in the middle of a project."

"What project?"

"A chair."

"A chair?"

"It's complicated, Jacqueline."

"The chair is complicated?"

"For your wife Beth. She's on the other line."

"Jesus Jones, is she still grousing about me not buying her that Higby piece?"

"But I've got an idea for a cool custom—"

"Her lipstick friends won't appreciate it. They all love that high-end Higby shit. You know I love your stuff. Just love it. It's the best. But for now just knock out that knock-off and fix the toilet. It's running. Still running."

"You only need to check the—"

"I've already left for the downtown condo and then a week in the islands with Gisele— I mean Beth— tomorrow. Just go over there. Fix it and I'll pay you whatever."

"Did you—"

"No, I'm not a plumber so I didn't. That's why you— look, please. The key's under the mat."

"Okay. Okay. I gotta go."

"*Ciao.*"

Click.

Click (off hold).

"Beth?"

"Yes?"

"I apologize for the—"

"We're going out of town. You've started the chair, yes?"

"Yes, I have," Jawbone says. "I'm at a critical stage when I think I can do something a little bit more custom, a bit more *feng shui* for your space."

"*Custom?* I want what I'm paying for. You've cashed the deposit check. I want that Higby chair that I pulled out of that magazine. Did you lose that picture?"

"No, Beth, but perhaps you can come by the shop and just take a look at the ideas I've sketched out."

"Whatever. Fine."

"Great, I'm at—"

"Text me the address."

Click.

"That chair," Jawbone says, "is going to be the death of me."

"Why don't you do one for her," Hector says, "and then build the custom one for yourself?"

"We can't do cheap Higby knock-offs."

"Why?"

"Because we have to teach the ignorant, Hector. We have to educate. About choices. About being original. Go big or go home."

"Gotta eat."

"Look, I'm eating fine."

"Ah, yeah. You got that grant money. Seventy-five G's. The City ever decide you could keep it or do you got to give it back?"

∞

Here's the deal concerning the seventy-five large:

Somehow Jawbone's pissed off every other furniture company and the royalties from her production lines are starting to dwindle, and she hasn't been able to place new designs. Not since Laxmie's asked her to take a smaller royalty rate. From 2% to 1%. *Click*. Or maybe it was Fuck You. *Click*.

The IAC grant money will let her leave the plumbing business. Leave her dad's shadow, her dad's loving— but old school— uncomprehending shadow. A dad that put away his saxophone and dreams when she was born and hasn't played since.

But there's a snag with that money, and until her lawyer says it's hers officially, she dare not spend it. Lest she have to repay it. That is the company line.

∞

"Building knock-offs, fixing toilets, *ese*. It's all the same shit seat, eh?"

Jawbone gives this a modicum of thought.

"Hey, maybe I do the chair," Hector says. "I got time. And skills, you know that."

"I'm sure you do, Hector."

"I'll come to your shop and bang it out."

"No one but no one gets in the cave. That's my Fortress of Solitude."[16]

"But you're going to meet this carpetbagger there?"

"Carpetmuncher, Hector."

"That's what I said."

"In the front office."

"Your shop has a front office?"

"Maybe I'll use your shop, Hector."

"You can't. Daisy don't like blacks. She'd take a bite right out of your ass."

"Is everyone in your family racist, sexist, and homophobic?"

"Nah, we're patriots."

Sigh. "You'd be willing to relocate for me, wouldn't you?"

"Okay. You can use my shop." He hands her a flyer. "As long as you come to my show."

---

16. Plus it has a rat and roach problem. Another thing she has to take care of before too long, for various reasons.

She stops, looks at the flyer for Hector's first big art showing. A feeling spreads across her face, oft-neglected muscles creaking. Her silver teeth shine in the morning light. "You got the show?" She hugs him and spins him around, planting a big kiss on his lips. "YOU GOT IT!"

"I did, I did," Hector says, blushing like a nephew whose tipsy aunt is taking things a bit far. "It's just a small—"

"No such thing as a small victory," she corrects. "What do we say?"

"Aw, come on."

"Say it."

Hector clears his throat. "This victory is mine. It is not a small victory. This victory will be celebrated, because we cannot let the bastards win."

"Close enough. Good boy."

"Thank you." He beams. "I'm renting a suit and everything."

"I'm proud of you." She beams, too. With joy. So much joy. "I'm so, so proud."

He blushes. "You can use my shop." He hands out a few flyers to the other scrappers. They nod appreciatively. "Hey, does she have big knockers, this carpetbagger?" Hector says. "If she does, I'll do the chair for you. Maybe she be extra *oo-la-la*. Sandwich her and her lady friend. Right in the chair. I got skills."

Jawbone throws a wet feather duster at the bravado of youth. It glances off his arm, leaving a stain. For a firecracker instant, she thinks it looks like an Impressionistic portrait of Harry S. Truman.[17]

∞

Hector does not tell Jawbone he is going to be deployed with his Guard unit soon. They're not sure where, but they all know. He says nothing because Jawbone is beaming, her metal teeth making a rare appearance in a smile. It is not a time to let bastards win. It is a time to celebrate. Hector waves his flyer to everyone. *"Free cervezas!"*

American Thighs

B drinks more. He's still at the ArtBar. Still waiting on the call that will change everything.

GO/NO GO.

It's a clinical type of drinking. He is already ahead of the celebration or commiseration. His drinking at this point is without context. A holding pattern. Where he reads and rereads that column. Rumination being a default of B's psyche.

The pink-haired waitress outflanks him again and sets down a double whiskey. From the smell it's the good stuff and by good stuff

---

17. As done with gun powder by Cai Guo-Qiang circa the early 90s.

we mean expensive scotch. He has not ordered it, but downs half of it in one motion. The taste of oak, peat moss, and charcoal fills his mouth. It's extra smoky. And smoke. God, B loves the taste of smoke.

Burn mother burn.

That drink will probably double his tab, but that's okay. His drinking has exceeded the amount of wrinkled singles in his wallet a dozen Old Styles ago. They'll call the cops and they'll take him to jail for the night and then he'll be back to zero. And probably be asked to never show his mug in here again. The only Chicago bar he likes. He hadn't thought of that. He likes this place. Even with the bad BBQ sauce and new menus and new waitresses and new TVs. Fuck. He looks around. For something, someone he can...

Fuck it.

Used to be he knew everyone here. Not so much anymore, so he'll sit here and drink until they close and deal with it then. He remembers why the bar is quiet: most of the regulars are across the street at the F-Hole for Honky-Tonk night. B enjoys honky-tonk like he enjoys sushi, as an occasional cultural experience, but not as a meal. Besides, he's already caught somewhere between lonesome and blue.

Another whiskey arrives. He looks up at the pink-haired girl. The word *water* is forming on his lips when she winks (someone must have coached her) and nods over to the corner.

A woman in funeral black hoists a Warhol highball glass with whiskey and downs it in one fluid motion. No stranger to the firewater of the Highlands, this one. But then her eyes bug and she belches. Regains her composure with a sip of beer.

Burn.

Then the woman in funeral black hikes up the hem of her skirt. Knocks him out with those American thighs.

Don't be the coward.

Grabbing the newspaper column, B carefully extricates himself from the wobbly chair, grabs his empty water glass and staggers over to his benefactor, navigating and tipping barstools like a beginner on a slalom course.

"Bob Bellio," he says by way of introduction.

"Emma."

"Thanks for the single malts, Emma."

"Sit down." She waves a bartender over. "Let's get something fruity and stupid."

∞

She taps the smudged *Chicago Shoulders*. "It was the most beautiful thing I've ever seen," Emma says. She fingers a small lock on the front of her leather choker. A small price tag still visible. "This kid."

B nods, encouragingly. If B were sitting alone he'd be nodding encouragingly. But now B is struck by the glowing whiteness of

57

her skin. Like a statue of marble. Or ivory. Or alabaster. Or soap. A deep plunging neckline splits her modest cleavage. A glowing white triangle where he could get lost. But B does not want to be *that* guy, that rude guy. Besides, he sees something in her eyes. Something sorely missing in his life. *Passion*. Excitement about something other than a baseball team. And the choker collar with the small lock. He won't ask. The mystery is enough.

"So, Timmy...?"

"His work was beautiful. I don't know if he was a prodigy or what—"

"Was?"

"He was killed," she says. "In a skating accident."[18]

B is drunk so a dark and private thought forms: *Good.* "Oh."

"But it—" she cuts herself off and looks at his greasy hat and red B and he sees that light bulb of a cute and inspired thought go off in her eyes. "Bob," she says, "can I call you *B*?"

Everyone does, he thinks. But he nods and smiles as though this is the newest, sweetest thing he's ever heard. And because of the way she says it, it is. Maybe she is a saint. A magnificent saint. He drums his fingers near hers on the newspaper.

"I felt flush, B, not like I was caught in the moment, but like I was having an out-of-body experience, this physical reaction," she says. "I

---

18. *Time moves in loopy circles. Stay tuned.*

was acutely aware that this was a *physical* reaction like— what is the biochemical thing connecting chocolate and love?"

B shrugs.

She mirrors his shrug. Not important, but: "I'm hooked on a feeling, B."

The pink-haired waitress sets down two piña coladas, leans into B, touching his arm and frowning when he doesn't look her way. The waitress throws stink-eye at this female intruder.

"Cheers," B says.

Emma smiles and they clink glasses.

"Thank you for picking up the tab," B says. "I think I was going to be a little light."

She dismisses it with the wave of her hand.

B wants to check his phone, but doesn't want her, this magnificent saint, to think he's bored and checking the time. "So why'd you buy me the scotch?" he says. "I see a few younger, hipper, eligible dudes in here. Little more suave and financially centered."

"Yes, yes, and every one of them has hit on me," Emma says.

Have they?

"You are in a bar." B smiles. His cheeks are starting to hurt from smiling.

"That's right. And I figure if I want a clown to cheer me up," she says, "I'd go to the circus. I *hate* clowns."

B laughs and piña colada jets out of his nose, soaking the newspaper. Tabby and Timmy's first ink.

On your mark.

"I didn't realize how heavy shame weighed," Emma says. "Such a burden."

B nods, blowing his nose clear of coconut, pineapple, and rum.

"And you look burdened, B."

He wads up the wet napkin. Looks to grab his drink. Sees it's empty. There is nothing to hide behind. She does not look away. He feels naked, exposed.

"So this kid, this child, this Timmy, I never liked him. I mean, kids are kids," Emma says. She pulls a water bottle from her purse hidden below tabletop level. "And you give them leeway," she says. "But they are crafty and cunning."

"Of course, they're kids." B is relieved he is no longer the subject of conversation.

"He was arrogant, not too smart, potty mouth, and LOUD." (She nails Timmy's volume and wrecked voice.) She unscrews the cap. Offers Bellio the bottle. "He could also be perceptive."

He takes a swig, but spits it out into his eternally empty water glass.

"Shit warm?" she says.

"Thanks anyway." He hands the bottle back to her.

She looks at the bottle with the practiced glare of disapproval saved for double-digit-preteen aged criminals and charlatans.

"I'll wait for Pinky Lee." B adjusts his greasy cap. Wishing he'd showered before leaving the house. Brushed under his nails.

"And he walks into this exhibit," Emma says, "at the MCA and they've got all this art stuff laid out and he creates this thing and I look at it and I'm seeing something I've never seen before, like when I first heard Hendrix or Pink Floyd or Tom McRae or the Flaming Lips. It was a unique experience and it made me"—she grabs his hand—"want to explode, to go to church, worship pagan gods, run naked in the street, all these conflicting things, it filled my heart and my womb." She tilts the bottle back to drink. Her lips touch it. Sensually. Suggestively. She takes slow, steady sips.

He realizes this is not a show. She has no idea of the arousal factor. She is simply being present in another moment.

"So what'd you do?"

"I went to the women's room and," she looks around, leans forward. Giggles. "I pleasured myself." She giggles again. "I *never* do that."

B clinks her water bottle. Drops dribble down her dress, the water disappearing in the whiteness of her darkened cleavage.

The pink-haired waitress brings a round of drinks and water. With ice.

Emma screws the cap back on, and the bottle disappears beneath the table. "And," she says, "it made me want to see the potential in things. It made me want to take a bit longer with my lesson plans. It made me want to connect with each student to push a little harder, and it made me ashamed that I hadn't been using all my potential. I never encouraged Timmy. I only criticized him. I was only damage control. I could have been a positive part of that piece. But instead—"

She clears her throat.

Get set.

Ticks them off on a finger.

"I want to be a better person."

Tick.

"I want to be a better sister."

Tick.

"I want to be a better lover."

Tick.

"I want to be a better teacher."

"A noble profession," he says. "One of the oldest."

She laughs.

"I can appreciate that," B says.

"It was either that or one of the other oldest professions." She winks at him. Awkwardly. Like a facial twitch. (B notes that he seems to be collecting winks this evening. A gesture he's never felt comfortable attempting and usually bewildered when receiving.) "And I want to create," she says, with a final tick. "With my hands." She takes a deep breath. He expects her to let out a deep melodramatic sigh, but instead she lets it out cool, calm, controlled.

She sets her glass down. Runs her hand down his bulky arm.

He pushes the destroyed newspaper aside to make room for her.

She takes his hand and turns it over. It's big and wide, with fingers like knotted rope. She traces a fake fingernail over his hand. A plastic fork over rough-hewn oak. "Like a gorilla's."

"A blacksmith," he says.

"Third oldest profession."

"Heh."

"B," she says and shudders. "Let me ask you this..."

B's phone vibrates.

"Have you ever had a plaster cast made of your cock?"

Go.

American Standard

From Jackie and Beth's bathroom, Jawbone calls her lawyer.

"Still working on it, Duchamp."

Jawbone hates it when her lawyer calls her Duchamp.

"I'm expecting the call later this afternoon. Meanwhile, don't quit your day job."

She hangs up.

Jawbone feels like a fraud with this deal. But this one she will be able to live with. Her new overalls vibrate and sing, her phone turning the bathroom tiled with *Cerdomus Pietra D'Assisi* into a Spaghetti Western. With our hero on the can, nude in a lesbian couple's house taking a mid-afternoon dump; she's been holding it all day. A trip to the restrooms at the MCA stymied by a frumpy woman obviously high and making 'come hither' looks at Jawbone. And while Jawbone was amused, she was not tempted, sexual experimentation not being part of her five-year-plan. She answers her phone.

"How's it hanging?" her lawyer says.

"That was quick. So do we get to keep the money?"

"What? Oh. No, haven't heard back. You haven't spent it, have you?"

"Why are you calling?" Jawbone hears her lawyer shuffle papers. Then a shotgun laugh.

"Listen to this: The City lost a sculpture. It's unaccounted for. You know they rotate them around the City and not all of them are on display at the same time. So it was time for this piece to be put out on display and when they went to get it, they couldn't find it. It's probably in a landfill outside Aurora."

"What's the punchline?"

"Guess who the artist was?"

Jawbone figures it out by the way the lawyer sneers when he says *artist*. More than his usual casual $250/hour sneer. "No way."

"Yes, fuckin way," he says. "Robert Bellio."

> *Robert B. Bellio.*
>
> *Bob Bellio.*
>
> *B.*

Jawbone laughs along with her lawyer, hoping the call doesn't come at this moment, while he is distracted. The call Jawbone loses sleep over. The call that will change everything.

∞

Here's the deal concerning the Call:

The Illinois Arts Council people wrote a check in the amount of $75,000 for Jawbone's *HOME DEPOT TOILET POLAROID DUMP SHOW* proposal. It was an error, of course, not only because it should have only been a check for $7,000, if, in fact, they were going to reward Jawbone for her application. But upon further investigation it was revealed that it wasn't an error as much as a misfired practical ha-ha joke of the people in the office. They took Jawbone's application in the folk art category (a category that has since been canceled) and tacked it to the wall for good laughs. Someone then typed up a letter explaining how they loved her idea and how they were pleased to announce the grant award. Someone took it a step further and then entered the check in the computer. All for laughs. Somewhere on a camera phone is a group photo of the office workers and grants coordinators gathered around Jawbone's application. From left to right, Jim, Erik, Michael, Caryn, Dana, and tall Dana and George the intern. The problem arose when George the intern was fired for lewd behavior and was replaced with that girl with pink hair, a real go-getter intern who prided herself on being "active, not reactive." And seeing the grant award for Jawbone's application and not wanting to bother people, but wanting to prove her initiative, the pink-haired intern sent the letter and check to Harriet "Jawbone" Walker.

Attempts to retract the erroneous award from Jawbone were met with several letters from her lawyer and one copy of a drafted letter to the mayor and a major PR company.

Indian Giver State Takes Back Money from Black Female Artist

The intern was fired and Jawbone asked her lawyer to negotiate a deal where she could keep the money, but complete a project to be named later for the City. Something, anything. Think of it as an advance. Stymied, the City pointed out that the AC is state run, but with offices in the City.

But because Jawbone's lawyer is a cousin to the Mayor, they agreed to look into it. This is called clout. Chicago runs on clout.

Jawbone yearns to create. Even if it means putting ramen noodles back on the menu. She's an outlaw artist. An outsider with no contacts, doing it on her own. She's had a few shows. They've been well received, but always overshadowed by a big event. An earthquake, a hostage situation. A tsunami. A baby being born with two hearts. The hottest comedian on the planet playing a surprise gig next door. A jumbo jet hits the 75th story. Always buried.

Should she get the green light that the money is hers, she will buy a round for the house at the ArtBar. Because that, mutherfuckers, is Karma.

∞

Jawbone rubs the tip of her index finger, which looks like the tip of a small toe since having lost it in a chop saw accident building a set for the kids' show *Catch a Shooting Star!* The blood never completely washed off the set and the kids thought it was cool and pointed it out to their parents after each show. Real blood, it spurted. *Right there.*

Bellio, she hears, now works out of a sun-filled loft shop in the West Loop. Complete with a padded freight elevator. Has pieces in three showrooms across the country. He's on Günther Adamczyk's short list of fabricators. He is a made guy.

The chosen.

Living on EZ Street.

Swimming in grants.

Approved proposals.

Sipping wine in a rooftop garden as the sun sets and his city glows in the magic hour.

She lifts the lid to the toilet. Untangles the chain to the flapper. She shortens the chain a link or two to prevent it from getting caught on the lift arm. The flapper flaps down and seals the flush valve and water starts to fill the tank.

A tank on a cheap toilet owned by lesbians.

In an expensive bathroom.

Filled with bad magazines.

In an expensive three-flat.

Filled with knock-off furniture.

In an expensive neighborhood.

Filled with happy shiny people.

In her expensive city.

The following is the Artist's Statement from Harriet "Jawbone" Walker's Grant Application for the seven grand fellowship in Folk Art: *Fuck Art*.

> *Fuck Bob Bellio.*
>
> *Fuck Richard Higby.*

She picks up a magazine. *Home Décor*. On the cover:

Happy Anniversary: YES, YOU CAN! Thirty Years of Painting with Ross Robards. And his round, cracked, and cratered face eager to help. She thumps the picture of the happy shiny man with metal legs.

And fuck you most of all, Tin Man.

Clouds

The cursor hovers over the blue square button SEND.

Duckworth's fingers hover elsewhere. Across the room, in bed. It is noon. Duckworth is both drunk and hung over.

Describe it, Duckworth tells himself.

It's indescribable, Duckworth protests to himself.

Describe it.

Spiritually?

Creatively?

I can't. It's indescribable now. The lucidity at the museum has faded like a dream, leaving only snatches and flashes of revelation. Duckworth pulls his covers up to his chin with one hand. Cups his scrotum with the other. In the background, a muted Ross Robards marathon plays. Vintage Video Toaster effects overlay crude text graphics including, but not limited to, YES, YOU CAN!

Duckworth's job, nay, *career* hangs in the balance. A killer story will save it.

But if not, then what?

Oh God, a blog?

He has attempted a few stellar columns and grand articles about Tabby and Timmy using first names only, but with his *Shoulders* deadline he has only managed to write a generic 'feel good' piece with no photos (Waylon having gone MIA). A piece that remains on his computer, unsent to his editor. A piece he is sure will be read by no one. He has to write *the* killer story. One he has assured his editor he is working on. Privately, should he get his shit together for the killer story, he does not want it published in the *Shoulders*. He wants it somewhere where it will get noticed, have an impact. But the killer story remains elusive amounting to several wadded up false starts sitting at the bottom of his blue trashcan. Each abortion ripped from his typewriter only deepens his morose week of fear and self-loathing. He can see the imminent summons to the *Shoulders'* editor's glass office, the fishbowl scolding.

What do you want, dimensions? Color? You want me to use words to describe color? Blue, indigo, azure, what difference does it make?

You're a critic. It's your job.

The feel-good piece cannot be his last testament.

Duckworth glances out the window. Cumulus clouds float by. Suddenly, he's seven years old in the principal's office.

"Your son has a problem."

"Yes?"

"*Da?*"

His parents next to him. The principal tapping his finger. His father is American. His mother Polish. They met when his father opened the door to a walk-in oven in Germany and said to the skinny naked dame: "I'm Corporal Duckworth, United States Army, and you're free." They were married ten months later.

"You see, he doesn't play outside with the other kids at recess."

"He's in trouble?"

"No."

"Not sure I cotton to your double talk, mister."

"He won't go outside," the principal says. "Because he's afraid of clouds."

"What?"

"He's afraid of clouds."

His mother starts to sob. She grabs her husband's liberating hands. "Oh Lord."

"We'll get through this, Barb."

The principal nods grimly. "I think we all know what this means."

His mother nods. His mother, who has seen indescribable things done to her friends, nieces, and sisters with gasoline, crushed glass, car batteries, scalpels and no anesthesia, she tears up and says: "He's going to be an artist."

The principal hands her a Kleenex.

The father shakes his head slowly. "D-Day. Auschwitz. Rock 'n' roll and now this."

Now, he's 9. Wins First Place at his grade school's Art Contest. Trenda Prather, the girl with the slight lisp, asks if she can touch his blue ribbon. Her boyfriend Jodie kicks the shit out of him. It is his first taste of celebrity.

He's 12 and a group of med students stare at him. The doctor with the x-ray of his head is white as a sheet. "Twenty percent of your brain is missing." Further tests conclude the massy sponge taking up residence there is benign. His mother says this is why he's afraid of clouds and is going to be a world-class artist. This is why Cpl. Duckworth opened her oven door, so that she could bring Jasper the Artist into the world.

At 13 he has a shunt placed in his neck to relieve any potential pressure build-up in his brain sack. He dabbles in abstract art.

At 15 he wins Third Place in the County Fair Art Exhibit.

Now he's 18 at the State Art Fair. He places fourth, which should be an Honorable Mention, but this is like the Olympics and thus he does not medal. He pretends he doesn't care and doubles down by getting a Black Flag tattoo on his forearm.[19] Thus begins his punk rock phase.

Six months later, second place is disqualified. That's how long it takes for someone to recognize a Kandinsky rip-off. He's bumped to Third Place, and Duckworth receives his ribbon in the mail, his cat, Chekhov, his only audience.

The School of the Art Institute of Chicago selects the new class of freshmen. Jasper Duckworth is not among them. He becomes a mosh pit regular at the Hell Hole, Abbey Pub, and Metro. No one wants to start a band with him. The term *poseur* is used. He starts a 'zine critical of the current wave of local punk bands.

He's 19 and buries his mother. Next to his father. He designs the funeral programs, which the funeral director insists is not necessary. He drops the 'zine and wears long sleeves year-round.

College. He studies the Old Masters; he knows this, that, and the other thing about Art. A summer spent studying in London on a student loan (he's defaulted) infects his speech with a slight British accent that never quite goes away. He writes two incisive, but unpublished, essays.

He's 25 and writes the Play about his parents. About their meeting, about its context in a larger world. It's specific in its nuances and detail with exacting dialogue and heartbreaking moments of staggering genius. He sells his punk vinyl collection to cover postage and submission fees. The exception being Black Flag's *Damaged*.

---

19. He hides the tattoo from his mother, conscious of her history with forearm tattoos.

He submits the Play to the Julie Harris Playwriting Contest. The resulting reader comments arrive the day before he buries his cat.

He submits the Play to a local start-up theatre play competition. Presumably without stiffer competition.

It makes the quarterfinals.

Everyone he knows who submitted makes the quarterfinals.

On a resume later, he adjusts the award to have made the semi-finals.

Then he adjusts it to have placed in the Top Ten.

Armed with this success, he targets several established off-loop store-front Chicago theatres.

He writes a short punchy query letter and synopsis.

Every theatre wants to read his Play.

Every theatre rejects his Play.

   Pass.

He's 35 and older, wiser. He loses most of his hair. He keeps the spine of the Play, but rewrites it. Then tucks it in a drawer for safekeeping, next to a black and white photo of his parents playing in the snow.

He's 39 and now the Associate Media Editor at the *Chicago Shoulders*. Writing reviews for commercials. Dissecting thirty-second beer commercials with the sharp wit and cynicism of his favorite art critics. He is read by a fraction of the people reading the movie reviews by the critic with the black turtleneck in the insanely pretentious headshot. Save for that one Super Bowl Sunday last year when the Chief Media Editor is hospitalized with food poisoning. That weekend Jasper P. Duckworth is a god. Two pieces of fan mail sustain him for a year.

He's 40. He changes the title of the Play.

At 42 he sends the Play to three major regional theatre companies. It is exactly what they are looking for according to the article in *American Theatre* magazine. Two never respond.

At 49 one responds with a handwritten rejection note: story is cliché, but writing shows *some* potential.

Pass.

Those who can't do: Bury.

Those who can't do: Kill.

Those who can't do: Destroy.

Those who can't do: Can't do.

∞

It is now late afternoon and behind the wheel of a rented SUV, Duckworth, now clothed and sober, fumbles with an honest-to-god gas station map. Scuff marks blemish the passenger-side tires where he has rubbed up against the curb. Duckworth has not been behind the wheel of an automobile in ages, taking advantage of Chicago's world class public transportation system. Besides, it seems so, well, gauche, to have to drive oneself (a driver being a perk he had only for his second contract at *Chicago Shoulders*). But now behind the wheel, he feels in charge. Eyes on the road, hands upon the wheel. He's got this.

∞

Let's peek back to see what finally got Duckworth out of his malaise and into the driver's seat.

Amid the sour burping of a Pimm's Cups brunch, he rolls over onto the TV remote buried in the covers, unmuting Ross Robards, his human hair paintbrush frozen in mid-stroke. The painter in standard definition looks right at the camera.

"YES, YOU CAN!"

Oh, Ross.

At his desk, the cursor hovers over SEND. Duckworth's finger hovers over ENTER. He can't believe his name is attached to the attachment attached to this email. There is nothing feel-good about the feel-good story he is about to submit. It is not a killer piece.

It may buy him time, though. Enough time to find Timmy. Enough time to pull himself up by the bootstraps.

SEND.

Because those that can't do instead champion.

∞

Now back in the SUV, the positive propaganda of Ross Robards cannot take away Duckworth's sour stomach. A stomach that rejects the roll of Tums for breakfast with a continued series of sour burps. He cannot take away the constant recalculations of rent and bills against a dwindling bank account. He cannot take away the knee-jerk mental critique of every fifteen and thirty second commercial playing in seven minute blocks through every pre-programmed radio station in this bloody SUV.

Duckworth makes a note to buy a used copy of Robards' *What Color is Your Art Chakra?*

Duckworth turns down Lake Cook Road and into a forgettable subdivision. Timmy lives here somewhere and with him Jacob's rope ladder out of oblivion. He's after something more than a killer story. Duckworth scrapes a curb and a plastic box of art supplies rattles in the back. Finally, he slows and counts down house numbers when—

CRACK!

Something violently hits his windshield, starring it. Duckworth squeals and swerves, hopping a curb and taking out an old-fashioned mailbox and blooming gardenia bush.

"Oh God, Oh God, Oh G—"

The airbag deploys, popping him in the face. The nose pads of his glasses dig into his skin. His cheeks and forehead and nose burn. Duckworth's heart pounds, resurrecting his hangover. But he is intact and despite not wearing a seatbelt, not currently pulling his head out of the cracked windshield. He takes a quick inventory and realizes things are fine. Everything in motion is safely at rest. Now only slightly stunned, Duckworth steps out of the SUV to survey any damage to the vehicle and see what it is that cracked the windshield.

Ponk.

A golf ball bounces off the side of the SUV.

Across the street, Timmy, decked in Native American-themed hockey gear and roller blades, drops another golf ball and on the bounce slap shots it out of the air.

Ponk.

The ball dings the SUV and bounces down the street.

"Timmy? Stay there!"

Duckworth hops back into the SUV. He backs it off the bush and mailbox with thudding and trenching of the yard, stopping askew in the road.

Ponk.

Duckworth falls out of the SUV and staggers a step towards Timmy. A tentative stupid horror movie move. "Timmy. I have to talk to you. Please don't— the balls."

Timmy yells "ALLAH AKBAR" and with a push of his right foot skates away.

Duckworth gives chase. Again. Although, it's not much of a chase— only about seven houses down. That's where Timmy zips up a driveway into a side yard. Timmy is cornered, stick raised.

Duckworth holds both hands up, weapons-free. Sweat mixes with blood around his eyes and nose and streaks down his face. Duckworth catches his breath. Timmy is here. Alive and well.[20] Nothing else matters. He takes a deep cleansing breath and reaches out to Timmy.

"Please, Timmy." Duckworth steps forward. "For the love of art, please—"

"Give me money," Timmy whispers.

"What?"

"Cash," Timmy says, "or I'll call the cops and tell them you touched my pecker."

Duckworth hands him his lunch money, a twenty. "Please— "

"I'M NOT JERKING YOU OFF," Timmy says.

"Don't talk like that—"

"PEDERAST! PEDERAST! HELP ME! PEDERAST!"

Oh. Good. Lord.

A huge looming medieval shadow behind Duckworth.

---

20. *We have now looped around. (See Nietzsche's Doctrine of Eternal Recurrence.)*

"DAD! THIS FAGGOT GAVE ME A TWENTY FOR A HAND JOB!"

This will not end well.

Duckworth turns. A mountain of a man. Bald. Goatee. Skull tattoos. Bermuda shorts and Hawaiian shirt.

"A HAND JOB, I TELL YA!"

Duckworth's brain fries. He can only say one word: "Aloha."

"Shut up, Timmy," the mountain says.

"OKAY, DAD."

"And give this man his money back."

"Uh, he can keep it," Duckworth says, realizing this will end just fine.

"That's nice of you." The mountain holds out his hand. "I'm Big Tim. Timmy's dad. Can I fix you a drink?"

∞

Duckworth tells Timmy's dad about the BE AN ARTIST™ exhibit. Tells him about Timmy and Tabby. About the feature he's going to write about Timmy. For starters. He doesn't mention the feel-good column. The column of no consequence already written. Already on the way to press.

"What about this Tabby woman?" Big Tim says. "Is she hot?"

Duckworth pauses. Finishes cleaning his scuffed up face with a wet-wipe. "Let's say I have dreams for Timmy. There was a connection with Timmy's piece. Not," he coughs, "Tabby's."

"I WIPED A BOOGER ON TABBY'S BIRD MOBILE," Timmy says. "IT WAS BLOODY."

"I have art supplies in my vehicle, and I'd like to see what Timmy can do," Duckworth says. "If you have time this afternoon."

"Sure," the mountain says. "Hey Duckman, what's your poison?"

"Water, please," Duckworth says, wanting to be receptive, but not indebted.

They walk through Big Tim O'Donnell's house (which smells like grilled cheese and cigars). The mountain pours himself three fingers of a chilled vodka and, obviously wanting to be hospitable, but not perfunctory, pours Duckworth a pink lemonade, for which the emotionally hung over Duckworth is grateful.[21] Duckworth takes a sip. Sighs. Mid second sip, he spots, proudly displayed on the fridge, several scribbles from a child's crude crayon. Colorful, but utter rubbish.

"These from Timmy?"

"Yip."

"Impressive," Duckworth says, unsuccessfully biting his tongue. "How old was he? Three, four?"

---

21. *Despite lemonade being the main ingredient in Pimm's Cups.*

"Uh, he did these this morning, Duckman," Big Tim says. "Bit autistic or something, isn't he?"

Oh. Dear.

Timmy comes skating up. He doffs his plastic Viking helmet in a cartoon curtsy move. "HEY FAGGOT, I HOPE YOU GOT INSURANCE," he says. "CUZ YOUR SUV IS ROLLING DOWN THE STREET."

∞

Duckworth again starts running down the street, chasing his rental SUV. He feels a squeezing in his chest and his stomach flips and he pukes up the sweet and sour tang of pink lemonade and two French crullers.

Timmy, trailing behind, jumps the puke with an "AKIRA LIVES!" He zips past Duckworth and grabs onto the back bumper of the rolling SUV. "GIDDY-UP, BITCHES!"

Duckworth jogs past the rear bumper, opens the driver side door, amazed that his feet have not given out and that he hasn't tripped on the cracked asphalt. He opens the door and pulls the steering wheel to the left to avoid a parked car. It's a cherry 1967 Cadillac. He glances down and sees the unsigned insurance form for this SUV on the passenger seat.

Bullocks.

The SUV veers harder to the left, and Duckworth falls into the driver's seat and stands on the brakes. The SUV comes to a sudden and power-brakeless stop. The box of art supplies flies off the back seat dumping everything everywhere. Under the seat, an ink bottle empties one wet *blub, blub* at a time. A neighbor smiles and waves at him. A neighbor fragmented through the spider-webbed windshield from Timmy's Titleists.

"BLOODY BOOGERS!"

Duckworth gathers himself. Starts the SUV. A square lights up in the console, and Duckworth realizes for the first time it is a GPS. He puts the SUV in reverse. Waves at the neighbor and guns it, looking down in time to see that the GPS square has now turned into a rear facing camera as he watches—

THUMP THUMP.

— a shocked Timmy disappears under the back wheels of the SUV.

Duckworth panics, jams the SUV into drive and guns it forward.

THUMP THUMP.

Oh, Timmy.

Duckworth sees the neighbor, slack-jawed and stunned.

Duckworth sees Big Tim running towards them, slack-jawed and stunned.

Duckworth gets out of the car, slack-jawed and stunned.

Timmy lies there, slack-jawed and stunned, a growing goose egg on his forehead. His plastic helmet cracked and useless. A broken nose, professional hockey player smile and two legs now spurred with the jagged pink bones of compound fractures. Timmy's eyes roll white. And he speaks:

> *"Fylliz fiorvi*
>
> *feigra manna,*
>
> *rýðr ragna siotasa*
>
> *rauðom dreyra.*
>
> *Svort verða sólskin*
>
> *of sumor eptir,*
>
> *veðr oll válynd*
>
> *Vitoð ér enn, eða hvat?"*

But because of all the commotion and screaming, Timmy's words are lost on a suburban breeze.

∞

It's a bit of a blur for Jasper P. Duckworth, that dream state of being guided from this form to that form and this report to that report and repeating a lot of information including addresses, place of employment, etc.

Officer Archie Reno who files the report sides with Duckworth. Timmy was a little shit and a spaz, a retard, a punk, and as evidenced by the spike in scorched animal carcasses this summer in the field behind his house, an arsonist psychopath. None of this is in the official report, but the officer who'd been thinking about leaving the force offers his card to Duckworth as a gesture of support. Right after citing Duckworth for a number of violations that will no doubt end up on his Permanent Record. "I hope you got a good lawyer," Officer Reno says, as he drives off on his way to a family reunion.

∞

Duckworth mute in shock, while Big Tim marvels at the hospital. He's never been in one. Even at birth, a stock tank catching his big splashy entrance. When the doctor comes out of the room in the back, he pronounces to Duckworth and Big Tim that Timmy is dead and would they like an autopsy performed?

Timmy is dead.

The doc is direct like that. He's got tickets to the Cubs and it's the only time he gets to see his mistresses. The doctor consults Duckworth with a look, and Duckworth, who is not a family member, demurs.

"Yes, I'd like an autopsy." The father lowers his head, a tear B.A.S.E.-jumping off his nose. He sniffs and turns to Duckworth. "You killed my boy."

Duckworth hangs his head.

"You killed my boy."

He hangs his head lower.

Big Tim produces a cigar from thin air, asks: "What was it like?"

völva

At first dawn, slipping between the cracks of dreaming and yearning, strange words come to Duckworth. Perhaps they are part of Timmy's last words. Perhaps they unlock that which we all know in our collective unconsciousness. Whatever the matter Duckworth is compelled to write them down:

> *vindold, vargold*
> *áðr verold steypiz*
> *Mun engi maðr*
> *oðrom þyrma*

And after several attempts at online translation, including Klingon to English, the words are deciphered:

> *A wind age. A wolf age.*
> *Before the world goes headlong.*
> *No man will have mercy on another.*

Duckworth stares at his handwriting for a long minute. The morning sun fades behind a patch of water vapor. He shuts down his computer. Burns the paper with his handwritten scrawl and scatters the ashes outside in his apartment building's courtyard before the cumulus clouds turn to cumulonimbus.

An Unkindness of Ravens

"We will never see an artistic genius like Timmy again," Duckworth says.

He sits, Jasper P. Duckworth, until a moment ago a man of silence, on the foyer steps of the Museum of Contemporary Art. He wears a dark trench coat, and despite the tripping hazard, its tails are spread out picturesque behind him on the steps like the cape of a fallen superhero. He will tell you otherwise, but he is aware of the melancholy picture of infinite sadness he has staged. (He wishes Waylon were here to catch the moment in Presidential Archival Black & White.)

But the Museum of Contemporary Art is a museum for contemporary art and thus he cannot compete.

> *Waylon, where are you? And your camera and your
> film of Timmy's masterpiece? Where is the Shot?*

He would like to have that picture with him when Officer Reno and his colleagues eventually haul him away for vehicular manslaughter.

A security guard with a walkie-talkie making minimum wage nudges the tails of his coat into a safer profile. The guard's sneakers cost more than Duckworth's coat.

∞

A young woman with pink hair and a nose ring walks by with a tight black t-shirt, on it a rhinestoned logo: FLUSH ART. She holds a book on Duchamp.

Duckworth says: "Miss, did you know Duchamp single-handedly severed the cord between art and merit?"

To which she replies in that air of disaffected "meh" coolness: "Like beer commercials?" She snorts and then moves on. Her space is immediately occupied in passing by a gaggle of loogie-hawking children and that teacher, Timmy's teacher. The shy one.

"How are you holding up, Ethel?" Duckworth says.

She doesn't hear him, so he repeats himself, louder, but with the exact same dramatic tone of wry resignation.

She stops and turns. "Go on, kids," she says. "I'll catch up. The exhibit is right through there. It's *Emma*, Mr. Duckworth."

He nods. "I apologize for not remembering your name." (But perhaps it's also that she is dressed slightly differently. A hint of thigh in her bland non-potato sack dress. And those elbows, how pronounced!) "That is rude of me," he says. "I was contemplating Timmy and his art project. The genius and the brilliance. I had this silly fantasy that I would introduce him to the world and that I would be famous alongside him. Trust me, dear Emma. We will never see his like again. Not in this generation. Trust me. I used to be a playwright. And now we don't even have a picture of his masterpiece." He turns his head upward, looking past her out the MCA windows. "There is a darkness approaching, I fear—"

"I forgive you for running over Timothy," she says.

∞

Emma takes Duckworth's head in her hands and plants a kiss on his airbag-burned forehead, his cheek, feels his stubble brush against her lips.

Does he ever shave down there?

Like Archie made her do. "What about Tabby?" she says.

Curiously, Duckworth kisses her hand. Tender. Genuine. But it is not enough. She needs more, to be closer to his vulnerability. To taste it. She kisses him full on the lips.

When they part, they stare at each other.

He tastes like lemon.

"Quick," she whispers. "What do you think of that African sculpture on the third floor? By the fountain." She swallows hard, her breathing shifts in anticipation. She will most definitely tell this story to Archie in the backseat of his squad car.

"Oh," he says, sort of distracted. "I'm not fond of ethnic art. Ooga chaka and such."

Emma touches his back lightly, a consoling gesture. He's muttering to himself.

She then excuses herself and goes to the bathroom, second stall, where she will shock herself at how easily she conjures a fantasy about being sodomized by that security guard and his walkie-talkie.

∞

Duckworth stands in a Red Line train car. Swaying with the car, not holding on, priding himself on great train legs. Flying without a net. Others hold onto poles or glass window ledges. He looks around the L car. Teens chatting on phones. And not to each other. They chat about the text they sent moments ago. He shudders at the guessed spelling or typos and inappropriate punctuation involved in that horrific butchering text-a-bet.

Timmy would have shown them the way.

Oh Timmy.

Duckworth knows he is doomed to remember the boy with the wrecked voice. But he files this away for processing later, perhaps for an article, essay, or even a memoir, because he currently rides another train of thought. The Tabby train.

Indeed, my sweet Emma, what about Tabby?

∞

"Howard is next. Doors open on the right at Howard." A male voice, with no discernible accent or dialect, what they call a general North American broadcasting voice. Friendly, generic, but intelligible, announcing the next stop on the (e)L(evated) train. The recorded voice belongs to an actor who is from Milwaukee and not Chicago. A tourist guiding tourists.

His phone pings with a text message: **ur fired.**

Brilliant, Duckworth thinks. Though now he wishes he could have made a scene in that fishbowl office. Display an exit worthy of social media.

Duckworth checks the address again. Get off at Howard, turn left past the Cub Foods. Apartment on Linden. Third floor. He tried to call beforehand, being brought up better than that, though he did not call Timmy beforehand. And, of course, Tabby's phone answered with yet another actor's voice informing him that her phone had been *disconnected or was no longer in service.* And in the end it was probably best, as this was a discussion that relied on face to face.

Hello, Tabby Masterson, I'm here to see if, in fact, you are an artistic genius. I have to see that you are the real deal. I have to convince you to let me discover you. Manage your career, guide you through the oh so cutthroat and fickle art world. Oh, and I can't rep Timmy, not only because he is young and stupid and out of control, but also dead. I ran him over. Twice. (Pause) Have I lost you?

And how will a seventy-three-year-old woman respond to that? Disbelief that she can stir such emotions with her art, Duckworth surmises. She seemed a bit of a rube at the MCA.

But he needs her.

And she needs a champion.

They will show everyone: Les and the museum board or committee or whatever it is they have, that ignorant, power tie wearing committee of businessmen and hippies and trust fund sycophants, the editors and moronic people whose tastes come from a stack of magazine subscriptions and whatever haircut their hairstylist mentions. Duckworth, of course, is more sensitive to this than most, having received two sessions of hair plug transplants before running out of money. So bad were they, the students stared. The girls laughed or giggled, the eye contact of a serious conversation or lecture thrown off-track by his faux hairline. Damn plugs. So he's taken to shaving his scalp. More so on the top than edges, sometimes letting the horseshoe grow and extend down into a beard. Very professorial.

He needs— what does he need, oh yes, he needs Tabby and he needs her by his side. Then he'll see those wankers, naysayers and disbelievers, he'll see their eyes light up. At Tabby's art. At him. Because *he* discovered her. *He* nurtured her. *He* championed her.

∞

Turning the corner onto Hill Street, Duckworth runs into not only an unseasonably chill wind, but a gathering of his worst fear: art students. A mass of them holding a candlelight something, vigil, protest, what? Hand-painted posters and banners of WE LOVE YOU BITHA reflect in the flickering glow of a thousand hand-sheltered, hand-dipped candles, the folk artists finally getting the call from their haughty counterparts.

OUR GODDESS.

WE HAVE MIGRATED.

SCULPT US.

MODEL US.

CREATE US.

A car with a plastic ART OF PIZZA bubble pulls along the curb. A pink-haired girl (it's that one) breaks from the crowd and takes the pizza from the driver with a quick exchange of paper money. She waits for change. She heads back to the sidewalk of the building. Opens the cardboard pizza box, but instead of taking a slice for herself, she places them in a shallow bucket. Another fellow with long hair and angel wings hooks the bucket to a line and tugs it. The Lorax bucket is hoisted to the third floor.

As it reaches the window lip, the window opens. A man reaches for the bucket and pulls it inside. Empties it and returns the bucket to the hook. He gives them a perfunctory wave, slightly disappointed. He shouts: "MORE BEER! AND SOME WEED!"

And the bucket zips down in a near free fall.

The shout carries through the crowd: "MORE BEER, MORE BEER. AND SOME WEED."

Various students hop on bikes and tear off on their missions, military surplus Israeli paratrooper bags decorated with safety-pinned Clash patches slung over their shoulders.

Duckworth looks back up at the window, at the man. It takes him a minute to place him (being this far out of context) and then it clicks: It is the *LA Times* art critic. Eyore or something.

∞

Duckworth makes his way through the candlelit crowd. People look up at him. A murmur grows. "The Messenger. It's the Messenger." Someone thrusts a copy of his column and a Sharpie at him. Duckworth, having seen enough movie premieres, signs the column and smiles.

The Messenger?

The pink-haired girl approaches him, head lowered. "Forgive me," she says, "for the beer commercial remark." Her FLUSH ART shirt replaced with a BITHA (also spelled in rhinestones) shirt. Tears stream from her face. "Please."

Duckworth looks around to see if there are any more autographs to be given.

∞

He buzzes the doorbell.

"It's been disconnected," the fellow with angel wings says.

"Can you tell her the, uh, Messenger is here," Duckworth says.

The one with wings nods towards the bucket currently being loaded with Goose Island beers and dime bags of stinkweed. Duckworth pulls out one of his dog-eared business cards and with the Sharpie writes: *I'm here. I would like to see Tabby.* And then as an afterthought. *Please.* He drops the card in the bucket and pulls out a beer. It's domestic, but ice cold. A quick tug on the line and the bucket ascends.

An excruciatingly loud and obnoxious rattle clangs and buzzes next to Duckworth's ear. He'll lose half his hearing in that ear for the day, but the door is now open. As he enters, the one with wings speaks. "She will be punished," he says nodding towards the pink-haired girl, her tears creating twin puddles at her feet. The one with wings now with a Ping-Pong paddle. He's drilled holes in it.

Duckworth looks around at the crowd. They all stare at him in anticipation, expectantly, for his verdict. Duckworth acknowledges the crowd, the pink-haired girl now on her knees, ass popping. "Use your best judgment," Duckworth says, chugging the beer.

∞

Duckworth blows on the tea and watches steam roll off it. Earl Grey. Tabby is not such a rube after all and maybe even a bit cultured. This might go well after all. He sets the cup on the saucer and steeps his bag a little more, loving this simple gesture. The tea warms him and chases the chill from his ears, though the left (which had been against the buzzer) is now aching.

"Eyeopetitknot2cot," Tabby says.

"I'm sorry?" Duckworth says and turns his good ear to her.

"I hope it's not too hot."

"Not at all." Duckworth raises the cup and blows again. Tabby is a grown woman and he cannot use his talking-to-students mode. As in poker, you simply cannot bluff someone who isn't paying attention.

The apartment is vintage with three huge bedrooms, the size rooms you wouldn't find closer to the City. Magazine clippings lie here and there, an artist's layout, sketches of larger works, sculptures in miniature, all scattered about. Clearly, there had been no attempt to clean in the moments from buzzing Duckworth in to him arriving on the third floor, slightly winded.

Tabby excuses herself to pour a new cup of hot water. He looks around the room again. There are framed articles and photos and essays from obscure art reviews and magazines. All about her piece *Migration*. The articles grow in length and reader base. The last item is a framed feature from a magazine founded by a Chicago resident and talk show host whose tastes are— well, the exposure is good. It's only been a month. Duckworth finds his column buried under something tacked to the wall. Evidently, while Duckworth was slaving away on word choice, a machine was put into play. All this in a month? The lead times on the magazine alone would require— wait, the *LA Times* critic. He has connections.

But I discovered her.

His hands shake, rattling cup and saucer. He reminds himself he is *the* Messenger. And he is here now in the tower. A deep breath and cup and saucer remain unchipped.

He hears something from the back room, a rustling— no, more like jostling or heavy furniture being moved somewhere down the shotgun hallway.

Must be her studio.

Tabby comes back. The circles under her eyes seem darker as though she's started wearing eye make-up but forgotten how to take it off completely. Traces of smudges, spots here and there. She refills his cup. Her hands are rough, chapped and stained with various inks and cuts, and they shake. She retreats to sit on a simple footstool. She looks tired, and not a satisfied tired. Gaunt. Sick-tired.

"So," he says, indicating her hands, but ignoring the articles and clippings. "You look like you've been keeping busy."

She sighs and nods back in the direction of the hallway and towards another distraction. She shifts on the footstool as though it is uncomfortable to sit. "I'm up for a MacArthur genius grant," she says. "They short-listed me. Expedited the application. There were fistfights among the committee."

Duckworth coughs into his tea. Still hot. He looks around. Tabby nonchalantly tosses him a stained rag, the spilt tea the least of her concerns. "That's fantastic," Duckworth says, a drop of tea clinging precariously to the tip of his nose. He thinks of Big Tim's tear.

She glances up at him. Looks him up and down. "You're all in black."

Duckworth looks at himself. Back at her. "I'm in mourning," he says. The perfect opening, he thinks, to use the Timmy story. So sad, so bad, but *you*, Tabby. I knew you were something special, he will say.

But she doesn't reply mourning for what? She says: "The Foundation wants to see my second piece."

"That should be—"

"They want a *second piece.*"

"I imagine you have several to pick from." He says this with a sweeping hand gesture.

Tabby sighs.

Duckworth leans forward, clasps his hands. Nods. "I know how hard it can be for an artist to select a 'representative' piece from a body of work— each a child, no? Each representing a stage or various stages, each one piece represents where they are and their stages of growth— stages of different influences, different thought processes, different techniques. Different moods, this altered by an interior landscape, that as a reaction to the world and its mood or lack thereof. Trying to distill an artist's representative piece to two for something as huge as a MacArthur must be very, very difficult. I do not envy your task."

He touches her shoulder. It is a sexless gesture without artifice or drama. "Perhaps I could help you select," he says, nodding to the hallway. "May I have a look?"

She blinks her consent.

He is excited as he follows her down the hallway, the fame and fortune that was hitched to Timmy's dead star fading with each step. The air seems to grow with electricity; he hears the high-pitched sound of a TV nearby.

They enter the room. The radiator in the corner hisses like a cat whose territory has been invaded. Duckworth unbuttons his coat. This room is even more of a mess. Paper shredded, ink spilled, clay dried, abandoned canvases of paint, half-finished sketches strewn about.

A door opens behind him. He turns his head. *LA Times* Chief Art Critic Eyal pads nude down the hall, his buttocks collapsed under the weight of a fleshy mudslide. In his hand a camcorder, the black padded grip crossing over the back of his hand like a seatbelt. Eyal enters the bathroom down the hallway and swings the door partially shut.

Duckworth hears a small beep. In his mind's eye, he sees a red recording light come on, followed by the sound of a stream of urine hitting the deep end of the toilet.

He turns back to Tabby who is crying.

"They want a second piece," she says. "Was *Migration* not good enough?"

His eyes flit over the various half-finished projects. The hair on his neck lies flat. There is no electricity, no joy. No excitement.

No potential.

Nothing special.

His eyes land on the Play-Doh® sculpture from the MCA. *TIMMY!* But it is not Timmy's piece. It's a desperate failed recreation, a vague shadow of Timmy's piece. There is nothing of note here. Nothing of value. Nothing of worth. Nothing worth the paper, ink, or time spent. Time the septuagenarian will never get back.

Duckworth turns to her. Their eyes lock, and she can see the future. She breaks down and sobs. He finds himself holding her. Her back spasms with the crying, and he holds her tighter, consoling her loss. His loss.

Finally, they separate.

"What happened to me?"

Answerless, Duckworth slides over a more comfortable looking stool, a padded job. Gestures for her to sit. A partial sculpture of wood, paper and clay currently nests there. It resembles a Harryhausen centaur from a British movie made decades ago. She sits on it. The sculpture cracks and falls apart, parts of it disintegrating into gray ash. She does not care, and he has not answered her.

"What happened?"

He squats down, facing her eye to eye.

She looks at him wet eyed. "It was the water," she says. "Wasn't it?"

"What?"

"It was the water at the MCA. It's tainted, isn't it? I knew it when I drank it. I felt it tingle, I felt high and depressed all at once, I felt like I was capable of anything."

"Tabby, it was not the water. That's absurd and not in a Dada kind of way. That's just silly," he says, but he can see the hurt in her eyes.

He places a hand on her shoulder. Squeezes. "You alone created *Migration*. The sky is your limit. Nay, the stars your destination."

"But look around," she says. "This is all poo."

Duckworth does not need to look around. It *is* all shit. "It's just a phase," Duckworth says. Just a phase, he prays. Though the broken sculpture catches his eye. It's not a centaur, but Waylon in miniature, on horseback. His eyes dark and hollow. Facial features distorted in a grotesque mask. The horse is bone white. A pale bone white, but there are hints and tints of red, black peeking through a coating of gray ash. Duckworth's stomach tightens. He expects a revelation to dawn on him as he stares at the ghostly distorted face of his photographer.

But nothing is forthcoming.

"I need to take *another* drink of water," she says, breaking Duckworth out of his reverie. "I can't go back to my old life." Her eyes glaze and then clear. Tabby gets up and leaves the room.

With his foot, he pushes the broken sculpture under crumpled newspapers and out of sight. Duckworth follows her to the kitchen, also a pigsty, leaving behind the broken horseman of the apocalypse.

∞

Tabby pours a gallon of two percent curdled milk down the drain. Wraps a scarf around her head and pulls a Russian fur hat over her ears. "I have to go to the MCA." She pulls the now empty jug from the sink. A thin film of milk still coats the side. "I have to get another drink. From the fountain. Another drink that's all I need, right?"

"Uh, well, yes, that would probably do it," Duckworth says, almost convincingly. "That would probably enable you to unlock whatever, er— creative firing your synapses are capable of doing."

"You think I can do it?" she asks.

"Yes, you can," Duckworth says, melodically.

"Otherwise, she's a one hit wonder?" A croaked voice. Eyal takes a swig of beer from a bottle. Duckworth can see the silhouette of discarded cigarette butts swirling in the bottom. It is not nearly as alarming as the drop of urine still hanging off the tip of Eyal's penis. He walks past Duckworth with no embarrassment. Leans down and with one hand tilts Tabby's chin up and kisses her deep and long.

A cell phone rings.

"Don't fool yourself into thinking that the fountain water merely creates something out of nothing. You are the conduit, Tabby," Duckworth says with Shakespearean actor bravado, the impact slightly diluted by the incessant phone ringing.

"Please get me another drink of water, Jasper." She looks up at him. "And please don't tell the MacArthur people. It has to be our secret. And the kids downstairs. They need something to believe in."

Eyal answers the phone. "It's for you, my love," Eyal says.

She looks at Eyal who looks at his phone. She looks from Eyal to the phone. He hands her the phone. Tabby looks at Eyal, kisses his cheek. He squeezes her hand and then proceeds to roll a super joint from the bags of stinkweed.

Duckworth is confused. He clucks his tongue.

There is short, hushed conversation. Tabby hangs up the phone. Eyal holds the lighted joint to her lips. "That was Dr. Yassa," Tabby says and then inhales.

Eyal holds her closer. "I won't leave you."

On the exhale: "I'm dying of brain cancer."

Duckworth's head spins. His heart chakra flares and dims.

"Please, it's the water," Tabby says. "Please, get me another drink of water. Before it's too late."

The Art of Drowning

The Museum of Contemporary Art is far, far away from Tabby's residence, so Duckworth buys three bottles of water from a nearby coffee shop that helps far-away kids with distended bellies stay far away and dumps it into the milk jug.

Then there's the killing of time and then another parting of the throng of vigilant artistes, and perhaps another autograph or three, and Duckworth presents the water to Tabby. She takes a sip. "This is not the fountain water," she says. "I can taste the difference. Are you trying to fool me, a dying woman?"

"No, no, of course not, Tabby. The fountain on the second floor, yes?"

"Third," she says.

"Oh, dear, my mistake. And you won't leave her side?" he says to Eyal.

"No."

"And you don't want the, uh, kids downstairs to get you any?"

"They need something to believe in," Tabby says. "I said that already."

Duckworth clucks his tongue, for he has done a bit of thinking. Even dead, she'll have worth if he can get the rights to *Migration*. He can *champion* her lost potential, her tragic potential. (At least she didn't heave *Migration* over a cliff, like that epic fail of a little wanker Timmy, may he rest in pieces.) Careers have been built on less. He could write a book. A tour. Lecture circuit. He'll have to move out of the City. Somewhere where housing is affordable, but near a major airport. "If I get you the water," Duckworth says, as though the thought has suddenly occurred to him in a semi-joking kind of har-har way, "will you let me, the uh, Messenger, represent you, represent *Migration*?"

"Yes."

∞

The next day, Duckworth assumes his perch on the MCA foyer steps. That Tabby woman is crazy. Probably from the brain cancer. Duckworth can't believe his shite luck. First Timmy and now this. Oh Timmy, you were the one. But he will, nonetheless, fill a bottle with fountain water for Tabby. Shortly. In a few minutes, after they finish mopping the third floor. If the cops don't haul him away for vehicular manslaughter.

A new gaggle of kids flits through the museum on the way to the BE AN ARTIST™ exhibit. He looks for Timmy, half expects him to be there, anticipates the ghost of him, that tear-jerky post-traumatic stress disorder flash, and is slightly disappointed with the gaggle of urban youth's absence of another small Aryan psychopath. But perhaps there is a Basquiat in their midst.

Erma or Ethel or— *Emma*! turns the corner and escorts five of the gaggle up the stairs past him. She has traded in burlap for color blocking, a Piet Mondrian inspired trench coat dress.

"I'm thirsty," a boy says.

"I'm sure you all are. That old school bus was hot and stuffy," she says. "Water is this way." And off she leads the children.

Duckworth waits for her to turn and talk to him. To recognize him. But she's too busy wrangling. A moment later, the thirsty kids come back by. Duckworth follows them into the BE AN ARTIST™ exhibit.

∞

A handful of fifth graders and their chaperons stand behind each of their art projects. Every one a masterpiece.

Could it be?

Duckworth pulls up his mental masterpiece criteria checklist of five boxes, each with a subset of fifteen boxes. On first scan ten of twelve art projects fill the five boxes and then nine of ten fill every box in the subset of the main five, but a mental sunburst obliterates this mental critical criteria, and Duckworth simply knows on a primitive level that yes, this is a room full of Timmys and Tabbys, and before he can find the language, another sunburst (this is where the word "dawning" comes from— as in it "dawns on him"), a sunburst of energy within Duckworth's heart chakra blossoms instantaneously and in turn opens a tear duct. His sinuses flush with snot. Like a sickly snail, it creeps for his mustache. He is overcome with the Beauty of it all.

This is not possible.

This cannot be.

Duckworth's head spins; he can't let this slip away. Not this time. Not like Timmy. Oh, Timmy. My son. Suddenly, he is humiliated by his avarice, by the thought that he would plot to exploit Timmy or Tabby.

Emma mutters: "Oh Jasper. Do you see it? We are once again present at the Creation. Together. We must never be burdened again. Never be so, so cynical."

With the word cynical, Duckworth reflexively snorts the snot back into his sinuses and swallows the snails.

Emma prattles on: "My whole life spent—"

SMACK.

"Pull yourself together, woman."

She gasps and shudders.

And while the Beauty is overcoming, and Duckworth is on the verge of his heart chakra opening to three times its normal size, he cannot swallow the Truth of it. "This cannot be. These are *children*."

These underprivileged, undercultured, underfunded, undereducated children cannot be responsible for this Beauty. This is not a snowflake paper doll, a random commotion of colors that might represent something if you squinted. Duckworth recognizes the technique in half of them. Techniques you have to learn through training, trial and error, years of working through homages, tributes, imitations, mentorship, advanced degrees. Things he's attempted and failed, resorting to the typewriter machine and the questionably infinite combinations of twenty-six letters.

"They're so beautiful," Emma says. A red handprint swells on her cheek. She runs her hands down her thighs. "The children. The art."

He looks at each of the kids. "Something's not right," Duckworth says. "What is it? *What is it?*"

One kid takes a drink of water. Water streams down the corners of his mouth. The other kids, the gaggle. They have empty water cups.

Like most epic epiphanies the human body responds with the blush response, a tingle in the scalp, a drop in the gut, that weirdly wired circuit between the crotch and belly button that thrums instantaneously and the head knows the phrase before the lungs exhale the air through the vocal cords like an orchestral woodwind. His lips form the simple two syllable word:

"Foun-tain."

And then the adrenals kick in and the rest of his epiphany comes out in a breathless, uncontrolled rush:

"Upstairs.

"On the third floor.

"It's the water.

"Tabby is right.

"It is the goddamn water.

"Holy bloody fucking shit.

"It is the *fountain*."

And with this realization, Duckworth's Critic(al) Head Chakra kicks in, booting the open outreached hand of his Heart Chakra which shrinks back to its nominal size.

One of the parents' cell phones rings. She answers it in a cool pleasant voice, which belies her tears of joy and wonder. "Just a minute, honey, let me move to better reception. We're leaving about now."

Duckworth sees a big red button under a Plexiglass box. EMERGENCY ONLY. Duckworth flips the box and hits the button. Steel gates crash down, sealing them in the room. Outside walkie-talkie matching long-sleeve shirted employees with FEAR NO ART™ silk-screened on them goose step up to the exhibit, forming a high school grad minimum wage security force.

The kids scream and then laugh in delight.

"We're trapped like Mouse Trap!"

"They're going to gas us!"

∞

BANG.

"The water?" Les the curator says, tapping a golf ball into a regulation-size hole in an expensive portable office putting green.

Slightly beyond where Duckworth has thrown the first chair.[22] "Seriously, Jasper?"

"Yes."

Duckworth steps aside as two movers wheel in a stack of crates.

"Put the furniture over there," Les says.

"It's the water," Duckworth says, to Les. Again. "It's the fountain on the third floor by the ethnic art."

"What are you talking about? I still don't understand."

"Whoever drinks the water gains the ability to create one of these." It is one of the gaggle kids' pieces (Duckworth has brought it up and set it next to the putting green. In retrospect, he should have put it *on* the putting green). An anti-war statement, though none of the artist's relatives has even been in combat.

"Don't be preposterous."

"We have to call a plumber."

"Why?"

"To shut off the fountain."

"You're being preposterous."

"No, I've seen it. A half dozen times. Timmy drank the water."

---

22. *The unimaginative or deconstructionist would say it is essentially an argument over plumbing. But Duckworth and Les, as with you and I, are neither.*

"That's just randomness, Duckworth. Eventually a monkey monkeying around with art supplies is going to make something halfway interesting."

"A thousand monkeys at a thousand typewriters will only throw their own feces at each other. You saw Timmy's piece."

"No, but I heard there was a picture."

"Ahem. You saw *Migration*."

"Beautiful."

"You mean to tell me that Tabby Masterson is so intuitive and empathetic that she created that piece of art out of thin air?" Duckworth says.

"Yes," Les says. "And that's what you wrote in your column. You called her a 'genius.'"

"That was before the fountain. That was before I knew she was juiced. And she can't replicate it."

"So what? She's created something—"

"She has a following." Duckworth pulls out a 'zine. An underground magazine made by the art students who were there at the unceremonious unveiling of *Migration*. And because they are computer savvy and art students you would think that the 'zine is professional print quality. It is not. Each one is hand-lettered, hand-painted, and unique. A tribute to the Goddess *Bitha*. "Do you want to be the one to tell these kids that it's all a sham? That they only need to take a swig of water to be able to obtain this status?

I don't think you understand. If people keep coming here and drinking the water... What about craft, sacrifice?" Duckworth says. "Instant Picassos. Monets, Gustavs, Drudeskys, Bontecous, Fasgolds, Arakelian. Springing up like weeds. We'll be overrun with one-offs."

"You sound like that's a bad thing," Les says, sinking a nine-foot putt.

"These works of art have ripped my heart out. They've reduced my life of words to a joke, a child's book, a waste of time. I've been rendered useless. And by what? Instant Art. My profession has gone the way of the dinosaur. This is my asteroid—"

"What?"

"The asteroid that wiped out the dinosaurs."

"I thought it was global warming."

"No, that's what's killing us now, was, before the fountain."

"I thought a flash freeze wiped out the dinosaurs." A six-foot putt.

Duckworth throws another chair.

BANG.

"We're all going to die. We're going to die surrounded by indescribable pieces of beauty. Don't you see?"

"It's good business for the museum." A ten-foot putt.

"I am in a room with a man with no vision," Duckworth exclaims. "I'm calling a plumber." Duckworth reaches for the receiver of Les' phone.

Les stops him with a well-placed tap of the putter to his hand.

"There are artists who have sacrificed, who are on the cusp of greatness," Duckworth says. "But now you can just add water."

"Are you lamenting for the artists or the fact you think your occupation is over?" Les says, banking and sinking a fifteen-foot putt off the anti-war piece, which emboldens him to say: "Besides, no one has been able to duplicate their success."

"What?"

"One masterpiece. That's all it produces. Everyone has a masterpiece in them, Duckworth. When that's out, it's out. We're a universe of one-hit wonders." Les polishes his expensive putter (a Maruman Majesty Prestigio Milled). "But *marketable* one-hit wonders."

Duckworth steps back in shock. "How dare you, sir!"

Les looks up, smiling. Bleached white Nirvana. "And we own all the rights to those creations."

"What??"

"For your ten dollars you get to create a work of art in the Be An Artist™ Exhibit. You get your picture taken. And you give us all the licensing rights. How do you think non-profits stay in business? We own *Migration*."

113

"How dare you!"

"Good day, Mr. Duckworth."

"It's an *atrocity*, this exhibit; an atrocity *exhibit*!"

∞

Security is fairly rough, but lazy, only escorting him to the front foyer, not wanting to walk all the way past the Greek statues and down the vast stairs to Chicago Ave. and then back up.[23]

Duckworth cannot tell Tabby. He cannot tell her about the truth about the Fountain. He cannot destroy her hope. He cannot remind her that the museum owns the rights to her masterpiece *Migration*. The cups, the calendars, the t-shirts, the posters, the baby mobiles. The global market. That there will be no encore to *Migration*. No second act to this American life.

"My teachers, when I was young," Tabby will say. "They would send slips of paper home to my parents."

Tabby is special.

Tabby shows great potential.

"They said I was gifted," Tabby will say, slurring her speech. "I showed great potential."

Duckworth's eyes will blur from tears of recognition.

---

23. Our friend Hector took off early today, having one of those good news/bad news kind of days.

A cell phone will ring somewhere. Her lawyer squaring away her estate.

"The water," Tabby will say, "it helped me reach my potential. I need more water. One more drink. I need to create one more miracle."

Les's words will echo in Duckworth's head. *We're a universe of one-hit wonders.*

"It just gave me a boost," Tabby will say. "Just the edge I needed. Is that so wrong, Jasper? Is it any worse than those dead junkie artists the world worships: The King, the King of Pop, The Man in Black?"

Duckworth will swallow hard. Take her hand in his. "No, Tabby, it is not. I'll see what I can do." He will say this looking into her dim eyes sinking into her cancerous skull.

∞

The Fountain hums, thrumming umbilicaled to a generator unseen and unknown, levitating with a razor-pitch frequency, suspended against the wall by invisible means, this older model, not merely a Project Blue Book UFO sink jutting from the wall, but a fully vented, dented John Glenn High School-locker-chipped-gray paint utilitarian object; not modern enough for art, not retro enough for kitsch— Stalinesque, if you will, and if you were to stare at it as Duckworth is now and then turn your back you would not be able to describe it, let alone answer these elementary questions: Which side is the spout on? Did it reach the floor? What color was it? Was there a pedal for the water release or a mineral deposit flecked button?

But Duckworth has not turned his back on it. He stares unblinking at it, burning it into his mind's eye for so long the walls of his peripheral vision darken and sparkle with tiny stars and the sides of the Fountain expand slowly and contract in rhythm to his own breathing.

In.

O u t.

In.

O u t.

Chinese Take Down (MORE)

Jawbone puts one finger in her ear to block Hector's thundering industrial fan and presses her plumber phone to the other ear. Her lawyer always calls both phones, never remembering which is her art phone and which is for Walker & Sons. She plays the voicemail from said lawyer.

"*Sorry, Duchamp, you gotta return the money. The mayor's office said...* (a shuffling of notes) *the mayor's office said, 'No dice.' Yip. 'No dice.' That's a quote. Hey, no charge for the phone call, okay? And I was wondering if you weren't busy—*"

Click.

Jawbone's shoulders pull tight. She drops the flip phone. It hits square on the stained cement floor of Hector's tiny shop, and the back panel pops open like a jet canopy, and the battery ejects itself. An ache blossoms behind her right eye. Her tongue, a piece of useless jerky, grafts itself to the roof of her mouth. Her silver teeth turn electric in self-defense. The trigger finger on her left hand fires round after round of imaginary bullets from an imaginary gun at the disabled phone. The light lunch she had turns sour, and her bladder threatens to turn loose as her bowels grumble and shift. Thin snot escapes both nostrils so quickly that she has to catch it with the crook of her rolled up flannel sleeve. Her face and chest flush. She unhooks her overalls— overalls she'll never be able to take off. Not for the foreseeable future, and Jawbone can see ten years into the future. She turns to the industrial shop fan and rips her shirt open, buttons popping and spinning like Ed Wood UFOs. Two of them *pling* and ricochet with bullet velocity as they hit the 500 rpm grime coated steel fan blades. A sudden puff of dust and a piece of one of the buttons catches her above the eyebrow. She feels the drip drip of blood, but only stands there as the sweat on her exposed chest is either absorbed by her ill-fitting bra or evaporates at the insistence of the fan's blast. She draws in a deep breath.

This is the end.

117

In her shirt pocket, her artist phone vibrates like a defective pacemaker. She answers with a closed mouth, *"hmm."*

"Ms. Jawbone, it's Beth; where the fuck is your shop? I'm over at Belmont and—"

"No, no," Jawbone says, working her tongue loose. "I'm at a different shop. Mine is being fumigated. Damon and Clyburn." Jawbone feels her cool performance is forced, but adequate. Then she realizes Beth is not one to pay attention to nuance.

"I'll be there in an hour or two," Beth says. "I've got to finish these errands for the trip with Jackie. You're almost done with the chair, yes?"

"Yes, I told you—"

Click.

Jawbone's second phone meets a tragic fate as it is thrown down and stomped on with the heel of her steel-toed boot. Jawbone cannot stand to be hung-up on. Blood drips into her eye.

Fucking Beth.

Jawbone leans over the slimy slop sink. Blood splats the bottom of it. A layered fog of water-stains clouds the chipped mirror above it. Her image is a fuzzy impression of coffee skin, dreadlocks and silver teeth. Her carefully conceived trademark look. The look that gets attention from across a sea of bodies through a lens of cocktail glasses when she crashes gallery openings. Branding.

There's Jawbone.

A tear of blood hangs in her eyebrow like a fly trapped by an exotic carnivorous plant. Jawbone finally staunches the cut. But she can't see how deep the cut is in the fuzzy reflection. She cleans the mirror with a fistful of blue shop towels, and the image sharpens as new water removes the ghost of old. Now her image, though sharper, reveals too much. Crow's feet from too many days squinting at small details. Despite the lack of daily smiles her mouth is bracketed by two deep lines. The permanent furrows of judgment carved between the eyes. The small gathering of mini-ruts above the Y of her cleavage, wrinkled like a neglected houseplant.

Who wants to live forever?

Jawbone cranks the mineral stained faucet handles and douses her face with water, feeling the calluses on the edge of her palms scrape her cheeks.

∞

Her reverie over, Jawbone dials another number on her plumber phone, now reassembled with duct tape, the little plastic tabs on the back panel having broken off. The phone's ringing has a new quality, like a distant space ship beacon circling the edge of a black hole.

"Pick up, Hector," Jawbone says.

It rings.

Jawbone stares at the argon gas tank she hauled with her to Hector's shop. It's empty. Hector's argon gas tank is empty. This renders the MIG welder useless, relegating the chair designs for Beth's Higby-knock-off-but-not-if-she-can-help-it to Flatland. And Hurricane Beth going to make landfall here as a Cat 5.

Pick up.

No dice.

Hector does not pick up.

With a flat carpenter's pencil whittled sharp, Jawbone scratches Hector's name off a quick list of cats who might have a MIG welder, might have a spare tank of argon gas. She works her way down. It's late evening. She has got to make headway on the fucking chair. Now.

No dice.

Jawbone can't reach Hector or anyone. She flips through her sketchbook. Makeshift glued-in pockets hold old ideas, receipts, and contact sheets. She pulls out ancient pages, stiff with stains, fingerprints, coffee, and seeds and stems.

Searching.

Muttering as she does.

"Shit shit shit."

Searching.

"Shit shit shit shit."

Searching.

"Yes."

She finds it. The bloodstained Cast & Crew contact sheet for *Catch a Shooting Star!* At the bottom: Robert B. Bellio's cell number.

The B Variations: Round 1

"Who is this?"

"Walker."

"Who?"

"Harriet Walker."

"Who?"

"Jawbone."

Click.

The B Variations: Round 2

"Don't hang up."

Silence.

"You there?"

Silence.

"Fuck you want?"

Click. (Jawbone hangs up)

The B Variations: Round 3

"I need a solid."

"A what?"

"A solid. A favor."

"Uh-huh."

Silence.

"I'm outta gas."

"Call AAA."

Click.

Fuck.

The B Variations: Round 4

"For my MIG."

Silence.

"What are you working on?"

"A chair."

Silence.

"Call Higby."

Click.

Cocksucker.

The B Variations: Round 5

"I know you're fucking with me, B."

"Who is this?"

"Else you wouldn't be picking up."

"Is that so?"

"Am I right?"

"Heard the shit you slingin' about me at ArtBar."

Silence.

"I'm a mean drunk, B. I'm trying to stick with herb lately."

Silence.

"I'm a jealous bitch, B."

"You want I should make you a medal?"

"And a bit uncentered lately. Look, I'm working over at the Sangamon Ave. building."

"What did you say you're working on again?"

"A chair."

"What kind of chair?"

Silence.

"A Higby knock-off."

"Heh."

"This client wants a knock-off, and I'm trying to convince her to go with something original."

"Hmm."

"Her partner's a good client of mine."

"Oh?"

"I need the gig."

"Thought you had a couple of furniture designs with Laxmie's."

"They're doing mostly Higby pieces now."

"Heh."

"I need the gig. I don't have pieces in showrooms across the country."

Silence.

"Hello?"

"I remember when I did furniture. Tough racket."

He does not hang-up.

Silence.

"I need this gig, B."

Silence.

"Please."

Silence.

(muffled) "*Jesus*, that plaster's cold."

Then nothing. No *click*. No nothing.

Dead and silent as a black hole.

Chinese Take Down (CON'T)

Jawbone lights a joint of skunkweed and American Spirit tobacco. The cut above her eye is dry, but throbbing. She chills on an Eames lounge and ottoman she found in the alley on the North Shore and had reupholstered with cowhide for Hector for his birthday. She should have gotten him a new fan.

No dice.

She can't believe she's going through this. This chair. This client. But like Jawbone said to B, she's a bit uncentered. And now she's starting to simply embrace the fact that her life is out of control, and the worst that Beth, that fucking Beth, can do is yell at her. And maybe legal action. But not tonight, and Jawbone knows Jawbone is judgment proof. But that's not entirely true, she thinks, picturing the sanctuary of her real shop. The tools and machines of value that would be auctioned off for pennies on the dollar.[24]

Still Jawbone has a rep to maintain and this new blaze of glory forming in her cloudy brain could be epic.

∞

Jawbone cracks open a Red Bull and chugs it. The sweet medicine taste pops her taste buds. She looks at the can.

> *Everything's getting smaller or bigger. Whatever happened to medium?*

---

24. *And part of Jawbone thinks, again privately and way off the record, that she deserves this misfortune, that she's brought it on herself. A blame the victim mentality. She apologizes silently to herself.*

I'll just sit here wrapped in Eames, she thinks. Feet up. Drink the bull and smoke the red. She looks at her chair designs. Her original, not that piece of shit Higby knock-off.

That chair is going to kill me.

She tilts back the can and spills into her nose. She's stoned, you know. Jawbone flops her feet to each side of the ottoman and leans forward snorting and coughing.

This would not be a good death.

She moonwalks over to the table. Her legs feel like a kangaroo's. Literally. And she does not fight the feeling, but instead auditions for a Ministry of Silly Walks musical. She uncaps the bottle and sips the water from her FUCK ART bottle, clearing the snot and gravel burning at the back of her throat. She takes another hit on her spliff and holds it.

"Kangaroo," she says, smoke streaming from her mouth. "Kang. A. Roo." Such an awesome word. She hops back to the Eames, her head almost touching the 18' clear ceilings. Her stomach growls and suddenly she remembers in a flash:

There's leftover Chinese in Hector's mini-fridge.

A carton of cold shrimp fried rice, a fitting Last Meal before Hurricane Beth.

Hallelujah, Mr. Cohen. Hallelujah indeed.

∞

Beth stands, hips cocked, arms folded across her chest pushing her small breasts askew. "The party's postponed a week or so," Beth says. "Jackie has to travel for work now instead of our vacation. I hate her work travel. Jesus— it's so dark in here— so I need that chair by then," Beth says, tapping the ripped-out magazine picture of a Higby chair.

Jawbone mirrors Beth's posture and taps her chin thoughtfully. Between bites of cold MSG. "Maybe we can get Bitha to do your chair? I bet she can replicate this like no one's business. You've heard of her, yes?"

"Oh my god, yes," Beth says. "I know she'd be great, but no one has her contact info. I even called the newspaper and that critic." She pauses, imagining the possibilities of owning a Bitha-designed Higby knock-off before all her friends do. Now that would totes fuck with Gisele.

Jawbone can see these thoughts floating up in cartoon bubbles above Beth.

They pop and Beth turns coldly back to Jawbone. "I'm giving you One. Last. Chance." Punctuating each word with a stubby finger at Jawbone's chest.

Bitches have gotten roughed up by Jawbone for less, but right now Jawbone can only see that Beth is dressed in the safe, bland, muted primary colors of an actress starring in a carpet commercial.

"And don't forget the Higby mark," Beth says, flipping her hair. "Gisele will look for it, that *cunt*."

Jawbone looks around for the audience Beth seems to be performing for. "I won't forge a Higby signature," Jawbone says, but is thinking:

This rice is awesome.

"What?"

"I won't forge a Higby signature." The word *forge* comes out with a spray of rice and scallions.

"Look bitch, you've cashed the check."

"Yippers," Jawbone says, spooning in another caked scoop of shrimp fried rice.

Beth sniffs the air. Then Jawbone's dreadlocks. "And are you stoned?"

"Still don't have to call me a—"

"I can smell it."

"No, I—"

"Ms. Walker. I can smell it," Beth says, hands held high and dropping them for the thigh-slapping emphasis of a community theatre actress who has starred in one local carpet commercial. "No wonder you have missing fingers," Beth says, leaning into Jawbone's personal space, and although she misuses the next word, Beth says it because that is the only one she can summon as a period to her statement.

"Hack."

Everything in the room downshifts for Jawbone. Slows down with that body leaning forward motion of braking for a stop sign that's snuck up on a soccer mom juggling a cell phone and PMS while trying to distribute a bag of fast food burgers to the hungry crying losing soccer team. Jawbone sees everything slow. Even Beth's lip-plumper plumped lips slow down, novelty desktop wave machine slow.

Status Report: The IAC money is going back to its maker. She could take that money and run. But she hates packing and doesn't own a car.

The production line has dwindled down to a lawsuit for which she can't afford the filing fee.

She's spent the chair deposit, the last of it represented by the weed, Red Bull, and stale Chinese food in her hand.

Ross Robards is in town shooting a 30th anniversary special. The rich production company of his is run by former interns. She could have been an intern. Back in 1983.

Jasper P. Duckworth touts the masterpiece artistic genius of a dead ten-year-old discipline case. *Photo Coming Soon!*

And "Bitha," an old woman with a cult following of snot-nosed, ironic, sarcastic trust fund head cases, is up for a MacArthur.[25] Original hand-screened BITHA t-shirts are selling for hundreds of

---

25. Speaking of, those MacArthur folks returned Jawbone's applications unopened. The FUCK ART rubber stamped on the envelopes a barrier to entry.

dollars, if you can find one. The MCA is selling out of *Migration* t-shirts, calendars, magnets, and watches. The same MCA where she is contracted occasionally as a fill-in plumber.

And finally, she's also spent all the IAC money. All seventy-five grand.[26]

Jawbone's only recourse now, regarding Beth, is to bitch slap her. But Jawbone suddenly recognizes Beth's weak spot, the missing scale in her dragon armor. Jawbone knows the perfect thing to say to deflate this ego and allow her to keep the chair money. Nothing pops an ego like a well placed laugh. Jawbone chews the last of her shrimp fried rice, eager to spew forth this perfect razor. The perfect playground burn. Jawbone swallows the half-chewed rice, the words forming on her lip. But the rice stops halfway down her throat. Despite the focus on Beth's rippling lips, Jawbone feels her esophagus expand, closing her windpipe. A lump. She picks up her Red Bull and takes a swig to wash the hard cold three-day-old rice down. By doing so, she essentially makes a wet sandbag in her throat.

Jawbone flashes to a Saturday morning cartoon dog telling her that she'll be fine as long as she can make any kind of noise.

She cannot.

To prevent the danger of choking, the dog says, be sure to practice the following:

Cut your food into small pieces.

Chew food slowly and thoroughly.

---

26. Disregard any previous statements or thoughts or lies. That money is gone, baby, gone.

Avoid laughing and talking during chewing and swallowing.

No air comes in.

Help mom and dad with your little brothers and sisters: Keep marbles, beads, thumbtacks, and other small objects out of their reach and prevent them from walking, running, or playing with food or toys in their mouths.

No air goes out.

The dog says cross your paws at your throat for the universal choking sign.

Not this.

Get someone's attention.

Beth now faces the table, the new plans. Tapping her chin. Possibly reconsidering. Possibly considering the trade-off of going off the Pill: Regularity versus a quick ten pound weight loss.

Jawbone's heartbeat thunders in her ears.

The dog says before you deep throat your first cock, practice slowly on vegetables. Cucumber. Carrot. Rice. Shrimp. Watercress.

Two dollar delivery fee. Limited delivery area. Must present coupon.

Beth's phone rings. Last summer's chart-topping dance tune.

Remember: lubrication, extend tongue, flatten back of tongue, force throat muscles open, go slow, and be patient!

Jawbone takes a tentative step towards Beth, who answers her phone and steps away guarding her privacy. Jawbone takes another step, the sandbag in her throat weighing her down. A dark cloud blooms in her mind.

This is how it ends.

"*No.* No," Beth says. "No, Jackie. Please..." Beth's shoulders start to hitch. She's crying. "Gisele? *Gisele?*" It's that rapid boil sucker punch break-up cry. "No. No. No. No. I love you."

Jawbone throws her take-out Chinese container at Beth.

She misses wildly and Beth does not look up.

No dice.

A wet pffft of air escapes from Jawbone's throat. Thank god. She takes another swig to wash the sandbag down. The liquid fills all the gaps in the rice. The loose sandbag slides, tightens, swells and lodges deeper, forcing her windpipe closed as easily as stepping on a garden hose.

I had it.

The autopsy, no doubt, will not note this second fatal mistake.

Not like this.

Jawbone throws the Red Bull can at Beth. It glances off her head.

"What?" She turns to Jawbone, tears and snot dripping from her pointed chin.

Here's how you perform the Heimlich maneuver, the dog says, wrapping its paws around the belly of a cat.

Jawbone turns and backs up into Beth, rump to crotch. Beth only knows that Jawbone is mocking her broken heart and doing it in her personal space, ass first. She shoves Jawbone away.

Jawbone staggers forward like a runner trying to break the finish line tape by a nose. One, two, three steps, then the tip of her boot catches on a crack in the floor that was to be filled in next week, and Jawbone crashes to the floor face first, breaking several teeth. She slides a few feet to a stop, coming eye to swelling-shut eye with the Chinese take-out container.[27] The bright energy efficient lights glint of the dull polish of the thin wire handle of the container. It's from the last Chinese joint in town known to use containers with wire. And slowly that glint of light drifts and fades behind a garden of billowing inky clouds forming her last mental word:

Kang-

a-

---

27. She realizes now with the origami nature of the container it is meant to unfold and take the shape of a bowl. *How did I not see that?*

THE 1983 INTERVIEW FLASHBACK
(A Merman I Should Turn To Be)

Bobby Bellio is nervous.

He never gets nervous.

But it's 1983—set your watches back—and Bobby Bellio is in his early twenties and it happens.

This interview must go good. It must go *well*. Bobby Bellio needs the internship. He doesn't want to intern for a photographer, a painter, though he himself is one. He wants to intern for Ross Robards the sculptor. He's studied Robards' sculptures. He's read Robards' book *Rice Paddy Pudding*.[28] Robards has already been labeled difficult to work with. Demanding this and that: special foods. Ethnic girls. Drugs to keep him awake for seventy-two hours at a time, working, experimenting, living the life. That's what Bellio's heard anyway. It doesn't matter. Bellio needs the passion of a mad scientist.

A gallery owner mentioned by name in *Rice Paddy Pudding* is now a shoe store manager, and he slipped Bellio Robards' number.

"Robards is fucking crazy, kid. And slow."

"Mentally?"

"No, I mean that output wise. He'll never generate enough stuff to keep anyone solvent."

"I hear he's going to be pitching a TV show."

---

28. Finding that autographed first edition book at a second-hand store had been time consuming and cost Bobby Bellio his drinking money.

"He doesn't even own a TV. Good luck, kid."

∞

Bellio checks his watch. Realizes the band doesn't match the color of his belt or shoes. Should it matter? Would *he* notice? What does that say? What does it say about him? Eccentric artist, but oblivious to his own colors? He slips the watch off and puts it in his pocket.

Minutes pass. He taps his foot. Waiting. Bellio pulls out the watch, looks at it. Damn. It's moving so slowly.

He wants to ask Robards about Tex, Benedict. About the tattoo parlors. What the hell ever happened to Brooklyn? To Honky Tonk?

He tries to think if he should crack a joke, or give a real firm handshake. One that would crush Robards' hand. Let him know he means business. He should certainly make eye contact, but not stare. Will he be wearing his legs? Should I squat down to his level? Look away when he ponders his answers? Should he give each question thought or should he answer with the first thing that comes to mind?

What if Robards says: An artist must consider all possibilities or art must be instinctive?

Bellio goes with instinct. That was how it was in 'Nam for Ross. Instinct. And training.

On the other hand, there's stuff you can only learn on the streets. In the field. In Country.

He slips the watch out. Ten minutes late.

He will not tell a joke. He will keep his head down.

He pulls out the piece of paper in his pocket, shifting his portfolio to the other side. He looks at the number 6. He looks at the number on the door: 9.

Fuck.

He takes a few steps down the hall to the door with a 9. Bellio realizes he is the one who might be late. Wrong address? Late train? Accident? Had to finish... what? Fuck, now he's late, *unreliable*.

The door bursts open and two bodies come tumbling out. A white male and an exotic female. Arms and legs akimbo. They roll like ninjas, then disentangle, coming up on their feet. The white male punches the female in the jaw. Her head snaps back. Unfazed, she swings her portfolio roundhouse style and catches the male above the ear. He drops like a sack of root veggies.

"That's quite a jaw bone," Bellio says. "Heh."

The man doesn't move. Bellio assumes he is another potential intern. Doesn't seem to be breathing, so Bellio pulls a small mirror out of his bag. Checks to see if the unconscious male is only unconscious and not dead. The mirror fogs up and Bellio, satisfied, steps over the body and towards Ross Robards' studio door.

The young black woman cuts him off, looks Bellio up and down. Her hair juts out from her scalp as if made from charcoal cheese puffs. A silver tooth glints as she says, "Good luck, hack. Nobody but me getting the gig. I'm gonna live forever. Dig?" Laughing, she brushes past him, portfolio tucked under her arm.

Bellio whistles. You don't get firecrackers like that on the Fourth of July. Heh.

∞

Bobby Bellio enters Robards' studio and there's Ross Robards, he thinks. At least his silhouette. He stands in the corner on his stumps, pissing into a bedpan.

"I'm Bob."

"Bob?"

"Yes, sir."

"Come on in, Bob," he says, even though Bob is already in.

Bob steps further into Robards' studio loft. There's a cot, a hookah. A dozen stained and leaking bean bags. A mass of ornate floor pillows. Yellowed newspaper clippings from who knows when. There's a string of dried fruit by a metal worktable. The place smells of tobacco smoke and metal and lacquer and oil and pot and sex and dead spiders and cheap perfume and paint and fuck you freedom.

It smells perfect.

The loft features windows that almost reach the ceiling. Almost touch the floor. Around them, mortar is falling out. The windows are cracked, held in place with chicken wire. Damp cement reminds him of childhood storm shelters in Oklahoma.

Bob walks over to the windows. Frames of wood crumble to the touch. One window has been painted. It's a heart, anatomically correct, but with double the ventricles. As though *in utero* twins had absorbed each other and this was the harvest. The cracked glass adds to the effect. Next to the painted window, a weathered note card says I HEART HEART YOU. And a price tag of $450,000.

Bob looks back over at Ross Robards. He wears a dirty hemp tunic. Hair hangs in his eyes.

"That's the cost of the building," Robards says. He rubs his red-cobwebbed eyes and walks on his hands over to the floor pillows. "The painting stays with the building. You have to buy the building to get the painting." He snorts and flops down into the pile of stained pillows that look stolen from the set of a porn production of *One Thousand and One Arabian Nights.* Henna tattooed arms and shapely legs peek out among the twisted sheets. They belong to two women, if Bob's toe and finger calculations are correct and allowing for the fact that Robards is not wearing legs at the moment.

Melting into the pillows, Robards takes a hit on the hookah and sighs, releasing sweet acrid smoke.

One of the women cups the smoke, waves it over her face as she breathes deep.

"Conjure my car keys, intern," Robards says and fades away, lost in a desert sky.

Conjure my car keys.

Bob picks gingerly through a pile of junk scrap metal, looking to see if a set of keys that would open and start a car may have fallen. The junk is precariously stacked, like a mobile without strings. Bob pulls a small flashlight out of his pocket and shines it around, looking. Nothing. He cranes his neck and hears it pop.

I'm too young for this.

He looks around the studio. There's a desk. He puts the flashlight away and studies the desk. A hodgepodge pattern of paint splatter, welding burn marks, and swollen rings of veneer from swag coffee mugs and imported beer bottles hide the cheap particle board beneath. A fine layer of dust betrays months of stagnation.

Conjure my car keys.

Bob picks up a stack of unopened letters and envelopes. He half expects there to be fan mail. But it is all bills, Final Notices, an IRS letter, and a twice forwarded unopened letter from Bob's school, probably regarding his internship.

Bob tosses the stack back. Looks around the studio.

Sees a sculpture.

A beautiful sculpture.

Of a car.

The car is parked.

Conjure my car keys.

Bob cracks open a jar of paint. It's crusty and molded and bad. It smells like sour apples. There's nothing here that isn't old. Bob figures Robards must steal his paints. He looks through a few more shelves and finds an old paint splattered apron. ART'S SUPPLIES. He guesses one of the tattooed women works there.

Conjure my car keys.

Bob Bellio is technically a painter, but an artist first. He picks up a pair of tin snips and finds scrap sheet metal. There is a grinder. Not-so-old patina. Gun blue. A hammer. He has not done this before. He's watched. He's observed and maybe even made a mental note or two.

Bob pulls the necessary objects together. Clears a little workspace out of the line of sight of Robards. He doubts the screech of the grinder will be heard up on the magic carpet. He pulls a pair of scratched and cracked goggles from a pile of plastic Tupperware, caked with the remnants of the remains of the remnants of something that may have contributed to something of beauty. Once. Back when Robards gave a shit.

∞

He scratches his chin, feels the scritch-scratch of flesh rubbing against a 150 grit beard. He looks for steel wool, finds it easily. Then with slow deep breath, he starts.

Within moments, Bob Bellio falls into a hole. A tunnel where time distorts and becomes a distant notion. Once, maybe twice, he consciously uses a technique he learned from somewhere; the rest of

141

the time it is pure instinct. Pure flow. Pure energy. He does not know the time or place of where he is. The earth is a scratched stained wooden table. The sky behind him, a place where the sparks of tiny pieces of metal from the grinding wheel shoot up like tiny rockets escaping gravity to become comets. Their ghosts dance and linger in that phantom zone of his periphery.

∞

Bob Bellio finishes the car keys. He stares at them, and the world around him seeps back in like water coming under the door. The sights and sounds and smells now welcome his new creation into the world like a newborn lion cub in the jungle.

He wipes his brow, smearing grit and soot across his forehead. It will never wash off. He sets down his tools. He hears moaning and giggling. He cleans his area, putting all the tools and leftover materials where he found them, buried under this and that, leaving only footprints and fingerprints in the snowy cobwebs.

∞

Robards lolls slightly, still riding the magic carpet while one of the women goes down on him in a slow wet fashion.

Bob, embarrassed, sits quietly. Finally, he pulls out pieces of a broken mirror and expired paints. He paints a mineral spring fountain, a fountain he saw years ago on a road trip with his parents. Turner Falls in south Oklahoma. They took the scenic turnout. It was hot. There were high clouds and a telescope you could look through for a quarter. There were castles or the remains of one in the distance. What they were doing in Oklahoma, he never asked, letting his imagination satisfy his curiosity. His parents admired the falls, while Bob's fascination was held by the smaller less majestic fountain. His dad gave him permission to hike down there. While they never went down to the falls, he spent his allowance on the twenty-five cent telescope, framing the view of the fountain. He pressed against the eyepiece trying to get closer and chipped his glasses. Glasses too thick for such a young age. For at least a month, he managed to hide the mishap from his dad. Then he got the belt. But in the meantime, he lived in the dream circle of the telescope. Such a vibrant private postcard of possibilities.

This is a painting that Bob delights in, but would never show anyone. It is rudimentary, a grade-schooler could do it, but it makes him think of his mom, that summer, the open road, the waterfall and the fountain. It has a child's purity and it pleases him.

Enough that he signs it: **B.**

Now the smells of the loft remind him of distraction, addiction, and decay. He decides he will not intern with this knucklehead. There is nothing to learn, and Robards is already a burnout. The worst kind of artist. Afraid of his own potential. Using the guise of an artist as a year-round Halloween costume.

And B now wants to explore the path that is open before him: Sparks, heat, metal, hammer.

∞

The giggling stops. B sets the mirror painting on the desk, next to the stack of overdue bills. The mirror painting is far too wet to slip into his bag. And it will be the last painting B ever does. He peeks around the corner.

One of the girls wipes cum off her lips with the shirttail of Robard's hemp shirt. The other twirls her fingers through Robard's shoulder length hair. "You should grow even longer," she says to Robards. She is Asian and speaks in halting English, but with a beguiling French accent.

"Yeah," B says. "Use it as a paintbrush. Heh."

"Your hair as paintbrush." The girls giggle. "That great idea."

Robards says, "Who the fuck are you?"

B tosses Robards his new car keys.

Robards catches them. For a moment clarity defogs his stoned and watery eyes. The Asian girls lean in for a closer look, and Robards elbows them roughly out of the sunlight streaking through the double heart window. B sees now that the string of dried fruit hanging above the worktable is a string of dried human ears.

Robards extricates himself from the pretzel of his nude sirens, though this task is rendered somewhat easy with Robard's legs ending above the knees.

B picks up his bag.

Robards pulls on a pair of rudimentary VA-issue artificial legs and Robards grabs B's waterfall mirror painting, the future. Drops the newly sculpted keys, the past. "You're the one," Robards says.

"Heh."

He pulls a long thin object from a side slit on his left leg. "We're going to live forever."

B opens the door to leave. "Heh."

But not before Ross Robards sticks him in the back with a bayonet.

∞

B knee jerks himself awake. Emma does not spoon up next to him, comforting him for the third evening this week. Instead, she is sitting in the tub mixing a new batch of alginate. Next to the tub is a bucket of pigmented silicone and a casting tube. B lies there. This is not his bedroom. Squinting through a you-mixed-your-booze haze and his own genetically poor eyesight, B sees her dresser. His phone blinks with a new voicemail. His stomach tightens as he fumbles for his greasy glasses, and in the sienna sodium glow from the street, he can see, standing at attention on the far corner of her dresser, a half dozen curing casts of his own erect and disembodied cock.

Screen
Malla
Ecran

First Intermezzo: WURLITZER PRIZE

Lovely Dark & Deep I

Waylon rolls the film canister between his palms. Kicks over an unopened can of beans. He stokes the campfire with no vigor, but sparks pop and soon a flame dances and backlights his boots. The temperature is dropping as well. He should get more wood. He should take another drink.

Instead, he sits back on his ass. Stares at the tips of his duct-taped cowboy boots, a bottle of tequila jammed between his knees. The framing is off. He knows it. It has to be. The only known picture here on this roll of film and it wasn't perfect, wasn't demonstrative of Waylon's best work. How could he show this? The piece, the Timmy piece, deserved so much more, a more invisible style, a better eye. The light, what could he have done with the light? The flaming pencil was lost. Shot straight on, it was like taking a picture of a sundae and framing out the cherry. He was unworthy. The small hole in his cheek, his penance.

∞

Waylon, having forgotten a can opener, takes the business end of a tire iron to the can of baked beans. He sets the now somewhat open can right onto the fire, then moves it to the side of the flames, rotating the can and stirring it occasionally with a stick stripped of its bark. He drains the bottle of tequila and suddenly the worm tickles his tongue. He chews it once. There's a soft pop, and he swallows it.

He stares at his shit kickers as the worm works its magic.

∞

Walk a mile in my boots.

These boots were made for walking.

Puss in boots.

A squirrel bounds up to the edge of the campfire light. Onyx marbles staring at him.

Waylon, the squirrel says.

Yes.

You suck.

Yes, Waylon says, rolling the film canister. I know.

You're not good enough. Waylon.

I know.

Look at you. Cowboy. You're from Minnesota. You lived in Texas for two months.

I know.

You're not a cowboy.

You're not a rough-around-the-edges photographer.

I know.

You won a photo essay contest in college. Did you think about the fact you were fucking one of the judges?

I know but . . .

But what?

I've been working. I've been making a living. Waylon fumbles the film canister.

Yes, you have. You've been grifting and scamming them with your camera. You're a—

Don't say it.

You're a *fraud*.

I know, he says staring at the film canister. The undeveloped celluloid. The last thing he shot.

You've fooled all these people.

I know.

And now look what's happened. A child has created something you never will. A masterpiece. And you couldn't take a decent photograph of it.

I know, Waylon says, picking up the canister. The only known record of Timmy's masterpiece.

If he got it.

If it's not blurry.

If it's not out of frame.

If it's not f-stopped correctly.

153

Say it.

I know.

Say it.

I'm a fraud.

Good. You're a fraud. Don't you feel better?

...

Ahem. Don't you feel better?

Yes.

Lighter?

Yes.

Unburdened.

Yes.

Good.

He pulls a bottle of Old Crow out of his duster and finds it empty.

That's right, I'm already drunk.

He wants to call that Emma. Sweet wholesome Emma. He wants to confess to her. I'm a fraud. Hold me.

But it's the shame.

I have no talent. I am not worthy. I am too old to contribute.

I'm from Minnesota. I have a Texas accent.

I am a fraud.

This is where it should end. This is where they should find your body, the squirrel says. They should find you in the back of your pickup. They should find you with your brains blown out. They should find you.

But is that the answer? Shouldn't I sleep it off?

Like every other time? Waking by looking out one eye to see if anyone's noticed you're a fraud. That you don't have a good eye. That your compositions are *pedestrian*. That your ideas, your homages, are rip-offs of everyone that's come before you. That a child could do your job. Has done your job. Will do your job. Vintage equipment, your props. The dark room, your wizard's curtain.

But I'm reliable. I've never missed a deadline.

Yes, you're a good cog. Sacrificing art for speed. A paycheck for perfection.

Point and click.

Push a button.

Pull the plug.

Say good-bye.

How will they remember you?

He was a true professional.

I remember this photo he took. Got it in barely under the deadline.

Reliable.

Professional.

Dependable.

Good eye.

Good hang.

Oh yes and very professional.

A pro.

An artist. He won a contest.

Once.

In college.

Is this the lie you want to leave?

Waylon shakes his head. A calm washes over him. So easy to let go. His timeline will stop here. He looks to the darkening sky of twilight to the west. It is a good place to die. He will kill himself tonight.

I will kill myself tonight, he says.

Excellent, the squirrel says.

But you know what picture they'll run? My staff photograph. That's the image they'll remember me by.

It's a lousy photo, the squirrel says. You're much thinner now.

I need to take a self-portrait. One without pretense. My last shot. Yes, at sunset. During the magic hour. Or with a flash, high contrast black and white as though shot during a lightning storm.

That will be my testament, Waylon says. Not this roll of failure. He tosses the film canister into the fire. It bounces off glowing coals and lands on the far side of the pit.

Yes, this would be a good death. A fine death.

A good photo. A fine photo. The back story of his suicide will only enhance the drama, his skills.

My testament to life. My testament to art.

My sacrifice.

Yes.

The squirrel nods.

Yes.

Die with your boots on. Waylon rolls his duster around him and lays his head on a flat rock and slips further into darkness as the sound of burning beans hisses at him like the end of an old vinyl album on his parents' stereo.

∞

Waylon awakes at first light. His head pounds, but it is a distant pounding like thunder in the next county. He stares at the horizon, the graduation of blue to black above him. Pink and yellow will follow.

A good day to die.

He would first like to go to that little diner and get himself grub— eh, *food*. (Let's not continue the folksy charade.) And a bottle of something. To celebrate his release.

Tonight's the night.

Thunder in the distance. Maybe he'll get rain. That would be a nice effect if it is still light. He could see the image in his head, clear this time. Not like the other times when he approximated someone else's work. When he shot roll after roll and dug through the contacts looking for that lucky shot. And Waylon has been luckier than most. Until the MCA.

No, this one is distinct. This last shot will be all Waylon. This will be the one they remember him for. This one will make him immortal.

He'll have to leave notes though.

How to develop the film. Where to develop it. Not to open the camera. But if the police find him, it'll be evidence. But not of a crime. Who will own the photo? Should he will it to himself? The newspaper? Emma? Jawbone? Duckworth? Is there even a post office nearby?

He has to make sure it's seen. What if the cops see it and toss it? What if it's only the crime scene photographer's photos that survive? Their flash-lit close-up exploitation-type photos. And autopsy photos.

No.

No.

No.

He'll have to leave his instructions in a suicide note. But the note will be made public. It'll look like he was *trying* to be great instead of *being* great. He wants the sacrifice to count but he doesn't want it to be *the* story.

They'll quote the note.

Not if you ask them not to as a last request. The squirrel is back. A smattering of beans on its snout. Or get a witness.

Yes, a witness. To take the film, the camera. Ensure that it gets developed and taken care of. A trustee. An assistant. An executor.

His stomach growls.

I'm hungry, too, the squirrel says. Let's go eat. It turns and bounds away.

Waylon looks down and sees his sock-clad feet. His boots are gone. Nothing. No signs. No footprints. No drag marks. No cigarette butts. It is as if Jesus himself walked into the camp and stole his boots.

∞

"Denver omelette, extra cheese, a side of sausage, a pot of coffee and extra cream," Waylon says. He pops his tattered socked feet up on the opposite booth. "And a cup of the soup *du jour*."

"Denver omelette, extra cheese, a side of sausage, a pot of coffee and extra cream," she says. Her voice has the honey tinge of someone from the South. "And a cup of *oui oui*." Her nametag reads: TRUDY. "For the cowboy at table 7."

She looks down at his feet. This waitress. "Looks like you could use new socks."

Waylon shrugs. "I woke up and my boots were missing. My truck died four miles from here. They, my socks, made it about half way."

"I think we got that song on the jukebox. You ain't got a dog that run off with them boots, did ya?"

"There might have been a squirrel, but no. Just the boots. And the truck."

She winks at him. "Be right out, Cowboy at 7."

∞

He downs his cup. Refills it. Extra cream. Extra sugar. Ice.

She appears again quickly. One hand behind her back. "I'll bring you a new pot." She glances outside. Dark with incoming storm clouds. "And if you want to hang around 'til my shift's over I can give you a ride to your truck, Cowboy."

"Yeah, okay."

"Here. On the house." She tosses something at him. He catches it in front of his face. She turns and walks back to the kitchen.

Socks.

Fluffy thick white and cotton heaven.

∞

She drives a little car, a domestic based on a foreign design. A little red wagon. It drives smooth. But is a little cramped.

Waylon squirms at how close the road seems after all the time driving in his truck. "Never been in a clown car before," he says.

She stares at the road ahead. "Watch what you say about my f'ing clown car."

"Thanks for the socks," he says in self-defense.

"I always keep a new pack in my locker. Never know if I'm going to pull a double, or spill coffee in them. I give them about a month before I throw them out and buy new ones. Get them in bulk. One of the few splurges in life. There are a few things you don't cut corners on."

"Sure."

"One: toilet paper. I get the double cottony whatever. Two: coffee. If you're going to drink it might as well taste it. Three: my feet. These sneakers are outrageously priced, but I spend most of the day in them so I've got to keep the tootsies happy. Four: my bed. Slept on a futon for two years in Paris. I'm what they call "Gaulier-trained". That's a humble brag."

"I don't know what 'Gaulier-trained' means."

"Like I said 'humble brag.' But it mucked up my back. Now I got one of them space age foam jobs. Cost a fortune. But think about it... where do you spend most of your time? On your feet, if you're a waitress, and on your back—"

Waylon's cheek pulls his mouth up into a crooked smile. The pucked hole in his cheek stings.

"I saw that. On your back when you sleep. Which some dipshit says we should do eight hours a night. He must have been well funded and shit I'm runnin' off the mouth." She runs the windshield wipers to clear a fresh smattering of bugs. It does no good. "What happened to your cheek?"

"Stray pencil."

"This world..."

"I like the tone of your voice, Trudy."

She smiles, sort of puzzled. "Beg pardon?"

"The tone. You have a unique tone. Like a cool singer/songwriter. I like it. Unique."

"My mom used to tell me to watch the tone of my voice when I was back talking her."

"I'm just saying."

"That's an unusual compliment."

They drive in silence for a mile.

"Can I ask you a favor?" Waylon says.

"You mean after the free soup and socks and ride?"

"Yes. After the free soup, socks, and ride. The socks I can give back to you after—" he stops himself.

"Sure, go ahead seein' as how I'm in a generous mood."

"Must be a full moon," Waylon says.

"Must be," she smiles, baring her teeth.

"I need help killing myself tonight."

"Oh."

"I don't need someone to pull the plug or push the button, but I need someone to handle the film."

"Oh."

"Take it to a place to have it developed and maybe published."

"Oh."

"So you wouldn't actually be pulling the trigger or pushing the button."

"Oh."

"Or pulling the plug."

"Oh."

"You could even close your eyes. But I have to make sure someone I can trust gets the camera. With my last picture on it. I'm a photographer."

"Oh."

"Will you help me?"

A quarter mile of gray road passes beneath them.

"Okay," she says.

∞

"So that's tonight?"

"At dusk."

"What are your plans the rest of the day?"

"I don't know."

"I reckon that's one way to kill your last day."

He laughs. "It is kind of a waste."

"I'll say."

"I do have a few things to get in order. Call to my lawyer. Run to the store."

"That's a couple hours spent. Still got the rest of the day."

"True."

She pulls out a cell phone. Hits a speed dial number. After a moment, she speaks. "Trudy, my back's twitchin, I'll pick up your double Saturday if you cover me tonight. Fine. Don't tell Don, just show up. He'll be cool. Thanks, Trudy." She hangs up.

"You're not Trudy?"

"Nope. Just wearing her nametag."

"I thought your name was Trudy."

"That's what you're supposed to think." She laughs. It is throaty and child-like at the same time. "Do you feel tricked?"

"Slightly. But more of a shame on me. I never asked."

"You didn't."

"I assumed."

"You did."

"Huh." He wiggles his toes. Something catches his eye. He bends down and picks it up. A red ball. He squeezes it. Soft. He squeezes it again. There is a small slit in it. He feels a metal spring clamp buried in the material.

"That's my clown nose," she says.

∞

They arrive at Waylon's truck still stranded and straddling the shoulder of the road and the pavement. Waylon feels the need to not only not abandon the truck, but that it be used as a piece of the background or actual set for his last photo and even perhaps death.

"So you figure a jump will do it, or should we call for a tow truck?"

"Doesn't seem very dignified. A tow truck. We could use my car, but I need the ride to work and I don't think that's the last picture you want."

"Yeah, I could use your car and the clown nose. That'd be—"

"You making fun of my clown nose?"

"No, I just—"

"After the request you asked of me?"

"I just— it's a *clown nose.*"

"I think that's a bit mean-spirited of you."

"Are you serious? It's a nose; it was rolling around on the floorboard. A clown nose was not what I expect to see rolling around on someone's floorboard. Just— and okay. Yes. I was rude and thoughtless. It was purely a defensive comment to mask my—"

"Mask your what?"

"Nothing. Sorry about the making fun of the, uh, clown nose."

"Apology accepted," she says, dryly. "I have to warn you. Some things I don't have much of a sense of humor about." She pulls out her phone and engages someone in a quick conversation about a tow, a possible dead alternator, a kid's birthday show, and yes, she knows what shark pool pants are, and they need the tow ASAP. She hangs up the phone and looks at Waylon. She takes a deep breath. A cleansing breath. Waylon figures it has to be that kind of breath, because her body language softens and the next thing she asks is: "You thought about a last meal?"

∞

They walk through Garden Good, a small organic grocery store.

"I'm not sure they'll have everything you want here. We may have to drive up into Milwaukee."

"I took this motorcycle trip out of college," Waylon says. "Three months. Wasn't a big bike, but I had saddlebags. Slept in a tent. Picked up odd jobs, tending bar and waiting tables. Whatever. Ended up in the French Quarter. Fun time. But I was young. Anyway there was this place with the best food, I can't even remember if it was officially Cajun, but it was so fresh, so hot. All these different flavors. I didn't know something could taste like that at the time. And I don't remember the specific flavors now, but I remember being satisfied. With everything. I don't know, must have been a good day."

"What was the name of the place?"

He pauses. Snaps his fingers. "King Bee's Blues Crib."

"Nice ring."

"Yeah." He stares off. "It's somewhere across the country." He's lost in the memory. She lets him remember. Not tapping her foot or looking at her watch. After a long minute, she gently tugs his sleeve, and they wordlessly resume shopping.

He stops walking. Picks up an apple and a pomegranate. "Now on one hand I could go with comforting food. Food I've always enjoyed, food that reminds me of mom, or college, or my first love."

"And on the other?"

"I could go with something I've never had. Experience something I've never tasted, new sensations. New combinations. Something that would truly be worthy of a last meal. Or I could go with something like lobster and steak."

"Something vulgar."

"Yes. Something vulgar, which I might allow seeing as how my last two meals were a greasy spoon omelet and soup, granted a good soup."

"I didn't cook it. No skin off my shin."

"And a can of beans." He holds the apple up. "Something safe and warm and satisfying." He holds up the pomegranate. "Something risky-edgy fraught with great disappointment or a great surprise."

"How about a sampler?"

He thinks for a moment. Then shakes his head. "No, I want to make a commitment to the moment."

"Respect."

He cocks his head, looking at the fruits. "I have no idea."

"When they do the autopsy, they'll know what your last meal was," Not Trudy says. "Needs to fit the theme."

He points at her. "I hadn't thought of that."

"Glad to be of help."

Lovely Dark & Deep II

An hour later with the back of the car filled with bags and bags of Garden Good groceries. Everything that looked good, or might look good or fell into the category of "I have a recipe for that" had been plucked from the shelf and dropped into a basket.

The car wheels crunch on the gravel road as they pull into a flea market, consisting mostly of a few series of tin shacks adorned with various talismans of rope, cow skulls, and barbed wire.

A few people scattered here and there, mostly senior citizens and young children.

"What are we doing here?"

"Shopping," Not Trudy says. "I think you might want to check out that far shed."

"You're not coming with?"

"I'll join you in a moment. I got to pick up something in that one on the other side."

"Okay then."

Waylon gets out of the car and heads towards the far shack. He turns and catches Not Trudy loping with a laid back stride, hips swinging freely but not for show. All her movements utilize an additional five degrees of body movement, giving her not an exaggerated effect, but one of a body enjoying being in motion. No one but him watches. She takes a few more steps and without breaking stride, like a magician produces a cell phone and credit card seemingly out of nowhere.

Hey, buddy.

He turns back.

Don't forget the beans.

The squirrel stares at him. A totem atop a wooden post. Black little eyes. Ebony marbles.

Tick, tick. It says, making a little gun with its little paw and pointing it to its little head. Tick tock.

Waylon feels his jaw muscles tighten. He bends to pick up a rock, and the squirrel zips off.

He shakes it off and goes into the shack. Looks at his watch. Eight hours and counting.

The shack is a used Western clothing store for all intents and purposes. On one side, shirts and faded jeans stained with life. He wanders around touching things, the fabric, not sure why Not Trudy directed him here. Unless she wanted privacy for her phone call. He turns the aisle where it opens up into a sitting area with a broke back couch.

And racks and racks of worn, banged up, scuffed and beautiful cowboy boots.

∞

A kaleidoscope of smells fills the car. Herbs, fresh bread, etc. Waylon's stomach growls.

She giggles.

"You heard that?"

"I have to warn you, I'm a lousy cook." She drives, tipping her new old cowboy hat back. It suits her well, as though it'd been a part of her whole adult life.

He wiggles his feet, the new/old boots now a second skin.

"How they feel?"

"Perfect," Waylon says.

"They used to be my dad's. He died last week. I gave all his stuff to Jeb to sell, except for one of his shirts. I sleep in that."

"I bet it's comfortable," he says. And then, "I'm honored. Thank you."

"Yeah, I gave away everything, but his shirt and his pistols, so you know, we won't have to go buy one of those for tonight." And then, "You're welcome."

"Pistols?"

"He's got an antique Peacemaker. I figure you'd want a six-shooter. They're not too accurate past fifteen feet, but I reckon it'll blow your brains out."

∞

The smoke alarm sounds for the third time. Waylon waves the copy of *Log Cabin Designs Magazine* and clears the smoke. He hasn't bothered to put the magazine down since the first time it's gone off. Because, one: it's a shrill annoying sound. And two: he is particularly fond of the Outdoorsman model floor plan. It seems cozy, yet roomy; stylish, but modest.

For a third time, he stares down the hall where the closet is cracked open. Showing are the tips of what he figures to be a pair of floppy red shoes. But remembering she doesn't much have a sense of humor about some things, he wisely keeps his mouth shut.

"Maybe I should take out the battery," he says.

"I'll forget to put it back in, and die in a fiery pie baking accident."

"Fair enough."

He waves a magazine in front of the smoke detector and clears the shrill alarm. It shuts off. She surrenders and cracks a window. Enters the room holding something that thirty minutes ago might have been on the cover of a gourmet magazine. "Uh, this one didn't make it either."

∞

They sit on the patched couch in silence. She slices pieces of apple from the core and hands him a piece, which he dips into a jar of oily organic peanut butter.

It could be worse.

He could be alone.

With a can of beans.

She looks at her watch. This is not the first time she has recently looked at it. She's getting nervous the closer it gets to dusk. He understands this, but she was attentive when they went over the instructions for developing and delivering the photo. He's decided to sign over the rights to her for helping. It might cover any court costs or fines if something goes sideways. Then again no one may give a shit.

"Nervous?" he says.

"No, why?"

"Because you keep looking—"

There's a knock at her door. She cannot hide the smile. She gets up. He gets up. She points at him. "Wait here."

After a brief exchange at the door, she brings in three brown bags and sets them down on the coffee table, knocking aside the jar of peanut butter with an apple slice protruding from it like a small sail. It smells delicious. He cannot place the smell. He thinks he can, but then that would be crazy.

Like a talking squirrel.

She tears open the bag and pulls out three large Styrofoam containers. Opens them. Steam escapes.

"No way," he says.

"Way."

She throws him a stack of napkins. And goes to the kitchen.

Printed on the napkins: King Bee's Blues Crib.

∞

She strides in from the kitchen, two beers in hands.

Waylon is still shocked. It's still hot. "How?"

She traces its path punctuating the air with a finger. "Phone call. Courier, cargo, courier. Credit card. And I might have to go out with the manager when he comes to town."

He reaches for his wallet. "How much?"

She hands him the beer. "I'll get the bill next month. We'll settle up then." She winks at him. "Dig in."

∞

Waylon is full and satisfied. He does not even know her name. He does not want to ask. He must focus on the task at hand. He goes over notes with her again while she drives his pick-up. Where to take the film of his last portrait. Who to deliver it to. Answers to other questions that might be asked. He keeps one eye on the road and the other on his notes for fear she might take a sharp turn and drive him away from his destiny. But she doesn't. She fiddles with the radio slicing through static until a woman's voice tells them that it wasn't God that made honky-tonk angels.

They turn into the campground. The gate is still open. A sign says it closes at sunset during the week. This is Thursday so they'll have to be quick and precise.

"We'll have to be quick," he says.

She taps her finger to the beat on the steering wheel and sings softly.

She reminds him of a country singer, now long dead. That song "Crazy." He opens his mouth to tell her—

Suddenly, the truck bounces up and down. There's a metallic crunch.

"The hell was that?" Waylon says. He looks behind them, but sees nothing in the gloaming.

She shrugs.

He pats his duster. The six-shooter's still there.

∞

They find the spot. She's memorized the notes. Steps back and lets him set his lights. Check his light meter. They're chasing the sun as they say in the biz, but he knows what he's doing.

He's calm, lucid. Everything seems sharp and crystal. He notices things. A nick in the bed of the truck. A mole above her lip. A torn cuticle. A new grass stain on his boot. She holds things when he asks, sometimes anticipating his hand-off like a professional caddy.

It's all set. This will be a fine death, a fine picture.

This is destiny.

This is fate.

The squirrel is right.

The squirrel is destiny.

The squirrel is fate.

Beat this, Timmy. Beat this with your Play-Doh® sculpture.

Waylon taps the tripod into the cold earth. She loads the camera with film. Puts new batteries in the flash. A few more minutes with a little trial and error and they manage to rig a pull string for the gun trigger made out of 20lb fishing line.

Waylon hops on the tailgate, pulls out the Peacemaker. Threads the fishing line around the trigger and the guard. Puts it in place. They are set. "Trudy, I want to tell you, well I mean your name's not Trudy, but whatever. This has been the greatest day of my life."

She frowns.

"What?"

"I was just thinking."

"Yeah?" He looks at the sinking sun. Fading fast. A few more minutes at most.

"Authentic. That's the aim?"

"Yes, in a perfect world."

"And you're only going to get one shot at this."

"True."

"Maybe you should shoot a couple of practice rounds. Not with the string, but do regular target shooting. Those are real cowboy boots you're wearing and that's a real cowboy pistol." (She always says pistol and not gun. Ships have guns, her daddy used to say, being an ex naval man.) "Be a shame to kill yourself and not have fired it a few times. 'Sides, you need to get gunpowder on your hands."

He looks at his watch. Takes it off, hands it to her. Looks at the sun. Two minutes, maybe. "Okay, but quick. Over there. There's a bunch of cans by that old campfire."

She jogs over to the campfire. Picks up a few cans, cradling them like a baby. Then finds a partially melted film canister. She holds it up. "Wonder what's on this?"

"Probably nothing," Waylon says. "Toss it."

Not Trudy shoves it deep in her jacket pocket. Gathers a few more cans. "Where?" she says.

Waylon motions to a few old fence posts connected together with rusted wire like broken and busted guitar strings.

She sets the cans on posts. Hurries back.

He steps up, sights down the barrel. The pistol is smooth in his hands.

His fate.

His destiny.

He looks over his shoulder to Not Trudy.

"Uh, it's a double action," she says. "You can pull the trigger or you can cock the hammer with your thumb and then pull the trigger."

He cocks it with his thumb.

BLAM.

CLANK. The can flies.

Cock.

BLAM!

CLANK. The can flies.

Cock.

BLAM!

CLUMP. It flies, but not as far as the other two.

"Clump?" Not Trudy says.

They walk over to the third can. Baked beans. It's punctured on one side, but not blossomed on the other. Not Trudy bends down. Waylon bends down. Not Trudy picks up a stick and uprights the can, forces the misshapen lid open. Something brown inside. Brown and red mixed with the residual beans.

Two lifeless black marbles.

It's a squirrel.

"I guess he done met his fate," she says. She stands. Wipes her hands on her jeans. "Darn. Looks like we lost your light," she says.

Waylon stands still, staring at the can of baked bean squirrel. "It's okay."

"So what do you want to do?"

"I'd like to build a log cabin."

"How about tonight?"

"I don't know," Waylon says.

"We could rent a movie. Eat leftovers."

"Yeah, I'd like that." Waylon hands the pistol to Not Trudy. She flips open the cylinder and dumps the shells out, stuffs them in her jacket pocket. Next to the film canister. They walk back to the truck. Not Trudy looks back at the can. Waylon looks back. They look at each other.

"Stupid squirrel."

, 19   16, 17   22   24   23   40   41   21   10   35   8   3   14   13   7   7   6   25   13   12

Screen
Malla
Ecran

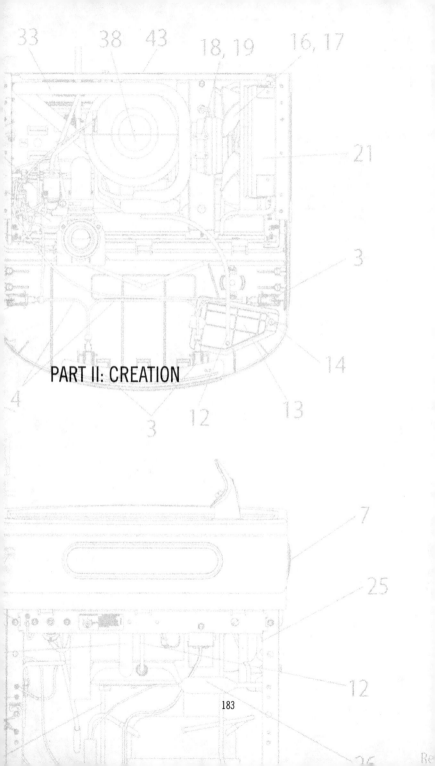

PART II: CREATION

Shipbuilding

Crack.

Crack.

These sounds: even in the haze.

Crack.

Jawbone's ribs.

Powerful arms pull her to her feet. Oak pistons again pound up under her ribs as she levitates off the floor. A god light fills her hazy vision revealing a Dutch angle of ghost shapes and lines and patterns. Her vision whips past an Edvard Munch screaming female and then back to an abyss.

Pressure. Lift.

Crack.

A wet violent expulsion.

A pearl diver breaking the surface of the ocean with a gale-force inhale.

∞

B holds up Jawbone. A full tank of argon gas in the doorway. Beth holds a blood-soaked rag and two of Jawbone's bloody silver teeth in the newspaper clipping of Duckworth's column. The trio stand there silently, save for Jawbone's wet choking, but now breathing gasps, staring at the floor at the Rorschach splatter of shrimp fried rice and Red Bull.

Jawbone sees the beginning of the next chapter of her life.

B sees an organic Franz Marc's *Fate of the Animals.*

And fucking Hurricane Beth, she grabs a mop.

THANK YOU
(Falettinme Be Mice Elf Agin)
GO

Surveying his shop, B cracks his knuckles. It is here for a few minutes of silence that he gathers his thoughts, focuses on the journey ahead. Visualizes the process. The end result. And his phone rings. It's Emma. Again. B turns on the band saw, slowly pushes a piece of stray hardwood through. The wood and metal blade clash, producing a cloud of—

"Hello?"

"It's me, B," Emma says. "What is that cacophony?"

"Mahogany," B shouts.

"When can I see you again? Tonight?"

"Sorry, Em, I'm swamped with this deadline. I told you about it. If I don't make headway on this commission, there will be no more gigs. I might as well go dust in the wind."

"I took more Polaroids for you," she says.

"What? I can't hear you."

"Polaroids," she shouts in a shouty smoky voice. "Black and white this time."

B found the color Polaroids interesting and a bit exciting at first. But there are worlds you live in and there are worlds you like to visit. And B is ready to return back to earth. "Emma. I have work to do."

"Come home. Come stay the night. Please. I'll call a friend. He can take pictures of us. He's open-minded. And a cop."

"What? I can't. I have to finish this."

Clank. Something breaks and the bandsaw screams and dies. Shit. B pulls the plug. The sudden quiet rings in his ears.

"Please, I had a bad dream," she says. "I had a dream of a great flood. And we were drowning. I think it might have been from a river."

"It was only a dream, Em," B says. "The only river near us is the Chicago River and it runs backwards."

"What about the Tigris?"

"I have to *work*."

"Will you text me?" she says in her sad little girl voice.

187

Click.

He tosses the mahogany into a scrap bucket. His phone rings again. She won't give up.

"Yeah?" B answers with not-so-forced annoyance.

"B, it's me."

"Who?"

"Jawbone."

"Oh." B shifts, aware of metal shavings in his boot. "Hey."

"Listen. ArtBar. Me and a couple of friends," Jawbone says. "Buy you a drink? I owe you. Or are you busy?"

B looks around his shop. A new shipment of iron and steel lines the walls like hundreds of oily hand rails. Two tons of steel. Three gallons of cutting oil. A stack of 2x4 lumber for custom shipping crates. Three, now two tanks of argon. A carton of cigarettes and wholesale bulk size canister of shitty instant coffee. Twelve apple pies and a case of granola cereal bars. A box of wet wipes. Two three-packs of underwear. A six-pack of new wool socks. And under a tarp marred with cigarette burns, an army cot with a ratty sleeping bag and a new feather pillow already tattooed with handprints. Next to that, an old portable CD player and a used audiobook on CD of *Dogs of God* as read by that guy who does the insurance commercials.[29] A broken band saw he must repair himself. A calendar with a drop-dead deadline in red Sharpie. And a set of design blueprints for twenty-six skeleton cartoon creatures for a wealthy insider artist who farms out his creations Sol LeWitt style that B now has to convert from metric into American. Despite the exchange rate, B is still more expensive than several Polish counterparts, but this artist, the one and only Günter Adamczyk wants to buy American. If B fucks this up, the job gets shipped overseas. Every job that follows will be shipped overseas. Behind him, even the clock from his grandfather's shop is *tick-tocking* a war march.

GO/NO GO

∞

The ArtBar is dead; most everyone's swinging over at the F-Hole across the street. A cheap poster says this week's treat is the rockabilly stylin's of Death Spoon, E.S.A.D, and The Vegas Cocks. B tells himself two drinks only and then back to the shop. But B is a smart man and knows that the third drink will more than likely be on the house and then he will be obligated to buy a fourth. So he will go

---

29. *The one with the talking tree and a man about to commit suicide that Jasper P. Duckworth has deemed witty, subversive, and, despite being shockingly funny, more suited to the stage. He ended his review by declaring the ad a— wait for it— a complete failure as a commercial. This, despite the catchphrase becoming a part of pop culture including two references in two major motion pictures. But Families Against Suicidal Teens sends a letter to their respective congressmen and the ad is pulled, but wins three Clio Awards. At the ceremony, the Creative Director of the ad, Michael Tannhauser Sapieja, refers to Duckworth (who is present as a guest, but not present as a presenter) as "that British wanker in the bow tie and hair plugs" and salutes him with the backwards peace sign. The ad agency Sapieja Shop doubles in size overnight.*

with a large 24 oz. PBR in a can with salt sprinkled on it old-school style and call it good.

B walks past a woman anchoring a bar. She says his name. He turns and looks right through her until she waves. But confusion slows B's ability to raise his hand and wave in a timely manner or to say the person's name.

"It's me," she says. Then B recognizes the arched eyebrow, now with a small pale bandage. "Jawbone?" She's chopped her hair. He looks around. She's alone.

She stands gingerly and gives him an air hug.

"I'm grimy," B says. "Sorry."

"No, my ribs are taped," she says. "Hence the dress." (It's a loose brightly colored pattern of sunflowers affair. This pattern almost hides the myriad wrinkles betraying its storage history.)

"Oh. Right. Your ribs."

"A crack a lackin' good time," she says with a grin.

"Ah. Wondered why you're out of costume," he says and she smiles bigger, covering her mouth with her hand as though it's an offensive gesture. "And you're making me feel underdressed and dirty," B says. "I mean, aware of the fact I'm dirty."

She rolls her eyes. Her hand moves and touches the bandage on her eyebrow.

B now sees her teeth. All of them are brilliant white, like foam against her cappuccino skin. And this strikes B as odd. He sits at her wobbly bar table.

"What are you working on?" Jawbone says.

Bob shrugs.

"I hear Günter Adamczyk has a new Italian project."

"Hack," B says without a second thought. He stares. "You look...?"

"Girly?" she says.

"Approachable."

They both laugh. She tears up with pain. Pulls a brown prescription bottle from her purse (a purse!), which B recognizes is actually a canvas tool bag. A Bucket Boss Brand 06004 GateMouth Tool Bag (even better!). "Generic Vicodin," she says.

"I'll try not to be funny." B glances around. "Where are your friends?"

"Hector got called into work. The MCA's had an uptick in attendance."

"And your others friends?"

She counts on her hand. "There's Hector. My buddy Waylon."

"Who?"

"Waylon Nagasaki. He's a photographer."

"I know his work. All film."

"Does my portfolio. Internet pics."

"Good eye."

"He's MIA. Off the grid."

"You selling on eBay?"

She shrugs.

"How's that working for you?"

"Same as everything else."

He nods sympathetically. "No one needs art." He finger combs his hair. "So, Hector, Waylon, and..."

"And..." She starts to count again and shrugs. "I don't have any other friends."

"Oh."

"Can I still buy you a drink?"

"Okay."

"You hungry?"

"Yeah. Famished. Let me wash up."

"Hang on," she says. Jawbone fishes into her deep purse. She digs for a moment more before dumping the contents onto the table: Maglite. Multi-tool (probably a Gerber or Leatherman). Tape measure. Box knife. Crescent wrench. White grease pencil. And a Baggied bar of Lava soap. She hands the Baggie to B. He takes it with an appreciative nod. Even though the ArtBar stocks them in each restroom, they're usually down to that useless nugget of grit. B looks back over his shoulder and catches her just looking away.

∞

When B returns, Jawbone has moved to a not-as-wobbly table, and appetizers and a shot and a beer await him. In fact, almost one of everything on the limited appetizer list is there, arranged like the picture on the pen and ink menu.

"You said famished," Jawbone says.

B's stomach growls a response for him. He nods and grabs a drink. "To Franz Marc."

Jawbone smiles, a bit unsure, but the way he says it, looking away, glancing at her makes her head buzz.

∞

It's a good hang, and B realizes he is not holding his stomach in like he does when he's around Emma. Then again, Emma likes mirrors and Polaroid cameras. And Jawbone, Jawbone seems to be content to be breathing. Slowly and tentatively. They chitchat about the ArtBar's décor and the new owner. That fuel runs dry quickly so B jumps into the deep end and brings up politics.

"I don't pay attention to liars and thieves," Jawbone says, with a wave of her hand. "Wearing suits." She watches B demolish the apps, reluctant to test her new dental work.

She brings up sports. It's a sports town and B is a man. A man who works with metal. But B, once a die-hard North Sider fan, has given up.[30] And although he is fairly well versed in the lore and current line-ups, he only keeps up with it as part of his job on those rare occasions when he meets a potential client who is a Fan. He dismisses the ballplayers with a wave of his large hand.

"I can't root for cry-baby millionaires," he says. "And cheaters."

Jawbone decides that the pair of first baseline Sox tickets tucked in her purse will remain there. Tickets she traded for with a nice piece of art.

They talk of food as B puts aside his menu while glancing about for a waitress. Jawbone shifts painfully, still studying the menu. "I'm sorry I'm taking so long," she says.

B nods. "No hurry." He pulls out a tattered and smeared copy of the Duckworth column. The one from the floor on Hector's shop. He spreads it out on the table.

Jawbone's cheery voice drops a notch or two in the sunshine department. "They don't have soup," she says.

B can see a thin layer of sweat on her upper lip. Eyes scanning, scanning the menu for something soup-like. "We can go somewhere else," B says.

---

30. 2010 AD

She hesitates. Replaying something in her head. "I'm going to go for it," she says. "BBQ."

B flags down a waitress that does not have pink hair.

"Pulled pork," Jawbone says. "With extra sauce."

"Pulled pork," B says. "No sauce. For either of us."

Jawbone cocks her head. B winks and she giggles.

Dr. Heidegger's Experiment

And on the other side of the bar, a man in a coat too heavy for the weather with a plaid bow tie and bad hair plugs downs small glasses of clear liquid. A few more patrons chatter away. Mostly new ones (probably tourists), as they actually seem to be looking at the ArtBar's temporary exhibit of hanged, random multimedia hodge-podge paintings and other pieces. With "things" protruding like a, like a sickly porcupine. Or a snared— come on, chap— pufferfish.

Where is your discipline? Duckworth thinks. Your craft?

And in addition to the new patrons, it's the artist of the temporary exhibit himself and his slouch-shouldered, belly-shirted muse of the week. Both in black (ack!). Their names are Daniel and Calliope. He is a synesthete, and she is a med-school drop-out, but this is not their story. And next to them a middle-aged Latino with prison tattoos is pitching woo to a younger woman with meth mouth. He talks of when he was a "Voicer" for Steinway pianos. She rubs his thigh and talks of a Van Cliburn competition. They break into song, a drunken twinkle, twinkle little star.

Duckworth looks at the empty seat next to him. His watch. *Where the devil is she?*

Outside, a siren sounds and Duckworth jumps. They're coming for him. It fades. He is still safe from the law. Not that he's a fugitive, but he knows it's only a matter of time before they come for him for running over the hopes and dreams of the Chicago art world, Timmy.

Duckworth now realizes that the jukebox is silent. The ArtBar's that kind of joint where the patrons dig music, but don't feel compelled to feed the Wurlitzer constantly. Its soothing unpretentious lighted presence is enough. And maybe that's because the new owner has switched over to classic rock. That's what the bartender tells Duckworth anyway. And no the bartender won't turn up the TV's volume. Damn him. This bartender is staging his own stand against the Man. But Duckworth has that feeling that he will be taken downtown and booked today and he does not want his exit music to be the chattering of this group. So Duckworth staggers to the jukebox. He does not recognize anything, but the Beatles, but fancies himself an Elvis man (but the owner does not and thus the King is not among the selections), but Duckworth recognizes a song that seems to be the winner in terms of length and Duckworth is nothing if not budget-conscious what with his unemployment benefits being contested, so he slips in a five dollar bill and within moments the

ArtBar rocks to the progressive and somewhat psychedelic rock sounds of Rush's *2112*. [31]

∞

By the third go around, Jawbone pulls the plug, or rather, kicks it out of the socket. She glares at Duckworth, who has turned his attention to their table. She shakes her head slowly. "Cut. That. Shit. Out."

Duckworth inhales deeply, lets out a melodramatic sigh. One designed to gather the attention of those who aren't paying attention. Not that the meager crowd smells bloodlust. Jawbone in her current incarnation is invisible in her camouflage to the few patrons who don't feel like swing dancing across the street at the F-Hole. "My muse," Duckworth says. "My muse has left me. And Art (big A) is dead." He loosens his bow tie. Rotates on his stool. Now facing away from the bar and towards B and Jawbone. "All of you craftsmen, all (four, maybe five, excluding our heroes) of you artists with your touch of the poet, you're wasting your time. It's over. This period in history is over," Duckworth says. He takes his knock-off Chihuly glass and pours the water into an open hand with the flourish of an amateur illusionist working from a poorly translated book of magic. The water splashes over his hand and onto the floor. "Just add water," he utters in a whisper, but it's a stage whisper and the back row of the Mercury theatre would be able to hear him. "All this gone," he says. "Like tears in the rain."

Jawbone and B exchange glances.

---

31. Side A, natch.

The waitress steps over the puddle of water with their food. Duckworth demurs while they rearrange their plates and condiments.

Jawbone takes a bite. Frowns.

"Heh." Then it finally dawns on B. "Your teeth."

"Got 'em replaced. No silver. New dentist."

"Looks nice."

She smiles, deflects. "Why no sauce?" Jawbone says.

B grabs the waitress. Scribbles something on a napkin and hands it to her. She looks at it and nods. No problem.

"What did you give her?" Jawbone asks.

"A cut list," B says.

As quick as the waitress is gone, Duckworth takes the floor, a performer with an unwanted encore. "There's a new wave coming," he says. "A storm of Masterpieces, a Renaissance of Art so stunningly beautiful, I can't, let alone *you*— you most certainly won't be able to describe it. And all your hard work, your sacrifice, your schooling. Your trade." (Dramatic Pause.) "Gone." He takes a drink. Pulls his bow tie off as he wanders out to the middle of the bar, working the room. "I never much liked any of you," he says. "But at least I respected you. Tried to champion the best of you. And now." He tosses his trademark plaid bow tie to the ground. "We're rubbish."

There is no applause to his soliloquy. And perhaps a few dismissive groans.

He stumbles over to Jawbone and B. Looks Jawbone up and down, dismisses her and turns to B, clearly the artistic one. "And what's your name?"

"Guess. Heh."

Duckworth: "Robert Bellio. I know you."

Jawbone snorts.

"Then you must know Jawbone," B says.

Duckworth turns to Jawbone. "Ah, 'Fuck Art.' Indeed. And the *Home Depot Polaroid Art Display.* So scatological. Marcel Duchamp would be proud," he says. Pauses, though not dramatically. "You clean up well." He sighs and this seems to throw his vision out of focus. He puts a supporting hand on their table. His shoulders slouch, the performance finally over. He is now with friends and family who have been guilted into attending and getting stuck with SRO tickets. Though he is now offstage, he is clearly still lost in his personal after-performance postmortem. A dropped line, missed blocking. A late entrance. Finally, he looks to B and Jawbone. Looks at their water glasses. Leans forward in that conspiratorial posture that signals to anyone who's ever heard a good bar story that this is not to be missed. They lean closer while maintaining their balance should a quick escape be necessary.

"I am Juan Ponce de León and I have discovered the *Fountain.*"

B and Jawbone exchange looks.

"The fountain, eh?"

"Whomever drinks from this Fountain shall be able to create a masterpiece of art. And only one. Regardless of skills, training, heart, and dare I say, soul. Instant immortality," Duckworth says. He says it like that. Decree-like. He stops. Story finished.

"Bullshit," Jawbone says.

"Is it?" Duckworth says and taps the newspaper column on their table. The one about Timmy. The one about Tabby, the new *it* artist. The artist that has had more success (as defined by media attention and financial reward and fans) in a month than both B and Jawbone and their many, many years put together. Then he slaps down a handful of clippings and print-outs of other articles. Other critics. The Elite. *"Is it?"*

B starts to say something when a large man in a Hawaiian shirt strolls in with a tire iron.

"Duckman!" Big Tim says. "Can I have a word with you? I, uh, got a flat tire."

B can see Duckworth eyeing the tire iron as he straightens his jacket and nervously buttons his top shirt button. Then Duckworth follows Big Tim outside.

"I told them they shouldn't sell real absinthe here," Jawbone says.

The waitress brings a bunch of small shallow plastic cups.

Jawbone recognizes a few things: brown sugar, whiskey, coffee.

B mixes it quickly, tasting it here and there. "Please, nuke this for two minutes," he tells the waitress. Before she can take the brown concoction away, B retrieves the original cut list scribbled on the napkin.

"Is that a recipe?" Jawbone says, sipping her water.

∞

Outside, Big Tim rushes Duckworth, who embraces his death. Finally, the father exacts his revenge for his only son's death. The irony of the tire iron is a bit much, Duckworth notes. Big Tim's arms circle his waist and squeeze him and lift him off the ground. "WOOOOOOOOO HOOOOOO!"

And then Duckworth is on the ground, on his feet. Big Tim shakes his shoulders. "The autopsy came back, Duckman," Big Tim says. "Timmy died of a hole in the heart. Not from you running over him. Twice."

"Wh— what?"

"Doc said it was only a matter of time."

"What?"

"You're off the hook, Duckman."

"Oh. Uh, what about the funeral? I'd like to say my farewells."

"Ah, I've already cremated him. Things just get awkward at funerals."

"Oh."

"Congrats, Duckman. It's a win-win."

Duckworth feels his mouth curl into a smile. His lips tingle. He thinks of poor Timmy. A hole in his heart. He then thinks of Tabby. Cancer eating a hole in her brain. Then he remembers spilling the fountain's secret to our duo moments ago and fears his loose lips may sink his ship.

∞

"Instant masterpiece?" B says.

"Bullshit," Jawbone says.

"Hmmm."

"I'm just saying," Jawbone says. "People are going to know bullshit when they see it."

"I don't think so," B says. "You take one look and bam. You're sucked in."

"But we don't live in a vacuum," Jawbone says. "Take this water glass here."

"What about it?"

"How much would you pay?" Jawbone says.

"Fiddy cents."

Jawbone moves it to a spot at the bar where a light shines down.

"Maybe a buck or two," B says. "Maybe."

"Now what if I told you that Marilyn Monroe had used this glass?" Jawbone says.

"That's memorabilia— not art."

"What if I told you this was hand-blown by a guy with no arms or legs and one eye, and that the tiny dot on the bottom of the glass represented a point in space in which he could see himself through the prism of... whatever."

"Wow. That's cool."

"Or this plant over there?"

"It's artificial," B says. (He once ate a leaf on a bet.)

"Okay," Jawbone says. "Cheap and from China we can surmise, but what if I told you it was sculpted by a guy with no arms and legs with only a toothpick. And that each toothpick had to be replaced every seven strokes."

"By a spider monkey?" (B has pirated cable.)

"Sure, a spider monkey."

"Hmmm. I'd have to have that plant."

"See, we don't live in a vacuum any more," Jawbone says. "I'm saying I don't give a shit what water you drink," Jawbone says. "Or what art you create. Fuck, Robards has made a fortune on that stupid waterfall-on-mirrors bit."

B downs his beer.

"Hell, that bow-tied asshole outside tells people if commercials are good, are funny. *Commercials.*"

The waitress comes back with a new sandwich and B's sauce.

Jawbone drizzles the BBQ sauce on her pulled pork sandwich and tastes a small bite. "Oh my god, this is good," Jawbone says. "Really good." Another bite. "I'd buy this off the shelf."

"It's rough," B says, beaming inside. "Using a microwave. I usually make my own catsup and Worcestershire sauce."

"You can make Worcestershire sauce?"

"We have the technology," B says.

"Wow," Jawbone says. "This is great. Thank you."

"So the chair, this knock-off for Beth...?"

"It's not going to be a knock-off. And well, Beth she's blah, blah, so I got nothing. Best hope is to sell it on commission at Highenders."

"They'd take it?"

"Said they would," Jawbone says. "But I'm kinda not sold on the current design. I think I was stoned when I sketched it. And I'm not doing shit for a few weeks," she says indicating her taped ribs. She looks at the Duckworth column. "And all I'm saying is this fountain thing is bullshit."

B has also perused the clippings of the Bitha crowd. The MacArthur. The Goddess. The masterpiece *Migration*. No previous experience. No training. No trial and error. The masterpiece created at the BAA exhibit at the MCA.

"So you wouldn't?" Jawbone says, tapping the clippings.

"What?" B says.

"Drink from the fountain if it guaranteed you one masterpiece."

"Nope."

"I mean, you're good, B. A talented sumbitch. But how about a splash to get over that X-factor hump? Land a big one? You wouldn't do it?"

"No."

"Why not?"

B shrugs.

"Hmmm." Jawbone sips more of her water. Sorts out her thoughts. "I hate to think that after I croak, all this shit I've made, my children are going to be boxed up in crates and hauled off to the junkyard." She sips more of her water. "Are we just making junk?"

"Hmmm."

"What?"

"It's an interesting question," B says. "Coming from someone who so recently faced her own mortality."

Jawbone looks at her plate. She's cut everything into toddler sizes. She's been chewing every bite at least thirty-two times.

"Fuck art?" B says, slyly.

Before Jawbone can respond to B, the women's restroom door opens and a woman emerges, rocking fishnets and what looks like a sheer top under a weathered Chicago Police Department jacket. Her heavy eyelinered eyes narrow, lock on B. She changes course and zips his way. She's wearing stiletto heels and B recognizes the not-so-inexperienced, not-so-unsure gait attached to those gams scissoring towards him.

Emma.

B finds himself clutching his butter knife— blade down, along the forearm, in a defensive position.

And sucking in his stomach.

Naked Girl Falling Down the Stairs

"B, who is this?" Emma says.

"This is my, uh, acquaintance."

"This is your big go/no go gig?" Emma says, pointing a Midnight Black tipped finger at Jawbone like a locked and loaded 10mm

Glock. "This is the thing you had to work on, if this one doesn't go well, there are no more gigs, this one? This, this—"

"I'm Harriet," Jawbone says.

"This *hussy.*"

Everything downshifts to slo-mo. B cannot account for both forks on the table and knows Jawbone must be palming one and were she to backhand Emma from this position, B can clearly see the pale white patch of skin between the choker collar and the sheer top where the tines of the fork would bury themselves in Emma's jugular.

And then it happens.

"Hussy?" Jawbone says, and laughs. Laughs uncontrollably which causes her great pain. Maybe not great pain what with the generic Vicodin, but she does clutch her fractured ribs. "Hussy. Hus-sy."

B does a quick calculation of the number of empty beer bottles and realizes that Jawbone has probably had a couple painkillers before she got here, in addition to the beers before his arrival.

"B," Emma says, "how could you?"

"Emma," B says, preparing to rip off the psycho-sexual Band-Aid.

Emma flings herself at B. Takes his earlobe in her mouth. "I'm sorry," she says. "So sorry, I was so lonely. You left me alone, B. I can't stand to be alone. Please forgive me. I'll do anything."

"Emma, it's okay. Go, go and enjoy."

"You have a right to be furious," Emma says. "I fucked him."

"Emma?" Duckworth says, reappearing. He slips an arm around her and plants a kiss on her cheek. "Where the devil have you been?"

"The bathroom," Emma says.

"Oh," Duckworth says, consulting his watch. "I have great news—
"

"I sucked his cock," Emma says to B indicating Duckworth.

"What the devil is this?" Duckworth says.

"But I was thinking of you," Emma says to B.

"I refute that," Duckworth says, to deaf ears.

"It was always you. Please, I'll make it up to you." She leans in again, pulls B head closer. A dirty whisper: *"My younger sister is in town from college. No freshman fifteen. I'll slip her a roofie. I'll go down on her. You can take pictures. We can do anything. She's pretty. She'll do anything. Please B. No one has to know."*

B looks to Jawbone, who cannot breathe with her taped ribs though her mouth is wide open, howling with a laugh that cannot get out. There is no panic in her eyes so B turns back to Emma, who turns back to Duckworth. "This is my Master," she says, indicating B. "He owns me, body and soul." She lifts her hair at the nape of her neck. There above the collar, tattooed in Halda Smashed font, the letter **B**.

Jawbone slaps the table, laughing.

Emma leans into a bewildered Duckworth, chin up. Defiant. "You want to punish me, don't you? You want to hurt me, don't you?"

Duckworth smiles with a how-the-bloody-hell-did-I-get-here look. His brain resets, and he sidesteps Emma and with ode-to-joy tears in his eyes says: "I didn't kill Timmy. He died of a hole in the heart. The autopsy. It wasn't me. Thank God. Oh Timmy."

At the mention of Timmy, Emma's emerald eyes open and turn opalescent and milky. Like the louching action of ice water in absinthe.

Big Tim leans into the ArtBar's doorway. "Come on, Duckman, bring the slut, and let's go celebrate."

Emma pulls a leash out of her purse and clips it to her choker collar. She leans into B, her jacket opening with the pressure. Hands him the end of her leash.

"She didn't just do that," Jawbone slurs. "She didn't."

Emma fingers the small gold lock on her choker collar. "B has the key," she says, matter-of-factly.

"It was late," B says to Jawbone. "I didn't want to be rude."

Jawbone slips off her stool with laughter. And pain.

Duckworth shifts, but this Emma defeat is mitigated by the other victory. He feels the need to put this whole thing in perspective and gain the spotlight. "Big Tim says it's a win-win," Duckworth says.

Jawbone resurfaces and B hands her the leash.

"Oh, and that thing I said about the fountain," Duckworth says. "That was the liquor talking. Seriously. Bollocks," he says, his lips moving awkwardly around the word. "A fountain with magical properties. Pfft."

"Pfft," Jawbone echoes, still trying to cut through her giggles.

"Check your barn doors," Big Tim says.

Duckworth zips up his pants. Starts to say more, but now the victory seems hollow. Emma's posture has straightened to a prideful one, a dominant one. B sees for the first time the posture of a determined teacher. Of Timmy's teacher. Tentatively, Duckworth reaches out for Emma's hand, but her Goth eyes warn him off. He gives them a polite nod and with that Duckworth leaves them, slipping into the encouraging and shoulder-wrapping arm of Big Tim.

"Wow," B says. "That was quite a show."

Jawbone mutters under her breath, "oh lord, oh lord." She pops another pill. Jawbone tugs on the leash, testing it.

"I can take you there," Emma says.

Jawbone stops tugging the leash.

Checking his watch, B says, "It's getting late. I should—"

"The Fountain isn't bullshit," Emma says. She says it direct like that. No smokiness. No little girl voice. Her instructive voice. Her teacher voice. No longer a voice from the back of the room. Eyes now clear and lucid and glowing against the heavy eyeliner of mock desire. "I can take you to the Fountain now."

"No," B says.

Jawbone says, "Please."

Deus ex Monarch

B still feels a slight buzz as they shuffle down the sidewalk, but now he's not sure if it's the large iced coffee he pounded before leaving the ArtBar or the booze. Or both. He takes the keys from Jawbone who is clearly medicated out of her mind. At least Emma isn't fucked up. Not any more than usual. B used to have such a clear vision of the future. Now with the events of the last few weeks, that future is gone. Not in the sense that he doesn't have a future, but in the sense that he cannot predict it with any certainty. It's as if he's caught up to the universe's plan for himself. As if it had everything mapped out up to this point and B has dutifully followed with his head down and without complaint. B raises his head. The next step is his to take. "Where the fuck is your car, Harriet?" He trips on a curb and drops the keys.

∞

Emma scoops up the keys. Jawbone points out her car at the end of the block. It's an old school VW Bug. Painted green with airbrushed rivets and the custom motif of the smiling shark mouth of a WWII P-40 Tiger Shark fighter plane. Emma leads them. Despite the heels, her gait is steady. She feels pressure on her collar as the slack disappears between her and the other end of the leash in Jawbone's hand.

"Last time I saw you," Emma hears Jawbone slur, "you were wearing a dress that might as well have been a potato sack. And now you look like a— what do you call them, dominatrix? But you're a submissive, right? The collar." There's a light tug. Emma stops. Turns, reels Jawbone in like a fish, pulling her close. "I. Am. A. Switch."

∞

Jawbone doesn't know what Emma means. But the way she says it so, serious, in command, Jawbone understands. Emma is a tiger on a leash made of yarn. Jawbone cannot summon the energy to laugh it off. Emma vibrates and Jawbone feels wave after wave of energy wash over her. Jawbone's breath shortens. She gets in half a breath when she catches a whiff of Emma's breath. It smells... Jawbone can't place it. Not mint, not alcohol, not bad, but earthy? Organic.

Like a wood nymph.

The image and thought slips away as Jawbone watches Emma walk; her legs devastating. Hips swaying unconsciously to an ancient beat. Those legs. Jawbone studies them. Emma's a little thick in the ankle. The thigh. Belly a touch too big. But that's only if Jawbone stares at a particular point on Emma. The overall affect of Emma is one of pure sex, a nebulous cloud of pheromones. Jawbone thinks Emma's legs aren't that much better than her own. My stomach seems almost as flat— almost. My boobs are bigger. But, Jawbone realizes, Emma does not care. She is not self-conscious among mortals. And when Jawbone blinks and takes in Emma as a whole, she cannot think of any one male or female that she knows is sexier. She is timeless. Greeks and Romans would have slaughtered each other for her.

A wave of melancholy hits Jawbone, wilts her. A streetlight blinks out as she passes it. Jawbone looks up. The constellations mock her.

∞

Emma drives. The leash trails to the backseat where she has insisted B and Jawbone ride like two kids on a chaperoned date.

Jawbone leans into B, her shoulder snuggled up against his. Her hands in her lap, playing and picking at the leather leash's stitching. "B, my best received piece in college," Harriet "Jawbone" Walker says, "came to me as I was sitting on the toilet. Do you think that's going to impress anyone at a gallery? They'd prefer I tell them I had an epiphany as I was climbing Mt. Hood and I did tell them that. And while they would say it was high altitude sickness, I told them it was because I was closer to God. I was a fraud even then."

"Hmmm. What about your favorite piece?"

"No one gave it a second look. I put it in the alley for the scrappers. Since then, I've been 'fuck art.' Twenty-five years, B. I've been holding

213

myself back." She looks down in her lap. "Twenty-five years holding my own leash."

∞

In the front seat, still driving, Emma digs through her purse. Finds a packet of wax paper with small stamps of black and orange sandwiched between the layers. She licks a finger like she's done a dozen times today in various bathrooms, slips it delicately into the packet, touches one of the marbled squares and retrieves it. It sticks to the end of her finger, a Monarch's iridescent wing.

Reverently, she says: "Until our work is done, we are immortal."

She touches the tab of acid to her tongue.

The Bacchae

Blocks away, the MCA looms. They must be launching something new, B thinks, as the building looks like it has been tagged with a thousand stars. A million points of light scattered across the building. B imagines if the City were to go dark this building would blend into the starry night, camouflaged in the universe.

Greek gods flank the steps to the MCA. An odd contrast to a museum of contemporary art, but before the MCA was a museum of contemporary art it was a classical museum. When the City took it over, it contemplated moving the Greek god statues to another area of the City, but the move was overruled when a local Greek Alderman grew tired of deferring to the whims of the Italians and Irish and Polish and Russians and decided this was something he could get his considerable girth and small political clout behind. He got to keep the statues there, made sure they added a small plaque with his name and a poorly written paragraph about the wonderful Greek culture. And to placate the neoconservatives, the naughty bits were covered with a monthly theme for modesty's sake and to add a contemporary touch to the statues. Funny, this didn't seem to be a problem until recently. This month's theme evoked 70s style superhero costumes. Bright neon and plastic-looking belts and boots. A large red B in a clean 70s professional lithograph style, on one of the females, smack dab between her chiseled breasts. Only one drip from the base of the B betrays that it is a late night guerilla spray paint addition and not a sanctioned costume change. For a moment, a deep private intimate moment, B thinks:

That's my B.

Only for a moment.

At the base, partially hidden by a loose undulating tarp is the text:

B thinks "everyone" should be two words. B does not know how they are going to get in. He thinks at this point Jawbone or Emma will simply take their cue from Big Tim and get a tire iron from the frunk of the VW. Smash in the front door. Despite his endurance training with Emma, B is feeling the burn in his legs, just from walking up the steps. He starts breathing through his mouth, which is for the best, as the pungent smell of thousands of dead fish wafts from the other side of the building. A few blocks east towards the lake, those damn Asian carp have beached, finally taking matters into their own hands.

∞

Emma takes the stairs two at a time, steadily to the entrance. B hangs back a bit from Jawbone who seems to be walking as if wearing a long black veil. B's instinct is to run up beside her and guide her, but instead he hangs back, if only to cushion her should she fall backwards. Beyond that, this moment is hers and hers alone.

Inside the MCA most of the overhead lights are off, leaving a scattering of illuminating pools. One pool of light takes Jawbone's attention. She pulls out the small Maglite from her purse. Directs its beam at the other pool of light. A figure nods awake at the front desk. Jawbone paints him with her beam, revealing a security guard uniform. Disoriented. It's Hector. Jawbone waves her light at him.

Suddenly, lights streak past them like slow moving tracer rounds. There is a muted *thimp thimp* as insects hit her flashlight. Then the glass doors. Fireflies, hundreds, then thousands of them kamikaze into the building.

A few hit B, Jawbone, but not Emma, glancing off them and exploding against the MCA. B realizes that the building is not stippled with phosphorus paint, but with the smeared bioluminescence of their mating signals. Hector quickly lets them in and now they stand now on the inside of the MCA watching this brief phenomenon. Emma is wide-eyed and smiling, the greenish deaths reflected in her glassy eyes. Jawbone presses her hands together as though in prayer as she looks away, flinching with each muted *thimp*. B thinks of his ex-wife, the courtship and marriage lasting as long as these streaking fireflies, doomed like they are, the guts of misguided love splattered across a life in the arts.

∞

Hector's fingers are stained from colored chalk. The open sketch pad under his shirt is printing pastel mirror images on his white security guard uniform. His tie hangs loosened and limp, off duty. "I've been in the Be An Artist Exhibit™," he says. He holds up a montage of Duckworth's *Shoulders* columns; columns Hector's used to create a canvas, a primer coat for his sketches. It is Hector's first stab at postmodernism. "I thought it would inspire me," he says. The birthplace of Bitha and *Migration*. He shows them his sketches. Desperate, random, and fearfully symmetrical. "I have to cancel my showing," he says, shame pulling his face.

"Hector has his first showing next week," Jawbone says with prideful and tired eyes.

∞

The gang take damp steps to the second floor, continue past the Be An Artist™ exhibit, its doors chained shut. Up to the third floor, up slick stairs, up towards the Fountain. Everyone seems slightly dazed as though expecting bad news, or good news, or awaiting biopsy results. "It's all bullshit," B mutters, grabbing a handrail.

The kid Hector brings up the rear keeping one eye on B, sussing him out. "So what are you working on?" Hector says to B.

"Not a goddamned thing."

∞

Suddenly, B is ten. He hears the falls, the fountain. He looks up and birds are silhouetted against the sun. Zipping, darting and twisting like a knotted ribbon up in the thermals. The sun refracts a prism through his chipped glasses, a blinding rainbow across his eyes. He never went down to the falls, he never climbed down those rocks and rolled up his pants legs, never stepped into the ice cold water, water that would send goose pimples up his legs in numbing defiance of the summer sun. Never crossed the stream, stepping gingerly from mossy rock to mossy rock, each lift of his leg persuaded downstream by the rush of the current, course-correcting with every step. He never did this. We can go down, his dad had said. We have time. But Bobby Bellio shook his head, chipping his glasses on the eyepiece. I'm fine, he said, feeding another quarter into the telescope. After all, the car was here. Right there. And it was oh so far down. He could slip, he could fall. And there were buzzards or vultures or other birds of prey overhead. He didn't want one of them picking out his eyes or mucking about in his intestines. It's kinda dangerous looking down there, Dad. Don't be the coward of your own life, his dad said. But Bobby headed for the car, careful to keep his head and glasses away from his dad. Next time, dad. I promise.

∞

Back at the museum, the sun is gone. The birds are still there. Swirling on the thermals, which B realizes now is caused by the HVAC system. The birds are *Migration*. The creation of Bitha. The creatures too delicate to share the earth with these clumsy bipeds.

Hector mutters to himself, gazing at *Migration*. "How can I compete, how can I compete?"

"You didn't know what was possible until now," Emma whispers in his ear. "You didn't know we could do this. Did you?"

Hector shakes his head.

Emma acknowledges the confession with a slow stroke of his cheek. "Yes, it's beautiful," she says. "We can be beautiful, too, Hector."

Jawbone says something softly, and B can't make out what she's saying. He leans forward when he realizes the water sounds, the lapping and splashing, have not stopped. He can still hear his childhood.

∞

B hears it clearly before he sees it. The living ambient sound of water seeking its own level. Touches his chipped glasses. There is the Fountain. Bubbling a bit, the water coming off it like a waterfall,

219

pooling into a large lake. A large lake of water on the third floor of the MCA. "Emma," B says, "is this your dream? Is this the flood you saw?"

She giggles, and begins to remove her shoes, which to Jawbone seems sensible. She does the same. Everyone rolls up pant legs. Feet abandon the ships of shoes and socks.

∞

Playing in the water. "It's beautiful," Emma says. "It's all so beautiful. We can be beautiful, too. Oh Hector, are you experienced? Have you ever been experienced?"

Hector pulls off his nametag. It falls and disappears in the calf-deep water.

Tears stream down Jawbone's face, twin waterfalls of shame and regret. She whispers to B. "Thank you for saving my life."

B shrugs.

Within sight of *Migration*, Hector rips his sketches in half. They fall, then float like leaves, the colors running and swirling against the overcast tile. A liquid autumn.

Emma shrugs off her clothes, a useless chrysalis, and invites them with open arms to enter the water. "Come, children, let us be gods and goddesses."

∞

Hector slides first, as children are always the first to dive in. Then Emma dives into impossibly shallow depths of the water. She reappears across the flooded room. Water beads and forms and rolls off her hips, her breasts, as though she has the skin of an eel. She says one word, but her whisper glides along the surface of this impossible lake, reaching B as a gentle vibration.

"Master."

A wave of déjà vu passes through B like a ghost. He stands paralyzed until he realizes his companions have become a living breathing postmodern recreation of a Lucas Cranach oil painting titled—

"Master."

B snaps out of it. Turns to Emma. Light plays off the small lock on her leather choker collar. Her head is tilted back, presenting. B tosses Hector the key. While it is in midair, Emma disappears into the water. Hector reaches out for the key, but Emma reappears rising up and intercepts it. She looks to B. Then Hector. Then Jawbone. This against the meditative sounds of water. Nature free. She places the golden object ceremoniously in Hector's hand and offers her throat. Hector almost drops this golden ticket. His tongue pokes out of his mouth in concentration.

After a moment, the choker collar and lock disappear in a splash. With one fluid motion, the otherworldly creature known as Emma rips open Hector's security guard shirt, revealing a Bitha t-shirt. She gathers two sections of this shirt and it too is ripped from his body. She does the same to his pants and takes him down to the water, the floor, straddling him. Hector takes the Lord's name in vain for the first time in his life. Emma lowers her hips onto Hector. He divides her, adding her, and they are one being, both bodies glistening in a baptism of now.

∞

Hector's vision dances with sparks and lighted streaks of color and sound. He tastes blue. Hears red. Smells yellow. Primary primitive. His senses rewire themselves. Doors open. She bends down, this goddess, her breath in his ear. *"Your work, Hector, is not done."*

∞

A spent Hector floats on his back, born again. Emma glides to the Fountain. The Fountain responds by shooting a jet of water. It washes through her hair. Her body. She showers in it. The liquid adheres to her skin, now a glistening quicksilver of porpoise skin. Emma leans her head back. The Fountain's jet arcs over her body then into her open mouth.

∞

"It's just a fountain, right?" Jawbone's hands shake. "Right, B?" She reaches out to him for support, but her reach is short and B is a universe away.

Emma approaches B. He doesn't need to look at the works of art on the wall. The works not created by the Fountain. He does not need to look at *Migration* and its special merchandising exhibit. Emma advances, offering communion to B; his turn to be born again. When he'd been thirteen, in church, they offered him communion. He'd seen his aunt prepare it in the back kitchenette. Whole wheat bread cut into squares. Grape juice poured into tiny glasses, smaller than his grandpa's shot glasses. When she'd left he'd poured himself a glass of juice. And made a PB&J from the bread. But in the pew later that same bread seemed to vibrate with energy, an energy of infinite possibilities, but B had not yet been baptized, and felt fearful to accept the Body and the Blood. Cannibal and Vampire. He rejectred the Communion.

He now rejects Emma's gift with the same terse one-two shake of his head.

B stands as still as the Greek gods protecting the MCA. Hector floats still, merrily along a dream. Splashing water echoes through the chambers of the museum, like a reflecting pool in the Temple of Syrinx.

Emma now presents to Jawbone. Dark eyes flash pure predator. Jawbone cannot move. The edges of her vision tunnel and darken and her existence is the creature Emma coming before her. A water creature walking on its tail, no splash, no wake, the water a part of her legs. Jawbone sees Emma and only Emma, only a primal urge. It is simple and her body responds. Her knees quiver, her bladder protests, her crotch surges as though Emma has whispered something erotic in her ear. Emma smiles, water leaking from her mouth like immorality from a succubus. Emma is coming to give a gift, not to take. Jawbone wishes she had followed Emma into the women's bathroom an eon ago, wishes she'd been open to the possibilities.

Wishes she'd never recovered from the fried rice. Her arms tremble as she raises them, open arms to this water nymph, daughter of Zeus. She wants to embrace the freedom Emma emanates. She does not want the next twenty-five years to be like the last twenty-five. No more searching for those wasted years.

Emma slips into Jawbone's embrace. There is no pause, no longing look in the eyes, no moment of unspoken communication. Words are long past, useless now. She kisses Jawbone. More quicksilver spills from their lips. Deep. Soulful. Jawbone moans caught up in Emma's incandescence, pure and cleansing. Drinking from Emma's lips, Harriet "Jawbone" Walker swallows fire.

Pointillism de Léon

Hector's shop. Neat, tidy, and a tad too small for B's taste. More of a studio with power tools. Hector is a dabbler. Still finding his way, so B says nothing, even though Hector is not present. He smells dog shit, but cannot locate the source. Jawbone closes the door behind them.

There's a brief moment where B scans the floor as if looking for a chalk outline of a dreadlocked body and a Chinese take-out container. Sees the dark chocolate smear of blood from Jawbone's fall near the drain in the center of the floor. B sidesteps the blood towards Jawbone's original chair designs (not the knock-off from

Hurricane Beth) sketched out on the backside of a concept for what looks like an eco-friendly shipping container home.

Ribs protesting, Jawbone places a leather apron on over her sundress and slips on her steel-toed boots as if they were house shoes. A flash of the old Jawbone demeanor pops through with the new ensemble. The clenched jaw, the furrowed brow, the half sneer of an impending deadline.

They're going to finish the chair. That fucking chair.

She drank the water.

B swats the gnat-like thought away. Jawbone cannot finish the chair by herself. Not with cracked ribs. Ribs B cracked giving her the Heimlich. It's the honorable thing to do, helping her with the chair so she can sell it at Highenders. Make ends meet. B doesn't mention his own deadline for Günther Adamczyk. They don't talk about the Fountain.

∞

Jawbone clicks on a small radio. Every song sounds like it's from 1947. Tinny. Basic. Raw. B ties Jawbone's bootlaces for her, circling them around her ankles, cinching them tight and spark proof. B tears off a sheet of vellum, crisp and clean. Slides it over her chair design. Takes the flat carpenter's pencil he's been nibbling on and quick strokes three lines, steps back. Jawbone takes the pencil, wet and all and makes one line. It is stronger than B's three lines, opening a door he did not see. B takes the pencil back, pulls out a mechanical pencil eraser. He removes one of his lines and adds a correction. B's ideas are spark points for Jawbone or so he thinks, wishes, as she builds on his ideas. B is self assured and confident and graciously defers to her because it is her gig and if he's being honest with himself, because he recognizes her ideas are simply better bolder. Standing on the shoulders of his ideas. His are old, recycled. Hers are inventive. No, reinventive.

She drank the water.

Swat.

B has one final spark of an idea. He hesitates but puts in on paper.

Jawbone nods, pats B on the back. "Now," she says, "it's time to shut up and drive."

∞

B starts gathering raw materials, while Jawbone starts a cut list for the various pieces, aided with a slide rule and B's gnawed pencil. They occupy each other's space. There's no other way. They get dirty. There's no other way. They are working.

B suggests a few alternations mid-build in his style, she tweaks it with a bolder idea until it becomes something new to both of them.

Collaboration. Alterations.

Behind goggles. Behind masks.

Her hand guides his occasionally. Lingers.

This takes place over a week's worth of evenings.

He thinks about her.

She drank the water.

Swat.

∞

Frequently, B anticipates a call from Emma that will not go well. B will not tell Emma that the reason he didn't call her late last night was because in a drunken stupor he'd painted Harriet's toenails. Electric Blue #132, if she asks. He'd like to explain it's because the cracked ribs prevent Harriet from doing it herself. But the truth of the matter is he liked it. He liked painting again.

I can't believe she drank the water.

He liked using his skills, his precision, taking it seriously, this toenail-painting business. And okay, he wasn't even drunk. Two, maybe three margaritas. Cupping her foot. Blowing on her toes. Making secret measurements of her little piggies to make her a metal toe ring. All the while Harriet kept begging him to make her more smoky tangy BBQ sauce, to which he'd playfully declined.

But Emma hasn't called.

B only anticipates it out of habit, and he cannot equate the water creature from the Fountain with Emma. The Emma he knew.

Emma drank the water.

∞

Now, Jawbone and B just lack finishing the chair. B has a bottle from Champagne and stashed in his bag, a card: "The most glorious moments in your life are not the so-called days of success, but rather those days when out of dejection and despair you feel rise in you a challenge to life, and the promise of future accomplishments." B pulled the quote out of a *book*. It was easy enough to find online, but B wanted to quote a book. It seemed important in a way he did not understand at the time.

"It's beautiful," Jawbone says. "Our child."

B lifts the leather apron off Jawbone. A bridal dress.

She pinches his cheek, then pulls out her new pay-as-you-go cell phone. Dials the pick-up number for Highenders. B reaches over and stops her. "Tomorrow," he says. "Let's knock out the finish." She sets the phone aside. "What do you see?" B goes through the list so quickly if you were to watch him you'd think he walked into the room for an audition. "What do you see?"

Images flash through their heads.

Raw

Clear

Satin

Gloss

Semi gloss

Wash

Painted

Lacquer

Gun blue

"What do you see, Harriet?"

Harriet "Jawbone" Walker opens a yellow metal cabinet designed for flammable materials. Pulls out two paintball guns. "Pointillism."

"Heh." He sees it, too.

You drank the water.

"I like your style." And locks and loads a gun.

"You and me, kid," Jawbone says.

A Ross Robards three-note jingle plays on the radio, but wait it's a *four*-note jingle. Modified.

"*YES, YOU* STILL *CAN.*"[32]

Jawbone sees B's jaws clench. She goes to kiss his cheek when he turns to her to say something. Her kiss lands flush on his lips.

The jingle sounds again.

YES, YOU STILL CAN! ROSS ROBARDS TV SPECIAL TONIGHT!!

---

32. *Another homerun for Sapieja Shop. One hundred grand for fifteen minutes of spitballing. Michael Tannhauser Sapieja is only mock disappointed when they are nominated, but do not win a Clio. Having received the news on his phone somewhere on Lake Como. The same phone with which they recorded the jingle.*

B spins and fires. The radio falls off the table with a splat of Burnt Sienna. A crack lightnings down the casing making the one working radio two non-working radios. But B still hears the jingle.

> *Yes, you still can.*
> *Drink the water.*
> *Yes, you still can.*
> *Drink the water.*

B clomps over to the broken radio, the exposed dull metal of his steel-toed boot flashes like a police shield.

> *Yes, you still can.*
> *Drink the water.*

He raises a foot . . . .

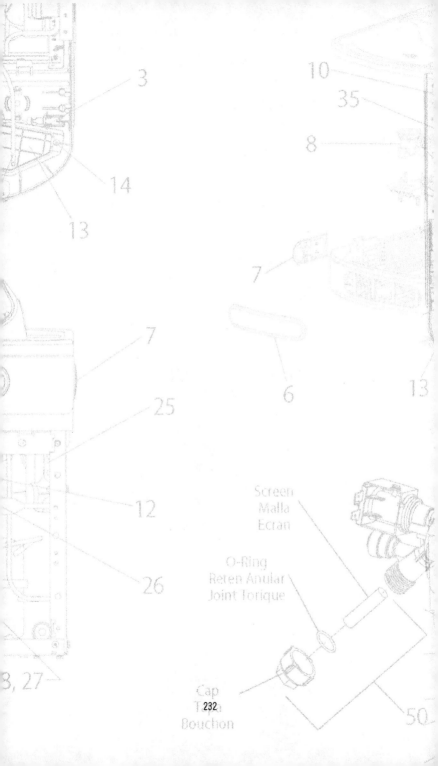

3

14

13

10

35

8

7

7

6

13

25

12

26

Screen
Malla
Ecran

O-Ring
Reten Anular
Joint Torique

8, 27

Cap
Tapa
Bouchon

232

50

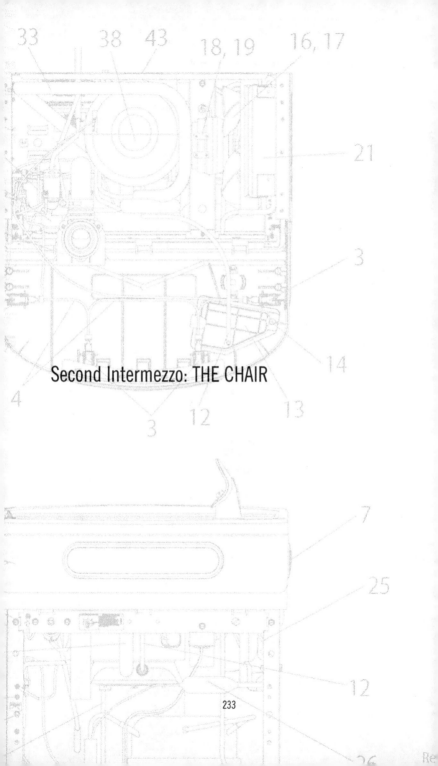

Second Intermezzo: THE CHAIR

233

A Mean Caucasian

A new chair.

Too arty. Not comfortable looking, not inviting.

Vladislav Vladislavovich Glinski scoffs at it here in the front corner of the high-end furniture store, Highenders. Next to a collection of limited edition Higby pieces. And what was that smell? Varnish? Lacquer? "Bah, those kids," Vlad mutters. "What happened to *craftsmanship?* Hand tools, *da?*"

In his day, Vladislav would build a solid chair and it would last. Become an heirloom. This one looks flimsy, leafy, half finished, or abandoned like a tree with rainbow blossoms growing through a rotting wine barrel. Perhaps it could have been exquisite. Poof, like something the rich or the rich sons would have, never their heads filled with want or worry, but only how to spend, how to drink, how to mock. How to fuck.

Sigh.

Vladislav used to know how to fuck. How to court the women. There were plenty; more than enough to keep him warm. Enough to develop a reputation. Enough to get the occasional slap in the face.

Vladislav smiles, thinking of a particular slap.

Natasha.

Young Natasha. A wicked slap. Vladislav slaps himself lightly. His palm and cheek tingle. Natasha. With the birthmark, the big lips,

235

and that high-pitched cat's cry when she climaxed. Natasha was a young girl, maybe fifteen, sixteen, but she was a big girl, as in stout, tall. So young, so full.

He remembers the first time she climaxed, the screeching voice.

Come, Tiger.

Oh my.

This strong curvaceous young woman, squealing. Unearthly.

It had shocked him. He'd lost his rhythm, but quickly found it again.

Later, he would gag her with an old sock. Tie her up with oily rope, lightly at first and then tighter, to the point where her eyes flickered with a hint of panic. A hint of danger. But he could tell by the way she curled her toes, it was mostly for show. And he appreciated it. Then he would tickle her big feet which always smelled like oranges. And she would laugh and they would fuck, and the squeal would not be so bad the second and third time. Not with the cotton in his ears. And in this closed chamber in his head, he would call her *Morana*, Goddess of nature. And death.

∞

Vlad shifts his weight from one leg to the other. The leg on the cane side. And then there was—

something stirs.

236

His penis twitches. The twitch is the biggest downcountry reaction of Vladislav Vladislavovich Glinski's in years.

He thinks more about Natasha, tied up, the look of fear, her laugh. An R. Crumb wet dream, her body taking up so much space, great-sized ass and breasts all in proportion, all defying the earth's gravity. The smell of orange sexy orange.

Now it is gone. No more stirrings.

Nothing.

But his mind still yearns, still lusts.

A girl passing on the street, a woman on the train. The L stop with all the young business women wearing their tailored suits and cheap tennis shoes. Perhaps their stiletto heels of their work shoes poking out of their bags. He'd stand on the train platform for hours at a time. Sometimes they would speak Russian, usually none of the women in the suits, but he would hear it. In the evenings as the second shift launched. The cleaning crews. It makes him long for his youth, when a smile and a wink would melt the iciest of them.

Now they look through him. He is an old man. Not capable of any impact on their lives. He is a ghost. Like the blind men on the train. People stop their conversations when they near, get quiet. Don't want to touch. He used to do that: ignore them.

∞

Vladislav does not want to be a ghost. His back stiffens. He shifts his weight. His cane does not work. The young do not realize that your body ages and breaks down, but your mind stays young and sharp long after. Why do you think grandparents love playing with their grandchildren? Because we are still young, Vlad thinks, tapping his head in a gesture with no audience.

A recorded voice announces Highenders will be closing in a few minutes.

"Sir, we'll be closing in a few moments."

"I heard. Thank you. I heard."

The woman sighs and rolls her eyes.

"I do not mean to bother you with my business," Vladislav says. He bends over to inspect this poof chair and his back seizes with spasms. "Ah, God."

The woman stares at him. Lets him bend over. Waiting for him to reach the point where she can't ignore him. The point where he becomes visible.

Stooped, he reaches out for support, finds it on the chair. NEW ARRIVAL. The tag says: A JAW-B PIECE. He leans back. Reaches the point where his center of gravity hands his fate over to the earth, pulled down by the forces that could not defeat Natasha's globes. He braces for impact, for the wooden slats that would cut into his bony legs and ass, for the leafy branches to scratch his arms, for the angle of the back support to mock his lumbar, his time in the Vorkuta Gulag.

Goddamn chair.

He lands on the chair. His spine cracks. Like a kid pulling a funny straw straight. His vertebrae scream, and extreme pain rips up and down his crooked spine and bowed legs, like a trail of ignited gunpowder. Or an electric chair. No trial. No jury. Just 10,000 volts of ride the lightning.

Goddamn chair.

Then quick as that, the pain dissipates. He takes a breath, bracing for his ribs to protest. But they do not. The chair hugs him, supports him. He sits up straight. Another vertebrae cracks. A single gunshot of fireworks and then a slight rush of blood to his head. He feels lightheaded, but not unpleasantly so. The sensation creeps through his body, warming his arms his legs.

Like his first shot of vodka.

Like his first time with Natasha.

"Sir, we're closing." A faraway voice.

When the sensation hits his toes, it travels back up his legs. His thighs warm. Then his scrotum, and then his penis grows erect. Painfully erect. Stretching and filling to the size of the Primorsky Krai.

Oh my.

Come, Tiger.

It tents his pants with a genuine pole. Not since his early twenties has he been this hard. His head floats for a moment. His sensory input and processing operations now operate through his extremities and his crotch.

"Sir, we're closing. I'm going to have to ask you to buy something or leave.

"Sir.

"Sir.

"Sir.

"Sir, please.

"Sir, can I help you?"

Another sensation building.

Natasha's smile.

Oh my Moscow beauty.

Building.

Natasha, I'm hard.

She stands before him.

Yes, Vladislav, my love. My big lover, fill me. Her sweet ass up in the air begging him for her. She starts to squeal.

Building.

"Sir?"

Building in his scrotum, building the pressure.

Come, Tiger.

Oh my. It can't be. Vlad thinks: I'm going to have an—

"Sir?"

The salesgirl touches his hand.

Natasha vanishes. The erection remains.

"Sir—"

"What? What? *What?*"

"I'm going to have to ask you—"

"I want to buy this chair." Vladislav stands and his spine holds. His erection holds as well, and standing straight now for the first time in decades, it leads the way. He looks down. "I want to buy this chair right now."

The girl looks down. A look of awe and shock zaps across her face like the strobing of a TV with too many channels.

Oh boy.

He winks and smiles at this young counter girl. "I want to buy this chair, my dear." Vladislav turns to the chair. His erection wanes. He pulls the fabric of his crotch and pushes down with his thumb. His erection softens a bit, enough to decrease its angle, but stays filled enough for a threatening bulge. He does this out of courtesy for the young girl. He puts on his jacket, which hangs down to his knees, but he does not bother to zip it up. He does this out of pride. His cock. This cock. Natasha's joy. He struts up to the counter.

The girl follows. Calculating her commission already.

He winks. Pulls out his wallet. "Big like baby's arm," Vladislav says.

She blushes, alternately repulsed and intrigued. She giggles.

"That's goddamn right."

She walks over to the chair, checks its price. Comes back. "Six thousand dollars," she says.

Vladislav blinks.

"We do have a lay-away plan."

"*Nyet*. It's coming home with me today."

"Then it's six thousand."

He winks at her. "You're very beautiful."

"I can take off 10%."

He smiles. "I bet you must have many men wooing you."

"I can take off 15%."[33]

"*Spasiba*."

---

33. The wiggle room of the standard mark-up employees on the floor are permitted to negotiate.

∞

Vlad looks at his tattered wallet. He has $143. And his checkbook. He smiles and winks. "Wonderful. I'll write you check." He fills out the check, leaning over the counter. As he does he feels his back tighten, feels his scrotum shrink and his penis soften. His smile falters.

"We can have it delivered tomorrow," the girl says as she punches numbers into a square gray machine.

"*Puzhalsta.*"

"Thank you for shopping at Highenders."

"*Puzhalsta.*"

The girl looks at the check and punches in more numbers. "We just need to verify the check with your bank." The machine beeps. She stands waiting for an electronic response.

∞

Outside, Huron Street is dark and cold. Vladislav knows dark and cold. But this is a different dark and cold. Closer to the dark and cold of the Vorkuta Gulag. It is the cold you imagine outer space to feel like. Without the starlight.

Vladislav stands stooped over, leaning against the window of Highenders. The chair sits there. Center stage in a pool of light cast by a stupid looking lamp no one with taste would ever buy. He tries to will the chair to move to the front door. It ignores him. He is invisible.

∞

Vlad makes it home, unnoticed and feeling sick to his stomach. He flops down on his sunken bed and box spring. His stomach hurts. A low dull throbbing in his balls. He feels sick to his stomach.

Blue balls. I got goddamn blue balls.

Another pang and he squats on the toilet like a sissy girl and pees. A moment later a viscous fluid follows and he pees again.

∞

He slaps himself. Lightly. Pours vodka. Sips it. Slaps himself again. Lightly. Oh Natasha. His hand snakes into his flannel night clothes, but nothing happens. A crooked penis of pure anatomy. Formed, but functionless. A useless old man. He downs his vodka, but through the bottom of the glass he sees a small black book under his dresser. A cracked address book.

∞

The stairs. Goddamn stairs. Stooped and taking a half step at a time, Vladislav makes his way down, his elbows wearing at the mismatched patches of his wool-lined coat. As he descends to a stained door below grade level, a faint smell hits his nose. His stomach growls and he realizes he's not eaten since yesterday. Before the Chair.

∞

"Jesus, Vlad. Ten grand?" Marek says. "For what?"

"I need it."

"You sound like a junkie, Vlad. What's the money for— is this about a woman?"

"I did things for your grandfather," Vlad says. "For your father. I could do things for you."

"Like what, Vlad? You're retired. I can't put you back on the payroll. You could barely make it down those stairs."

They were watching.

"No. You've been good to us, Vlad. I'll give you six grand. It's all I can do."

Vlad coughs in mock disgust and then checks himself.

"Call it a post-retirement gift," Marek says. "And a little something extra to protect the gift."

"Spasiba. Spasiba. Spasiba."

"I hope she's beautiful, Vlad. I hope she gets your dick hard, my friend." Marek nods his head and a matronly woman appears with bowls of steaming Zharkoye and pumpernickel bread. "Now eat first. She can wait."

Vladislav looks at Marek, the bowl. The steam from the bowl warms him. The smell. He leans back. He rubs his hands on the table. The worn smooth surface. He looks at Marek. "I made this table," he says.

∞

Pawing against the window. My love, my Natasha. Vlad looks at the sign on the door. A preprinted sign filled in with loopy handwriting.

Open at ten.

∞

Sleep does not come. He stands in his kitchen, reaches into the brown bag, pulls out the second gift from Marek. He opens another bottle. The good stuff. He drinks deep. Like when he was young. He opens the humming icebox. With his crooked toes, the nails cracked and curling like talons, Vlad opens the bottom crisper drawer and like a vending machine, he is rewarded as a moldy orange wobbles into view. He peels the green and white spotted rind and holds the pulpy fruit under his nose. Natasha. Between deep inhalations, he takes another swig from the bottle.

I'm coming, my love.

∞

The cab honks its horn. In a Pakistani accent the driver asks from the curb outside Highenders: "Sir, I am for leaving or staying? Please tell me."

Through the vodka haze Vladislav answers: "Scram, Patel."

The driver puts his battered former police cruiser into gear and vrooms away.

Vladislav pulls a tire iron from his jacket. Swings at the glass door.

∞

There is no foreplay, no touching the chair, no caressing it, no taking in its smell, the way the light plays on its finish against the grain, the whimsical pattern of polka dot explosions. Vlad has had over eight hours of anticipation.

Looks at the tag. A JAW-B PIECE.

His hand slips into his pocket. He unwraps an orange wedge from a moist paper towel. With sticky fingers, he slides the wedge over his upper and lower teeth like a mouth guard. He breathes around it, the smell exiting his mouth under his nose.

Natasha. Oh Natasha.

It's like sitting on a heating pad. But the heat radiates from within his core. Up and down. Natasha. His body relaxes. His spine straightens. His calves loosen, his toes uncurl. His penis becomes erect.

Come, Tiger.

It is greater than anything he has ever imagined. An out of body experience trapped inside his body, a new body, a body disregarding age, gravity, cell degeneration, atrophy, bone shrinkage, a body that is shouting fuck you to the world. To this country. To the years lost in the Gulag. A body alive and transcendental. A body building to critical mass. A body that is not a ghost. A body that will not be invisible.

He should stand up.

He should take the chair home.

He should throw out his old rocking chair.

He should be at home with the Chair.

He should place the phone by the Chair and order take-out three times a day. Never leaving the Chair. Leaving the door unlocked and tipping well.

He should leave now and come back and buy the Chair.

Only six more hours until they open.

Would have should have could have Natasha.

∞

Glass crunches underfoot at the front door. The police officer is a newly transferred second year patrolman responding to an alarm at a small furniture store. His name is Archie Reno. The perp will be long gone, he thinks. He'll talk to the owner, assess what is missing, help fill out a report for insurance purposes, and maybe discreetly pass a card with the number of a board-up company owned by his brother-in-law to fill the void vacated by the shattered door.

Officer Archie Reno steps up to the door frame. Hand on the butt of his weapon, the other shining a large Maglite. But he doesn't need it to see the old man sitting in a funky chair swaying and bucking as though in the throes of a beyond-your-officer-training seizure.

∞

Natasha squeals, squeals for Vlad the Tiger to raise his hands, to get down on his knees. Why is her voice changing? Vlad thinks. Natasha, what are you saying?

She's saying get down on the floor, now motherfucker.

Such language from Tasha, unheard of.

Now or she'll shoot.

Natasha's face starts to fade, but her yelling is louder now. More like Marek's grandfather, that drunk dog. The vodka haze dissipates. Vlad's body relaxes save for his cock. Still hard, still throbbing. But the building orgasm is gone. Sinking beneath the surface, disappearing like a mythical leviathan.

"Hands in the air, old man."

∞

Officer Archie Reno calls for back-up. It's an old man, probably drunk, and he feels bad yelling at this man. The same feeling he gets when he yells at his kids. Or Belle. But his training does not waiver.

The old man's eyes flutter. His teeth are orange.

It's not a seizure. He's on something. The officer holsters his weapon and pulls his Taser. "Sir. Sir, raise your hands and get down on the ground," he says. He knows the man can't hear him. He should wait for back-up, but the man in the old thick suede wool-lined coat is harmless. And on something. He should wait to tase the man, and wait for his back-up to cuff him. The Taser will only drop him for a second or two. He should wait, but he should be able to cuff the man. He is old.

He should not have pulled a double shift.

He should not have divorced Belle.

He should not have introduced Emma to his kids.

He should not have told Emma he loves her.

He should not have given Belle her first cigarette.

He should not have stubbed it out on her hand.

He should have taken a nap.

He should have called Belle.

He should have told her about Emma.

He should wait for back-up.

∞

"Old man."

Someone calls him an old man. Vladislav blinks his eyes. Clear and lucid. Sharper than they have ever been.

Come, Tiger.

There is a cop standing in front of him. With a gun. The cop is here to take the Chair away from him. The Chair that takes away the pain, the Chair that gives him Natasha, the Chair that makes him visible. Young.

"Old man."

Vlad has outrun cops faster than the one before him, he has outsmarted the KGB. He has beaten three raps in NY, Chicago. He has never been caught, never convicted. Back when he was visible. Back when he was young. Vital. A force to be reckoned with. When only throwing him in the Gulag for political reasons could stop him.

Come, Tiger.

He is young.

Vital.

A force to be reckoned with.

Vladislav holds up a hand, palm open. "Wait. Wait."

"Sit, old man."

Vladislav reaches in his jacket.

"I said sit, old man."

"My name is not *old man*. MY NAME IS VLADISLAV VLADISLAVOVICH GLINSKI!"

∞

The glass crunches behind Officer Archie Reno.

"Oh my goddess," a female voice says.

Officer Archie Reno glances back involuntarily. It's a girl with pink hair. Not a threat. He turns back to the old man.

Vladislav Vladislavovich Glinski squeezes the trigger on Marek's second gift. The bullet catches Officer Archie Reno above the bridge of the nose. He drops as if all the strings puppeting his life are cut with a giant pair of shears. Because his heart still beats, a small fountain of blood squirts from the center of his destroyed face.

∞

Officer Archie Reno's Maglite falls, its beam blinding Vladislav. In the light he sees Natasha, hears her.

Come, Tiger.

He hears her scream, scream with delight and come in wave after wave. Vlad does not hear the back-up officer arrive. He does not hear him scream at him to drop the weapon. He does not hear him scream officer down officer down. He only hears the girl. Natasha Natasha. Screaming and screaming, as he defies gravity.

Now, Tiger.

Her orgasm sounds like a gunshot.

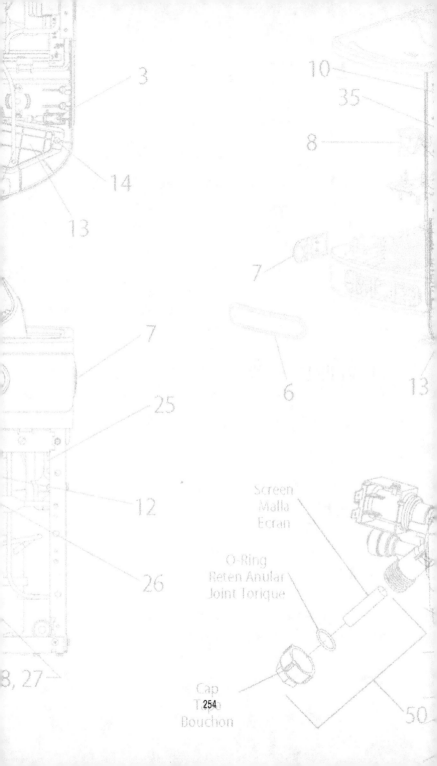

3

14

13

10

35

8

7

7

6

13

25

12

26

Screen
Malla
Ecran

O-Ring
Reten Anular
Joint Torique

8, 27

Cap
Tapa
Bouchon

254

50

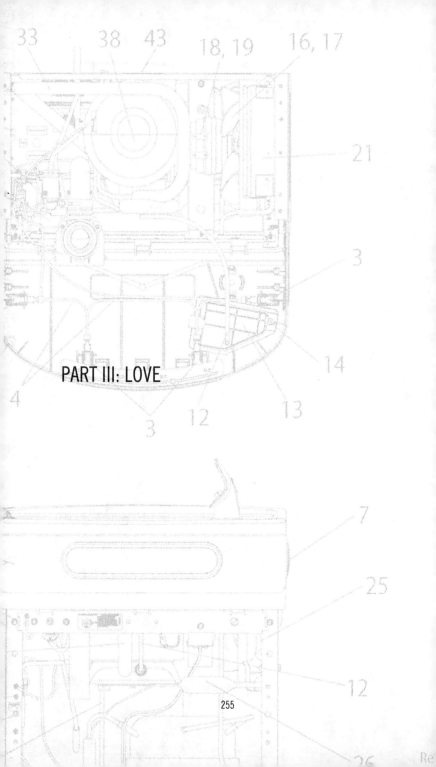

PART III: LOVE

255

MIA

...and with a pair of $14,000 Manolo Blahnik alligator boots, Mia Tam Robards stomps down on the PDA. Or cell phone. Or Blackbeard. Or whatever it once prided itself as being.

His assistant had gotten it for him. Trying to keep him a little more connected, as Ross Robards is a busy man. Robards realizes he has never seen these boots on his wife before.

Mia Tam Robards screams at Ross Robards. An orchestration and matriculation of limbs and lips, which despite her middle age and constant anger is unmarred by wrinkles, a product of good Asian genes and expensive face cream. "We get one day a month," she says. "One day a month and you're checking work email. *On a phone.*"[34] All this in a French accent, which is still beguiling to even those that know her, but not their Vietnamese history.

"The special is today," Robards says.

"I'm today. I'm today," she says. "This is *our* morning. Our morning. Breakfast tacos. I'm fixing you breakfast tacos this morning."

"So, I forgot breakfast. The special is tonight."

She glares at the empty box of Krispy Kremes on the worn wooden table.

"I have to tell them about wardrobe," Robards says, pointing at the detritus of a message interrupted mid-thumbing.

---

34. *Again circa 2010. And Robards is not an early adopter. Unless you count Mia.*

"Wardrobe? You're going to wear the same goddamn jeans you wear every time. You have a dozen of them. They're all the same. Your assistants splatter them and distress them with bleach and sandpaper."

Ross Robards, an unwitting subscriber to Mia's symphony season, recoils at the overture, but knows the melody will be the same.

"I *never* see you," Mia Robards says. "I'm lonely."

It's true. Ross Robards is a busy man. Despite the laid back TV production style, he runs a tight ship and rarely gets off the boat (goddamned right).

"I only want you," Mia says. "I want spend time with you."

"Mia," Robards says, nonchalantly. "If you'd just get on a goddamn plane occasionally." Robards spends a significant time away from his Chicago home at various studios scattered across the country.

She stiffens with the verbal slap. His wife, Mia, does not travel well. It's an inner ear thing and despite the offers from Ross to let her forego a day job, she refuses. "You think I care about meal ticket?" she says. She drops words when she's angry, and she knows it and it frustrates her more.

Robards knows it too and takes it like a sailor bracing against this storm. Or a Buddhist. He listens. He breathes. He finds a safe Zen spot (a red dot painted years ago; there is one in each room of every property Robards owns) and pulls the universe in around him like a child's homemade blanket tent or a pillow fort. He finds a small happy place of sound and colors. He imagines her face a palette of colors and swirls that he can paint and redefine like—

"NO!"

Mia's yelling prevents the colors— they won't come for Ross Robards. He nibbles on the end of his five foot ponytail. It used to taste different, organic, when it was his real hair. But his real hair (now much more thinning and brittle despite the hot oil treatments) ends at the 18-inch mark where it is woven/spliced into sable hair specially treated and highlighted to look like his real hair. The real five-foot ponytail has not been active since season six. Or somewhere in there. But now he cannot summon the colors. The kaleidoscope genie will not come out of the bottle. He cannot summon the blue of the Scottish Highlands sky, or the greens of Ireland. He cannot find a primary anything, as she continues to—

"You've abandoned me," she says.

Everything shifts to gray, a washed out wet gray. Ross Robards, TV personality, prays he's having a stroke, because she's never used this word: *Abandoned.* The weight of the word. The source of the word. From her. A Vietnamese orphan. The things Ross S. Robards carried. Nothing is heavier at this moment than this word. Abandoned.

"LISTEN TO ME!" This is when Mia slaps him. Hard. Despite her size, it rocks his head.

Ross sees red.

Then black.

∞

When he comes to, Mia writhes in a chokehold. She is breaking the tiny bones in her hand banging them against his artificial legs.

Dear. God.

Ross Robards releases her.

Goddammit.

She slips to the floor and crabs away from him, slowly climbing back to her feet.

Why can't she understand? He has to do this. He has to do this. He has to keep rolling. He cannot gather moss. He cannot stop. And in this split second, he knows she will say something they will regret. Something that will be brought up again, something that will carry more weight and consequences than any of the thousands of intimate moments they have shared.

"I lost my legs over there, Mia. Can you not cut me a break? Today? *Today?*"

"There's one more thing you should have left over there, Ross Robards."

"And what's that?"

"Me." And she shoves him with her unbroken hand.

And Ross falls back and because he is not strapped in tightly, he falls out of his legs. And now she is taller than him.

"I loved you." She says it like that. Past tense.

"Mia—"

"What happen to love and cherish? You promised to *cherish.*"

And now Ross is eye level to her torso. Scarred and flesh-patched. When did she get her belly button pierced? "My work," he says. "My real *work*. Is that a tattoo?"

But Mia is quick. "Books, DVDs, mall appearances, reruns. You don't need to work. You don't need to work *all* the time. You're in syndication for Fred's sake."

"Those things fund the A4V," Robards says. Ross does, despite the crazy schedule, divert an extraordinary amount of time and resources to this pet project. Essentially a comprehensive art therapy project for Vets old and, God help him, young. Young like he was when he slipped off a M113 Armored Personnel Carrier tank and fell under its tracks. Crushing both his legs into jelly. "They have to know, Mia, they have to know they can contribute, they have to be able to get the things, that *thing* in their heads— things you would *never* understand," but as he says this he knows Mia understands.

Mia with third degree burns over thirty-two percent of her body. Mia who still self medicates with the best medical marijuana money can buy. Mia, a burned fourteen-year-old. Mia who came to visit Ross every day in the hospital when they decided the colonel's son next to him was more important than trying to figure out if they could save Ross' legs. Ross sold his stateside GTO and brought Mia home, borrowing money from a wealthy widowed aunt who painted landscapes and paint-by-numbers to set them up in Chicago. To make a home with his child bride. Mia.

"They have to know they can create things.

"Things of beauty.

"That they can express.

"They have to get that thing, Mia, *OUT OF THEIR HEADS!*"

But Mia who spends most of her day playing online poker and editing industrial videos in an editing bay that can only be described as an isolation booth goes all in. "Art therapy, I get," she says. "I get it when you were artist. But you're not artist. You don't care any more about being artist. You used to be an artist. Working in metal. You were pure, political. What you did mattered. Was important. The only thing you sign are your cheap DVDs. You don't even sign my birthday cards. The flowers I get, your assistant is good, but I know you don't close your R's when you sign. You don't sign anything. Twenty-seven years. Not since *that*," she says pointing at the mirror. B's 1983 mirror painting. "That's where it started."

Ross vibrates.

She grabs one of his artificial legs and rushes to the special place in the open loft area where the mirror hangs. B's 1983 Turner Falls mirror. B's last painting before he turned to the craft of shaping metal. She takes that leg of Robards' and despite the wrong cultural reference swings it back like the eighth samurai left on Kurosawa's cutting room floor. But she is not a samurai and the swing of the leg ends up shy of the oil-painted mirror by several inches, and is now several inches in the drywall (narrowly missing the exposed brick which seemed oh so important when they first toured through the space with their realtor) further aggravating tiny broken bones in her hands. The mirror slips along the back wire on the hanging screw and slides down coming to rest at a lower 45 degree angle. The signature R. Still in the corner, now teetering like a sienna cattle brand for the Lazy R ranch.

∞

Ross sees that R. Sees the bottom of the R, where he painted over the bottom of the letter turning Bellio's B signature into an R signature.

Mia limps into another room, cradling her hand against her chest like a broken wing.

Ross gorillas on his hands over to Mia's secret stash and rolls a joint. His first in twenty-seven years. Since he gave up the drugs. Gave up the red meat. Gave up the pleasure of an unnatural altered state. Gave up the satisfying anger of metal work.

He inhales deeply.

His head buzzes.

His body.

His phantom legs.

The intercom buzzes. "The limo's here for the show, sir. Congrats again on your anniversary."

He exhales.

∞

Mia returns from the master bedroom.

Is the master bedroom over there? Ross thinks. He's confusing the layouts of the Chicago loft with the other loft in that other city.

Mia's rolling a big suitcase. Heading for the door.

"It's our anniversary, Mia. Our 30th."

"It *your* anniversary. And it only the 27th."

"Thirty counting public access," he says.

"Of course, Ross. You are correct."

And then he knows he's going to say it because he has to say it. He owes her that much of a gesture. Because that is the script. And when they look back at the transcript he can point and say, I said it. She can't accuse him of not.

The intercom buzzes again. "Sir, the limo's here. We're waiting."

So Robards says it, a hoarse whisper: "I can't live without you."

∞

Mia pauses, but doesn't turn. The skin grafts on the neck and shoulders visible. Loathing the melodrama, the reduction of two unique individuals to this, to *this*. The only options: Slam door or close it. Softly, she walks through the door, leaving it open. Over her napalmed shoulder, she says: "Yes. You can."

Karma Police

They walk into the mall with the guns in plain view. Barrels down. But they've taken the time to paint the tips a bright Hunter Orange so it looks like a toy gun to most and a paintball gun to the few enthusiasts there. Enthusiasts who would never paint the tips of the barrels Hunter Orange as paintball guns are not toys. Security guards don't give them a second look. Too busy watching the cameras and lights of Ross Robard's *Yes, You Still Can* 30th anniversary TV special. Too busy pointing at mirrors already painted from previous seasons. How simple. How easy. Let me show you. To kick things off, Robards starts with a classic mirror painting: A serene sunset and log cabin by a pond filled with:

"Happy hungry trout."

B frowns. The painting Robards starts is essentially B's 1983 painting; Robards' template for success. The color. The composition. Swapping out objects for variety: a cabin instead of a fountain. A grove of trees instead of a water fall. A pond instead of the stream. B flushes with indignation.

Robards leads the excited or bored or curious mall crowd in the chorus.

"Happy hungry trout."

Jawbone frowns. "Trout live in rivers," she says under her breath.

"Everyone," Robards says, stoned but holding steady.

They all join in.

"Happy. Hungry. TROUT!"

∞

It hits him in the chest. A center shot, a kill shot. Permanent Carmine Red blossoms like a flower.

"I'm hit," Ross Robards screams, *"Medic."*

Another hit. Another blossom.

Where is the shooter?

Robards staggers backwards, arms aflail. He drops the wooden handle of his paintbrush, the slender dowel fastened to the tip of his trademark silver ponytail. All five feet. He treats it as a third appendage, a limp prehensile tail. Ross Robards is a rich man. And his only luxuries other than his vinyl record collection and penthouse apartment and studio in Ireland and his state of the art artificial legs are the weekly spa and pampered hot oil treatments for his hair. He's not had a haircut since being In Country. The tip is tainted with Indanthrene Blue. His Viridian Green shirt streaked with color. His famous blue jeans spotted and starched with the dried paint of countless paintings. Countless mirrors, countless TV shows and books. The famous paints. His famous hair brush. His famous jeans. His blue jeans, he tells his audience with a wink.

Those flailing arms strike his easel. The mirror with the still wet serene sunset and cabin by a pond filled with "fat happy hungry trout" rocks unsteadily and then falls to cheap mall tile.

Shatters.

A million pieces.

A million little pieces.

A million little trout in a million little ponds.

A million little happy hungry trout.

"Trout live in rivers, you hack mothercrutch!" someone screams from above.

Another blossom.

Oh God, I'm dying.

Ross Robards cries for a medic. He hears the choppers coming.

This is it.

Ticket punched.

Farm bought.

Number up.

Drive on.

Don't mean nothing drive on.

Here comes the Rooster.

People scream as Ross lays dying. They scatter. Someone yells *sniper*. Mothers push strollers away seeking shelter in an Orange Julius. Teens flee to the Gap with their primary colors so hopeful so cheerful so happy so commercial. Texting as they run inside. Other teens dive into the multiplex. Find seats in the back. Breathing hard. As they were surely almost killed. Did you see what happened to that guy? No baby, I only knew to drag you away. We're safe now. As a hand slides up a blouse.

∞

Back at the battlefield, the falling easel hits another and another. It is a domino effect. The stage manager had warned them this might happen, but Ross Robards, who is stoned out of his gourd, likes seeing his reflection in those dozens of mirrors as he paints.

Another paintball whizzes by the stage manager's head. She's standing there staring at Ross on the ground screaming at ghost choppers. Everyone is running. She looks up and sees the black(?) woman with the CO_2 gun and feels a pang of racial profiling guilt.

Dreadlocks bouncing, the assailant's silver teeth shine as she screams: "Rivers, *ri-vers!* Get it right!" She fires again and again at Ross, at his paintings. The man in greasy overalls next to her with an honest-to-god red bandit bandana says nothing, meticulously firing at the mirror paintings one by one.

∞

Paintballs zip by like circus meteors.

A waterfall is hit and finds itself dammed with a sunburst of Carbazole Violet.

A Burnt Umber cabin in a Montana snowfield finds its door obliterated with a Quinacridone Purple splotch.

A wooded glade finds its Emerald Chromium Oxide defiled with the shit brown smear of Mars Brown.

Robards sees the sniper. Hears the *thock* and *thock* of the weapon.

He's hit and his work, Ross Robards' life's work, is hit and hit. A center shot, each one.

He touches his wet chest. It stings.

> *Must get up.*
>
> *Medic.*
>
> *Medic.*
>
> *Charlie's in the trees, Armstrong.*
>
> *Oh God, why didn't I run to Canada?*

His long silver ponytail.

A security detail comes running. They are screaming into walkie-talkies. They have forgotten their weapons, their helmets.

Where's your weapons, soldiers?

Cpl. Ross S. Robards turns onto his belly. He sees the low wall surrounding a botanical Japanese garden. Crawls for it. If he can pull himself into the Bush, he will be safe. He tiger crawls over a broken cabin.

A sharp snowfield of Titanium White.

A million hungry trout. They are nipping at him. Hungry. Feeding.

A little further. A little farther.

Like an animal he crawls.

He slips on his blood. Scarlet and thick. Oh God. Bright red. Arterial blood.

Another shot by his head. Debris flies, everything goes Cadmium Yellow and he is blinded.

A little further.

Like an animal he crawls.

A shot to the head. He cups the back of his head. Holding in his brains.

Robards crawls to find a place to die.

Like Tex from Oklahoma.

Like Benedict from West Virginia.

Like Hobie from Portland.

Like Armstrong from Georgia.

Like Brooklyn from Austin.

What do you call a guy with no arms and no legs on your doorstep?

Matt.

What do you call a guy with no arms and no legs nailed to the wall?

Art.

What do you call a guy with no arms and no legs screaming in a rice paddy?

Pfc. Cooper Armstrong.

Cpl. Ross S. Robards holds in his brains. Reaches the wall. Rolls over. Curls into a ball.

"Mia," he whispers.

Benny.

Hobie.

Tex.

KIA.

MIA.

He's touched all their names. Engraved on the black wall. He's made charcoal impressions of all these names. He wishes his name were on that wall.

"Mia, I'm sorry."

He blinks his eyes, the Cadmium Yellow stings. He knuckles his eyes clear and scans the treetops, which are in reality a railing for the second floor of the shopping mall. A railing with a clean field of fire for Ross Robards' painting exhibition.

Next to the screaming woman, Robards sees a man dressed in greasy overalls and a ball cap with a blue NY and big glasses lob a grenade over the rail at him. The man is laughing.

"Heh. Heh. Heh."

Laughing at my death.

"Heh. Heh. Heh."

I know that laugh.

The grenade explodes mid-air. A dozen tissue parachutes open and its message is a foil-covered four letter word.

Each word the same.

Raining down.

In front of the cameras and live TV audience.

A million little screens.

HACK

They float softly landing in a million broken ponds.

The Escape

The masked gunmen explode from the emergency exit door. An alarm sounds, an annoying buzz ignored by the people of the City. The alley, swamped with puddles, mirrors the running figures. Everything shines like glossy magazine pages. There is even a bit of steam smoking from a manhole cover. It is like a movie set.

And B thinks:

> *Damn it. This is an* authentic *experience, not a movie set. We have pulled triggers and revolted and protested and committed civil disobedience.*

Okay, maybe not civil disobedience, and were they to be caught, their public defender might be required to mount a defense against:

1. Assault & Battery (raised to Felony because of the paintball guns)

2. Intentional Infliction of Emotional Distress

3. Vandalism

4.   Destruction of Private Property

5.   Breach of the Peace

But they have had an authentic experience. They did not do it online, they did not hunt elk on a farm stocked with specially bred elk whose antlers are the best in all the land, nor did they shoot them with remote controlled guns viewed through a monitor, nor did they read *Into Thin Air* with the cold environmentally corrosive air-conditioning turned way up wrapped in a goose-down comforter on their Ikea couch.

∞

B thinks: *Did I see a boy with chipped glasses?*

Jawbone thinks: *I drank the water.*

∞

They did not assume the identity of an electronic avatar and have cybersex with another avatar on the other side of the planet. They did not buy a replica jersey of a Chicago Bears player and watch the game from a golf club house. They did not take their Hummer to the grocery store. They did not become politically active by clicking a donation of $5 and hoping for change. They did not experience Lee Bontecou or Andre Gursky or Frank Lloyd Wright by flipping through a coffee table pop-up book. They did not experience Thomas Pynchon by reading an essay on his works.

∞

B thinks: *He seemed scared.*

Jawbone thinks: *I drank the water.*

∞

They did not live their lives as a forecast of the future six months from now. They did not read the movie critics' review of the Cremaster cycle. They did not order their margaritas frozen and without salt. They did not experience the Ring Cycle in their sweats in a movie theatre. They did not say they would pray for a sick relative and then not bend a knee and talk to God. They did not make Thanksgiving pie from a can. They did not distress their CBGB t-shirt with sandpaper. They did not blog about someone else's blog. They did not steal Bill Hicks' comedy routine.

∞

B thinks: *Please, don't be scared.*

Jawbone thinks: *I drank the water.*

∞

They did not travel Europe and experience foreign cuisine by DVRing cable. They did not talk about making a movie, writing a play, singing a song, learning the guitar, or learning to paint or sculpt someday. They did not wish they'd always stayed up late hand-crafting tissue paper grenades with parachutes and loading paintball guns with custom filled paintballs using a syringe from a junkie friend. They did not wish they'd assaulted the hack artist Ross Robards in the middle of a packed mall while he smiled and painted from muscle memory the same painting he'd been replicating for twenty-seven years that he found one afternoon on his desk painted by a potential intern who left after a few hours and never left his name.

∞

B thinks: *I never crossed the stream.*

Jawbone thinks: *I drank the water.*

∞

Here, present in the moment, they *did* it.

And not being military trained, they whooped and hollered through the alley like soccer hooligans.

"A cab ride away," Jawbone says. Her dreadlocked wig bounces.

There were photographers. There will be pictures. And the gawkers, they got the best thing ever: a story.

Jawbone pulls up her mask and flashes her faux metallic teeth, a prop she bought herself for this evening's commando raid as a tribute to her old self. They shine in the streetlight like the sapphires she used to wish they were.

"Kill shot," she says, laughing.

"Hack and slay," B says.

"Slay hack," Jawbone says, hawking up a clear loogie.

They laugh at the pun fueled by adrenaline and the privacy of the moment. Two bodies hurling through the noir alley into the deserted streets of the City known to eat its young. Now to catch a cab, get back to ArtBar and watch the news.

B wonders if the kid in the thick chipped glasses will be in the clip.

He slips on something in a puddle. Something slick. It is like stepping barefoot on algae on a rock in the stream at Turner Falls in his youth. Or what he imagined it would have felt like had he had the courage to walk down that steep hillside. If he had run downhill, timed his jump he might have cleared the stream. But he'll never know.

B's arms windmill and he falls forward bent at the waist, clomping steps propelling him forward. He squeezes the trigger of his paintball gun.

Once.

The ball of Permanent Carmine Red strikes Jawbone up and to the left of her right temple. The ball bursts splattering upward into the matted hair of her wig.

"Oh shit, B," Jawbone says. Dropping to the alley.

B recovers from the potential pratfall, but wonders why Jawbone is now falling as though he has handed off the pratfall baton to his teammate now running the anchor leg. Jawbone goes down. Her dreadlocked wig falls off. She goes down for the second time in so many weeks. She goes down laughing, then coughing.

B laughs.

Jawbone rolls over, dropping her paintball gun.

"Come on. Let's go."

In the streetlight, Jawbone looks like she has been the movie victim of a headshot. She coughs. Hacking wet. She doesn't stop coughing. Her metal grill falls from her mouth in a glob of mucus.

"Come on. Let's go."

Jawbone raises her hand like a fallen football player looking for an assist in getting to her feet. Her mouth is wet and dripping and her eyes glaze over like potter's clay.

"Harriet?" B grabs her hand, but is surprised at the strength in Jawbone's grip. It is a death grip. "My ride is here," she says, through a bubbling slurry. "Love..."

"What? Wait? What?" B drops to a knee. Pulls off his bandana. Leans close to her.

She caresses his cheek. She gurgles something. A wet whisper.

His ear to her mouth now.

A bubble forms on her lips. It pops, obliterating her last word.

The Fountain Period

From Wikipedia, the free encyclopedia

The Fountain Period was a 21st century period of art originating in The United States of America in 2010. The peak period only lasted from 2012 to 2013, but the repercussions were felt for a decade. It was thought during that period that a drinking fountain ("Fountain") on the third floor of the Museum of Contemporary Art, Chicago, IL would grant the imbiber the ability to create one artistic masterpiece. But shortly thereafter the artist would die, usually of accelerated natural causes. [1]

During this period most every exceptional *created* work of art was questioned and its merit or means of production challenged. A trend emerged where a large number of arts organization, galleries, museums, and media seemed to place a moratorium on celebrating art. If a work of art appeared to be exceptional or had an exceptional quality, it would not be officially displayed for up to two years. This would allow enough time to pass to see if the artist would expire. [2] Of course, this raised ethical issues about artists that had, in fact, created exceptional works of art and died of natural causes not associated with the Fountain. But since no test was ever devised or implemented there was always the question of guilt by circumstance.

In response to this, Ross Robards, former host of the long running painting show, Yes, You Can!, founded the Artist Guild. The Artist Guild, a non-profit organization, would deploy a legal and critical team to defend certain works of created art based on a non-disclosed criteria established by Robards.

"'Gut instinct'—it's what kept me alive in 'Nam," Robards said, adjusting his metal eye patch. "It's what going to save us in this bullshit time." [3]

Robards eventually expanded his interests and created the new artist collective War Machine Works ("WMW").

Congressional Hearings

An investigative Congressional hearing was convened in Washington D.C. on October 31, 2011 Senator Cooper Armstrong. A one-time comrade in arms of Robards, Armstrong (rendered a quadriplegic by war injuries) summoned members of the arts community to testify regarding the Fountain. The hearings were canceled on the second day during the testimony of Vladislav Vladislavovich Glinski, a former Russian art prodigy. Glinski, as a sign of his absolute belief that the truth of art was "art being the thing itself regardless of where it came from," set himself on fire. [4]

Many galleries (and organizations), reluctant to choose sides, closed when seemingly most artists pulled their works and set them on fire either in solidarity of Glinski or in protests of Glinski. [5] Glinski, at the time of his Congressional testimony, was under arrest and recovering from a gunshot wound by a Chicago police officer. Glinski was being held for the alleged Second Degree murder of Chicago Police Officer Archie Reno. Glinski had allegedly broken into a furniture boutique. Investigating the break-in, Officer Reno was shot after Glinski refused to remove himself from a "chair."

The Chair

The Chair is thought to have been one of the original sculptures or works of art created under the influence of the Fountain. The creation of the Chair was a collaboration between Chicago underground artists Harriet "Jawbone" Walker and Robert "B" Bellio. [6] Subsequently, the Chair was placed in Oz Park near De Paul University where it lasted thirty-five days until a group of vandals killed each other in the park. Witnesses say the vandals seemed determined to destroy the Chair when members had a heated change of heart and turned on each other with metal grinders and blow torches." [citation needed] The Chair was removed by the city and is in secured storage pending negotiations with the Smithsonian. [7]

B is listed as the only person still missing from the Great Chicago Flood centered at the Museum of Contemporary Art and is presumed dead. [8] Survivors of the Flood who were in the MCA include Ross Robards, an unidentified woman, and Jasper P. Duckworth.

A marginal critic at the time, Duckworth found himself at Ground Zero with the Fountain, having personally experienced the death of two of the Fountain's early "vessels"— Timmy and Tabitha, later known as Bitha. Timmy's creation was destroyed only moments after its creation by the artist himself. No known photo exists. Bitha's creation *Migration* was destroyed in the Great Chicago Flood. Duckworth did attend the Congressional hearings, but did not get a chance to testify. He did remark to a TV reporter later that Glinski's immolation was a "derivate piece of performance art. Though his timing was perfection." [9]

Since beginning his fifteen-year prison term for the kidnapping, assault, and maiming of Ross Robards and B., Duckworth has not commented on his experience with the Fountain. Instead, he recently issued this statement: "I am looking forward to the upcoming production of my first play, 'The Art of Drowning' with the underground Chicago theater company Visions & Voices." [10]

The Written Word

The Fountain seems to have had little effect on the written word: plays, novels, short stories, et al. According to Amazon publisher Darren Callahan, this is "due to the general publication/production lag which acts as the industry's own moratorium."

"That's a misconception," Whisk(e)y Tit publisher Miette Gillette said, though she did not deny a "water taint" clause has been added to their boilerplate contracts, only affecting royalty rates. *[citation needed]*

Even rival writers were known to question whether their fellow authors, scrambling for the few meager dollars left in publishers' coffers, had "tasted the water," exacerbating the rumor that this act might "enhance the work" while dodging death. Looking at the New York Times Best-Seller list, the late author Bret Easton Ellis said, "I can point to a few 'S&S'ers.'" [11]

Despite the controversy raging in the art world, publishers have freely admitted that a great story is a great story and whatever sells well keeps the industry alive. "We can't fact-check a name, let alone investigate a drink of water," a leading publisher said, anonymously. "And if we banned every writer who ever wrote under the influence, well, I'm just saying." [citation needed]

"I tell you one thing," best selling author Stephen King said, "I wish these yokels would just shut up and do the goddamn work." [12]

Found Art

While the Fountain effect did not hinder the publishing world, it did lead to resurgence in "found art."

Found art is the "creative" practice where an everyday ordinary object is taken out of its normal context and presented with a new moniker to the masses as art. The movement lasted a brief time, generally being dismissed as antiquated and a poor attempt at recycling of Dadaism.

A few critics theorize that some of the Fountain water may have survived. A fellow cellmate of Duckworth's stated that Duckworth had mentioned that he had managed to store several gallons of the water just before the height of the Bitha and *Migration* phase of the Fountain Period. [citation needed] Ross Robards has suggested that perhaps, "Mr. Duckworth is simply biding his time, perhaps for generations, before drinking Fountain water and unleashing a "bullshit Holocaust story on us. But I'll be there as long as I still got one good eye." [citation needed]

Music

"Love hard, motherfuckers," said Wayne Coyne, lead singer of Grammy award-winning rock group The Flaming Lips. "You die at 27 or you don't." [13]

The Great Chicago Flood

The Great Chicago Flood happened on July 23, 2010 destroying virtually every work of art at the Museum of Contemporary Art and washing it into the Chicago River and into Lake Michigan. The flood also caused the deaths of hundreds of members of the Illinois National Guard [14] and the massive group of protesters AKA "Seekers." These two groups represented the majority of the Flood's victims. Engineers have suggested that the flood was caused in part by a collapse of an underground tunnel similar to the flood of April 13, 1992. But this fails to explain why water rushed from the third and second floors of the museum. Downtown property and loss of business damage totaled 6.7 billion dollars. One hundred percent of the insurance companies involved invoked a *"Force Majeure"* clause. The loss of the works of art is generally regarded as priceless."*[citation needed]*

The following year the MCA was demolished. A new museum has been planned and designed by Chicago designer Richard M. Higby, but budget disputes at the city, state, and federal level have delayed groundbreaking indefinitely. Currently, there stands a makeshift and weathered memorial of a pile of mismatched and discarded chairs.

Legal Ramifications

The Right of Art case is currently advancing to the U.S. Supreme Court, which expects to hear the case within the decade. The argument is that the government could not deny a person the right to choose to create a work of art regardless if it meant certain death. This right to choice argument was based largely on the taped video testimony of several artists and/or relatives of Seekers or lay people (who wanted to create art) killed in the Great Chicago Flood of 2012. The legal argument has next to little outcome for personal rights in a practical matter since the Fountain was destroyed in the Great Chicago Flood. The case is largely seen as a movement to vindicate and legitimize the artists who chose to use the Fountain's properties as a way to enhance their artistic, and many would say, financial standing in the art community. "Nonsense," said lead attorney B.A. Hill. [15] "This is about a person's right to choose. Period."

External Links

http://robertbellio.com/

www.richardhigbydesign.com

http://www.nea.gov/

References

1. ^The official total number of Fountain deaths not attributed to the Great Flood is currently listed at 39 with 1 MIA. The official death toll for the Great Chicago Flood is listed at 2,999.

2. ^Conservative critics and politicians decried this as a collective liberal hoax to pressure the federal government for an increase in funding for the National Endowment of the Arts.

3. ^Time Magazine Online, September 2014.

4. ^The incident was broadcast live on C-SPAN 8.

5. ^The largest of these groups were the Tabula Rasas.

6. ^At the Congressional hearing B denied ever having drunk the water and swore that the chair was originally intended as a knock-off, but that after the original client dropped the project due to personal reasons, he and Jawbone collaborated on it for an original piece. When asked if he and Jawbone had a romantic relationship, B responded, "I painted her toenails. Does that constitute a romantic relationship, Senator?"

7. ^As a result, the rise in the number of knock-offs of the Chair by unnamed artists calling themselves "Opiate for the Masses" grew to a staggering proportion. Another group "DeathbyArt" took to doing quick knock-offs and painting them a ghostly white and leaving them scattered on street corners as makeshift memorials to the death of artists whose works were influenced by the Fountain. Ironically, another black market was created for these chairs, which were often stolen and replaced with even cheaper knock-offs by artists not associated with Opiate and the original knock-offs. Germany and Nova Scotia were the primary markets.

8. ^His disappearance (and presumed death) after the hearings weighs heavily on the side of the argument that both B and Jawbone had imbibed water from the fountain and created the Chair, still posited by Ross Robards and WMW to be a true masterpiece.

9. ^This chaos and confusion during the National Guard confrontation with Seekers allegedly allowed Duckworth to kidnap both B and Robards at gunpoint. Duckworth denies this, stating it was the spectacle of "seeing Waylon come riding up on a horse like a crazed cowboy." No eyewitnesses have corroborated this story.

10. ^Chicago Tribune Online, (Glenn Jeffers) April 1, 2019

11. ^New York Post Online, February 2013 "Swishers and Spitters."

12. ^Entertainment Weekly Online, December 13, 2013

13. ^High Times, November 2015

14. ^Many critics point to the deployment of National Guard Troops as the main reason for Gov. Theodore Nugent's (R) reelection defeat.

15. ^Texas Monthly Online, June 2017. Brian Alan Hill is a Texas attorney and former Chicago stage actor, who starred as "Dan" in the critically acclaimed production of "[the] Violent Sex." His most successful television role was Dr. Max in the TV mini-series Asteroid.

Whet Stone

The steam clears Ross Robards' nose, countering the clogging of his sinuses by the alcohol thinner. He stares down at the drain of his *Cerdomus Pietra D'Assisi* tile-lined shower. He hates it. It should be polished black granite from Bangalore, India. The same granite used for the Wall.

H(ooch)

Permanent Carmine.

Quinacrinone.

Indanthrene.

Cadmium.

A(V4)

He takes a bottle of hundred-dollar handcrafted shampoo. Mixes in paint thinner and applies it to his scalp and Payne's Gray runs down his body down the drain. The color of mud baths now available to tourists in Vietnam.

Permanent Carmine.

Quinacridone.

Indanthrene.

Cadmium.

C(-rations)

Bruises and welts from the paintballs pockmark his body. They hurt. All the colors swirling, a kaleidoscope of feelings, emotions. He tries to hold them back. His name should be on that wall.

Permanent Carmine.

Quinacridone.

Indanthrene.

Cadmium.

K(IA)

His tears mix with the steam and evaporate and condense on the shower stall. His brother in arms.

Don't mean nothing.

Drive on.

Permanent Carmine.

Quinacridone.

Indanthrene.

Cadmium.

[drain]

He reaches for the hunting knife from its sheath on the Italian marble windowsill. His only trophy from the conflict. He left two legs, but took a knife. And a child bride. Who as a woman went MIA.

∞

As if at an altar, Ross Robards genuflects before the TV. He has a box remote connected by a fat black wire. The rabbit ears are bent and twisted, a creature from a dark fable. The dial *clunks* as he turns. He has thirteen channels. He has not watched TV in twenty-five years. Only his show.

Clunk.

Consume.

Clunk. Fear.

Clunk. Sports.

Clunk. Consume.

Clunk. Celebrity.

Clunk. Threat level: Yellow.

Clunk. Beautiful people breaking up.

Clunk. Beautiful people making up.

Clunk. Beautiful people making beautiful babies.

Clunk. Safer now.

Clunk. Threat level: Orange.

Clunk. Hard work.

Clunk. Fear.

Clunk. Consume.

Clunk. Fear.

Clunk. Smile.

Clunk. Hearts and Minds.

A Bouncing Betty.

Clunk. Just do it.

A tunnel.

Clunk. Live richly.

MREs

Clunk. True.

Oh Jesus Christ.

Clunk. Think outside the bun.

Flashlight and a .45.

Clunk. An Army of One.

Hands and knees.

Clunk. Impossible is nothing.

In the darkness

Clunk. No Fear.

A tripwired Claymore.

Clunk. I'm lovin it.

Chunks of his legs, his friends here there and everywhere.

Clunk. Build your own.

Pulling Armstrong onto the chopper.

Clunk. But wait.

Applying four tourniquets as he wears two.

Clunk. What you don't know could kill you.

He searches in vain for his show. Something familiar with a familiar tempo. Not the now, now of now.

Clunk. Whaaaaassuuuuuuuuuup?????

Is this normal, he thinks. Is this what surrounds his show? This dross, this dreck...?

This...

His breath shortens.

This...

Fight or flight.

This is victory over communism?

Waterloo

Let's loop back to Jasper P. Duckworth already in progress and see what he's been up to these past few weeks.

— does it with a slight smile, a roll of the eyes and a small shrug of the shoulders. Hector the desk security guard sees this, sees Duckworth carrying two full five gallon collapsible jugs in each hand. Shuffle walking as fast as he can.

It is not the look of someone sneaking out ten gallons of H_2O from the third floor fountain. It is the look of someone who has a Plan B. It is the look of someone who figures to win, to have an impact, to not be "cut out of the loop." It is someone who has decided that even if philosophically he loses, financially he will win. Though there are no bullet points of further action in Plan B, he will have Fountain water on demand. Access. Perhaps a black market— after all, his father turned a tidy profit during WWII. Enough to bring his skeletal mother to the States.

Duckworth's look, shrug, and eye roll says can you believe the stuff we have to do? The things we have to do for Tabby. Tabby who has a cult following. Is becoming a viral hit. A household name (for those with cable). Tabby who has asked you to be her water boy.

∞

Hector, who in a few days will have life-changing sex with a water nymph on the flooded third floor in the presence of the Fountain, half nods and smirks at Duckworth. He is a Critic and Hector is an artist. It even says so with a tattoo on Hector's right inner bicep,

ART, so Hector has to let Duckworth know he knows with a not-so-subtle flex.

∞

In the back of Duckworth's brain he acknowledges Hector's look and tattoo, but is filing it for processing later. Duckworth thinks I can have a legacy as a true Critic. I *will* have a legacy. Because what is his legacy now? A bunch of newspaper articles pissing on others' work. Reviews of TV commercials. A drawer filled with a dusty manuscript. A therapist's notebook tucked away with the line *afraid of clouds* underlined. He isn't sure what he will do with the water. He only knows that he needs access to the water. The water is power. Tabby is dying. And thus she is of no use to his legacy. Not that he is heartless. Duckworth has already priced a spray of flowers for her certainly imminent funeral.

Now he is stuck within the revolving doors, and the water is leaking from one of the jugs like a pesky pissing schnauzer.

∞

Duckworth takes a deep breath.

What to do now?

He looks out the window of his fifth floor Lincoln Park apartment. Lake Michigan beckons to him. With tiresome effort, he tries to open the window stuck with dust and grime. He's fired his maid, a robust Russian woman who had taken the finish off his hardwood floors inadvertently two years ago with the wrong detergent when she washed it the first time. He chastised her. And in her broken English she asked to make it up to him. Suddenly, she'd gone from an immigrant worker to a foreign beauty with a tigress' sexual hunger. Not that he knew what a tigress' sexual hunger was. And of course, she didn't speak good English and maybe she wasn't offering, um, sexual favors, but he knew she knew when this tall creature bent over that her cleavage showed. He took her from behind. She screamed: *Come, Tiger.* He didn't know what that meant, but he liked it.

As they finished, he had a brief moment of panic as the feeling of confidence and power shifted to legal thoughts. She had presented, yes? She didn't tell him to stop, right? They'd left things unspoken. She'd straightened her skirt and thrown her wet panties away, looked at Duckworth, given him a kiss on the cheek.

"You no Vlad," she said. "But you got potential."

∞

Talking to himself.

Art does have the right to children.

It does, it does.

Everyone will be its children.

Everyone will create a masterpiece.

And when every work of art is a masterpiece...

All will be equal.

And nothing will be a true masterpiece.

Unless *someone* tells them otherwise. The museum will own the rights to the pieces, but not to Jasper P. Duckworth. He will own his own legacy. He will have his story. Book rights, movie rights. His life rights. A documentary perhaps. Maybe even a reality show (though the thought does sour his stomach a bit). They don't own *him*.

Plan C formulates with a lucidity that only comes with skydiving and rock climbing and combat, none of which Duckworth has ever participated in.

I will be a champion of the Fountain.

He will encourage its use. He will critique it all. He will write with a heavy heart of the pieces that fail to move him. A gentle critic. He will champion certain pieces, his critiques tantamount to emotionally resonant poetry. Poetry that will be permanently laminated with good heavy plastic mil and be proudly displayed alongside the creation. People will look to Jasper P. Duckworth to be the authority, to nudge their own inclinations into a sound judgment.

Ah yes, I thought so. Just like Duckworth.

And then... and then he will, uh, he will, yes, yes he will then resign. Retire, weary, and empty.

Oh so empty.

Art is dead.

And he will go off and live abroad.

And become a Seeker.

And he will grow his hair out, plugs be damned, his beard; he will burn his bow-tie.

And he will work on his Play.

But first, he will let the world know. It will be his last column, and he will lead them all to the Fountain. He will tell them what they can accomplish with a drink of water. The followers of Bitha will become their own gods and goddesses. It will be dangerous. They will try to stop him; this important thing he has to do. He unties his bow tie now. Strikes a match and holds it to the plaid material. His trademark tie smokes, melts and finally disappears in the meager flames, among the toxic fumes of a cotton polyester blend. He coughs twice, this Prometheus.

∞

Jasper P. Duckworth retrieves a ream box of 32lb 100 percent cotton bond paper. It has been vacuum sealed since college. A gift from his father who said: "Someday you will write your parents' story."

He brings it over to desk #2. Next to his typewriter. He slits open the paper. (Desk #3 is the one in the corner. The one where that maid— looking to maybe move in— suggested he turn it into a breakfast nook. What a waste!)[35]

Duckworth rolls in a crisp sheet.

The snap of the roller.

The whack of the paper against the platen.

He sees the shape of it already forming in his head.

It is going to be good. It is going to be outfuckingstanding. Eh, Timmy?

---

35. On desk #1 is an Underwood typewriter circa 1922. It's in good shape having been restored by that machine shop on Montrose. The keys are snappy and the platen yielding. The owner collected and restored old typewriters and newer 'electrical' ones. When Duckworth told him he was a writer, the owner tried to sell him on a portable typewriter (weighing only ten pounds). The shop is only open a few hours a day. How do you stay in business, he asked the owner. Ah, I've tried to retire a few times, but the cops won't let me, see they still use typewriters and no one else can fix them. Got an accommodation certificate from the captain, he said pointing at the wall. And there it was. (This shop has since closed.)

But the ribbon on the Underwood is dry. So over to desk #3; a solid oak job bought at an antique store on Madison Street in Forest Park and on that desk is a 1941 Royal. The Royal still sports a small metal plate of another shop long closed. The carriage isn't as visible as it is on the Underwood on desk #1 (one he has not sat at in two years), but it is beefy, tank-like. Indestructible. Except Jasper has lost a key. The 'X'. His former maid Natasha professed (in her grunts and broken English) to know nothing about it, but there it was missing suddenly after her last cleaning session. This typewriter would be perfect for this manifesto. But how do you type without an X?

So, he sits down at desk #2. He typed all his Editorials from his college days on this machine, a lime green 1967 Sears Chevron, when he wrote for the college art magazine Art Fag. Somewhere in there he typed the occasional poem or two. (They're kept in a folder under the ream box, if you feel like snooping.) Perhaps romantically, the other typewriters would be more suitable, but this modern job wins out for nostalgia and a fresher ribbon. Plus, it has a '1' key, whereas the others do not and instead you have to type a lower case 'L' to get the effect of a '1'.

This *manifesto*.

He walks around the small apartment, flicking off all the lights, save for a small faux antique lamp that could have come off a desk in *The Maltese Falcon*. (Duckworth often lamented the fact he should have bought a real antique lamp. He lamented this fact often. Lamented that he lamented this fact and lamented that he lamented so much.)

But no more.

This is the end of regret.

His stomach grumbles like an old man watching hucksters and yucksters present the local news. Perhaps he should have a splash of water (tap). He fills a glass. Antique, of course. He settles back down. The water is cold and his teeth ache. His stomach growls again. Maybe he should eat a little something. You try writing a Call to Arms for the disaffected, misguided cool kids on an empty stomach. He quickly microwaves a burrito. Sits back down with a plate and fork. He cuts a bite out of the middle.

Jesus, who puts peas in a burrito?

He sets the plate aside and focuses.

Time to work. The seed has germinated, his head bursts with ideas and focus. Now to let them spill out onto his machine, let them power the mechanics of his 1967 Sears Chevron Typewriter. (Physically, one does not need to pound the keys. With a fresh ribbon, one only needs a solid tap to create a crisp image. A hard tap produces a ghost double image of the letter. Merely tapping the keys in a constant steady rhythm keeps the letters crisp and clean.)

Duckworth burps. His throat burns. He jogs to the bathroom and crunches a couple of Tums. He feels flush. The apartment heat is still on (mental note: call landlord). He strips down to his boxers and manages to crack the window across the desk.

It must be erudite.

It must be inevitable.

It must be shocking.

It must be moving.

It must be pithy.

It must be perfect.

It must be a masterpiece.

The manifesto.

He sits. He types:

The fFountian

Or

An hour passes.

He types:

Art Has ~~The~~ A Right To Children

by

jasper ~~O.~~ P. Dcukworth.

A red dot skims his hand. Then is gone. He stops and turns his hands over. Top and bottom. Front and back. Nothing.

Get up. Stretch.

He blinks and now he's in the kitchen holding a glass in one hand. A jug in the other. Pouring a finger of the Fountain water. Perhaps just a sip.

He settles back at the typewriter. Glass in his hand.

> *Why didn't I get the X fixed? I would have liked to use the Royal.*

He swirls the Fountain water in the glass. Holds it up to the desk lamp light. Studies it. Looking for something. A crystal rainbow swirl. Tiny grains of magic. Any sign. Nothing. Inhales its bouquet. Nothing.

The red dot again.

A sold painting, part of his mind says.

No, the other part of his mind says.

The red dot moves. Circles his chest. A tiny figure eight. Moving in the common pattern of a man holding a rifle and breathing. A laser sight. On a sniper's rifle. A sniper's red dot. They've found me, he thinks. The second thought is:

Who are they?

He will not be scared. He will ignore it.

He notes with irony that when the bullet goes through his face it will be essentially the body of his essay. And that, as they say, will do the trick.

Now wouldn't that be a hell of a final essay?!?

A final editorial. They'd have to publish a picture of it instead of his words. They'd have to use his own Chevron's font instead of the newspaper font. They'd see the 'it' as it was meant to be seen raw, unpolished. With guts.

And brains.

It would be a good death.

But until then he has a mission.

The manifesto.

My masterpiece.

He goes to the kitchen, pours more Fountain water into his glass. Now half full. Doubt:

Does it work with the written word?

Back at the typewriter. He tears out the blank paper with a satisfying zip. Rolling and snapping in a fresh sheet. The watermark centered and right side up. Surely a sign.

Do it.

Do it.

Do it.

Just a sip.

He's 50 and lifts the tall glass to his chapped lips.

The phone rings and three drops of urine stain Duckworth's undies. He picks up the phone. "Duckworth," he answers as though he is the front desk of a large company. Glass still in hand.

The red dot again.

A female voice.

Low.

Professional: "Don't drink the water."

And then—

"What the bloody hell?"

"The power in your building has gone out."

"Oh."

"Meet me at the coffee shop."

"Who is this?"

"Who is this?"

"The pink haired girl."

X-2-T

"Don't drink the water," Thalia of the pink hair says, rolling her small laser pointer between her palms. They are at a small locally owned and operated coffee shop. "It will kill you."

She's younger and Duckworth has already adopted the slightly condescending, occasionally self-effacing, slightly rude, slightly vulgar, world weary, randomly complimentary or positive observation mode. He does this alternating his attention between her and every person that walks in the door, and by flicking imaginary pieces of lint off his pants.

It will kill you.

"Don't drink the water," she says.

"Uh huh," Duckworth says, not sure her angle. Not sure he wants to know.

"May I ask you a ques—"

He taps the table in front of her. "What's that there?"

She slides over a stack of newspaper clippings and print-outs pulled from a fuzzy Sol LeWitt purse. She deals him the first story from the top. "It's a story," Thalia says. "About the Chair. We have reason to believe this Chair may have been watered," she says. "The artist Jawbone Walker was also a part time plumber. She did a job or two at the MCA."

"She was the artist who received the misawarded grant," Duckworth says.

"It was an oversight," Thalia says, curtly. Then recovers, blushing. "May I ask you a serious question?"

"Raised quite a stink as I recall," Duckworth says. "Whatever happened to that?"

Thalia blinks. "I don't know what happened to that intern."

Duckworth cannot see her remembering the scolding she received from Erik at the IAC after she erroneously mailed Jawbone the check for $75,000.

"I mean the chair."

"Stolen. I heard."

Duckworth doesn't know she was there at Highenders when Officer Archie Reno's ageism allowed him the opportunity to catch a bullet with his sinuses. But he can sense Thalia is attracted to power, figures of authority, and perhaps he will hear this story later. In bed.

"In your opinion, is it possible," Thalia says, "that this Chair could be a water masterpiece?"

"Is that your serious question?"

"No. But I would still like your thoughts."

"I think it is possible. Design-wise there is a certain history and aesthetic. After all, isn't a chair a sculpture?"

Her eyes light up. "It *is*."

"So," Duckworth says. "What is your *serious* question?"

She asks: "Would you mentor me?"

He leans back, rolling up his sleeves, exposing his fading Black Flag tattoo. Her eyes flicker with recognition.

"That's why you can't drink the water." Sad eyes. Slight pout. "We— I need you."

He checks her hands for rings, wedding, engagement, or leave-me-alone grandma jewelry. Finds none. He leans forward, places his hand near hers. Almost touching. She smells mildly of BBQ sauce and patchouli. Her hand moves slightly and touches his. Invitation accepted and microaggression averted, he takes her hand.

"You're a *seeker*," he says. "I can tell. So wise for a young woman. You're an old soul, I can tell. It's our soul age that matters, don't you—" His eye catches the top newspaper clipping. The word: "*written*" circled in the article. "What's this," he says, disengaging their hands.

"Oh," she says, blinking the spell away. "A little something about this kid, Matthew Luke, who wrote this poem. His teachers accused him of plagiarism, and they booted him from school, but they couldn't find anything online that would support the claim. I didn't read it too closely."

"The kid?"

"Always tested low. Don't get me wrong, the kid's spelling was shit, but the poem and words rang true. They faxed it over to a university English department to get their thoughts."

"They scoffed, didn't they?"

"Yes. They blamed the water."

"Privately, of course," Duckworth says, tapping his chin. Something eluding him.

"They claimed it was too emotionally complex to have come from such—"

"The Fountain isn't common knowledge."

"Yet."

"English professors. They profess nothing," Duckworth says, stalling as he searches for the source of a mental itch. "But wait a minute. The *written* word."

"You're not interested in that are you? As an art form."

Yes, Duckworth screams inside. The Play. *The Play*. But out loud he says: "No, no, I'm a critic, a connoisseur. The written word is merely a tool. For a *champion* of art."

When he read about the film critic who became a writer and director in Hollywood. Duckworth did not sleep for a month, nodding off while flipping through a thesaurus for the perfect word to add to his C minus review of the talking baby selling sandwiches it is not old enough to chew. The one his ex-maid thinks is *funny*.

"Of course." Thalia nods. "So you'll mentor me?"

The *written* word, Duckworth thinks. But he says it out loud. Clearly. He clucks his tongue dismissing his perceived faux pas.

"So, Thalia," he says. "That's a lovely name, means 'messenger of the Gods.'[36]"

"You're a wise man," she says. "I'd like to buy you a beer."

Duckworth's eyes narrow. He scans her hair. Her t-shirt. "You were at the MCA. When I was sitting on the stairs. We exchanged words. You were rather rude. I spoke of Duchamp severing the cord between art and merit and you, like most of your generation, searched for the falsehood." Of course, he doesn't mention her contriteness at the base of Tabby's apartment building. Duckworth sits back. Ogles the barista. But thinks:

Bloody Christ, the written word.

"I apologize, Mr. Duckworth."

"Hmmm." Duckworth turns to a mom and her young daughter, who have been scrutinizing brochures for Space Camp and Hula Camp.

The girl wears a curling sticker name tag: MACKENZIE. "I don't know which one to pick," she says. "Which one, mom? Hmmm? Which one?"

The mom rolls her eyes. Yawns.

Duckworth leans in. "Space Camp, Mackenzie. There's nothing of value on this earth."

The mom clucks her tongue. And the girl nods thoughtfully.

---

36. *Nope.*

"Uh," Thalia says. "I've been enlightened since then. Please mentor me."

"Hmmm." It's not enough.

"I now see the cord that exists between art and the merit of *critical* thought. I see that despite the Fountain water that that must not be severed." Her eyes water. "I apologize for wasting your time." She scoots her chair back. But does not stand. "I hope I didn't interrupt anything important."

"No, no," Duckworth says, talking into his teacup. "Just a manifesto I'm finishing."

"I'm an excellent proofreader."

"Hmmm."

"I'd love to read it sometime."

"The whole world will read it sometime." Duckworth hands her his handkerchief for her eyes. He shifts. Softens his posture. He says, "What do you study besides the newspaper?"

"Art, human behavior," she says, blowing her nose. "I'm a student."

He looks at her. Her small crow's feet.

"Grad student," she says.

He looks at her. Her openness.

She averts his gaze. Demurs.

"Apology accepted," Duckworth says, looking away.

She smiles and talks into her lap: "Going back to the newspaper clipping. The City looks like they're going to give Jawbone Walker a permanent installation for her Chair. Erase the bad PR and such. How do you feel about that?"

"She's dead and I can't very well champion her." But Duckworth doesn't say that out loud, he says this: "I think that it's a fitting tribute to this Walker chap—"

"Woman."

"Right, woman. And the world will be a richer place for it. There's always room for—" he adds small amounts of creamer one drop at a time to his hot tea— "Truth & Beauty."

Her eyes water again with emotion. Such tender emotion, he thinks.

"I agree, but isn't the truth part of the equation neutralized if it comes from mystical water? Isn't it cheating?"

Clearly, she's angling for an answer. Clearly, the experience of seeing Officer Archie Reno gunned down because of the impact of art must not be tainted by a silly notion of interlocutory mysticism. Clearly. "If we embraced that notion," Duckworth says, "then we'd have to exclude any number of great works from writers/alcohol and musicians/pick-a-drug. We'd have to remove the Liverpool boys and Woodstock. These things are our culture and great works are often a product of all these, um, factors." He pauses, seeming to grab the next thought out of the ether. "We should judge the art, not the artist."

312

She wants to nod her head, it seems. She wants to swallow it, but is leaning forward, one eyebrow slightly cocked.

Duckworth adds off-handedly: "I'd never drink the water to enhance my writing. I suppose," he laughs. "You'd say I'm a bit of a purist. Unless, of course you, count tea as *illicit*."

A smile cracks her face.

"But I think people should drink the water," he says. "They should embrace their potential."

"It kills them."

"If they are truly artists..."

"I have much to learn."

"I wouldn't drink," Duckworth says. "I need to be the shepherd."

"You will shepherd them with your manifesto?"

"Yes. They will drink," Duckworth says. "Art is sacrifice."

Lambs for his resurgent career.

"You're so smart," she says. "I agree with everything you said." She pushes a scone around on her plate. "But there are rumblings that a faction of the Art students don't agree. They're embracing purity in art. One group goes so far as to declare performance art the only art form."

Duckworth scoffs. "*Performance art?* Those children need a good spanking."

"They think it must be untainted. Free of enhancement."

Duckworth scoffs.

"It might be challenging reaching out to them," Thalia says. "I fear they're not going to embrace this manifesto you've written."

"I just started it, really." He taps his temple. "But it's all up here."

"There could be a counter revolution, right here, right now," Thalia says, her voice rising with excitement. With possibilities. With vision. "We have to rally the people. The people need someone to show them the way."

"I agree. Totally."

Deep breath. Breasts heave. "And that's why I want to be a critic."

Duckworth spills his tea.

"Mentor me. Teach me the ways of the Critic."

"Um, well. I'm quite busy. The revolution and all."

"You could use assistance."

"Perhaps."

"I could apprentice."

"Can you learn by observing?"

"I'm very observant."

"How do you feel about personal tasks?"

"I'll be your personal assistant."

"Hmm."

"I'll be right beside you."

"So we're clear," Duckworth says. "I'll be the one showing them the way." It's a half question. The lilt of his voice at the end subtle and plausibly deniable.

"Yes."

Duckworth taps his chin. "There will be late nights."

"I have insomnia."

"It's a thankless job."

"I don't need gratitude."

"There will be hate mail."

"Love it."

"You'd have to drive me. You do have a car?"

"Yes."

"You'd have to fetch tea and meals."

"Coffee? Absolutely. Or tea."

"And I'm afraid you'd have to do my dirty laundry, but you'd be there every step of the way." Duckworth looks her up and down again, this punk rock girl. "You'll be right there beside me. In victory."

"That's what I want." She takes his hands. "I like being near you."

"I'm, uh, currently— I couldn't pay you."

"I'm a trust fund baby."

"Ah."

"And a massage therapist."

"It could be dangerous."

"Art *is* dangerous."

Fade In:

"It will kill you."

On one side of the typewriter: the title page of his manifesto and a half ream of blank paper.

On the other side: the Play.

The glass of Fountain water at his elbow, doubt plagues him.

Duckworth reaches out, hesitates. Picks up the Play. Yes, another draft, another pass. He looks at the glass of Fountain water sitting next to him. This would be his masterpiece. Guaranteed. His parents would achieve immortality. The Play. *The Play.*

There is a reason Cpl. Duckworth opened that oven and rescued his mother.

It will live on.

It will be his legacy.

It will inspire.

It will outlive that fat book of movie reviews.

He stares at the glass. Fingerprinted with one perfect set of prints. A ghost hand holding it upright, steady.

He thinks of Timmy: *Dead of a hole in the heart.*

He thinks of Tabby: *Dying of brain cancer.*

Then he thinks of that woman. Jawbone. The chair. Dead. From what, he didn't know. Hooliganism?

She drank the water.

He looks at the glass. The ghost handprint of the near dead. It would be so easy.

But he wants to live.

For now.

Perhaps a little later.

After everyone drinks their potential and he has judged.

The manifesto beckons.

∞

Now hours, days, or weeks later, he's still staring at the glass of Fountain water. He's reading his Play. Just once more for inspiration. Before the backbreaking work of the manifesto. The Play, however, is brilliant, ambitious, and the main character a post modern biblical G.I. Job. It only lacks a few more dots connected and a vaguely ambiguous button for the final dénouement (something that would confuse his deceased Polish mother who would have liked to have seen the happy ending she lived. His father would have pointed out his set designer didn't know shit). And then he has to solve what, clearly, is going to amount to triple casting, what with all the indispensable Nazis.

Duckworth once again thinks, maybe just an eye dropper of that water. A drop or two. He feels his writing, his eye, his taste, his sensibility are just that far from breaking through. A couple of drops. The precursor to a storm. He will be compared to Williams, Albee, Saroyan, Inge, Ibsen.[37]

And after Duckworth's hit, after the Play, he will go to Stockholm. He will shun interviews and articles. He will take a prestigious commission and disappear. Future scholars will follow the mystery of J.P. Duckworth and his overnight success and mysterious

---

37. Duckworth fails to recall his trip to NY. While in the NY Public Library he looked up the reviews of Williams' then-debuting works. And was startled to realize this: What is now known as the golden age of Williams' work, the plays received mixed to bad reviews. The majority of the glowing reviews of masterpieces belonged to plays and playwrights now lost. Most theatre-goers don't know who Saroyan is. And he was nominated for a Pulitzer. Especially the generation coming up now. They write sitcom plays because that's all they know. Lining up to land a spot on a reality TV show hoping to become a personality celebrity and land an endorsement deal is the top goal among graduating high school seniors. I weep for the future.

disappearance. He will be the JD Salinger, the Pynchon of The Stage. He will take Thalia with him. Groom her. Watch her grow. Watch her become a butterfly. Until he dies. Where, according to his last wishes, she will bury him with no service, no viewing, in their spring garden. Fertilizer. They won't prove he drank the water. Only that he disappeared. *Habeas corpus.*

Now.

He takes a swig of the water from the Fountain.

Swishes it around in his mouth.

Holds it.

He thinks he feels a little electric jolt down his spine, his arms, his feet.

He spits the water back into the glass.

He cannot swallow the fire.

He cannot swallow the fear.

Perhaps it will be enough. He breaks out his red pen saved for revisions. He puts the Play back in the drawer. Puts the red pen away. He thrums his fingers on the desk.

And he will carry with him a litre bottle of the Fountain water and in five to seven years he will drink the water and finish his Play. Maybe even a decade from now. Maybe.

And it will be a masterpiece. Out of the range, the pool, the collective era of other pieces. Maybe.

And he will submit it to the London Playhouse, the Goodman, and The Public, under a short handwritten note: Now.

Maybe.

Meanwhile he and Thalia (whose gentle snoring from the couch behind him is sweeter than the softest lullaby) will teach that everyone has potential. They have to let them unlock it. They will start a revolution. They will lead them to water. And they will stay above it all. They will judge only the art and not the artists. It will be difficult. They will have to spread the word and no doubt there are those who will try to stop them even though everyone has a right to realize their potential. Art does have a right to children. Such an inspiration!

Maybe.

He pulls The Play back out of the drawer. He pulls the red pen back out of the drawer. Sets them next to the typewriter. The beginning of the manifesto. The glass of backwashed Fountain water.

Please, God, give me a sign.

Artist or Critic?

Maybe he will slam the glass down in anguish. Oh slumbering muse, hear my anguish.

Duckworth squints, hoping tears will come. Tears that will add legitimacy to his anguish and perhaps rouse Thalia who will come to his aid and comfort.

Artist or Critic?

Tears that a much better looking actor might conjure on the movie set of his life story.

This moment.

This is the Oscar-clip moment. With a John Williams score. Or Randy Newman. Or Danny Elfman.[38] This is the moment.

Artist or Critic?

The moment of choice in what would surely be the Best Adapted Screenplay. And he imagines what that moment might look like:

---

38. *A future Duckworth might update this fantasy moment with a Jóhann Jóhannsson, Hildur Guðnadóttir, or Zöe Keating score.*

321

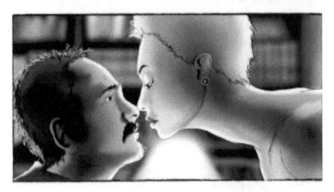

She places the letter **X**, clearly a stop sign, on his play manuscript. Duckworth knows this as he watches her movements with one eye open. His fate is decided. His muse has spoken. The camera has completed its

PUSH IN.

And now the camera holds on a classic Jonathon Demme close-up of the face of a Critic.

FADE TO BLACK

∞

Later that night, after more zesty lovemaking, Duckworth's dreams are filled with visions of death as a shepherd leads the masses to a large body of water and a baptism of slaughter.

The Coffin

The blue flame sputters, and B raises his welding goggles. Dark round mole-like lenses with a cracked brown leather strap. Goggles an aviator might wear if planes flew through the center of the earth.

GO/NO GO

He sets aside his torch and leans against his steel table. A piece of grease-smudged paper lies there, weighted down at each corner by heavy steel disks with holes drilled and tapped in the center. He looks over the sketch again. He goes back to his torch, turns a few knobs and disconnects the tank. He bear hugs it and carries it over to a stand-up dolly he's made during one of his many slow times. He loops the safety chain around it. In another corner, he undoes another safety chain and bear hugs a full tank. Carries it over to the torch and in a few seconds is back in business. Muscle memory takes care of business. It is the only way to function.

In the corner of the basement studio staring down at him is a half-finished sculpture of a twelve-foot child.

It is the commissioned piece based on the paintings of Günter Adamczyk. Günter Adamczyk has taken pictures with the Pope. He has been compared side to side to Van Gogh. In a glossy self-published book. Günter Adamczyk is a well-connected very rich and mediocre artist. A mediocre artist who is very connected and very rich and has a marketable back-story. Ten years ago, he was the owner of a chain of organic grocery stores when he was diagnosed with Shy-Drager syndrome, a degenerative nerve disease. So he rented a small place in the Caymans and turned to painting; the thing he's always wanted to do but never had the time or patience. He was a busy man and running a chain of Garden Good grocery stores is time consuming. Especially if you micro-manage as Günter Adamczyk does. He went to the Caymans to paint and to die. He painted for six months. He went swimming every day. Running every day. He bedded anything that would have him and tried every recreational drug he'd warned his sons against.

Every sunset was his last.

But it kept rising.

For eighteen months.

And finally, he went back to the States where a triumvirate of doctors said:

Ooops.

Sorry.

You're not dying. Hope we didn't inconvenience you.

Not at all, Günter Adamczyk said. He sold off his chain of Good Gardens and lived in the Caymans and painted and fucked young tourists impressed with his bohemian lifestyle.

At least that's what Günter Adamczyk's commissioned biography says.

Günter Adamczyk expects the piece to be finished today, packed up and shipped to Italy tomorrow. This is a trial run for B. If Günter Adamczyk is pleased there will be more work. If not a blacksmith in Poland where steel is much, much cheaper will find himself with work. Günter Adamczyk says he will call when he is upstairs.

GO/NO GO

But B is not working on Günter Adamczyk's commission.

B picks up a piece of rolled steel and lowers his goggles and turns on the gas. Squeezes a flint sparker and the tip ignites. He turns a dial, sharpening the flame, feeling comfort in the familiar hiss.

The flame paints the tip of the steel from red to a hot orange until it glows with a light and heat of its own. B glances at the sketch again of the coffin and sets the torch down. Picks up a hammer and lays the piece across his hundred year old anvil. He raises his arm feeling the weight of the hammer. Brings it down with a resounding clank. Sparks fly from the steel as it yields.

Clank. Shock. Sparks. His arm becomes a machine. The first machine. Clank. Shock. Sparks. Raise lower bounce. His other hand turns the steel slightly with tongs, a greater angle here, a flattening here, a curved lip there. His phone rings. Clank. Shock. Sparks. It is all eye/hand/muscle memory.

Reaching back 100 years.

Clank. Shock. Sparks. Hammer anvil metal. He could be in any time in any place in any country.

1,500 years.

His cell phone rings. Nothing exists but this. Man and metal.

2,000 years.

Clank. Shock. Sparks. A wayward time traveler could pop in and not be able to distinguish past or present or future.

2,500 years.

Clank. Shock. Sparks. B could be the first blacksmith— his phone rings— but not the last.

3,000 years.

Clank. Shock. Sparks. Clank. Shock. Sparks. Clank. Shock. Sparks. He reheats the steel. Cools it in an orange bucket of dirty water and repeats it. The water hisses like a serpent. His phone rings. He is meticulous. He is perfect. Out of respect.

3,500 years.

For his forefathers. For his craft. For the deceased.

Now.

For Harriet "Jawbone" Walker.

Emma

Burning.

She is burning.

She cranks on all the water faucets in her apartment.

Shower. Sink. Kitchen hose.

Buckets of ice. She cannot cool down. Ice packs melt instantly. She cannot put out the fire. The burning in her womb. Her breasts. Her head. Her chest.

Two butterflies on the ledge outside her window. It means something, what? She squeezes open the window. Finds the strength and steel to make a cage of her hand catches a butterfly.

Plucks a wing. Places it on her tongue. Smears the butterfly over her breasts. A smear of green viscera and iridescent powder. Wait? What? Where did you go? She catches the other one. Eats it whole.

She masturbates with each cloned cock. Duckworth's, B's, her doorman's, her maintenance man's, her boss', Officer Reno's, Timmy's.

If only she had one of Hector.

Beautiful Hector.

It is of no use.

She cannot put out the fire.

It is always burning.

Burning.

Daughter of Zeus

Thalia types her notes into her smartphone. Her notes about it all. Timmy. Jawbone. The Fountain. The water. She's interacted with Eyal, Bitha, Duckworth. A Russian's near death orgasm in the Chair. She's had a policeman's death-splatter stain her sneakers. She will write a book. Her thesis will be published. She has a special angle. This will be the book. She'll be the authority. And she thinks she knows how the water works. What it does, why it does it, and why you die.

She's written the tweet and e-blast and press release that she'll send tonight to her extensive digital database. A database filled with contacts culled from, among other sources, the IAC, the MCA, the ArtBar, and Robards' Rice Pudding Productions. Everywhere she has so "ineptly" interned. This tweet and e-blast and press release will gather the masses at the MCA. Line them up to drink the water. Because saying you have a right makes it so. And also hopefully, protesters with their sense of righteous indignation. She feels only a slight pang of guilt. It is for the greater good, after all. People have a right to choose.

And if they wait on Duckworth's manifesto they'll be sitting on their thumbs until the cows come home.

Tonight, they're going to go see a folk artist's show. She feels badly for the artist. Some Hector dude. For a moment. She knows no matter what Duckworth sees he will try to impress her with his acumen. It will make for good copy. It will contrast nicely with her review of his unpublished play he left sitting out. Actually, it isn't too bad. Has potential. But Jesus pleasus, another Holocaust piece?

Damn, won't he turn the air on in here? It's so fucking
hot.

She grabs the glass of water off desk #2 and chugs it. It's slightly warmer than room temperature. Doesn't cool her at all. Tingles. Sweat beads on her forehead. Darkens her temples.

Duckworth comes out of the shower. Natty towel wrapped around his waist. Girly slippers on his feet. He wasn't bad for a weak man. Not bad at all. She let him do most of the work. He seemed pleased. A few more days of this and she'll be done with him.

"Hello, love," he says.

"Hello, darlin," she says. Injecting a bit of honey in her morning voice.

∞

"I've been thinking," Duckworth says. "And yes, this is probably a bit premature and silly, but I've been thinking, just now in the shower, that maybe after our revolution, I could take a sabbatical. Maybe go to Sweden for a year. Work on a novel or my memoirs or something. Maybe you'd like to be my traveling companion. To flourish. To blossom." He wants to tell her that she is his muse, that she inspires him. That he is afraid he will never inspire another soul like she has inspired him. That at the end of it all, he wishes he could touch one soul and inspire them to greatness. For this he would be content. But the lighting is not right. If there was a candle or two burning. If there was just the small lamp. But now would be forced. The moment too raw, too unfocused. And then Duckworth decides that that doesn't matter. Life is now. And it is his to seize. "I'm rather taken with you, Thalia, and frankly, last night and today, my heart is—"

Then he stops. He's staring past her.

∞

She doesn't look. She knows he's looking at the Play. She must not have put it back correctly. She'll summon her little girl voice. It will be all right.

He's not looking at the Play. "Did you drink that glass of water?"

"It's a little hot in here," she says, turning to him.

Duckworth now pale. Ashen.

She feels her brow furrow. "What?" And then slacken as though someone has loosened a giant bolt in the back of her head a quarter turn. Her lip quivers and she can barely get the question out. "Was that...?"

"No," Duckworth says. "Of course not." He smiles. Mechanically. Gears shift. "Well, love, do you think you might have time this morning to go over my Play?"

"Ok."

"Give me notes, as they say."

"Ok."

He fumbles his red pen as he hands it out to her.

"Ok." She reaches out slowly for it. Eyes locked with his.

His lip quivers, his mustache dances. His eyes glass with tears and he retracts the red pen. Then he drops to his knees and wraps his arms around her thin young waist. He pulls her tight. Sincerely. "I'm a bad man," he says. "I'm sorry sorry sorry."

She feels it again.

"Oh Thalia. I love you."

The tingle.

And then she knows. She knows. She drank the water. Warmth radiates from her core. She tries to push Duckworth away, but he holds her, his face against her stomach. She can feel the wetness of his tears, the desperation of a soul in need, his arms pulling tighter, fingers clawing at her as though he is trying to burrow inside her for shelter. It turns her stomach even more. She digs her sharp fingernails into his armpits and manages to loosen his grip. He looks up at her with puppy eyes and she squirms free and rushes to the bathroom, to the toilet where she shoves two fingers down her throat.

The Inheritance

B opens the envelope from the attorney. Brown paper. A couple of fingerprint smudges. He recognizes the stain. Holds it to his nose. It's cutting oil. Tears open the side. There's a key and an address. Over in the West Loop.

∞

He finds the address. The secret hideout. His nemesis' lair.

Outside by the door, a weathered steer's skull. The jawbone missing. He turns the key and slides open the big metal door. It slides easily. Quietly. Well lubed, well maintained. A nice front office area. Modern. Clean. It reminds B of an airlock. Another key. Another door.

The shop is vast. Clean and organized, and as shabby a dresser as Jawbone was, her space is clean and efficient.

B hates order. Prefers chaos. Out of abstract pilings come ideas and suggestions. Here among all the right angles, the squared corners is order and for B a lack of possibilities.

"So," B says out loud. "This is how the other half lives."

He sees tools he's only read about. A kitchenette he can only dream about.

Jawbone's voice resonates in his head like a Christmas bell on a silent night.

Invest in yourself, B.

A twin-size bed with a feather bed and comforter. Shag white carpet underneath. There is a box of disposable booties from a hospital on the edge of the carpet next to a line of scuffed steel-toed boots, sitting at the edge like dogs on the porch with their noses pressed against a screen door.

In the screened-off kitchenette/living room area are dozens of small works of art. B adjusts his backpack. Aware of the 99 cent bottle of water poking him in the ribs. He inspects the sculptures and paintings. They are from other artists. B recognizes most of them before getting close enough to look at their signatures. Their marks. B knows most of them. He has drunk most of them under the wobbly tables of the ArtBar.

Liars.

Thieves.

Cannibals.

B knows because he is all of the above.

B notices a sculpture. One of a woman stepping out of a claw foot bathtub. The tub must be set outside as her hair is blowing sideways in an unseen breeze. The water and soap bubbles have been pushed to the edge of the tub, her pendulous breasts. B inspects more closely. It's beautiful. On impulse B lines up the woman's hair like a sextant and follows the line of sight of the woman's billowing hair.

Sure enough. There it is.

A small plate with metal soap bubbles ten feet away. Tacked in perfect position to the wall.

Brilliant. Heh.

He leans in to look at the object label:

Hector Antonio Vargas (b. 1999)
A Woman Bathing Outside, 2007
Hammered Copper, Clay, Patina
For Abuela.

Good for you, kid.

He marvels at it for several minutes. Where the woman has a touch of abstract surrealness to her, the tub is spot on scale.

Bastard. Heh.

B inspects the other works of art. All gorgeous and beautiful.

He gives each its due. Each gets a thought and inspection and a low whistle. B's work is not represented among the collection. His phone vibrates. He reaches in and turns it off without looking at the caller ID.

Next to the collection is what can only be described as a target range. The targets include: headshots of every art critic B has ever heard of, every pop artist with a television art or craft show, including Ross Robards, author of *Everyone Paints, The Picasso Within,* etc.

The titles have been altered in Jawbone's spiky script: EVERYONE FUCKS. THE PRICK WITHIN.

And finally, Robards having earned the top spot on her hit list, a dozen mirrors with the Wisconsin weekend cabins surrounded by magical ponds with happy hungry trout. B shifts his weight, uncomfortable for a moment.

All of the works have big splotches of colors, sickening neon eighties colors.

Target practice.

B scans the victims, part of him expecting to find his work among them.

But he doesn't.

The water bottle pokes his ribs.

I don't even rate.

B sets his bag down.

Invest in yourself, B. And Jawbone did. Good to see the seventy-five grand of disputed arts council money didn't go to waste.

A train rumbles by. B puts his hand on a stack of old rusty wrenches. He has a flash of inspiration. A vision.

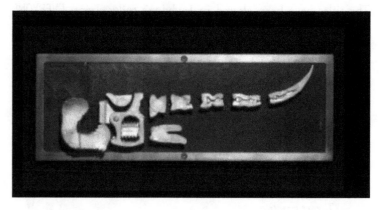

Someday...

A compressor in the building kicks on, firing like an old man's cough.

He feels a cool breeze.

It's a/c. She's got a/c.

B is not a religious man. Not in the sense that he has signed up and bought the books and tithes ten per cent. But on a weekend afternoon this space located in the Industrial Corridor with deserted parking lots and an empty harbor of old school parking meters is *quiet*. Sun streams in from high windows. Dust particles dance and swirl. The only foreign sound is his still calm breathing. A Zen wave washes over him.

It is the feeling he thought he would have walking into the Sistine Chapel. The St. Petersburg Cathedral. The Guggenheim. The Getty.

Where God should be.

Everything seems sharper, more acute. His head buzzes.

He could move in. He could never go back. He could stay here. He could let his phone die. He could let the bills pile up. He could let his landlord sort it out. He could let that crazy sexy alien file a missing persons report. He could curl upon that custom sofa and fall asleep in the peace of *being*.

He could learn a new set of tools. He could abandon his life up to now. Not assume Jawbone's life, but spin his own life, his own art into a new fresh direction. He could leave behind the Modernist style he's cultivated and honed to the point of reflex.

The point of being flat broke.

The point of rut.

The point of flatline.

The point of muscle memory.

The point of habit.

The point of being unknown.

The point of death.

The point of recycle.

Like most artists, B might have one great piece, or two. It may not be their favorite, it may not be the thing they are most proud of. It may not be the thing they slaved over. Night after endless night. In the mind's eye it is not the piece they see with their name in neon lights or whatever their individual marker for success.

But it is the piece that defines them to the world.

Defines the world's expectations.

Defines the manager's expectations.

The agents.

The publishers.

The gallery owners.

The magazines.

The executives.

The box office.

The audience.

The consumer.

And he is tired of trying to feed them. Not mad, not angry, not bitter. Just old. And tired. He was supposed to be in a different place in this, the graying autumn of his life. Physically. Artistically. Emotionally.

He could be reborn. Without the Fountain.

A thrumming sound nudges him back to this dimension. On the far side, a door. Not an exit, but to a room, perhaps. B walks through the rectangles of light on the floor from the high windows.

He's nervous.

He comes to the mystery door. Outside the door is a mat. A pair of grimy work boots, the toe leather worn to reveal the protective steel underneath shining dully. Next to it a small trash receptacle and another small box filled with disposable latex booties. He hesitates, but slips off his boots, dismayed at the permanently dirty socks he must peel off his feet. He sits and lets them air out for a minute as if there might be invisible gas emanating from them that would fill up the plastic booties like balloons and carry him into the slowly revolving blades of the industrial ceiling fans above.

His hand reaches for the door knob, the carnival reflection of his fingers becoming the size of sausages and that's when a car crashes outside the building. The impact is thunderous.

∞

B never panics and is good in a crisis, save one time while driving to his folks' house for Thanksgiving. It is a story he has never told anyone and will not be divulged here.

B, with no thought in his head to call 9-1-1 for no reason other than he does not have the thought to call 9-1-1, rushes outside to the car steeling himself for a gruesome sight. A small red car hugs the corner of the brick building with its nose. As though the tiny red beast has sneezed on impact, it drips a number of viscous alien colored fluids from its snout. Steam manages to add to the visual. B cannot see the driver. He/she/it does not stir. His bootied feet splash through the car's discharge as he comes around the side of the vehicle. He sees the white of the deployed airbag. Dripping red.

His stomach turns. His brain flips a switch. The same switch that paramedics and firemen and cops have switched on more times than not. The clinical switch. The matter-of-fact switch that permeates PBS specials on trauma in the ER.

This switch trips because B has seen men lose fingers in the shop. One lost the top half of his hand above the lifeline and another the tip of her finger on a kid's build in an incident that requires all four people who were present at said incident to adequately provide all four points of view, *Rashomon* style.

Again the switch. The switch flips because now B has a clear view of the car and its inverted V snout. Big dripping slushy chunks of raspberry and cherry colored gore and what B can only assume is blood soaked brains. It is shocking the amount splattered across the airbag and the front windshield where it drips down and pools on the dash.

He looks around. He's it. He's the only one here. He thinks of Oklahoma. Going home for Thanksgiving.

He thinks to himself, he could leave. He could go inside and wait for the whole thing to pass. But this is an industrial street. On a weekend. And he would be here for a couple of days. People would knock on doors. They would start a memorial pile of stuffed animals and plastic flowers and he would run out of food. Be forced to boil and eat the leather of his shoes.

All this in the span of a single footstep to the car.

He sees the driver. Cannot tell the sex, and not because of the red mass of human hydraulic fluid. But because the closer he looks, he sees the crazy white pancake makeup of a clown. With a red nose pushed to one side of the face giving the illusion of a Picasso.

Doctor, I'm sad.

The great clown Pagliacci is in town. Go see him.

But Doctor, I am Pagliacci.

B fights to keep the bile down. The switch is still on. He opens the door. An arm, still attached, flops from a lap to its side. Something falls from its hand. A cup dripping gore. The dead clown's arm swings momentarily before coming to rest. Because the switch is still flipped on, B reaches for the body, toward the shoulder as if to lay a reassuring hand, but then the clown speaks:

"Baise-moi."

It's female, this clown.

Now the switch is thrown to the off position and B throws up. Gut wrenching on his knees.

It's a mad world.

The clown stirs, leans its head back. Blinks its eyes. Then the clown steps tentatively out of the car. Neil Armstrong on the moon kind of slow. She wears a tuxedo top with a fancy, larger-than-life bow tie. Her pants are the comical bowl-shaped kind held up by tight suspenders with enough room for a baby shark to swim around her body.

In the blood dripping absurdity of it all, B can see the darker outline of her nipples beneath the soaked shirt.

The clown takes a step or two before collapsing against the car and sliding down its length. The waist of the pants pushed up in front of her chest like the steering wheel of a large truck. She grips the steering wheel at ten and two.

"Baise-moi."

Licks her lips. She dips her finger into the bloody mass sliding down her cheek from her matted hair. Sucks it clean. Her eyes flutter closed. B steps closer to her, crouching down when her eyes snap open. She beckons him closer as her chest heaves behind the hula-hoop pants. A red bubble forms under her red nose and pops. She again wipes a finger through the gore on the side of her face and this time smears it against B's lips.

His tongue flicks out on its own.

Oh God.

His brain cannot process, except these thoughts:

Cold.

Raspberry.

Vodka.

He looks at the cup. And it becomes clear. The gore is her forty-two ounce snow cone slushie. Splattered everywhere.

He holds out his hand.

She takes it. Squeezes. Clear lucid eyes. No potter's glaze this time. "Shine on," she says with a smirk. "You crazy diamond."

"Sail on," he says. "Silver Girl."

Body of Work

The body sits hugging its knees in the shower. Hot water steams her skin, washing away the pancake make-up and the horrifying red of a raspberry-cherry slushie losing the battle of the First Newtonian Law of Motion. Her body shudders. Whether from laughter or crying B can't tell over the sound of the shower. He scrambles a half dozen chased eggs and fries up a pack of bacon.

His cell phone dances with the vibration ring. It's probably Emma. He ignores it.

Sorry, honey. I'm nursing a clown back to health.

Her name? He picks up a gold nametag. TRUDY.

Yes. We Met Cute.

His phone buzzes with a voicemail alert.

∞

The body steps out of the shower, a towel wrapped around her torso. Her skin pink like a jumbo prawn. Her hair slicked back. The light freckles. The eyes that squint when she smiles. B makes an effort not to stare. To concentrate on flipping the bacon and now hard fried eggs.

"Smells fantastic."

"Hope you like it crispy."

"Is there any other way?"

(Heh.)

"I laid out clothes for you. Might be big."

"I think I can handle oversized clothes," she says.

(Heh.)

She dresses. Walks up to B and puts a hand on his arm. She wears Jawbone's overalls and a wife-beater t-shirt. She's found a clip of sorts and has pulled her hair back and up. A few wet tendrils frame her face. Natural. Raw. (Her wig and red nose seem to have taken the brunt of the airbag.) Her eyes shine, golden blossoms floating in an infinite sea of azure.

∞

B pours her a cup of tea, and they sit in silence. Food untouched. B steeps his tea bag. Chai spice aroma fills the area around the table. He slides the gold name tag over to her. "Trudy, I presume?"

She laughs. "No. Not Trudy."

B cocks his head, like a terrier.

"That's not my name tag."

"So what is your name?"

"Thanks for asking." She doesn't elaborate. Yet.

"Hmm." He pulls out his cell phone. Listens to his voicemail. Twice.

She looks around the place. "Nice. Like a church."

B nods. Yes. She gets it. He stares at his phone. "Well, Not Trudy," he says, absently. "What's up with the clown car? And the bootlegger slushie."

"A friend killed himself," Not Trudy says. "Coming home from a kid's party when I found his suicide note. On a napkin. And here I am. I'm looking for Jawbone Walker. They were friends. My friend and her. He wrote a letter for her."

"Oh." B pushes his tea cup away. Tells her about Jawbone. He tells her about Emma. About the Chair. The Fountain. The alley, the errant headshot. Stealing glances at his phone, he tells her everything.

"Oh, that's horrible. Dying by friendly fire." Sigh. "Was there ever a time when all we did was take care of one another? When did niceness become weakness? This fucking world." Her hand goes to her mouth. "I didn't mean to say that out loud."

350

B puts a hand on her arm. "It's okay." He taps his phone. "That was the coroner. It wasn't my friendly fire."

"Oh?"

"No. She drowned."

"Drowned?"

"Drowned."

"Oh," Not Trudy says. Her eyes spider web red, but she doesn't cry. She looks out the window. Seems to count swirling dust angels. "I'm so confused."

"How did your friend die?" B asks.

"Self-inflicted gunshot wound to the head. With my father's Colt Peacemaker. That's what we— he planned. I found this letter. Before he walked off into the woods."

"I'm sorry."

"I thought I'd saved him. And now they're both dead. I'm a dead letter carrier." Not Trudy nods to herself. "I guess I'll have to do it myself." She turns back to B. "This is a strange request, B." (She calls him B already. And why not?) "I'd like to hang around, but not be the center of attention. I'm keeping the embarrassment factor down, and you haven't cracked one joke and have only been kind. And forthcoming. It's kind of shocking, but if I could just sort of hang out and watch you work or hand you tools or something. I just wanna stay here for awhile. Before I skedaddle. Is that okay?"

"There's no rush, Not Trudy," B says. "We're both a little shaky."

She nods, grateful for a bit of *esprit de corps*. "Thank you."

He checks the time. "Upon further review, I do have to be somewhere later," B says. "But you can hang, when I go."

"Shotgun!" she calls and then laughs. Then seriously: "I do have one more silly request. For my eggs. Do you have any BBQ sauce?"

"Yes," B says. "Yes, I do."

She sips his tea, smiling gratefully. Then with a mouthful of crispy bacon: "So what's behind that door?"

∞

They stand at the mystery door in silence. The sun has slipped behind the clouds, and the headed-to-the-pub traffic noises have become more muted, as if the denizens of the neighborhood have migrated south. It is real time they are experiencing. Not half-hour TV time, not three minute pop song time. Not eight second video time. Not lost at the workbench for eight hours time.

Real time.

B looks at Not Trudy. She's perceptive enough. Smiles a hint to acknowledge that he has looked at her, and she will follow his lead. He opens the mystery door and finds himself in front of another door. This is an anteroom. The carpet, a beige sort of thing, has been stamped— well, more dusted with various boot prints as if the boot

352

were held above the carpet and tapped gently and the falling dust and dirt fell, like powdered sugar on French toast.

A few different sizes. Jawbone was not the only one who had been beyond this mystery door. It's curious.

Next to the second door is another empty shoe rack and a white cardboard box.

Not Trudy walks to it and pulls out another set of white plastic foot covers. Booties. She pulls out one pair, then two. Hands a pair to B. They slip them on, wordlessly. B opens the second door.

They are quiet and reverent as though standing in a church or mosque or synagogue or Druidic clearing. And in a number of respects it is. Off to the left is a tasteful stained glass window, probably stolen from a demolished church. Or a soon to be demolished church. Or a church now weeping for its stained glass. There are no religious figures in the stained glass, no virgin, no saints or angels awaiting the starter pistol crack of the Rapture, but instead simple flowers, simple patterns of colors residing on the left side of the spectrum.

And shine like it does on the rest of the empty room. Although the room is not entirely empty. In the center stands an altar.

Not Trudy gasps; her hand goes to her mouth like a freshly hired soap opera star. B glances around, his head jerking like a pigeon's, looking for something to say: this is a joke.

This is not a piece of art that Bellio needs to take in, needs to assimilate, needs to process, needs to ponder. This piece is family. One of his first born.

Little particles dance in the sunlight. Little angels and fairies flitting around the queen.

"My Lord," Not Trudy says. "It's beautiful."

The altar is Bellio's missing sculpture. His second thought: *She got the lighting right.* The first is: *Uh.* B looks around. He knows the piece inside out, but not its surroundings, this hidden altar. He finds the object label. A simple white cotton linen cardstock with Jawbone's spiky handwriting.

B. (b. ?)
The Standard, 2001
Scrap, Imagination, Inspiration, Hammer, Anvil
Stolen.

THE STANDARD.

I don't rate.

His previous errant thought repeats itself.

I don't rate.

Yet now...

The Standard.

"It's the most beautiful thing I've ever seen," Not Trudy says. Tears running down her face. She staggers a bit. B steadies her like a mourner at a funeral. She shakes him off gently, but with a lingering touch of reassurance. She goes to a knee and sobs. Convulsing body wracking sobs. The sounds she makes are without restraint or embarrassment. B drinks her in. Her reaction, not calculated, cloaked, or guarded. Pure and joyful. Child-like. There is no past, no future, no worry. Nothing, but the glorious present.

The dam breaks.

And Bobby Bellio also takes a knee.

Field of Gold

Three years ago:

Jawbone grunted and with a final heave the sculpture fell off the back of the heavy truck and splattered into the mud. Gulls noticed and squawked their disapproval, circling their mountains of refuse.

Hector arrived late to the heist— a job interview with the MCA coupled with Cubs traffic— right as the legs of the sculpture sank into the mud. "That is cool," Hector said, dropping the tailgate on Jawbone's little pick-up.

Jawbone hawked and spat, slipped the Teamster driver a hundred dollar bill and hugged him to the surprise of the Teamster who, though racially tolerant, was somewhat alarmed to find his left eye and nose buried, however briefly, in Jawbone's dreadlocks. The smell was decidedly sour. "I like this piece," the Teamster said. "It's amazing."

"Yip. It's the standard."

The Teamster drove his heavy truck away, escorted by a flock of squawks.

Jawbone unfurled ratchet straps. "Fuck art, Bellio," Jawbone whispered. "Drink beer."

Jerking his thumb in the direction of the departing Teamster, Hector asked, "That your boyfriend?"

"Help me load this into my truck."

"That your boyfriend?"

"Ain't got one."

"Why?"

"Because no one," she said, patting Bellio's sculpture, "is as interesting as mine enemies."

∞

Three years later:

Jawbone will design a custom BBQ smoker for Bob Bellio. The plans of which will be discovered after she is dead. In Jawbone's shop by a curious young woman after making love to B for the first time.

Burr Oak

A light rain falls on the mourners. Of course, it does. B wears a suit that embarrasses him. Too tight to button, two inches too long (when did I shrink?). He ignores the water wicking up the back and dampening his dress socks with a hole in the toe. And though there is a metaphor floating around in his head somewhere, he sticks with *my toes are cold.*

It's a small, but diverse crowd of cliques representing many facets of Harriet's life; a few ambassadors, privy and familiar with the cliques, move slowly from group to group shaking hands, eliciting a faint look of recognition and a smile. And then the inevitable small folksy joke or one-liner. This is the first time he's seeing most of them, having missed the wake— the church one, anyway. There's another at the ArtBar tonight. B tries to discern the groups. The artists are easy. Then family? Which is her father? The man he's never met, but wants to buy a beer for. Which ones were sisters? Did she have one, two, or three? Were they real or girlfriend-type sisters? Clients? A book study group?

Beth is here. Standing across from Jackie, who is holding the hand of a blonde[39]. Both wearing scarves and big sunglasses. Both stars of their own 40s movie. Posing on the backlot funeral scene from *Twilight in the Park.* Beth keeps glancing their way. Her bottom lip quivering, not holding the tears. She is not going to make it easy on them. Her whole body shakes and quivers, ready to burst. To collapse. B's instinct is to comfort her. But he doesn't.

---

39. *Gisele.*

No one comes over to B.

Do they think I killed her?

Didn't they get the call? It was walking pneumonia. That is the Official Cause of Death. She drowned. Her lungs filled with fluid. Natural Causes. But B knows it is pneumonia from the Fountain. The water. He could have stopped her and didn't. So they are right. He did kill her.

Another loner in the crowd is Higby. Jewfro mullet and all. The turned-up lapels of his bespoke jacket form a bevor, masking the lower half of his fact. Impossibly small glasses peek over, his eyes betraying nothing. Higby seems to be talking to himself. Crazy. The whole world has gone crazy.

Rain rolls into B's eyes. His sunglasses steam up. When did it get so humid? He reluctantly reaches into his pocket and pulls out his greasy, oily ball cap. With the red B. His toes grow colder.

A few people look over their shoulders at him. Whispering. A few even point in a half cocked gunfighter manner. He can't hear them, but doesn't need to.

"Is that Robert Bellio?"

"WTF?"

He pulls the cap lower, creating a cave for his face. Something to peer out of. He overhears someone say Jawbone's dad isn't present.

"Said he had to go back to the house for something."

"He ain't coming back."

"That bastard."

A thunderclap activates a number of black umbrellas, like the cue for a musical number. B has left his umbrella in the car with Not Trudy.

Finally, the hearse pulls in, backs up slowly. The bearers of the pall materialize from the crowds. One from each group. B nods to himself in approval. They take their positions as the coffin is rolled off the business end of the hearse like the conveyor belt of an art deco factory. It is the coffin B crafted. Crafted with materials earmarked for the Adamczyk commission. Materials Adamczyk does not know he has donated. B will burn that bridge when he comes to it. Now, however, steel and mahogany will carry his friend home.

The lid has been placed. People see the coffin for the first time, whole, complete. There are a few gasps. "So beautiful. Jawbone'd be proud. Wow." Low whistles. A few drunken claps. Heads nod. Scattered sobs.

"Beautiful."

"So beautiful."

B's gut contracts.

Oh no.

This is how they will remember the funeral. Not the handcrafted programs in their pockets. Not the cut flowers they meant to press or dry. Not the obituary her friend Hector wrote; stunning and humorous. B learned so much about her. She was a track and field star in high school. When it was popular, she donated her CD collection to the troops overseas. Played piano at her church in her youth. She lost an infant brother. She made little peanut butter things at Christmas. Something he might have discovered first hand. Over drinks. Over the holidays. At baseball games, because who can stay away from the ballpark? They should have used her tickets.

All this will be lost in this transient piece of art: her coffin. "So Jawbone, so perfect and fitting." He feels empty. The loss.

It stops raining as Hector looks up from his feet, his position at lead pallbearer. He acknowledges B with a nod of the chin. Hector knows the difference between a coffin and a casket. The others see the respect. They know B made the coffin. They nod as well. Visibly enough that others turn to him. There's a whispering that weaves and travels among them. B is uncomfortable with the attention. Especially now. It's the work. Always the work. Not about him. He'd rather them blame him for her death.

It stops raining because Not Trudy is behind him holding the forgotten umbrella over his head. She slips her arm through his. B lets the moment linger. This saint.

Duckworth.

B's eyes narrow. He's not sure it's Duckworth. The trademark bow tie is missing. The horseshoe of hair is shaved, his upper lip sporting a perfect cigar mustache. Duckworth's eyes and soul are hidden behind D&G (knock-off) sunglasses. His head raises in the direction of B. And stops. They lock eyes or the equivalent as both are wearing sunglasses. But they certainly have locked into each other's direction. Both expressionless— again as both are wearing sunglasses. Duckworth's are similar to big black safety glasses, the kind you wear after getting your pupils dilated or when you turn elderly and your eyes only welcome the light of a small TV or the tunnel that leads to your Savior.

B's are pharmacy clip-ons. He'd planned on getting prescription sunglasses finally, but instead used that fund for the coffin's silk and satin interior.

Duckworth strides towards B. Duckworth's hands are in his pocket and for a split second B imagines the critic pulling out a 9mm and shooting a few people. Instinctively, B steps in front of Not Trudy. But before Duckworth can close the gap—

A screeching voice: "Who's this hussy?"

The figure wears a black hooded rain jacket and mirrored sunglasses. "Who's this hussy?" It is the voice you'd imagine belonging to an evil stepgrandmother.

B glances around. What the hell?

The figure whips off its own sunglasses with a clawed hand. It's Emma. Her cloudy eyes almost invisible, retreating into her cadaverous head. It's Emma. Now an emaciated husk. A walking skeleton, her curves reduced to sagging waxy folds of loose skin. It's Emma nodding to Not Trudy saying: "Who's this hussy?"

"I'm Not Trudy. B's friend."

"'B' is it? Are you fucking her, B?"

"Emma. Shut. The. Fuck. Up."

Emma freezes for a moment, sensing an escalation she cannot possibly win, goes low. A conspiratorial whisper: "Is this the hussy you've been 'building furniture' with? Been 'finishing a project.' Look at her. She's a granola girl, she's not an artist. Christ, she has the ass of a twelve-year-old boy." Emma pats Not Trudy's ribs and backside as though frisking her.

"Excuse me," Not Trudy says.

B stiff arms Emma away from his saint. "Emma, this is not Jawbone. You know Jawbone."

"This isn't Jawbone? Then who the fuck is this, your little sister?"

"Emma, please."

Duckworth takes a giant step back. Red rover, red rover.

"I was working on a chair with Jawbone." He's lowered his voice, but the stares are starting.

"If this isn't Jawbone, who is?"

"Are you high? You met Jawbone. You took us to the fountain."

Her unfocused junkie eyes show only desperation and jealousy. Something has shifted. Gone is the goddess Little Miss Strange and in her stead a voodoo chile.

"Not here, not now. Emma, please go home."

"WHO THE FUCK IS JAWBONE? WHERE IS THIS BITCH? WHAT FUCKING CHAIR ARE YOU TALKING ABOUT? DID YOU FUCK JAWBONE? DID YOU? WHERE IS THIS BITCH?"

The gathered mourners gasp, exclaim, exhale, drop their programs.

"WHAT THE FUCK ARE YOU LOOKING AT? DO YOU KNOW THIS JAWBONE WHORE?"

"Get her out of here," someone says.

Hector comes tromping through the mud, a Godzilla mortar explosion with each step.

B grabs Emma's arm by the elbow and guides her away from the mourners.

"YOU'RE HURTING ME. You're hurting me. *Oh, B.* You're hurting me. Please, hurt me. Do you want to hit me? You can. You can hit me. I'll let you do anything. You can piss on my face, I know you're angry right now. I'll do it, I'll let you do. I'll drink it. Your girlfriend can watch. Please, B. Please. FIST ME. FIST ME."

B wisely decides there is no rational response to this. Not even a You're Crazy. You Need Help. You Are Sick. Emma has left the building.

Higby buzzes past him. B sees the blue light of a wireless piece in his ear. Not crazy. "Nice work," Higby says.

"Piss off," B says, though Higby keeps walking, oblivious.

Emma swoons a tad. "B, I think something is wrong with me," she says, coughing up iridescent powder. "Help me. Please..."

Behind them is Duckworth who cannot read a room: "I know about the chair, B. Did you make it, did she make it? Did you drink the water? Did she drink the water? That's not a bad thing, I say. I just need to verify. I just need to confirm. For the children's sake—"

Hector clamps a hand on Duckworth's elbow.

Duckworth: "Unhand me."

"Family only," Hector says.

"Unhand me. I'm not with that woman. I've never seen her before in my life."

"Artists and family only."

"Unhand me."

"Only our community."

"I'm in the community," Duckworth says. "I am a playwright."

"Pendajoles."

"Unhand me."

"I'm a playwright."

"You're a critic—"

"I'm a playwright."

"—and a hack."

"I'm an outstanding critic."

"You review beer commercials. Go—"

Emma interrupts, "Hector, I need your cock. I need it—"

B shoves his thick callused thumb roughly into Emma's mouth. Her lips clamp down and she shuts up, starts sucking.

Hector in Duckworth's ear. "You criticized my showing. My work. In front of my grandmother."[40]

Duckworth remembers this. Remembers doing it to show off in front of Thalia.[41]

"If I see you again," Hector says, "I will end you."

"I AM A PLAYWRIGHT, I—"

B turns to Duckworth. "THEN WRITE A GODDAMN PLAY."

∞

"Whole world's gone bugshit crazy," B says. The truck windows cloudy with the fog of their breath. Tired, he slumps in the passenger seat, blowing warmth into his chilled hands. His feet are cold and wet.

---

40. Hector's tattoo has since been amended. The word ART now preceded by the word FUCK. Part a memorial for his friend. Part in response to Duckworth's off the cuff remarks.

41. It's true. Duckworth used his byline to get a '+1' into Hector A.V.'s show, where he spoke loudly and clearly about a lack of form, style, and discipline and made borderline racist barrio comments. (Though he kept coming back to A Woman Bathing Outside.) Sadly, we were not on the guest list. Which is probably for the best.

Not Trudy sits in the driver's seat. "She looked sick or something."

B shrugs. "Something caught up to her." B watches Hector stomp back up the hill to the gathering. Distant tail lights heading west are the last of Emma and Duckworth who have been thrown together into a cab. "Good lord," B says, shivering. "I could use an Irish coffee." B sees Hurricane Beth walk by. He hops out of the truck. Consoles her for a moment or two. She hands him something. B reenters the truck.

"What's that?"

"Her card," B says. His stomach grumbles, empty. "She wants me to make her a coffin."

There's a knocking at the window. A graying black man in a classic suit with something under his arm. "Pardon me," he says.

B rolls down the window. "Yes, sir?"

"Is that Harry's funeral up that way?"

B nods. "Yes, sir. It is."

"Thank you, son," the man says. "Thank you." He opens his case and produces a tenor saxophone and walks quietly up to Harriet's final resting place.

Not Trudy reaches back into the jumpseat and produces a brown bag with two pulled pork sandwiches. "I added your BBQ sauce." Then says, "Oh," remembering something. She reaches again into the back seat and pulls out a large Styrofoam cup of steaming coffee. Hands it to B. "Extra cream. And two shots of Jameson."

Manna from Heaven.

"I forgot my extra socks."

B shrugs. It is all he can do to not hug her.

"By the way, I don't have the ass of a twelve-year-old," Not Trudy says. She smiles. Snaggletooth and all.

"By the by, Not Trudy, what's your real name?"

"Olive."

Olive.

They sit in silence. Somewhere up the hill a man breathes into a saxophone. Mourning and celebrating his daughter with grace notes so achingly conjured only a parent who has lost a child could truly hear. B looks at this bright beautiful creature next to him. It's raining. It's overcast and yet Olive's face glows as in full moonlight. A raindrop clings momentarily to her long eyelashes and falls, and B falls with it into a burning ring.

The Wakening

Small groups from the funeral have caravaned to the ArtBar for the postmortem. Most have parked blocks away. Construction and street cleaning. So they walk. B navigates between the groups, shoulders hunched. Hat low. Walking between the raindrops.

"That was a beautiful casket."

"How long did it take you?"

"Beautiful."

"Simply amazing."

B nods. His fingers dig into his pockets for something. Anything. His toe is still wet.

"A work of art."

"Thank you."

"Will you build a casket for me?"

Another figure at his elbow. An elbow in his ribs. It's Higby. Looking at him through nickel-sized lens. The pulsing blue light in his ear. Holding out a card. His wedding band is made from three kinds of wood. "Call me," Higby says. "I think we can do something."

The flock of mourners stops. Higby keeps going down the street. Touching his ear. Onto the next deal. Onto the next production line. The next revenue stream. The next success. The next critical acclaim. The next interview. The next magazine cover.

B tucks the card neatly into his wallet behind his Jewel card. His phone buzzes with a text message. It's from Günter Adamczyk. **YOUR FRIED.** And there it is.

Olive pulls up in B's truck. Despite the rain, she's had it washed. Detailed. Waxed.

"Where'd you go?" he says.

"Had to drop off something," she says.

"What?"

"A roll of film."

"Oh."

Suddenly the flock stops, grouses. B looks up. A sign on the ArtBar door. CLOSED. OPENING SOON UNDER NEW MANAGEMENT.

And because no one is from this 'hood and their favorite bar is not near and someone comments, "You do roll the dice with a big group descending on a neighborhood bar," they all hug and shake hands and exchange weary pleasantries and head back to distant parking spots or disperse among the buses, trains, and cabs. B watches them leave. Already checking their watches and phones. It's getting kinda late. Company picnics last longer. A familiar truck horn sounds. Olive has found rock star parking across the street. In front of the F-Hole bar. It's happy hour.

Cloud Gate

"You ready to cash in?"

B shrugs, still a little groggy from closing down the F-Hole with Olive. A night of drinking and telling Jawbone stories.

"B, that casket," Higby says, smiling, porcelain veneers visible. "Now *that* was a work of art. I have contacts, connections. CEOs. Princes in Dubai. All those—"

B thinks Higby is going to say a Middle Eastern racist locker room joke. Here between us boys. Instead he says, "Enterprising Collectors."[42]

Higby's headquarters is a loft. A massive loft. A massive loft with its own elevator. B would hate it if it wasn't so tastefully done. Exposed brick. Local art. WWII bomber nose art (similar to the paint job on Jawbone's VW, now Hector's). Real diner booths. Double booths, red with white piping. Complete with tabletop jukeboxes. Americana with a sense of humor. A required reading bookshelf filled with classics of every genre, every era. The spines cracked in multiple places. Multiple reads. And then running counter to the *feng shui* flow in an I-can't-help-it-manner: vintage 70s punk posters (are those real signatures??). And a couple of what must be choice electric and acoustic guitars hanging at the other end. Used, abused, and loved. Heh.

"Seriously?"

---

42. As opposed to the Trophy Hunters, the Connoisseurs, or the Aesthetes.

"There's a market for this kind of casket," Higby says tapping a Polaroid of the casket. When or where he took it, B has no clue.

"*Coffin*," B says, weakly.

"Pardon me?"

B clears his throat of intimidation. "Caskets have four sides, coffins six. Occasionally, eight. They're ususally cheaper." He nods to the Polaroid. "But not that one."

Higby appraises him. "Attention to detail; a Bellio hallmark." He lets the compliment hang for a moment.

"I don't know if I can mass produce," B says.

"That's the beauty. You work with the team in Indo-wherever and get the mass production down. The high end ones you'll handcraft. Hell, you can hire a team of carpenters to oversee. You just sign the caskets. It's the difference between a Fender Squire and a Fender. Ya know?"

"Oh."

Higby says, "We can keep the price point between X-Y. Mid-level to exclusive. No sense selling 25 for Z when you can sell 2 for Z^3. You see?"

"Yes. I do."

"This is going to be huge. No more underground outsider artist BS. Unless you enjoy struggling in obscurity."

"No," B says. "I've done my time."

"Hell yes," Higby says. "You've done your time."

Four gigantic TVs. Expensive. High Def. B has a small color TV. To his embarrassment, he has to watch movies in full screen to see what the hell is going on. Higby's running CNN, Fox News, Chicago's own WGN, and Comedy Central. (Look at that color!) The TVs must have inviso screens or tech camouflage as B did not see them when he first walked in.

As B's eyes are drawn to the TV screens, Higby undresses to his birthday suit, which is beyond B's level of comfort. B glances over. Higby is toned and tight and tantric. Of course he is. Higby slips into a designer track suit. Then speaks candidly about the Chair. How blown away he was by it. The cult status it's gained. The successful collaboration he had with his rival, *your rival*. "But you still put your soul into it. I could see it, B. I saw that Chair on the news and I saw you, your spirit. But your spirit co-existing with Jawbone's. How you survived that collaboration is God's own private mystery. Did you work on it at the same time?

"We did."

"Unbelievable."

Higby zips the jacket up to his neck forming a mini gorget. "That Chair—" He steps to thie wide CinemaScope window overlooking the Chicago skyline. Higby chokes up. Clears his throat. Nods to himself. "That Chair..."

B becomes an object of stillness, fearful of breaking a mood. Higby finds his voice and continues on about the Chair, his own backstory, his early career. Every anecdote looping back to the Chair. B feels himself inflating and shrinking at the same time. As Higby drones on, B wonders what the view from here is like at night. A view you don't get living on the ground floor. A new vantage point would do him good.

"B?"

"Yes?"

"You're going to get paid. Big time."

B thinks of things he could do with the money:

> *Out of debt.*
>
> *A new bandsaw.*
>
> *Drop his day job.*
>
> *Fix his mom's garage.*
>
> *Big screen high def TV.*
>
> *Travel. New Zealand. Australia.*
>
> *The Caymans.*
>
> *A new truck.*
>
> *A drawer full of fresh socks.*
>
> *A bigger TV. Anamorphic widescreen.*
>
> *Maybe one of them guitars.*

Peace.

Quiet.

A diamond ring for Olive.

"People are going to pay you for your product," Higby says.

"Product?"

"Apologies, *art*. Don't get indignant on terminology. That's the first lesson."

stant Masterpieces? WGN BREAKING: Controversy at the MCA
- Instant Masterpieces? WG BREAKING: Controversy at the MCA -

"That's fine."

"What is it?"

"It's the business. The Business of it."

Higby nods. Fingers steepled under his nose. A grin spreading underneath.

"How do you keep the—"

"Passion?"

B cringes at the word. It's a young person's word. It's a mid-life crisis word.

"Spark?" Higby offers.

"Yes."

troversy at the MCA - Hoax or Art? CNN TICKER: Chicago
Controversy at the MCA - Hoax or Art? CNN TICKER: Chicago Co

Higby takes out his Sharktooth ear piece, as if this is now all off the record. "Let me show you."

∞

"Look at these babies." Higby shows him a handful of fresh hops, honest to god hops. Large green pine cone shaped hops. "Smell them. Your friend Jawbone was right. 'Fuck Art.' This you can touch. Smell. Taste. It's fucking sexy. First batch I sold, I made in my bathtub. But now I have this." Higby leads B around a corner to three large cylindrical tanks with Jules Verne gauges and dials. Raises his arms Dr. Frankenstein style. "I. Give. You. *Beer.*"

Whoa, B thinks. "What's that?" B says pointing at a 5 gallon bucket of water with a hose dropping into it from the tanks. The water bubbles like a witches' cauldron.

"Carbon dioxide from the yeast," Higby says. "The water keeps the gas from going back in. If it does you contaminate the tank and get moldy beer. Moldy beer is no *bueno*." Higby takes a beer mug—

Where do you buy beer mugs??

—and pulls a tap (fashioned from an early B piece, long forgotten). Amber liquid flows in a fluid spiral, like a trained animal settling into place.

"Sip that."

B does. "Good."

"Right. Check this out." Higby takes him to a drafting table. Clicks on an environmentally friendly and energy efficient lamp. He shows him proofs of custom labels by local artists. The work pops.

B takes another sip of beer. "Damn good."

CNN TICKER: Controversy at Museum of Contemporary Art in Chicago - Hoax or Art? CNN TICKER: Controversy at Museum of C

"That's what I'm talking about," Higby says. "Design. Taste. Art. And up to 10% alcohol by volume. This is my passion. Come on, B, you're a Renaissance man. So what do you do to mark time besides make outsider art? What's the other thing?"

"I do a little work for—"

"Not your goddamn day job," Higby says. "What's that other other thing? The thing that gets your dick hard."

"Nothing," B says. "Work and work."

"Bullshit."

B pauses. Looks at the beers. The foam, the color. Caramel. Smoky.

"BBQ sauce."

"What?"

"I've been making my own bar-be-que sauce," B says.

"Hell yeah."

"From scratch."

"From scratch?"

"From scratch."

"Not the catsup and Worcestershire components."

"From *scratch*."

ICKER: Seekers Riot for Instant Fame.   FOX NEWS TICKER: Riot Cops Deployed. Second American slain in less than a week, officia

"No shit? Goddamn, B, you are a purist. I knew it! A fucking purist. You distributing it?"

"Still noodling with it," B says, not staring at the news ticker. Much. "I think it's close though."

"Yeah?"

"Yeah. It's good. Real good."

"I have a distributor. I'll hook you up."

"Ah, I don't know if it's that good."

"I've seen your work. I'm sure it translates to your sauce. Make me a couple of bottles. Seriously."

"Nah."

"I'll shop it around. Get you on the shelves at Garden Good."

"Nah."

"Why not? Take a leap."

B takes another sip of beer. It lifts him above the drab mourning of this cloudy day. So fucking good. He starts to shrug his shoulders. Say nah, again. But realizes this is only out of habit. Olive would have something to say about that. And she'd be right, so B says, "Why not?"

"Yes," Higby says, with a fist pump. "The world was built on 'why not' and 'hell yeah.' Let's make a batch. What do you need?"

"Now?"

"You got something else going on?" Higby picks up a pencil.

B's world floods with colors and possibilities. He starts to rattle off a list of ingredients. They're listed in his little notebook. A half dozen versions and variations. Chicken scratch marks here and there with each batch correction. He lets himself project into the future, letting the present springboard him. He sees the bottles. The labels. Higby's seal of approval. Standing in the aisle. Waiting, maybe with Olive, her belly swollen with child, for someone to buy a bottle. To strike up a conversation. Or even better yet overhear one. *No, no, this Smoky B is the best BBQ sauce.* It pleases him.

He holds his hand out to Higby to seal the deal.

But Higby is staring at one of the glorious high def TVs. Staring at the ticker.

Chair or Cheat? WGN BREAKING: Crowds gather at MCA. Line forms for fountain water. Chair or Cheat? WGN BREAKING: Crowd

He takes in all four screens in a blink. His brain processing quantum calculations. The Fountain. The accusations. The chair. The water. The cheating water.

"Is it true?" Higby says, ignoring B's outstretched hand. Ignoring it as it slowly deflates. Putting the Sharktooth earpiece back in. Official now. "Is it true?"

CNN TICKER: Flash mob at the MCA: Seekers or Destroyers? CNN TICKER: Flash mob at the MCA: Seekers or Destroyers? CNN TIC

"Is the casket a cheat, too?" Higby asks.

"No, Rich—"

"I think we're done here."

"Higby— *Richard*, I didn't. She took a drink; we needed the chair to finish for her commission. I never drank the water. I didn't. I never even took communion as a kid. I'm all me. All my work, it's only me. What I do," B says, pointing to the coffin on TV, "is what I am. Please, this thing you're offering me. It's the break I need. I can't keep doing it like I have been." B is surprised at the desperation in his voice. "The next ten years can't be like the last ten. They can't. Please, Richard. Don't nix the deal. Please..."

Higby stares at the TV.

B tries to read his face. His body language. Any nod, or shake. A shifting of weight on his feet. Something. Anything.

And there it is. A small twitch of a smile.

B exhales.

And Higby crosses his arm, turns to B. "But you knew she drank the water, Bellio. *You knew.*"

The gray of B's life seeps back in. The slow creeping cancer of falling short.

ficer Archibald Reno killed by Russian Mobster. FOX NEWS TICKER: Art linked to Officer's Death. FOX NEWS TICKER: Officer

B shuffles past the TV images of Officer Archie Reno leaving the morgue feet first. The parade of CPD decked out in Class A dress uniforms. White gloved salutes. He turns to Higby to beg, swallowing that final bitter pill of pride. *"Please."*

"I hoped for more from you, B. And maybe you're cool. Maybe it's all bullshit," Higby says. "But the optics are no *bueno.*"

Ding.

The loft's elevator doors slide open.

Going down.

The Queue & The Question

A man[43] on the TV smiles and laughs at his colleagues' joke. And without a blink launches into a story. *Art or Death. Details at nine.*

Robards sets his watch alarm.

∞

Nine.

The smiling man in a shiny suit staring at a teleprompter and wearing an earpiece tells the General Public about the Fountain. The Fountain on the third floor of the MCA. The magical, miracle Fountain. He reads the short punchy sentences scrolling in front of him, this man in a shiny suit that he does not own. Every sentence slanted to elicit a grimace, a shake of the head, a tear, or a laugh. And, per format, the serial killer VO: What You Don't Know Could Kill You. Which, finally, seems to be the case.

CUT TO:

A reporter named Belle Day (as the crawl at the bottom of the screen proclaims), who looks like she should still be in college, talks to a man named Jasper P. Duckworth. He is somewhat familiar. But something is different. It takes Robards a moment to realize it is because he is all in black (like those Gook NVA that took his legs in that ambush), and has lost that wonderful plaid bow tie. With his haircut he looks like a new recruit in the Corps. Or a skinhead. With a giant mustache.

---

43. *Larry. On loan from the* Morning Show.

Duckworth talks impassionedly. "Art has the right to Children. People have a right to art."

"Not just any art," Belle Day says, "but a masterpiece."

"Yes," Duckworth says, "how can that be destructive?"

"It's my understanding that the creation of a masterpiece will cause the artist to die within a short period of time."

"People have the right to choose."

"But you die." She has trouble with weighty issues.

"People have a right to their own bodies. As a woman, don't you agree?"

"Well, yeah, I guess," Belle Day says, and this is why she is still a weekend reporter. (Though she will blame her fumbling of this ball on the recent slaying of her ex-husband (Officer Archie Reno, CPD), the folks in the newsroom and Master Control will wonder how long her spectacular tits will continue to keep her on the air.) She pauses for a moment touches her ear with a trademark pink-mittened hand (rumored to be hiding a skin disease or ridiculously stubby fingers or Man Hands) where there appears to be a plug and wire running from it (her ear, not her mitten). "But who controls the water? Is it the State, the City?"

"The MCA is a non-profit corporation so—"

"But the source of the water, the City. Our wonderful Lake—" she gestures to the south then correctly east, "Lake Michigan." She gives it a beat and then to Duckworth: "Are you prepared to take on City Hall?"

Duckworth takes the microphone gently from her hand.

"People have a right to art.

"People have a right to choose.

"Choose Art."

CUT TO:

Belle Day gestures with her pink mittened hand to the line of people outside the MCA. They stand two and three deep deep in conversation with their companions. Most have water bottles, an Igloos, a few canteens. CamelBak packs. One man, a flask. From which he sips. Belle Day walks over to the people seemingly at random and asks them the Question, ready to give a camera-friendly reaction. (Fun!)

"Oh, I don't know," a woman says, clutching a toy poodle that despite being colorblind is offended by Belle Day's pink mittens.

"I want to write the world's best rock anthem." (Devil horns.)

"I want to— I don't know. My grandma used to quilt." (Aww.)

"Epic poem." (Hmm.)

"Gnarliest sick trick." (Skateboard lingo, Belle Day explains to her audience.)

383

"A book."

"A sermon. To bring people to Christ so they may be free." (Neutral smile.)

"A sermon. To bring people to Satan so they may be free." (Uneasy smile.)

"A stand-up routine."

"A sculpture."

"A rockabilly song."

"A political cartoon."

"An Oscar-winning performance."

"A birdhouse," says a little girl. "The best birdhouse ever." (Awwww.)

"The most pimped out ride. Then they can bury me in it. Fuck yeah." (Earthy language alert!)

"A love letter to my ex-wife. Move that bitch to tears." (Goodness, apologies.)

"A scrapbook for my unborn child." (Awww.)

"Conduct an upcoming performance with the symphony." (Wow.)

"Cable access show. I can do a whole season, right?" (I don't know.)

"Create an environmental detoxification capsule the size of a Tylenol caplet that could be dropped into any body of water, anywhere and restore the health of the ecosystem by decomposing the toxic sludge by-products of humankind's convenient lifestyle." (She nods, lost.)

"The best pick-up line ever." (Uh huh.)

"Sex tape." (Eww.)

"The ability to walk through walls." (Okaaaaay.)

"A World Series of Poker Championship bracelet winning hand." (You're all in!)

"1500+ SATs." (Hello, Ivy League.)

"A killer app. To make the world a better place." (Nice!)

"I don't know. I guess I'll wait to be inspired." (Patience is a virtue.)

"A perfect golf swing." (Fore!)

"Salsa. The dance not the dip." (I love salsa!)

"A perfect bowling game, dude. 300. I'd be so happy I'd die." (That's a lot of turkeys!)

"I don't know." (So many possibilities, right?)

"Cosmic sex." (She giggles.)

"What is up with your pink mittens?" (She moves on.)

"Negotiate a deal to bring peace to the Middle East. (Ambitious!)

"Why isn't the line moving?" (Touches her pink mitten to her ear.)

"I'm hungry." (Thank you.)

"I'm tired. We've been in line for, like, forty minutes. Come on." (Get out, the voice says.)

"I just saw the line and fell in." (Back to you, Larry.) [44]

∞

Now, Robards thinks. They don't even know what they're in line for. He unplugs his TV. But they want it *now.* No training, not even basic training. No patience, no skill. No demons. No exorcism. No injection of the self. No one wants to use the brush to ease the pain. No one wants to paint the world as they see it. No one wants to be transformed. No one wants to nurture. To water, fertilize, give sunshine.

They want their names in boldface. They want recognition. They want immortality. All those people. Standing. Standing in line on their own goddamn two legs.

Wanting.

Now.

Now.

They only want to Just Add Water.

---

44. *After the events of the week, Belle Day makes the talk show rounds, signs a book deal, launches a custom mitten line, fills in on the* Morning Show *before getting her own daytime talk show. It lasts thirteen seasons garnering a local Emmy and a Peabody. Bookends for her co-authored best-selling inspirational self-help books. (Sapieja Shop handles all her PR.)*

Seven years in the Hanoi Hilton.

Seven years of patience. Of torture. Of rice and water and dysentery and the madness of living in his head, watching his legs rot.

Just add water.

Ross Robards pulls out a tattered business card with a government seal. It is a chit for a life debt.

What do you call a guy with no arms and no legs who shits in a bag?

Makes a call. A woman with a whiskey voice answers. "Governor Cooper Armstrong's office."

"Put me through."

"May I ask who's calling?"

"Tell him—"

He unsheathes his hunting knife. His ghost legs itch. Draws it flat across his skull severing the ponytail. It falls to the floor. His scalp tingles with the freedom.

"Sir, are you there?"

Tell the Governor: "The Rooster's crowing."

∞

B squints, retying his robe. But it's not his eyes. Neither he nor Olive could figure out the new flatscreen TV Jawbone still had not unboxed. Part of her spending spree. B has brought his small TV from his shop. The static on the tube is like looking into a strobing snow blower. Standing in the snow blower is Ross Robards, droning on about the artist in each of us and that it only takes imagination and practice.

Mechanicus

Muscle Memory

Repetition

Machine

This is not a rerun of one of his shows. This is live. This is happening. His hair is missing. He looks haggard, thin. But something has him riled up, a dark passion rendering him almost unrecognizable.

Suddenly, Ross Robards stops talking. He always talks.

B thinks the audio has dropped out.

Robards finally speaks: "Fellow artists. There's something going on in the art world, in our world now as we speak, and it's not for me to judge. So I let it pass. And I stood here in my comfort zone in front of that camera. And I tried to pretend everything is okay. That it will sort itself out."

B leans forward, turns up the volume as his stomach turns sour. Because he knows. He knows what this is about.

388

Robards stands in front of Soldier Field, dressed in his old Marine Corps field jacket. "But it will not. This is a fraud, a sham. I've seen this before. The government intervention— the Police Action and cost of life. And I will not stand for it."

There is a tiny church mouse sneeze behind B. It's Olive. "I found this. Plans for a custom BBQ smoker." She reties her robe, a rolled tube of paper under her arm.

On the TV, a lightning fast slideshow of art pieces.

"It's beautifully designed," Olive says. Unrolling them.

Each one a sham. And others suspected.

Tabby's *Migration.*

"Jawbone must have done these," Olive says, smoothing out the paper.

The Chair.

The Coffin.

"Your initial is on it," Olive says, tracing the B. "It must have been a surprise for your—"

B shushes her, just as Robards takes a deep breath.

"THIS IS A CALL TO ARMS."

Olive lets the plans roll up on their own, now fixated on the TV.

"THIS IS A CALL TO ARMS."

"Duckworth has led the masses to the Fountain," B says. "Robards is opposing."

She slips a hand under B's robe onto his strong tense shoulder. "What does this mean?"

B: "War."

Olive: "I'm tired of war."

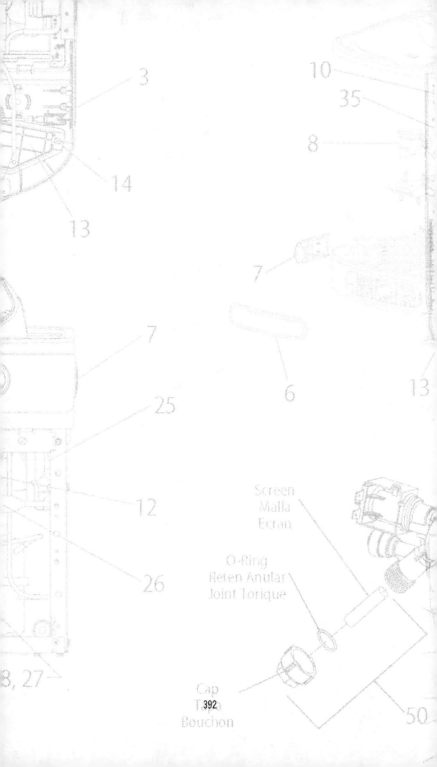

3

10

35

8

14

13

7

7

6

13

25

12

26

Screen
Malla
Ecran

O-Ring
Reten Anular
Joint Torique

8, 27

Cap
Tapa
Bouchon

392

50

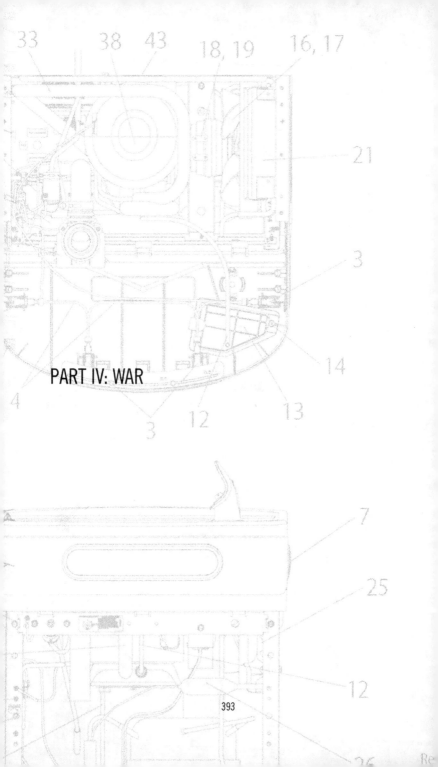

PART IV: WAR

393

Chaos

No one is sure who opened fire at the MCA. Or why. Maybe it was a garbled communication, maybe it was something said or done to professionally trained part-time warriors who out of uniform would have looked like couch potato dads, still loving their could-have-been-glory-days decked out in the officially licensed jerseys of athletes living their glory days.

And yes, we can argue that possibly there are artists among these soldiers. Sketch, tattoo. Maybe a sculptor or a photographer. Maybe even a woodworker. And maybe they had reasons for joining the military. An older brother, family tradition, honorable men doing their duty for love of country or for a government-paid education. Or maybe they were psychopaths, criminals. But right now, as with most mass gatherings involving the government and citizens, there are three groups:

Those with guns.

Those with shovels.

Those taking notes.

∞

Or maybe it was a firecracker.

Or perhaps someone in a black t-shirt raised a gun or a gun-like object. Maybe it was a paintball gun, though most of the Guard know the difference, or maybe it was someone cloaked in the digital camouflage of a forest and decided he didn't like the looks of someone else. Or maybe it was someone we know. Someone whose work was not finished.

Or maybe it was Governor Armstrong, who owed a life debt to Ross Robards.

∞

Earlier.

Another group forms. Wearing black t-shirts. With the white letter "I" slightly off center. If you're close enough you can see that the t-shirts say BITHA. But that the B THA have been painted over or colored in with drying Sharpies, leaving the "I" visible from yards away.

∞

As he arrives at the MCA from a quiet Soldier Field (a seemingly poetic backdrop for his cause, but clearly one lost on his viewers and supporters), Ross Robards realizes he should not have cut his ponytail. Without it and his "blue" jeans all tucked safely away with the wardrobe boy, he has rendered himself virtually invisible. Only his different gait would give him away as *the* Ross Robards of *Yes, You Can*. Hey man, he's got bionic legs. Yes, you do. But now this multi-millionaire king of the PBS empire is a civilian and he's not carrying a gun. So that makes him little people. Subject to elbows and jostling and jockeying for positions and sight lines.

He sees that reporter Belle Day, dragging on a cigarette between live segments. She's shorter than you'd expect (about Mia's height), especially in front of her tall cameraman. Ross Robards is comfortable in front of the camera. He should go to the camera and tell the truth. Speak the truth. Plainly. And apocalyptically.

∞

B realizes that Olive is no longer behind him. She's wearing a black Ramones t-shirt she conjured from who knows where. If she's here, she's blending in with the Bitha crowd at Seneca Park. He thought he'd be able to come here to stop something, to have a say. But like everywhere else, B is blending in. A part of the crowd, unnoticed, unacknowledged. Another tree in the sea. Another wave in the forest. B wonders if he should remove the battery from his flip phone. Remove all the names so they don't fall into the wrong hands. This is the thinking that a rally with armed troops always spurs.

He wonders vaguely if he is shot which picture they'll use of him on the news. A grainy snapshot, something with a beverage in his hand. A gallery opening. That stupid b/w photo for that PR thing he didn't have the money to pay off. The photographer still holding onto the negatives. His only copy with the words PROOF watermarked across it.

Proof he was alive.

Proof he wasn't anyone you knew.

Proof he wasn't anyone you'd remember.

Proof he never made it.

Proof he was only newsworthy in death.

He sees now that no matter what he says, he will not be heard. It's the younger generation. Their ideals, their risk, their willingness to stand up to oppression and bullshit. Shielded with naiveté blossoming with blood. Every generation, it's the young leading the charge. Into peace, into war, into change. These idealists have no future. But there is no future without these idealists.

"Hey, it's him." Fingers pointing at him. Him. B. The him to the her. Jawbone. The Chair. But these are only the protesters to the protesters. The hecklers. A minority group that seems unorganized and haphazard at best, like sprinkles thrown on a cupcake from across the room.

That fucking chair is going to kill me.

It's at that moment B is hit with a pang in his left side. It reaches up across his arm and back to his chest. And then up his neck and explodes.

∞

But where would he stand, where's his mark? There's no one with cue cards. Duckworth's now talking to Belle Day. But halfway there, Ross Robards realizes he needs to speak to the crowd and the only way to do that is to get a bullhorn, otherwise the TV audience will see he has no support and thus and so they will stay on their couches. Perhaps texting in a vote about the newscast. But Robards did not bring a bullhorn and the only one in use right now is being wielded by a pink-haired woman wearing a tight white t-shirt that says MUSE.

From a small makeshift rent-a-stage, she's taking charge, waving a bullhorn and a bottle of water. "DRINK DRINK DRINK."

∞

In the front row, a small group of baseball wearing beer-bellied doughy twenty-somethings are yelling: "TITS TITS TITS."

If paintball guns had laser sights these yo-yos would be lit up like Christmas trees.

∞

Vendors wearing MCA t-shirts and pictures of a Bubble Man leaning over the Fountain hawk bottles of "fountain" water. The labels being soaked and peeling off as they come out of plastic ice chests. "No waitin' in line. The real dealio. Come on, Picassos."

∞

Heartache. Not a heart attack. But the wave is sudden, explosive and nearly takes him off his feet. B suddenly misses his friend Jawbone. Feels her hand in his.

My ride is here.

He misses her.

He misses his friend.

Love...

And her final blood-popping word lost for eternity.

They should be standing together on the sidelines here with popcorn and Old Style. Mocking the extremists on both sides. Doing the only thing they've ever done and what they should only do, our lost loveable assholes.

Shut up and drive.

A hand on his shoulder.

It's going to be okay, B.

It's Jawbone's voice.

Go make things.

The hand is now gone, but B sees her. Out of the corner of his eye. He pushes past someone and sees that it's only a student with longer dreads and fifteen years younger. With a pierced lip. Smoking a joint. Still he walks up to her and wraps his arms around her. She senses his vibe. And hugs back. It calms him. This one last hug from a surrogate. The spirit speaks. "Peace be with you, brother," the student says, letting out a medical grade cloud of smoke.

He can't wait to tell Olive. To tell her he saw his friend, if only for a moment. To tell her he loves her.

I love Olive.

He turns away from the heart of the crowd.

This is bullshit.

He doesn't need this chaos. He's going to find Olive. He's going to take them home. Make love. Make art. Let these young idealists, knuckleheads, and weekend warriors sort it out. This, B thinks, is fairly sure this is what he should do.

"That was Robert Bellio," the student says, to no one and everyone. "He's got mad skills."

∞

Ross Robards rushes to Thalia with her bullhorn; he knows he can take the steps two at a time. Without his ponytail he feels lighter (and with the loss of Mia, he's already lost nineteen pounds), he's back in Basic at Camp Pendleton. All these young men and women. Standing in line. All those young faces he couldn't save. Nothing left of them now, but their names on a black wall of polished marble. He can save *these* young faces. No one should have to do this. No one should have to sacrifice themselves for art or country or anything else ever again. You only need a work ethic: Patience. Practice. And meditation.

∞

Another bullhorn squawks, this one with a Russian accent. The only man to ever have sat in the Chair is speaking. B stops in his tracks. The only man to know what it was like to sit in Jawbone's chair, B's chair, is only thirty yards away. The scent of gasoline excites his nose.

∞

Duckworth takes the stage. Takes the bullhorn from Thalia. "Fellow humans, we can all be artists, we can all create something of substance, of value, we can all be the children of art."

∞

B sees the wizard. The wonderful, wonderful wizard. B has to know what it felt like to sit in that Chair, to know what the Fountain is capable of. He must do this before he leaves the park, the City with Olive. Before his new life. He cannot leave this business unfinished. He cannot disappoint his dad. He shoulders past a number of people.

Murmurs mix with chants and shouts and become an audio menagerie of the Chair. The Chair. *The Chair is pure. The Chair is life. Long live the Chair.* And one voice leads them.

The Russian spins in a glowing robe indeed with wizard sleeves and talismans. The Chair is a conduit for life—"

"The Chair was watered," someone shouts.

"So be it," the Russian says. "Is not God in the water, in the air we breathe, in the earth on which we stand?"

"We're on concrete, you commie."

"Give that soul a drink of water."

"How do you know about the Chair?"

"Because I sat in it. I am Vladislav Vladislavovich Glinski!"

The crowd oohs and ahhs.

B's stomach flips. It's him.

Someone shouts, "COPKILLER!"[45]

Others make a peace sign and shout, "V, V, V, V!" They chant his initial. They see him. They hear him. They know him.

"God is in the water," Vlad says. "God is in the water."

Someone throws something at him. It hits him square, but it is a tapeball and thus falls harmlessly. "Get off the stage, old man."

Vlad's eyes light up. "Without water," he says, "without God. There is only death."

And with that, Vlad picks up a can of gasoline he has tucked between his feet, hidden by his robe. Douses himself. The gas stings, invading the bullet hole wound in his shoulder from Archie Reno's fellow officer.

The crowd oohs and ahhs. This time with a much more genuine concern and interest.

B grabs a few water bottles from a vendor.

Vlad strikes a long wooden match produced from one of his sleeves, and Vlad lights himself on fire.

The crowd oohs and ahhs, then screams with genuine horror. Holy shit. This is just like a movie. Phones record.

---

45. Freed on bail. A substantial bond, but freed nonetheless. The Judge will not seek reelection, content to have his family returned intact.

B swims through a sea of them to get to Vlad. The burning man. The sea is rough, and B swims against the tide. The changing tide of public opinion. Belle Day and her cameraman go live with a front row seat. And now he smells bad BBQ. Burnt Russian. B fights his way to the cleared-by-fire circle around Vlad. He douses the still standing wizard with water. It is not enough. The hiss and steam from Vlad's flesh exists outside of everyone's experience, but B has flipped that switch and tackles him. Rolling the flames out. Patting them out. Others now join in emptying water bottles on the duo. B and Vlad roll to a stop. Vlad's blackened robes plastered around B like giant bat wings. Vlad smiles. He smiles because his flesh has pulled tight and curled and burned and dripped away from his mouth.

"I made the chair," B says to the hole where Vlad's ear used to be. "I made the Chair."

Vlad's eyes blink, at least the one still with a lid. He brushes B's hair with a clawed hand, the tender loving touch of Grendel's mother.

"What should I do?

"What should I do?"

People of authority and training now reach out to B. To disentangle the two from their drenched and blackened embrace.

"What should I do?"

Vlad pulls B tighter. It is a death grip. Vlad's mouth near his ear. The sweet smell of charred flesh fills B's nose. Mouth. Lungs. Vlad whispers: *Pryzhok.*

∞

Someone screams. Then the crowd. A ripple of backpedaling widens a circle. The Russian is on fire. Black smoke chases after an escaped helium balloon animal version of *Migration*.

A bullhorn cannot compete with a fire. And Duckworth sees that the Guard will be moving in. He spots B staggering away from the downed Russian. B's cheek darkened with the ashes of human flesh.

Duckworth signals to the mountain. *Take him.*

∞

The shadow of a mountain engulfs B, and he feels himself pulled off his feet. Light as a bird, light as a feather from a tissue bird on a wire.

∞

Seekers.

Yes, their time has come, these greedy young ignorant gods and goddesses. Remember the white letter "I"? Remember if you're close enough you can see that the t-shirts say BITHA. Remember that the B THAs have been painted over or colored in with drying Sharpies, leaving only a glowing white "I." And realize that these Seekers might as well have painted targets on their chests. This is where symbolism loses out to marksmanship.

Little puffs of smoke will soon appear as though magic tricks are spontaneously happening in a crowd of digital camouflage. Spontaneously happening out of the barrels of oiled guns. Magic tricks happening as fast as you can shuffle a deck of cards. And it starts with a single shot.

∞

Upon a pale horse. Duckworth sees him first. A stranger in filthy clothes, ragged with dirt, leaves, twigs. The horse, though young, looks ridden past exhaustion, eyes white and wild, like their rider. A disintegrating duster flaps about his knees, an ashen shroud. It is as if a cowboy and his steed have been crafted out of gray ash and given the breath of life and dropped into a diorama of green army men.

Duckworth sees the man come a-riding; can nobody else see him or are they so in the throes of this Götterdämmerung that all is lost in a vibrating buzz of chaos? His heart is already jacked with adrenaline and his heady giddy with anti-establishment authority, but this vision propels his spirit back on a line to Tabby's studio, back to the Be An Artist˝ exhibit, to her cracked and crushed sculpture of his faithful companion, back to the moment of Revelation.

It can't be.

And now the rider slows his horse for a moment, a nostril snorting hesitation, and the rider's gray arm reaches out and seems to pluck from the crowd a lithe woman in a black Ramones t-shirt and a brightly colored backpack who suddenly and gracefully, like a gymnast, is airborne and landing lightly behind the rider on his gray steed, a steed now being spurred on, charging towards Duckworth.

Duckworth does not see Ross Robards rush the stage. Neither does the weekend warrior who has drawn a bead on Duckworth, who also doesn't see the two dozen paintball guns trained on them from across the park. Because not all art students (crafty and cunning, also) are ignorant about guerilla warfare tactics.

The horse's hooves grow larger as it approaches, faster and faster, the metallic clip-clopping rhythm, rhythm Duckworth has tried to reproduce unsuccessfully in both the bedroom and at the typewriter. And the great beast does not slow, and Duckworth can only raise the bullhorn to his lips, to trumpet the return of the king.

"OH WAYLON!"

And now the beast is upon him.

∞

And Duckworth certainly doesn't see the weekend warrior mutter two words: "Fuck art." He fires the first shot.

The rubber bullet strikes Duckworth's forehead, and he now falls off the crude stage, falling in mid-air as though he is a thousand feet above the earth. A stage the horse and its rider leap over with no difficulty, with no difficulty too over the falling Duckworth, and horse and rider and passenger continue on out of Duckworth's sight behind the MCA and towards the lake of decaying Asian carp.

Duckworth falls still.

Before he hits the ground, Seneca Park and the neighboring MCA Plaza become a free-fire zone. War.

The Fountain

"Haiku. Haiku. Haiku." Someone in a galaxy far far away is saying this: "Haiku. Haiku."

Something pops. It's B's jaw and his ears ring clear.

"Hey you. Hey you. Hey you," someone next to him says.

[Clank]

B lifts his head. It throbs and the blood sloshes around in his belfry, and the bats screech the early alarm. B cannot feel his hands. They are tied behind him. A miscast half-hitch, our late friend and Webelos, Timmy would have called: KNOT SO MUCH! B's numb ass throbs. He is tied to an Eames chair. From the furniture wing of the MCA.

"Hey you. Hey you."

B turns his head to Ross Robards. Ross Robards also occupies an Eames chair. This one a nice little cheetah print number. "Hey you," Ross Robards says.

"I heard you the first time, Ross Robards," B croaks. A silhouette of vultures shade and wipe his vision. They're waiting for him to die, to muck around inside his intestines. B squints at the harsh lighting and recognizes *Migration*. His head implodes to white with the second rotation, and B lowers his eyes to prevent what is sure to be the first of many migraines. Far off he hears a clanking. He doesn't need to strain to know it is the Fountain behind him. He can even envision the yellow UNDER CONSTRUCTION tape marking it off like a crime scene, the fornicating chalk outlines of Emma and Hector long since washed away.

The vultures of *Migration* circle again.

[Clank]

Ross Robards takes a deep breath. A calm controlling Zen breath. The air smells like stale tunnel air. It smells like a half a world away. Like three generations of music ago. Like the hair of a girl child named Mia. Like his old shop with the crumbling brick and the two hearts forever with their backs to the sun and the gift of an intern— "Robert Bellio," Ross Robards says.

B turns to Ross Robards. Squinting through the gobo of *Migration*.

"Robert B. Bellio," he says. "You were the one. The one who left me that mirror. Of the waterfall."

B grunts. (Yes. No. Maybe.)

"I owe you everything."

B grunts. (Hope you enjoyed it.)

Ross Robards clears his throat.

"Sorry about the mall," B says. "Heh."

"What?"

"The mall. Heh." It's a nervous laughter. "Heh. Heh. Heh."

"That was you. The sniper. And that woman. They hurt like a sumbitch. Those paintballs."

B grunts. (I apologize. I lost my head.)

Ross Robards nods. "The Chair, right? That friend of yours. She made the Chair."

B grunts. (We both did. Kinda.)

"That fellow what set himself on fire, you attacked him, too."

B looks, half his face in the shadow of *Migration*. "I tried to stop him," B says. "I had to know."

"Know what?"

"What to do."

"Did he tell you?"

B grunts. (Yes. No. It was in Russian.)

Footsteps down the hall.

B grunts. (I'm sorry about mucking up your TV special.) He stares off into the distance. Into the past. Into space.

[Clank]

Ross Robards knows that look. He knows Jawbone died in that alley. His driver called him on his new cell phone and told him. He hoped it was Mia calling. To check on him. But she has moved on. A survivor. Like himself. Like B here. Ross Robards knows the apocalyptic supernova of guilt and repression behind B's look. He wants to hug B. Hold him to his chest and tell him you are not alone, soldier.

[Clank]

The supernova dims to hospital waiting room brightness, and B's eyes focus. They focus on a table. A table you can buy for $20 at the hardware store. A table that would collapse were you to give one set of legs a swift kick. Then he sees what is on top of the table. "Futh," B says. His mouth suddenly so dry he cannot get his tongue off the roof of his mouth to utter: fuck.

Like a Kiddieland version of a Nazi torture chamber, the table presents several instruments designed to summon pain, religious conversion, and cries to mother. B's heart double pumps, and a jolt runs from his belly to his groin and back.

"Uhnah," B says.

[Clank]

Ross Robards' military instincts kick in. B's eyes go wide, and Ross Robards knows B knows the situation is FUBAR, beyond the obvious being tied to postmodern chairs sense. But he cannot make sense of what B sees. The table they are seated only a few feet from is laden with organized piles: watercolors, Crayola® crayons, Lincoln

411

Logs®, LEGO®, Tinkertoy®, glue, wire, scissors, Silly Putty®, a sketch pad and pen.

And a glass of water.

[Clank]

A big mountain of a man (as the witnesses will describe him) walks in. "Hi. I'm Big Tim."

Ross Robards looks from B to Big Tim. B hasn't looked up, still fixated on the glass of water. Ross Robards would like to use his cult of personality here on Big Tim. Big Tim looks like the kind that would respond to folksy good old boy charm. Except Ross Robards is smart enough to realize that B knows more about this particular situation and, thus, Ross Robards will keep his mouth shut until he knows what the shot is. Five years in the Hanoi Hilton will teach a man patience. Except Ross Robards is plum out of patience. "What the fuck is going on, Big Tim?"

"Wow, you look different without that ponytail."

"Hey, Big Tim?"

"Yeah?"

"What the fuck is going on?"

"Sorry, it's a secret," Big Tim says. "I'm not allowed to say."

B conjures enough spit to loosen his tongue. "The secret is," B says, "is that a hack critic is about to walk into that door and force us to drink a glass of Fountain water and make us create something which he'll take credit for. Am I right, Big Tim?"

"You're smart."

"Nah, but I can sense a coward. Heh."

[Clank]

"So, Big Tim, is he going to take credit for both our masterpieces?" B says. "Or are you getting one as a thank you gift?"

Before Big Tim can answer, footfalls silence the conversation. And then the thin faux British accent. "Welcome, gentleman, to BE AN ARTIST™ Redux."

And there's Duckworth, dressed all in black. Hair buzzed down with a number one. Mustache perfect. His Black Flag tattoo touched up with a black Sharpie. A black suit that with a few hours at a tailor's would fit him perfectly, but all of this personal grooming is lost in the literal shadow of the goose egg knot slightly off-center of his forehead. A goose egg courtesy of a less-than-lethal rubber bullet. He also wears plastic surgeon's gloves.

Big Tim notes this as he glances down at his own bare hands.

"I suppose you wonder what you're doing here," Duckworth says.

"They know," Big Tim says. Now staring at the goose egg, as though it is a partially absorbed in utero twin. (He's read about such things.)

"What?"

413

"They know."

"I told you not to tell them."

"The one in the hat knew." (B)

"You didn't tell him?"

"He knew. Said he could sense a coward."

"He did?" To B: "You did?"

"Yes."

Duckworth turns to Robards. "Did you know?"

"That you were a coward? No. But it makes sense."

"How's that play coming, playwright?" B says.

Duckworth's eyes narrow and his lips purse.

"I'm sure," B says, "it's got great potential."

Duckworth steps up and slaps B. It's vicious for a slap, especially with his father's wedding ring on his index finger hipster style, but B laughs a barking shotgun *HA!* Especially with Duckworth's bulging third eye. Duckworth nods to Big Tim and Big Tim clocks B.

WHITE.

∞

Cosmic starfish and flares. And good Christ, now he's choking. B hawks, and a tooth drops out of his mouth onto the marble floor. A quick tonguing of his gums and two more teeth float in his mouth.

Dental insurance. B would also have added dental insurance to his Christmas list.

He spits both teeth at Big Tim's feet. *Clink, clink* on the marble floor. "You better hang onto those."

Big Tim looks at his cut knuckles. Swelling. He doesn't complain as he picks up B's teeth and tucks them into his shirt pocket. "Sorry."

Satisfied he has the upper hand, Duckworth sits on the cheap table, crosses his leg and picks imaginary lint off his pants. Cool calm, while "American Waste" plays on repeat in his head.

"So, Duckworth," B says, spraying blood in a fine mist, "you got all the kids lined up to take a drink, knock out pieces of shit and then you get tired of anointing this one and that, you're going to present your new passion? 'Hey, look everybody, look at my secret passion that I'm just now going public with,' all filled with humility and aw-shucks. So is that going to be one," he looks over to Ross Robards, "or two masterpieces? To prove you're not a fluke, a watered one-hit wonder?"

Ross Robards says: "You could just practice." To B: "He could just practice."

B says: "He doesn't have the talent."

Duckworth slides off the table.

"But with practice..." Ross Robards says.

"Yes, Ross, but that requires patience," B says. "And that's awfully hard to come by when you don't have, what is it, Big Tim?"

"Heart...?"

"That's right, Big Tim." B spits a bloody loogie at Duckworth's feet. "Heart."

Duckworth kicks B in the chest, summoning some of that old mosh pit energy. B's chair rocks back. Duckworth kicks him again, and B falls backwards. B, who has stage combat training, tucks his head forward and thus does not crack his skull on the marble floor.

[Clank]

"How. Dare. You." Duckworth screams, "You don't know what it's like to watch gifted people throw away their talent on drugs and whores. It comes so easily to them, they don't think they have to work. They want someone to hand them the success, the money because they're 'talented.' When was the last time you wrote a marketing plan, eh? When was the last time you networked a little, or have you hoped someone like Günter Adamczyk would suddenly knock on your door and ask to see what you've been up to?"[46]

Ross Robards clears his throat.

"I'm not talking to you," Duckworth says. "You and your bloody sad sack PTSD PR back story. How did you really lose your legs? Your bio changes every ten years."

---

46. In fact, he did.

"Defending my country." Ross Robards glowers. "From all enemies foreign. And domestic."

"You're so, so, so brave. Look how brave he is. You don't know the pain and rejection I've felt." He says this staring at Ross Robards' artificial legs. He turns back to B. "I deserve this. I deserve it. I was supposed to be an artist. I was afraid of clouds. *I am afraid of clouds.*"

[Clank]

"What the bloody hell is that infernal clanking noise?"

"Clouds are just water vapor," Big Tim says, thankful for his legs and his full cavity-free set of chompers.

Duckworth grabs the glass of water from the table. Ladybug shaped drops land here and there. Duckworth takes the glass of water to B. "Lift the front legs of his chair," he says. Big Tim does. And even though he is already on the ground, now B's legs are higher than his head. "Drink," Duckworth says and starts draining the water onto B's mouth. And because of the angle, a splash or two drains into his nose.

"Stop it," Ross Robards says. "Stop it. Now."

B snorts and water sprays. Water mixed with the blood from his oh, so recently extracted teeth. B turns and thrashes his head. Grunting what can only be obscenities.

"GET OFF HIM," Ross Robards says.

Everyone pauses because that's what you do when a quiet voice you've heard on TV for twenty-seven years screams at you. "I'll drink

417

the water," Ross Robards says. "If you let him go. And I'll whip up something special. Something you can be proud of, Jasper. Just. Let. B. Go."

Duckworth, a bit more woozy than he'll ever admit from the rubber bullet, considers this for a moment. This easy path. One masterpiece, and Robards has certainly had his time in the spotlight. The nagging thought is that he needs *two* masterpieces. But wanting to savor the power, Duckworth turns to B to ask his opinion now of this man he called a HACK on live TV.

"I can't hear you," B says.

Duckworth leans in to repeat the ques–

And that is when B kicks like a mule. A mule wearing steel-toed boots. The boot catches Duckworth in the mouth, splitting both lips into halves. Another boot from B and the drinking glass shatters, tinkles down like a broken rain stick.

But Duckworth manages to summon a bit of that WWII/ Nazi surviving power from his deceased parents and fights through it. Duckworth beelines to the table. Grabs a tea cup from a box of miscellaneous Found Objects and fills it at the Fountain. "BIG TIM." Each word misted with pink from his quartered mouth.

Big Tim clamps his hands to either side of B's face avoiding B's gnashing loose teeth, squeezes so B's lips form a butterfly-shaped opening. Duckworth stands high above B's head avoiding his thrashing legs and pours the water in a thin stream into B's mouth.

B sprays it out into Big Tim's face. But Big Tim doesn't flinch. Timmy was a spitter until the day he died.

Duckworth refills the cup again, full, and tiptoes like an egg racer at the county fair over to B where he kneels down and pours the water into B's nose and mouth. Big Tim clamps his hand over B's face. Lifts the chair to a sitting position. B gags.

Coughs.

Swallows.

Coughs.

Swallows.

Swallows.

Swallows.

A Thousand Words

A thin sagging line of blood and saliva touches down from B's lip to his knee. Duckworth lets B catch his breath. His body tingles. His core radiates warmth as if he has taken a shot of the world's oldest Scotch.

Robards stares intently at the box of art supplies. Crayons, chalk, children's toys, sharpened pencils. The mis-tied half-hitch already coming loose behind his back.

"Is this where Timmy made his masterpiece?"

"Yes, Big Tim," Duckworth says. Arguably true as this is where Timmy drank the water. "This is the place."

"Do you mind if we have a moment of silence?" To B and Robards: "Do you fellows mind if we have a moment of silence? For my little boy."

Robards says, "Of course not. That would be fine." Working the knot.

[Clank Clank]

Duckworth looks over the various mediums and art supplies laid before him. How long ago was it? A few months? Weeks. Only days? Here with Timmy and that woman. Timmy. Oh Timmy.

Migration circles them.

[Clank]

Robards, meanwhile, continues to flex his wrists and hands. Loosening the cord. This POW will not go gentle. Not here among children's toys.

[Clank]

B thinks of Jawbone's last word. Lost in a bubble of watery blood. B thinks of Glinski's last word. His last word from charred lungs. If only B spoke Russian.

[Clank]

"Time's up," Duckworth says. Although Big Tim still has his head lowered. "Time's up. B, it's time. Big Tim, retie Mr. Bellio's legs nice and tight. And let his hands loose. Stay behind him."

Big Tim does as he's told. "What about Mr. Robards?"

"One at a time. But double-check his hands."

Big Tim does and quickly reties Mr. Robards binds. Smacks him across the head for good measure. "That," Big Tim says, "is for good measure."

Duckworth, growing impatient, walks behind B and pushes him and his chair up to the table, in a gentle first date manner. "Create."

B shakes his head.

Duckworth leans forward. "Create. Now. Let's see what great potential you have. Let's see the peak of your powers, the accumulation of all your training, patience, and heart." Duckwork winces. The bilabial plosive sounds of the P (and B) words agitate his mouth wound more than their sibilant counterparts.

"I'm a sculptor, you dumbshit critic. Metal worker. This is all kids' stuff." The shadow of *Migration* wipes his face.

"Was that"—Duckworth points up to the circling vultures of *Migration*—"kids' stuff?"

"I'm a metal worker. I can't weld Play-Doh˚ or hammer chalk. Where's your sense and sensibility?"

Duckworth backs off a moment. "Wait a minute. You're a painter. You used to paint."

"Fuck off."

"No. Emma told me. You used to paint when you were younger. Gave it up for altruistic reasons." Duckworth's lips flap. "We have paints. Paint, painter."

"No."

"Do it."

"No."

"Yes."

"I'm not a cheat."

"We can help you go gentle into that—"

"I'm not a cheat. You might as well kill me now. Jasper."

Silence.

Vultures circle.

Big Tim looks around the room. Settling on Duckworth. "Well, I guess that's it." He moves to untie B.

"HOLD." Duckworth says. "Last box on the table."

Big Tim lumbers a few steps and reaches into the box. Pulls out a paintball gun, hands it to Duckworth who loads it. "I was inspired after seeing the newscast of Robards' special," Duckworth says. "Yes, we can. Here's the thing, B. You create something. A painting. I don't give a bloody hell what it is. Or..." Duckworth places the barrel of the paintball gun against Robards' left eye. "I'm going to shoot out his eyeball."

[Clank]

B looks at Robards through his chipped glasses. It's always that easy for the ones with the guns, he thinks. He looks at Ross. Even kind of likes the crusty old fucker. B nods to Duckworth.

"Pass the oils."

Duckworth beams. "An oil painting. Like the Masters. Yes yes yes."

"B," Robards says. "Fuck that noise. I'd rather go blind than have this parasite take our blood." He spits this to Duckworth: "You hear me, *civilian?*"

Duckworth's paintball gun is a modified Spyder. It shoots 400 psi / 600 fps. And yes, this is enough to fuck up a human eyeball at close range. Or any range.

So when Duckworth pulls, not squeezes, the trigger it obliterates Ross Robards' eye.

Robards goes Zen. Takes the pain inside. Quashing the guttural moan rising in his throat behind clenched and grinding teeth. It holds for a moment. Then erupts as a battlefield scream.

Somewhere, Mia Robards cries in her sleep.

The violence of Robards' scream causes Duckworth to pull the trigger one more time and, thus and so, he shoots, in the middle of the chest, standing in the doorway, a clown. A female clown.

[Clank]

"Holy shit," Big Tim says. "A clown. A female clown."

And indeed, in full regalia, stands a female clown. Bowl shaped pants held up with suspenders, an oversize bow tie, red wig, white pancake face, and huge ass floppy feet. And the make-up is a big happy balloon lips *[Clank]* variety, complete with red nose. Contrasting with the splat of Emilia Blue over the left breast, a wet heart from Duckworth's errant shot.

Duckworth does not quite know what to do. A clown out of context can be a frightening thing. Especially in the commission of a crime— and let's be honest, that's what's going on here despite all the psychobabble. Big Tim looks to Duckworth for guidance, because, come on, a fucking clown. Big Tim takes a step back, and despite his size glances at the table for something to be used as a weapon. Nothing on the table screams Acme-Stop-A-Clown.

Robards continues his own scream. B looks at the clown, his Silver Girl.

The clown holds up a plain manila envelope. "Special Delivery—" she bows with a flourish—"for Mr. Jasper P. Duckworth, Esq."

Duckworth nods to Big Tim, who takes the 9"x11" envelope from the clown as though taking a wedge of Muenster from a better mousetrap.

[Clank]

Duckworth opens the envelope with a pair of childproof scissors. Inside is a full color semi-glossy 35mm print of—

"My God," Big Tim says, "what is that?"

Tears stream down Duckworth's face. He drops the paintball gun. Then his knees wobble like two shorting-out electromagnets. His hand goes *[Clank]* to his split lips. Touches his teeth through the petals of the top lip. Now he's on his knees.

Big Tim follows him down to his own knees, eyes locked on the photograph.

"This," Duckworth says, his body starting to convulse with sobs, "is *Untilted #9* or *Ragnarök and Roll*."

"That's—"

"Timmy's masterpiece," Duckworth says. "Oh Waylon, you got the shot, you got the shot. Dear sweet Waylon. You got a perfect shot of Timmy's masterpiece."[47]

Big Tim puts his arm around Duckworth. "My son did that?"

Duckworth turns to the clown, the messenger he has already shot.

The clown has produced a seemingly never ending rainbow string of knotted handkerchiefs. One end she holds gently to Robards' ruined eye socket and clutches him to her chest, the blue heart tattooing his cheek with one big Warhol teardrop.

"Where did you get this?" Duckworth says, back on his feet.

The clown shifts her big feet in a dead-fish-flop kinda shuffle. Consoling Ross with a French lullaby.

With no patience for the French or clowns, he interrupts. "Are there more?" Duckworth says. "Are there more where this came from?" He tears frantically through the empty envelope. "*Are there more?*"

[Clank]

At this time, neither Big Tim nor Duckworth notice a small door open behind them. You wouldn't notice the door or pay much attention to it or even be aware of it. Unless you worked security

---

47. *Waylon's photograph will be a finalist for Picture of the Year and the Pulitzer Prize for Spot News Photography. It will lose out to a cell phone picture of Vlad Glinski's immolation, but thankfully will later be widely recognized as inspiring a new generation of photojournalists. Belle Day tries to book Waylon on a one-hour special of* Good Day with Belle Day. *No dice. He will be purported to be stalking beasts in the Serengeti with a Polaroid camera. Or leading a drum circle in Venice. His photo will never be licensed for swag.*

for the MCA. Much like our friend Hector. Hector Antonio Vargas has recently lost his best friend. Hector has seen her embarrassed at her own funeral. Hector knows that being a folk artist will only get you so far in Chicago. Hector knows that the critical drubbing his art showing received in the *Shoulders* was Duckworth's way of impressing that chick with the pink hair. Hector knows that he is scheduled to be deployed to the Middle East this summer. Hector has cousins in Mexico. Cousins connected with the government, with the cartels. Hector knows this. And though he knows he's going to miss his dog Daisy, he knows he does not have to take this shit any more.

Your work, Hector, is not done.

At this time, neither Big Tim nor Duckworth notice Hector grab from the miscellaneous art supplies a sharpened No. 2 pencil.

Big Tim holds up the picture of *Untilted #9* or *Ragnarök and Roll.* "My boy did this."

[Clank]

Hector, though trained in knife fighting by the world's finest army, decides he wants Duckworth face to face. So, he taps him on the shoulder, and Duckworth squawks a bit as he turns, and then Hector, face to face with Duckworth's alien *[Clank]* split mouth and freakish forehead, hesitates a moment. Duckworth recognizes Hector, but has no training of any real use, so Hector's hesitation *[Clank]* is met with Duckworth's own hesitation. And that's when Hector's tattooed bicep *[Clank]* flexes and, he stabs Duckworth in the abdomen and kidneys a half dozen times. *[Clank Clank Clank Clank Ker Clank]*

[Clank]

Duckworth *[Clank]* falls to a knee. His legs shake. His arms shake. He must crawl crawl crawl somewhere anywhere, all four of his lips *[Ker-Clank]* vibrating with shock. *[Clank]* He can feel his mother peering down at him through damning clouds. His father next to her, shaking his head. For this I waded through Kraut viscera?

[Ker-Clank-Errrr-Errrr]

Big Tim has been in his number of bar brawls, knows these skinny Latinos, these pesky flyweights are nothing but trouble, can take a punch, are shit-quick and will not back down. But he does have residual fatherly pride and bum-rushes Hector. But Hector, at Jawbone's insistence to further feed his art, has studied his culture. Including bullfighting.

Olé!

And now, Big Tim's arms and legs splay out among the ruined and collapsed table and the kaleidoscope of cheap art supplies. He cowers, clutching Waylon's photograph of Timmy's masterpiece to his chest, and decides he is done, calling it a certifiable win-win. Though Robards, head still clutched to the lullaby cooing clown and crying out for someone named Mia, would disagree. B stares with murderous intent at Big Tim as Hector cuts B loose.

[Clank]

[Clank]

[Clank]

Duckworth tries to flee the scene by crawling on one leg and one arm. Hector sees this. He stabs Duckworth one more time with the pencil and then breaks off the lead-tipped half. OUTFUCKINGSTAN*[CLUNK]*

—the Fountain explodes.

The Flood

When the Fountain explodes, the shrapnel spray cuts *Migration* from its tether, and the origami birds fall to the flooding floor, the floor flooding with a volume of water that belies the size of the Fountain, as though Poseidon has tapped his trident thrice, and now the birds float out the room on a blood and water-colored chalk-tainted river, down the steps into the foyer, and out the front revolving doors turning like a vertical mill wheel where they travel down the front steps, past the Greek gods, engulfing the bulk of screaming protesters, the Guard, rubber bullets and paintballs, and tear gas and rioting, and ride the Fountain river through downtown Chicago.

∞

A little girl far from the chaos of the MCA points excitedly and yells: DUCKS!!! and dives fearlessly into the river that is now Michigan Avenue in an attempt to retrieve one. Her Space Camp t-shirt with MACKENZIE paint-markered on the front pocket. The current is strong, but a pink-haired corpse proves to be a reasonable flotation device.

Thirty-seven years later, this child will grow up to pilot the *Bradbury-Tarkovsky Maru* on the first successful manned mission to Mars. Tucked safely in the thigh pocket of her space suit, a yellowed and water stained paper-winged creature from *Migration*.

∞

As for the survivors, what happened next is next:

Oz Park

Olive lifts the mole aviator goggles from her eyes. Inspects her welds on the BBQ smoker, the unfinished gift from Jawbone. She shrugs off her leather welding jacket. Under a purple tank top, half-healed shrapnel scars mar her torso and arms. On good days she doesn't even use the painkillers. "Not bad for a clown, eh?"

B drank the water, so he sits out the rest of the game. Avoiding anything creative. Avoiding sudden death.

"Not bad indeed, Silver Girl," B says, his hands clean. No longer a craftsman. Now a teacher. It's Jawbone's design, but Olive's moxie. She's good. Natural skills. Every night, he kisses each and every one of those scars. He feels warm inside. B's heart is bursting.

∞

His truck is loaded, oil changed, windshield wiper fluid reservoir filled. The smoker hitched to the back on the custom trailer. Road snacks and drinks bought and on ice. The back covered with a new camper shell covering an air mattress and sleeping bags and clothes and a special ice chest with secret ingredients and a few books, including a guide to the best and most lucrative BBQ contests across America. Again, he'll supervise. Cooking being art and all.

Now, one last stop before hitting the open road.

∞

At Oz Park in the Emerald Garden, they find the Chair. The natural organic elements of it blending perfectly with the lush surroundings. A small creek frames the bottom of the postcard picture. B walks up to the Chair. Stops short. "This is close enough." Olive's hand, with grease under her nails, slips into his. The hands fit like they were cast together. Like they've always been together.

"It doesn't look as big out here," B says.

Olive says: "Now it's competing with the universe."

The Heartless

Four miles from Oz Park, Ross Robards steps into a sacred place. His old shop. The paint faded double hearts glow with the sunlight in the window. The smells of his distant past are faint. But still there. Acrid tobacco smoke and wood and thinner and sex and dead spiders and cheap perfume and paint and fuck you freedom. Perfect.

Under his arm, a slate of polished black granite with an *In memoriam* name inscribed. The steel will arrive in a few hours. He takes this time to strip down, buzz his head jarhead style. To suit up in old work clothes that fit like an old skin. To clean. To organize. To meditate on the new memorial, a steel chair. Soon, Ross Robards will be reborn in a shower of sparks.

Ross Robards will be meticulous.

Ross Robards will be perfect.

Out of respect.

For his lost brothers.

Tex from Oklahoma.

Benedict from West Virginia.

Hobie from Portland.

Brooklyn from Austin.

Jawbone from Chicago.

The Brick Road

One thousand four hundred miles away from Oz Park, countless millions of Monarch butterflies billow on their migratory path from Mexico to Canada. In the fall, they will travel back. A cloud of living onyx and tawny-orange. Not a single one will make the round trip. Some will be eaten. Some will simply out fly their life cycle, winding up with their dead brothers and sisters knee deep along concrete highway barriers. The trip will take three to four generations, but the females lay eggs along the way to ensure the future of the Monarchs.

Little Dog, Too

Hector will find the Monarchs inspiring as he enjoys a folk art hero existence on a small farm outside Campeche with Daisy his canine companion, painting and selling his work through an underground network of galleries and foreign representatives with the occasional local show for his *abuela*. The Guard lists him as AWOL, Hector having deployed himself on a more critical mission.

An agent in Hollywood he's never met face to face is a "big fan" and shops around the life rights to every major and mini studio. "Oscar bait" is a term used more than once. But whitewashing due to a lack of bankable Latino leading men frustrates Hector and he ankles the project.

The Soldier with the Green Whiskers

Big Tim. The big mountain. Shielding them all from the lethal shrapnel. It hurt, of course. There was blood. Through a morphine haze, he recalls the clown giving him mouth to mouth. A clown. A female clown. Recalls the dude with the metal legs (and dripping eye) and the sneaky pencil-stabbing bastard staunching his wounds with makeshift field dressings made of Play-Doh® and magic hankies. The other chair dude, the one he punched, making a quick stretcher of that cheap table. They all carried him through that emergency exit away from the flood. The pencil-stabber taking point.

Then he is here. They won't let him have a cigar, but a kind nurse brings him a big circus lollipop. Big Tim wonders briefly if they left Duckman behind.

He ignores the recycled TV news with footage (courtesy of Belle Day and WGN) of Duckworth leaning through a broken window pane on the fourth floor, pencils jutting from his body, a lumpy forehead, clothes tattered on one side from the blast, a broken bullhorn in hand, as the Fountain pours out in staggered waterfalls from the floors below him, his lips mouthing—*DRINK DRINK DRINK!*—as the sound and the fury of an irresistible force meeting moveable human objects drowns out his directive.

Big Tim sees none of this, instead fawning over another present from the kind nurse: a creased photo found tucked in his ruined pants. He smooths the photo with pride. The picture is perfect. Composition, lighting. Timmy's Masterpiece in mid-drop, the flaming pencil, the animalistic impression of the sculpture. Big Tim sees so many things manifest in the sculpture, as if he is cloud-watching. And in the background, leaning over the rail, is Timmy, arms spread wide open in victory.

My boy did this.

The Wicked & The Powerful

Two miles from Oz Park, the police, following a complaint of a strong smell and loud music, arrive at Emma's apartment to find Duckworth curled up next to Emma's iridescent locust shell of a body. They are partially under the bed and among a disarray of silicone cocks in a shallow, but widening pool of his blood. He strokes her hair asking her forgiveness. A jagged pencil juts from his body, vibrating with his thready heartbeat.

Near the bed, a turntable needle bumps and hisses and skips on a loop stuck in the grooves of Black Flag's "Thirsty and Miserable." A forensics expert will later notice a small tiger-striped caterpillar inching along the inside window sill.[48]

The Cowardly

Still at Oz Park, B removes his chipped glasses. The sharp edges of the world bleed into one another: a blurry mix of oil, water, soap and sand. The Chair disappears in the washed out watercolor of his middle-aged vision. It's as if it never happened. The Chair, the Fountain, Jawbone, Olive. If only he could function without his glasses. Leave the world a puree of bricks and leaves and maybe a slash of the nearby creek, leaving only a few things in focus, things right in front of his good field of vision, a scant eight inches, enough to double check the label on his beer, the small mole above Olive's lip as it rises to his.

∞

---

48. The coroner will discover hundreds of partially digested Monarch butterflies in Emma's stomach. The toxicology report will reveal a lethal amount of cardiac glycosides in her system, no doubt from the Monarchs' diet of milkweed. B will hear this story and think: no, it was the Fountain. Emma became a goddess and went supernova. She was her own masterpiece.

He puts his glasses back on. Sharp focus. He turns to Olive. Or where Olive used to be. He glances back to the truck. The door looks funny. B takes two steps before he realizes the passenger door is open. The sea bag he gave her for her stuff is gone. B stands there. For a minute. Ten. Fifteen. Gone.

She's gone, baby, gone.

A block east, a parking meter maid on a two wheeler sprints from car to car, checking dashboard parking slips for expiration times. B has not gotten one. One more ticket and he is sure to be towed. He pulls a maxed-out credit card from his wallet to pay the new parking meter monsters. They were only going to be here a few minutes. They were only going to be together a lifetime.

Perhaps it's a sign. Did he really think they'd be able to do this? It's the only City he's ever known in his adult life. The City that holds his roots. He can't possibly pull this off. Maybe he can get a job delivering steel. Grunt work welding. Maybe beg Günther for his old gig.

A child screams behind him.

B turns to see a young boy fall to the ground at the foot of the bridge spanning the small creek. A group of taller shirtless boys throw rocks at him. The boy backpedals, then scampers off the bridge to the far side of the creek. The gang stands there. He cannot cross.

B walks in that direction. Then double times it. The lost boys, losing interest, start scuffling among themselves. B sees the boy stop. Sees the boy judge the distance to get back across the bridge, the time needed to zip past them. If they are distracted enough. If he is quick enough. If he is strong enough. The boy decides discretion is the better part of valor. The boy hurries along the creek looking for a place to cross.

B mirrors his direction.

At one point, the boy stops, takes off his glasses. The sun reflects and refracts through them. Even from here B can see a big chip. The boy runs his fingers around the chip and then puts them back on. Blinking and squinting in the light. He scans up and down the creek. The easier section to cross is still wide. So very wide. And cold. And slick. He can't do it.

B glances back expecting to see a tow truck hauling away his life. His future. His options. But there is Olive. Waving a parking slip at the meter maid. Her voice on the wind. We're paid up, f'ing move on. Her bag at her feet open and purse strap hanging out. A coffee tray with two cups on the hood. She rolls up her sleeves, ready to throw down.

Bound by wild desire.

B turns back to the boy.

The boy retreats a step, shaking his head. This boy with the thick chipped glasses, he vibrates with fear. Backs up a step. Then three, four. The boy turns and runs away. Quick small awkward strides.

B takes one, two steps into the stream. His feet and shins numb instantly. *"Robert,"* B shouts.

The boy stops near the top of the hill. Turns. Tears streaming from his eyes. A regal butterfly flits past him, momentarily testing his glasses for nectar.

B stands there.

The boy stands there.

B's arms open.

The boy takes a tentative step forward. Towards B. Towards the creek. Then another. The hill adds speed and now the boy runs, he runs downhill gaining velocity, one step ahead of gravity, his chipped glasses bounce and fly off his nose and it is too late to stop, and the blind boy does not break stride and B now understands Vlad's and Jawbone's last word and his arms open wider and now the boy's toe hits the edge of the water, the edge of the unknown universe and B screams:

Jump

THE END

Acknowledgements

Writing is a solitary endeavor. Until it's not.

So here's my speech. We'll see if the band plays me off... I'd like to thank my parents who have been waiting the longest for this: William C. Hay and Susan L. Hay. So thank you for letting me stay up past my bedtime as long as I was reading. I haven't slept since.

Second, for this particular book, Brian Alan Hill, who first read a random mismatched set of chapters and tapped the pages and said: do it. It was that earliest encouragement that kept me plugging away in secret.

Third, Allison Moore Hay, my wife and partner in many crimes, and a fantastic writer, as well. She came into my life before *The Fountain* found new life, and has been nothing but proud and supportive throughout the process. She jumped higher than I did when I shared the news.

The Fountain was one of those lightning ideas that flashed hard and fast and I couldn't shake it. So I didn't bother to try. That's a lie. I did try. I worked in secret for years. A side project fed and watered between other projects. Finally, like a splinter, it worked its way to the surface. It ended up with me in the MFA program at Queens University in Charlotte where I met some truly talented and big personality writers: Anna "Banana" Dickson James, Stephen G. Eoannou, Bonnie "Brooklyn" Neel, Jeremy "Jeremy" Rice, Steve "Honky Tonk" Woods, Alison Wellford, Heather Startup, Abby Schaffer, Beth Uznis Johnson, and Hobie Anthony. They dug in with me and gave me their best.

Also to the Co-Director of that program Fred L. Leebron and my mentor Pinckney Benedict who went above and beyond and genuinely supported this book. They both knew when to push and when to get the hell outta the way. Occasionally at the same time.

The home team for support going way back: Tim Houchin, Carrie Hill, Barb Hazlett, Melanie Marnich, Courvais, Glenn Jeffers, John Beckman, Tiffany Scott, Bryan Kerr, Don Grail, Johnny Simonetta, Mike Noe, Lianna Greenberg, & Scott "Rabbi Bucky" Greenberg. (If you didn't see your name here, you're probably hidden in the book. Heh.)

I'd also like to thank writers David Barr III, Naeem Murr, Lauren Groff, Darren Callahan, and Jay Bonansinga, outstanding and very accomplished writers kind enough to not only give insightful feedback on early drafts but also offered to blurb for me.

Ron Drynan for donating his time and talent for the book trailer VO.

R.J. Inawat for all my legal needs. Jennifer Petrini for all my PR needs. I owe you both a round. Or two.

Mycki Manning (the Dorothy to my Scarecrow) for the Vegas photo shoot and laughs, then and since high school. Carlos Cobarrubias at Xquisite in Venice Beach for the hair and beard taming.

Fellow filmmakers and dear friends: Scott Storm who not only enthusiastically gave of his time and talent to create the storyboards used in the Duckworth daydream sequence, but also produced and edited the book trailer. Thank you to Joe Kraemer for the music and Anthony Miller who generously revamped my dusty website davidscotthay.com and provided laughs and IT support.

Extra Special Sauce Thanks to Miette, the heart and soul of Whisk(e)y Tit, who kept the faith and picked up the tab at that last crazy night in Jazz, TX before SHTF. And to Hobie Anthony who turned me onto this cool small press.

And finally, two other brothers in arms, who let me fictionalize them for my own nefarious purposes: Richard Higby, my friend, former boss and furniture designer. He knew. Richardhigbydesign. com.

And across the hall from the old woodshop, the sculptor Robert Bellio, who had no idea, and whose artwork proudly hangs in my home. Find him at robertbellio.com. Buy a piece.

Both men taught me much just in the way they went about their business and how they approached their Work.

I could write pages regarding everyone above. Thank you all.

If you've made it this far, free to drop me a line. Love or hate, it'd be swell to hear from ya.

–david@davidscotthay.com

About the Author

DSH is an award-winning playwright, screenwriter, and novelist. Born and raised in OKC, he lost the tip of a finger in a chop-saw incident somewhere in Chicago.

He makes a mean old-fashioned and the best ribs on the block. He currently lives with his wife and son and dog and chickens and a dozen typewriters in a valley between the ocean, the mountains, and the desert.

The Fountain is his small press debut. It will be translated and released in Russia in the summer of 2022. Davidscotthay.com for more whatnot.

About the Publisher

Whisk(e)y Tit is committed to restoring degradation and degeneracy to the literary arts. We work with authors who are unwilling to sacrifice intellectual rigor, unrelenting playfulness, and visual beauty in our literary pursuits, often leading to texts that would otherwise be abandoned in today's largely homogenized literary landscape. In a world governed by idiocy, our commitment to these principles is an act of civil service and civil disobedience alike.